Advance Praise for *Continuum*

"CONTINUUM is a marvelous pastiche which combines the suspense of a down-to-earth spy novel with an ethereal spiritual cosmology. The passages describing the realm of spirit are transcendent while the passages describing the evil logic of modern-day bioterrorists are all too disturbingly earthy and real."

~ Harry Arader, The Centromere Group

"From the novel's first page to its last, CONTINUUM's riveting subject matter and interesting characters grab the reader's attention in a surrealistic fashion. The mysticism and medical details realistically interweave the stories within a story, holding the reader captive to the end."

~ Richard A. Silver, MD, MBA

"A blend of romance, spy, science fiction, and the paranormal, CONTINUUM draws the reader into the thrilling realm of international bioterrorists close to the White House who can only be thwarted by the combined efforts of a pair of beautiful women gifted with the shared sense of premonition."

~ Patricia Lofthouse, Television Producer

CONTINUUM

Also by Marlys Beider

Fateful Parallels

CONTINUUM

For Sally and Steve DeAngeles -
Hope you'll enjoy reading this!

A NOVEL BY

MARLYS BEIDER

Best always -
Marlys Beider

Continuum

This is a work of fiction. Names, characters, places, and incidents are either products of the author's imagination or are used fictitiously. Any resemblance to actual events, locales, or persons, living or dead, is entirely coincidental.

Lyrics on pages 14–15 are taken from "Burning Love," written by Elvis Presley. Lyrics on page 245 are taken from "Ain't No Sunshine," written by Bill Withers.

Published by Hats Off Books®
610 East Delano Street, Suite 104
Tucson, Arizona 85705 U.S.A.
www.hatsoffbooks.com

Cover illustration by David Loew.

Publisher's Cataloging-in-Publication Data
(Provided by Quality Books, Inc.)

Beider, Marlys.
Continuum / Marlys Beider.
p. cm.
LCCN 2004108780
ISBN 1-58736-365-8 (hardcover)
ISBN 0-971-1748-1-4 (paperback)

1. Parapsychology--Fiction. 2. Precognition--Fiction. 3. Supernatural--Fiction. 4. Bioterrorism--Fiction. 5. Prejudices--Fiction. 6. Political fiction. I. Title.

PS3602.E377C66 2004 813'.6
QBI04-700291

I dedicate this book
to the memory of my mother, Ellen Schroeder-Pallenberg.

The eyes are the window of the soul.

~Proverb

ACKNOWLEDGMENTS

FIRST AND FOREMOST, I am indebted to my editor, Al Petrillo, for his talented guidance, encouragement, and patience. I could not have hoped for better.

Thanks to Patricia Lofthouse for putting me on the right course and for understanding what this book is all about.

I cannot fully express my gratitude to Harry Arader and Dr. Richard Silver, two superb brains behind science and business. Without your generous assistance, my rambling thoughts would never have become reality. Thank you both.

My everlasting appreciation to those who gave me unlimited ear time and shared their knowledge with me: Alice Licht, Francis Manley, Jim Driscoll, Georgia Curtin, Sharee Pemberton, Shay and Ken Beider, Lynn Wiese Sneyd, and Susan Wenger.

For their various contributions, thank you to Frank Perez, Rick England, Kellon Lovegren, Margery Rubin, Martha Sassone, Owen McCaffrey, Kathy McCaffrey, Dan Beider, Christine Hodson, Robert Hoyt, Sharon Millman, Kerry Stiles, Dennis McConnell, Julie Mekdaschi, and "Sharif."

Thank you to my dear friends who scoured the manuscript for flaws: Dr. Signe Kilen, Wendy Green, Aileen and Sid Howell, Jewel Spivack, and Bonnie Morris.

And, of course, my love to Jackie, Shay and Ken, Kelly and Mike, Lesley and Danny, Olivia, Samara, Hal, Cody, Jake, Jonah, Skyler, and Noah—all fifteen of you inspire me every day.

CONTINUUM

Prologue

Chantal Atwood woke her husband at two in the morning. Minutes later, State Legislator Edward Atwood helped his very pregnant wife down the wide stairwell of their home in New Orleans' Garden District.

Ella Laveau, properly dressed and prepared, waited at the bottom of the stairs. Usually grateful for her premonitions, that night she condemned the gift of clairvoyance she claimed had been passed on to the Laveau women for generations. She had always been treated as part of the Atwood family rather than a household employee and strongly sensed that Chantal and Edward would need her presence for what was to come.

Accompanied by Secret Service agents, the group arrived at Touro Infirmary Hospital where Chantal, the daughter of United States President Paul Pearson, and Edward, the son of Louisiana State Senator Ronald Atwood, received VIP treatment.

Edward and Ella were granted permission to remain by Chantal's side through the birth.

Listening to the fetal heart tones, the two attending doctors assured the soon-to-be parents that everything was perfectly normal. After six hours of relatively easy labor, Chantal delivered the first of her twins, a healthy baby girl.

A worried expression spread across the face of the nurse monitoring the heartbeat of the child still in utero, but before she could whisper her concern to the doctors, Chantal began to bleed heavily and the fetal heartbeat became shallow and faint. The doctors, deciding the placenta had separated or ruptured, performed a C-section. As soon as they delivered the second baby girl they saw that her respiration was labored. Recognizing her low APGAR level, they tried to resuscitate the already unconscious infant.

Edward begged the doctors to allow him to hold his dying child and pressed his lips on the infant's forehead. His tears stopped when the baby opened her tiny eyelids, emitting a mysterious purple brilliance.

Mesmerized, Edward and Ella silently began to pray. For a second they were surrounded by the purple luminance, and then they witnessed the slow extinction of the amethyst fire in the baby's right eye.

At the same moment, fifteen hundred miles across the country, Gloria Prime screamed curses during her final labor pains in the delivery room at St. Mary's Hospital in Tucson. She had never wanted the baby that had agonized her throughout the pregnancy.

Nineteen years old and separated from her parents in Mexico, she was in her third month when she drove herself to Nogales. Gloria knew she could buy female hormone stimulants in the dusty city across the border. For ten days she swallowed five hundred milligrams of the drug four times a day, and believed the abortion worked when she began to spot daily for one week. When the spotting stopped for three weeks she assumed everything was normal, but was perplexed when the bleeding started on and off, repeating itself for ten weeks.

When the man whom she had married in desperation complimented her on the fullness of her breasts and the roundness of her hips, Gloria became suspicious and went to see an obstetrician. She was six months pregnant.

Blinded by rage, she began jumping rope excessively, bounced furiously on a trampoline, applied saltwater and vinegar douches, and even tried to harm herself with a coat hanger until the pain stopped her from going farther. After another six weeks, when she realized nothing had worked, Gloria pounded her fists on her growing belly and damned the resistant and unwanted child in her womb.

It wasn't only the pain of labor that made her scream and curse in the delivery room; her wails released the anguish of abandonment and the rage of rejection. Gloria swore that she would inflict the same pain on the child, who she believed was the cause of her misery.

When the smiling doctor put a healthy female infant into her arms, Gloria sobbed tears of bitter resentment. Her convulsions only stopped when the baby opened her tiny eyelids and made eye contact. Gloria froze and deemed it a hallucination as a magnificent purple fire erupted in the newborn girl's right eye.

TUCSON

...in May—
twenty-seven years later

CHAPTER 1

EARLIER IN THE morning, while the sun was still in its infancy, Teeba Prime had realized this was the day she had been waiting for her whole life. During the afternoon hours she remained calm, even though she knew that before dusk a bullet would tear into her, a bullet meant for someone else. Throughout most of the previous night Teeba's dreamlike state had been filled with many visions, the most important revealing the beginning of a new circle. In it, people and events would collide, not only with her but also with the split part of her soul.

As in her previous lives, Teeba recognized she was one in a small number of the elect who could understand the mysterious system of teachings from a superior and profound purity. She had been waiting for the seal to be broken so the universal movements again could entrust her with a mission.

From the moment she awakened that day, Teeba's heart pumped fast with anticipation. Yet apprehension was in every other beat of her pulse. It was not fear of the foreboding that made her jitter; rather it was the anticipation of the calling. Though everything was still foggy, she was aware that the decision had been made.

"Thank you," she whispered, knowing that her gratitude was connecting with a world of pure spirit and intelligence, but aiming beyond and above in her quest to unite with the first sphere—the world of Emanation.

During the many transmigrations of her soul, she had been entrusted with enormous wisdom and powers, yet in every new lifetime some of the acquired sageness and strength remained untapped. "Thank you," she communicated again, "for letting me recognize the new mission and allowing me to release and use my energy today."

During the interchange, Teeba was aware that the purple fire in her right eye had been well hidden by the lowered eyelid. But the dialogue had birthed a mysterious glow on her face, and a prudent smile lingered on her lips while she read out loud:

"...So they came to the wheat-bearing plain, and thenceforth they pressed toward the end: in such wise did the swift horses speed forward. Now the sun sank and all the ways were darkened."

Teeba, the twenty-seven-year-old teacher at Tucson's Agave High School, gently ran the palm of her hand over the page she had just read to the eleven students in her classroom. She gave her students time to think while she enjoyed another minute of total silence. Her gaze still hugged the last sentence of Book III in Homer's *Odyssey* while her mind connected with an extraordinary intelligence that had taught her the significance of previous lives.

"Thank you," she transmitted again. "I am ready." Slowly, she lifted her eyelids and faced the students; the purple fire in her eye had already dimmed.

Extra curriculum classes were rare at Agave High, due to either quickly fading interest after one or two sessions or no interest at all. But for the past four weeks Teeba had been able to hold the attention of six girls and five boys in their junior and senior years; her capability of making an art out of any subject gave her students freedom of expression. It was only her second year at Agave High and Teeba already had been unanimously voted "Teacher of the Year."

When she first started at the old school on Romero Road, large classes of undisciplined, disrespectful, and even dangerous students faced her. They laughed at the young, 5'5" woman who looked more like one of them rather than the rest of the middle-aged, fatigued faculty. The students, who came from trailer park communities and modest residential housing areas, were a tough bunch. They were the offspring of mostly poor Anglo-American, Hispanic, and African-American families.

But Teeba's small stature was soon forgotten as her reputation swelled with the impact of her presence in the classroom.

Teeba's eyes drifted away from Homer's poetic words, and she placed her own beautifully bound volume of *The Odyssey* on the desk. She raised her chin, letting her students know it was time for discussion.

"Gawd, that dude Telemachus really has a problem, doesn't he? He's so *totally* unsure of himself," a girl's dragging, nasal voice opened the dialogue. "*Totally!* Always bitching about his plight." Nikki Barnes slid her skinny body from a lounge chair position into a slouchy, semi-upright posture. Her skimpy black tank top revealed plenty of ghostly white skin, and she drew more attention to her almost hollow stomach as she played with three small silver rings that pierced her belly button. Her forehead crinkled under the short, raven black bangs. "Gawd," she repeated, "Can someone explain his problem to me?"

Otis Brown spoke up. "Hey, the k-k-kid's still young and i-i-immature. G-g-give him some time, he's..."

"Bullshit," Christopher Snow seethed. "That character starts out to be a screwed-up sissy because he was raised only by women. What do you expect?"

"What's wrong with that? You were raised by *just* your mother." Candy Perez emphasized "just" as she snapped her gum. "Does that make you a sissy, too?"

Christopher's eyes narrowed. He felt his temper rising but did not want to waste his energy. Candy was not worth it. Without turning his head he groaned, "Sleazy runt," but extended his middle finger in her direction. He knew he was the only one in the class who had finished reading the legend of Odysseus, the warrior, returning home from the Trojan War. Christopher had devoured Homer's classic and already formed his own interpretation.

"Sissy or not," he said, briefly pausing for the effect, "Telemachus inherited his father's genes and knows he needs to learn how to be aggressive. He admires Nestor and wants to be a leader just like him."

Christopher was proud of his scholastic achievements. His hungry mind, together with his outstanding athletic ability, had earned him a scholarship at USC, and he was the only one in his graduating class leaving Tucson for a distinguished university. Because of his baseball skills, he had received offers from various teams to go to the minor leagues right after high school, but he had set his goals higher and often talked to his friends about the fame and fortune he guaranteed for himself.

Raising his chin, Christopher continued, "Telemachus is learning fast. He's in awe of the way Orestes avenged his father's death by murdering the killers." Christopher looked provocatively at his teacher. "Therefore, I believe Junior is thrilled at having inherited the same bloodthirsty gene from his famous father and is striving to emulate him." Christopher paused and pursed his lips. "What do *you* think, Ms. Prime?"

Teeba stiffened as a sharp prediction pierced through her extrasensory perception; deep shadows were forming a shroud of darkness over the student. In a fraction of a second she realized that Christopher represented a link in the cataclysm of events to unfold.

And even though she was filled with excitement, she instantly grasped the impending sadness of the upcoming reality where good and evil would collide. But as quickly as the other dimension had opened her highly developed additional senses, there now was a halt again.

CHAPTER 2

"I PREPARED SOME challenging questions on these sheets, covering the first three books," Teeba said. "I look forward to your ideas and interpretations." She slid off the desk's edge and handed copies to the students.

Christopher sat in a comfortable position. His left leg had taken possession of the empty chair in front of him; his right leg was stretched into the aisle. He had flung one arm around an empty chair and casually extended his right toward the passing teacher. As Teeba handed him the sheets of paper, he held on to her hand. "You didn't answer my question. You ignored me," he smirked.

The other students had already assumed their after-school mentality and were paying no interest to Christopher and the grip he had on the teacher's hand.

"Hey, g-g-good class, Ms. P-P-Prime," Otis Brown stuttered before he left the room.

"Thanks," said pale and skinny Nikki Barnes.

"Bye, see ya next week," mumbled Candy Perez, still chewing her gum.

"Bitch!" Christopher muttered when he saw Teeba smiling at the departing students after freeing herself from his hand.

He waited until the last student had left, stood up and stretched. Then, he slowly walked toward Teeba, who was straightening the piles of paper on her desk.

Christopher's clipped light-blond hair contrasted with his handsome suntanned face. His eyes, blue like the glaciers of Alaska, helped him look wiser and older than eighteen. His tight, washed-out blue jeans had a few stylishly fraying holes that were intended to reveal glimpses of his muscular, strong legs. The white tight T-shirt showed his athletic build.

"You didn't answer my question," he demanded as he stood in front of her desk.

Teeba lifted her head and her gaze met his.

Startled, Christopher stepped back when he saw a bolt of purple fire shooting from her eye into his. He felt examined, like the mysterious fire was X-raying his thoughts; he cringed from the notion. A unexplained dizziness made him reach out for the edge of the desk.

He blinked several times before he found his voice again. "Do you feel trapped between the blackboard and me?" With his hands on the worn desk, he leaned his upper body closer to Teeba. Their faces were only a few inches apart. He let out a short nervous laugh. "Why don't you speak?"

"Looking at you, I couldn't help but think about sweet Timmy and the great progress he's been making. You should be very proud of him."

Christopher jerked his body straight and squirmed. Strangely, his younger brother had been on his mind all day long. He breathed heavily and spoke fast—it always happened when he was getting mad—letting the words run into each other.

"Whatareyoutalkingabout?" His face turned a few shades darker. "Ihardlyeverseehim," Christopher yelled. "You're the one spending more time with him than I do!" He kicked the desk with his heel. "That's the problem! He's always more important, isn't he? Everybody's always more important! You seem to take time for everyone but me. Why?" He walked around the desk and towered over her.

He wanted to grab her and say that he'd had a crush on her since sophomore year, but her determined, calm voice stopped him.

"You're a very intelligent young man, Chris. You have a talent that gives you the freedom to go into Homer's mind. You might surprise yourself and find out you'll be able to answer many of your own questions."

"Did you give your fancy words wings?" Christopher quipped. "Well, they're flying right over my head." Meanwhile, his gaze was glued to her lips and his mind fantasized; he was one of Homer's powerful gods and she was his Aphrodite.

"Yes," she said, "I intend for my words to have wings. Whole new worlds would open up for you if only you'd be willing to fly with them."

A loud voice interrupted. "Hey, you comin' bro?" Chip Olson stuck his huge sweaty head through the door. "We're starvin'. Let's go, dude."

"You show me how and I'll fly with you," Christopher whispered before he took his books and left the classroom.

CHAPTER 3

TEEBA WALKED TOWARD the windows. Two were open already, but she needed more air. As usual, the swamp cooler was not working. Agave High School had its problems. The wear and tear of the desert sun with its drying powers, the severe downpours during monsoon season and the carelessness and abuse of the students had done their damage. Money was tight and only the most necessary repairs were made. It was the beginning of May and within two weeks, the much-anticipated vacation would start.

Teeba leaned into the lower part of the window, manipulating the handle while pushing against the metal frame; it worked and she cranked it open. The fourth window was painted shut. The classroom's windows were already in the shade and the warm breeze rushing in created a welcome cross draft. The heated desert air brought with it the smell and steady hum of the cars and trucks whizzing by on Interstate 10. Only a parking lot separated the school from the freeway.

Outside, four husky seniors, the backbone of Agave High's baseball team, walked toward a worn and dented car painted in psychedelic colors. Teeba overheard the boys teasing Christopher for being alone with her in the classroom. She watched as a student thrust his pelvis forward, shouting, "Oooh, yesss, baby."

Christopher appeared to be flattered rather than annoyed by the attention and in an exaggerated Elvis Presley gesture, he wiggled his hips and sang,

"Hey baby, I ain't askin' much of you
No no no no no no no no baby, I ain't askin' much of you

Just a big-a-big-a hunk o' love will do."

"I wish I could let you know how misguided you are," Teeba whispered. "I wish I was allowed to change things, but you've already entered the circle and have chosen your decline."

Teeba lifted her head toward the light blue afternoon sky and a serene stillness spread over her face. She had waited for this day for a long time—the day in which her life's mission and her enormous strength and knowledge would be tested again. She remembered the secrets that were taught to her under the seal of mystery, which needed to be protected so two worlds could continue to exist: the world she lived in and the world that was to come. In less than two hours her physical body would be at rest while a powerful transfer of energy took place. This was the day when the circle that formed the day she was born would open for the players to enter: men and women. Good and evil.

She let her gaze drift back into the classroom and took a deep breath. Despite the incident soon to occur at Agave, there were many things left for her to do. But nothing could stop the events from happening during the upcoming nine months.

Teeba sat down at her desk and began work on the remedial English tests composed of multiple-choice and two essay questions. With her photographic memory, she grasped the contents of each set of answers instantly, marked the mistakes, and wrote short-phrased praises. She usually rectified papers in the after-hours of the school day but no one was aware how little time it required. It was one of her many secret gifts. At least for now!

CHAPTER 4

FORTY-FIVE MINUTES later, a car screeched to a halt in the parking lot and four young men got out. They had filled their stomachs at the nearby Taco Bell and were ready for the next hour or more of practice as they walked over the hot asphalt toward the gymnasium.

"Shit, I forgot my new cup. I gotta stop by my hall locker," Christopher complained, and turned in the other direction.

"I'm comin' with ya. I gotta stash these away," Chip Olsen responded, pointing to his pocket. Knowing the consequences of violation, Chip didn't dare bring the pack of cigarettes into the locker room.

After stopping at their lockers, they proceeded toward the gym, passing Teeba, still sitting behind her desk with her eyes closed. The two students stopped and stared.

"If I was still a kid, I'd believe in Sleeping Beauty," whispered Chip. The glow from the late afternoon sun shrouded Teeba in a mysterious purple aura.

"Go ahead, dude. I'll be right there," Christopher ordered, winking at his friend. He walked into the classroom and stared at Teeba's peaceful face. As he approached, he had the illusion of caressing her smooth bronzed skin. He fantasized about loosening the rubber band holding the thick pile of her hair together so he could run his fingers through her long black tresses. He pictured her trim naked body kneeling in front of him in a field of blossoming desert wildflowers. He heard the moans, felt the touches, and tasted the sweetness. He started to shudder with desire.

Just then Teeba opened her eyes. She did not say anything, but her look suddenly frightened him again. It was disconcerting how the intensity of her eyes had this immense impact on him. He blinked and took a deep breath.

"You're still here," his voice cracked. "I thought about what you said and really would like to have a long and serious discussion with you. You know, about Homer and *The Odyssey*." He tried to sound sincere. "My mother's not working tonight and I can pick up the car after practice. How about if I swing by your house for an hour or so? I think a one-on-one dialogue would really reduce my confusion."

"Oh Christopher," she exhaled. "I promised to have dinner with my father tonight but," she paused and lifted her chin, "I now must give priority to your confusion." She rose slowly. "You'd better hurry to the field before you get into trouble with Coach Kalkbrenner."

"I don't get into trouble. What's he going to do? Kick me off the team?"

The Agave High School baseball team was in first place for the AIA 5A State Championship with only one game left to play. Without Christopher, the team would face a struggle in order to win the State Championship again. Christopher knew he was invaluable.

"Yesss!" he triumphed as he ran toward the exit. He was taking the shortcut across the parking lot to the locker room when he saw his mother's faded brown Ford F-150 pull into a spot.

"What the fuck?" Christopher approached the old pickup. "What are you doing here?" His facial and vocal expression showed disgust as he watched his mother assist his eleven-year-old brother from the vehicle.

"Chrissie, I need help tonight." The butter-blonde, thirty-six-year-old Sugie Snow looked up at her son while holding firmly onto Timothy's hand. Timothy's head was twisted toward his right shoulder; his eyes stared past his older brother into nowhere and his body rocked rhythmically.

"Is Teeba, I mean Ms. Prime, still here?"

"Shit, how should I know?" Christopher lied.

"Someone didn't show up for work and they called me to fill in. I need the money. I thought Teeba could be with Timmy until you get through with practice. I'm sure one of your friends can give Timmy and you a lift home. You have to stay with Timmy tonight." She looked worried, expecting an outburst.

"Dammit, Mom! You always know how to fuck things up for me, don't you? I need the truck tonight, okay? I won't babysit for *him*. No way!"

"We need the money, Chris! Tonight's a big drinking night with good tips. We need the money, okay?" Her raspy voice cracked as she tried to speak louder.

"I don't give a shit. I need that car tonight, get it?" His mind was working fast, trying to figure out how he could rearrange whatever was happening. "Take him with you and let him sit in the kitchen; you've done that before. Nobody will even know he's there. I'll get a ride to the lounge to pick up the truck after practice."

"I can't let Timmy stay there until past midnight!" Sugie protested. "And how am I supposed to get home at that hour?" She fumbled for the pack of Virginia Slims in her purse and lit a cigarette, all with her left hand—her right never let go of her rocking son.

"It's all *his* fault! Dad only left because *you* insisted that this freak of nature stay with us." Ignoring the mascara-stained tears rolling down his mother's sun-toasted cheeks, Christopher pointed his stiff index finger at his younger brother. "Look at him. He's screwed up all of our lives. God, I can't wait to get away from all this shit."

"Can I help?" As if out of nowhere, Teeba stepped between them. She bent down to Timothy and made eye contact with him, gently taking his free hand. With that, the boy let go of his mother and stopped rocking.

Sugie Snow and Christopher stared at Timothy. The child seemed magnetized by Teeba's eyes. Soon, his small strained face relaxed and his mouth turned slightly upwards, hinting a smile.

Within the first six months after Teeba had started her teaching job at Agave, she established the Special Education Program for the Learning Disabled. Sugie tried to enroll Timothy in the program but was rejected. Feeling compassion, Teeba took Timothy three times a week after school and worked with him on an individual basis. The child's progress had been phenomenal, and the teacher only recently had assured Sugie that Timothy would be accepted into the Special Ed program.

Sugie blinked away her tears. "I know it's not a night where you usually help out with Timmy, but I had a call from work and I thought, perhaps…"

"Of course, I not only want to, but I must take care of Timothy." Teeba bent down to the child's level, caressing his head. "How about if you and I go and work a little in the Special Ed room, Timmy? There's something new and exciting that I know you'll like very much."

"Areyoupurposelyscrewingwithmyhead?" Christopher ranted as a jolt of rage surged through him. "Youhaveadatewith*me*, Ms. Prime, or have you conveniently forgotten already?"

"No, I have not, Chris. But this has become an emergency and I know I *must* be with Timmy." The deeper meaning of Teeba's words was lost on Sugie and her older son.

CHAPTER 5

CHRISTOPHER KNEW HE had to hold back the bitter taste of bile and the barrage of obscenities gurgling in his throat. "Arrrgh," was the only sound he managed to release. He stormed away in the direction of the gym.

Smirks greeted Christopher as he came running into the locker room. Hardly out of breath, he was still grim-faced and his fists were clenched. "Assholes!" he roared as he stripped off his clothes and yanked his practice uniform out of the locker.

"Whoa, Snow!" Buzz Nolan said. "What's with you and Teeba Prime? I thought you don't like to eat brown meat?"

"What the fuck you talking about?" Christopher asked, choking on the insult. "She's as pure Caucasian as you and I."

"*Ay-ay-ay-ay-ay,*" Ramon Garcia sang, mimicking some sexy Lambada steps. "Rumor has it her fancy mother is really a purebred *chiquita.*"

"Yeah? From my own experience and not from a rumor, your mother sucks cock!" Christopher spat and flung a half-full can of Gatorade at Ramon.

"*Chinga tu madre.*" As Ramon charged toward Christopher, Coach K appeared.

"Get your lazy asses on the field. You guys are late."

During the next twenty minutes Christopher had trouble concentrating. Even though his mind was not on the game, he had a pleasing satisfaction as he swung the bat. His anger only made him hit harder and run faster than any of his teammates.

His resentment for his autistic brother had reached the boiling point. He knew he needed to rid himself of the steadily growing hindrance in his life. "The time has come!" he whispered. "I've got to put an end to him now. It'll be a relief for everyone." The thought loosened the tightness in his chest and the once-nauseating idea now seemed to be relaxing every raw fiber in his stomach. Like an antacid, it smoothed and coated the pain, allowing his mind to sharpen and shift into high gear.

Then another flash coiled his insides. "Teeba prefers to be with an idiot instead of having a productive evening with me." He spat. "Is she really a Spic?" he asked behind gritted teeth. "What does Garcia know that I don't?" Christopher's grip tightened around the bat. "So she's lied—she's been trying to hide her Hispanic background!" he snarled. "The fucking Spics are everywhere."

The thought of an intimate relationship with anyone other than one whom he believed to be purebred from a superior species was nauseating. He grunted and spat again before swinging his bat. "I'm a racist and proud of it!" he hissed as the ball spun across the field.

Christopher had secretly joined The Order of American Aryans and admiringly read and reread many books on Hitler's Third Reich. Through these ideologies he also developed an of-no-use-mentality for any living being either physically or mentally impaired.

Christopher remembered the days when he lived in a small but decent home, vaguely recalling happiness and comfort. He was only nine when his father left with no explanation and without saying good-bye. Gary Snow's departure came shortly after Timothy was diagnosed with autism. Christopher bitterly thought of the day when they moved into a cramped, stinking trailer.

Shortly after the divorce, his father married Paula—or Ms. Perfect—as Snow proudly referred to his new bride the few times when he phoned his older son. Christopher was told that his stepmother was pretty, meticulous, and obliging, and also owned a brand new beauty salon. Within twenty-one months after their wedding, Ms. Perfect had given birth to two healthy children.

A year after his second half-brother's birth, Christopher received an invitation to Los Angeles. He went there with high hopes of being asked to move in with his father and new family. But as soon as he stepped off the Greyhound bus there was immediate resentment between stepson and stepmother. It was Christopher's only visit. He had not seen or heard from his father since.

Soon after Snow left, Sugie began to work two jobs. The money she made from her day job as a cashier at Home Depot went almost in its entirety to pay for Timothy's care. At night she tended bar at the Desert Moon Lounge. Just ten years old then, Christopher dreaded watching his mother get dressed for that job. She put on heavy makeup, and her tight outfits always revealed too much of her butt, breasts, and bare legs. "You don't need that, Mom. You're much prettier without all the yeechie stuff on your face. I like you better in jeans and T-shirts," he used to tell her.

"I know, honey, but I'm only doing this for you so we can live a better life. I make good tips looking like this." That explanation only had caused Christopher to be more resentful of every tasteless detail in their pitiful lives.

Ignoring the sounds around him on the field of Agave High, Christopher didn't feel the perspiration on his skin or the dust on his tongue. And even though he concentrated on the pitcher, his mind's eye led him from the painful glimpses of his past to the recent picture, less than an hour ago, when Teeba lovingly caressed Timothy's head.

"Deceiving Spic bitch—go to hell!" Christopher cursed. In his heart he knew that Garcia had been right. "How could I've been so blind and not notice her Hispanic characteristics?" Oblivious to his mood swings, Christopher forgot that only a couple of hours ago he felt the desire to be noticed by Teeba's large dark eyes and to touch and caress her bronzed olive skin. Only a couple of hours ago he wanted to kiss her full moist lips and the slender curves of her body. Instead, now her delectable attractions had abruptly turned into despicable features.

Christopher's anger had created a fireball that now boiled his blood, cooked his mind, and turned his eyes ablaze. The time had come. He had to act.

"Hey, Chris!" Coach K called out. "You're looking great! Now hustle up, take some grounders."

Christopher ran over to his coach. "Listen, I'm having trouble with my new cup," he lied. "My old one is still in my hall locker. Can I get it?"

"Make it fast."

Chapter 6

Blinded by his steadily increasing rage, Christopher raced toward his hall locker. From inside a rolled-up pair of socks tucked into an old gym shoe, he retrieved his prize possession—a shiny new Walther P99, given to him on his eighteenth birthday by one of his fellow Klansmen. In no time at all he had proved to himself that he was as good in target practice as he was on the baseball field.

He ran through the dark empty hallways toward the Special Education Center. He stopped and held his breath when he saw them. Timothy was standing in front of an oversized easel, putting different shapes and colors on a Velcro-like board. Teeba, just a few feet away, was observing and praising him.

Silent as a predator, Christopher positioned himself. The pistol's cold metal caressed the palm of his hand. "So smooth and so perfect," he whispered. "Everything will be smooth and perfect from now on." Slowly he raised the gun and curled his index finger around the trigger. His aim was automatic and he heard himself snarl, "This gift is for you, you hopeless idiot. You'll be better off."

As soon as Christopher pulled the trigger, he closed his eyes and exhaled. He could feel the tension leaving his body and he smiled. In his euphoria he failed to notice that Teeba's body was faster than the bullet as she flung herself over Timothy's small frame.

"Gotcha," Christopher heard himself say from seemingly far away and in slow motion. When he opened his eyes he was confused. The classroom seemed ablaze in a purple fire. He tried to blink the strange vision away, but through the brilliant haze he saw two bodies lying on top of each other. "What happened?" he stammered. "Did I fire two shots? Did I kill them both?"

His breathing quickened and he felt sweat running down his spine. Like a robot, he abruptly turned away and stiffly began to run. But with each step, he forced his legs to become lighter. He empowered each new breath to widen his chest more, thus allowing his heart to release frustration, anger, guilt, and hatred. He replaced the grim look on his face with a smile as he envisioned his father embracing him into a new life. His mother would gratefully give up her sleazy night job. She would never have to embarrass him with provocative clothes and makeup again. Life would be good. Christopher had freed himself.

Sprinting through the dust on the field, he stopped next to the coach. "What do you want me to do next?" he asked, hardly out of breath. Everything had happened so fast, Christopher could tell that no one was aware he had ever left.

"Hop to it, take some grounders," Coach K said absentmindedly. His eyes were glued to the action on the field. He was more than pleased with the performance of his about-to-win-State-Championship team.

The loud, resonant clanging of the mop against the aluminum bucket echoed through the empty hallways of Agave High School. Alonso Cordova was mopping the floors while pushing the cumbersome tub. The clamor he created had drowned out the single shot. But now, Alonso stopped. He listened into the direction of two eerie sounds—a high-pitched repetition of screams and the recurrent banging of a door. Alonso dropped the heavy wet mop and ran toward the chilling noise. As he turned into another hallway he froze at the sight of the blood-smeared child. Alonso's own blood started to curdle as he witnessed the horrifying emission of unarticulated shrieks of fear that took turns with the slamming of the door.

Baton Rouge

...in May

Chapter 7

When she saw the flashing lights from the squad car behind her, Angela Atwood smiled and accelerated. Pedal to the metal, she thought and laughed before making a sudden turn to the shoulder of the Interstate Freeway. She daringly hit the brakes hard, almost causing the police cruiser to crash into her. She looked into the rearview mirror and, with a teasing twinkle in her eyes, watched as the state trooper slowly approached her fire engine red Porsche.

"Officer?" She lifted her head; her large, black-fringed eyes challenged the middle-aged, husky highway patrol official.

Since he never removed his sunglasses during the day, he surprised himself by involuntarily taking them off. His watery gray eyes were drawn into hers when a glorious purple fire erupted from her left pupil.

The magnetic lock of their eyes only took a few seconds and left the burly trooper with a blank stare. He rolled his eyes before he found focus again. When Angela offered him a bright smile he was unable to return the favor. He did not know what had numbed him.

"You have a wonderful day, Officer. You deserve it." She raised her window and through the rearview mirror watched the perplexed look on the state trooper's face as he scratched his temple with the arm of his glasses. She knew she was leaving the man in a state of confusion, as if he had daydreamed the encounter.

Angela, the twenty-seven-year-old daughter of Governor Edward Atwood and First Lady Chantal Atwood, threw her head back to free a short, throaty laugh. Then, she turned serious. "I've got to quit doing this," she scolded herself. "I'm definitely abusing my abilities by cuisinarting people's solid thoughts. It's not right and I should know better." As she pressed down the gas pedal, she ran her fingers through her shiny bright copper hair, allowing a glance into the mirror again. She liked the new color and the stylishly short textured cut.

The already high humidity in the mid-morning air had found its way into the car. Angela knew it would only get worse. She lowered the air conditioning and welcomed the hissing force of cold air. Then she picked up her cell phone.

"Mama! It's me."

"Angela, darlin'. Where are you?"

"I'm on the I-10 on my way to see you with only forty-five miles to go."

"That's a wonderful surprise. We didn't expect you until tomorrow. Is everything all right?"

"Everything's fine. But I had the strangest dreams last night and when I woke up this morning, I had the strongest urge to be with you and Daddy," Angela said. "Are you going to be home when I get there?"

"No, sugar, I'm leaving in a few minutes. I'm the guest speaker at a lady's luncheon for the Citizens Preparedness Council in Lafayette. Why don't you head straight up there? I would adore having my beautiful daughter at my side. How about it?"

Angela loved listening to her mother's lulling voice with the unmistakable accent of a true New Orleans native. "No, Mama, thanks. I'll take a pass. I've spent a lot of time in Lafayette lately and tomorrow's the big day and I have to be there again. I think I'll just relax and chat with Ella."

"Oh, Angel!" Chantal's voice increased in intensity. "I almost forgot! Daddy and I are hosting a dinner for Phillip Portal, his wife, and Dr. Hakan Öztürk tonight. There'll be a few others from PIGR as well. Their Los Angeles office only informed us late yesterday that Mr. and Mrs. Portal and their entourage are arriving in Baton Rouge this afternoon. So, Daddy invited them for a rather informal but authentic Louisiana food extravaganza tonight."

"Mama!" Annoyance and disappointment forced Angela to lower her voice.

"I know you hate these dinners, darlin', but you're an integral part of this whole new project. How thrilling that you're going to be with us tonight."

"Oh, Mama!" Angela said again, dreading the idea of sitting through yet another dinner with brilliant scientists who only showed excitement when the conversation revolved around their work. For the most part she had stamped them as lifeless and boring. It did not even intrigue her that she would finally meet Phillip Portal in person, one of the world's most prosperous individuals.

During Angela's many meetings in the recent past with PIGR officials, Phillip had given credence to his reclusive and neurotic reputation. He usually consulted on videoconferencing screens while working in seclusion at one of his many compounds somewhere in the United States. It was during one of these videoconferences that she learned of Dr. Hakan Öztürk and briefly made the Turkish scientist's acquaintance via the big screen as well.

The powerful and influential people she would dine with later did not intrigue Angela. Instead, she had envisioned a cozy, quiet afternoon and evening with her parents.

"Well okay. Fine then," she acquiesced. "I guess I have no choice. But I insist on some just-you-and-I-time between now and tomorrow. Deal?"

"It's a deal, precious."

Thirty minutes later Angela parked her car in the pleasantly cooled garage of the Governor's Mansion, located on Capitol Lake in Baton Rouge.

CHAPTER 8

"WELL, LOOKIE AT you, sugah!" Ella Laveau tilted her head and walked around Angela. "Sometime I jus' have trouble recognizin' you."

"Oh come on, Ella. Just tell me you like it." Angela blocked the older woman's circling path.

"I like it jus' fine. Whatever and whenever you do somethin' new to your hair or face—whatever you put on your body…to me you still the most beautiful 'n unique creature the Lord put on this earth." Ella drew Angela into her arms. "Feels good," she whispered. "Feels good to have you 'round, Angel."

"Come with me, Ella. I need to get comfortable."

After Angela hung up her hastily packed clothes, she sat across from Ella in the sitting area of the bedroom. Taking the older woman's hands into hers, Angela said, "It feels so right being here. When I woke up this morning, I somehow knew I'd be sitting next to you later during the day." She stopped and listened to her thoughts. "Mmmh," she frowned. "Now I'm curious to see where this gut feeling will lead to. Any hunches, Ella?"

The older woman leaned closer. "Look me in the eye, child."

Ella was only sixteen when she started working for the Atwood family. Her mother trained her in the culinary arts, preparing her to take over whenever the time should come. During those years, Senator Ronald Atwood, his wife Barbara, and their fourteen-year-old son, Edward, were living in one of the most beautiful old Victorian mansions on First Street in New Orleans' Garden District. Just a few years older than Edward, Ella watched him grow. She followed his education and charismatic career from becoming the youngest state legislator to the office of the president of the Louisiana State Senate. When Edward decided to run in the gubernatorial race, he won by a landslide and now, in his third term, proved to be the most popular governor in the history of the State of Louisiana.

The day Ella turned twenty-five, her mother died unexpectedly. Even though Ella was young, she never regretted making the commitment to continue preparing her mother's popular recipes, following a longtime tradition. Heritage, custom, and practice of her own culture were important factors in Ella's life. She claimed to be one of the many descendents of the famous and powerful Voodoo Queen Marie Laveau, who was born in 1794 in New Orleans. Ella never tired of telling stories about her feared yet respected ancestor who remained a figure shrouded in mystery. Like Marie, Ella considered herself a devout Catholic. Although she regularly attended church in Baton Rouge, once a month she made the trip to New Orleans. There she would have a silent twilight dialogue at Marie's tomb in St. Louis Cemetery No. 1. She never forgot to leave a white magnolia among the many offerings from other visitors. A mass at the Cathedral always followed her regular ritual.

Ella did not need to cultivate her inherited clairvoyance; she declared it a gift passed on from one generation to the next. "I have a talent one cannot study for," she exclaimed whenever she was asked. "I don't rely on my senses of reasoning, rather I respond to somethin' unexplainable. Some folks call it a blessin', others believe it's a curse. It always depends how one looks at it."

Now searching Angela's eyes, Ella shook her head. "Take out that contact lens. I need to see the true color."

Angela removed her left tinted lens, which she always wore in order to match the deep dark color of her right eye.

"Somethin' is happenin' but it's vague. The fire of the amethyst is still dim. What is it that you're feelin', child?"

"I don't know yet, but it seems there's an inevitability to my intuition for being here today," Angela offered. She filled her single contact lens case with cleaning solution and dropped the dark lens into it. "You've always told me—and somehow I've known it all my life—that I came into this world to accomplish something extraordinary." Angela was silent for a moment. "And even though I've had great success in my career and was able to perform other unusual things in my twenty-seven years of life...the bigger purpose is still unknown to me."

"You'll find it. And who knows, today might be the beginning of the journey."

"I don't know why, but Ebony's been on my mind lately. How is she?"

Ebony was Ella's thirty-year-old daughter from a short-lived marriage to D. J. Petitjean, a prominent jazz musician in New Orleans. Besides his musical talents, D. J. was also blessed with good looks and good genes. His good looks attracted an endless stream of female fans and his good genes kept him alive despite his perpetual drinking and smoking habits. He still played the clubs in New Orleans, but Ella never saw him again after the divorce twenty-six years previously.

"Ebony got engaged a couple of weeks ago, but I don't see anythin' good comin' out of that relationship. She fell for the wrong man, jus' like I did. I've got strange vibes, if you know what I mean," Ella pondered. "It ain't gonna last. That's my prediction."

"It's a pity we have not seen each other for years. Is she still in Tucson?"

"Yep, still nursin' and workin' hard, tryin' to make a livin'. She seems lost, though; says she's lookin' for the true purpose in her life. She ain't gonna find it in that man," Ella stated and shrugged her shoulders. "Nuttin' I can do. She's gonna find out for herself." She paused. "You hungry? How 'bout a li'l of my gumbo and some dirty rice? There might even be a few fresh beignets left."

Angela loved Ella's cooking. Her traditional yet inventive French meals were always a multicourse extravaganza, but over the years Ella had also worked on enhancing the two famous classics of Creole and Cajun cuisine. She experimented by combining both ethnic cuisines and called the results Louisiana Food. Her concoctions surprised even the most critical connoisseurs and were applauded by dignitaries and friends who visited the Governor's Mansion. Angela had spent many hours at the stove with Ella, observing closely and learning the older woman's skills. Whenever possible, Angela looked forward to assisting her longtime friend in the kitchen.

Happy and content, Angela leaned back into the chair letting the last bite of the delicious beignet melt in her mouth. "This was delicious," she praised, as she experienced a sudden fatigue. "I think I'm going to take a little nap. Please wake me up when you need my expertise in the kitchen for tonight's meal," she teased, trying to suppress another yawn. "This is really unusual for me to feel so tired in the middle of the day."

As soon as Angela laid her head on the soft down pillow and closed her eyes, she was drawn into another dimension. The vague intuitions from the early morning hours would become clear and Ella's prediction would unfold. Angela's journey was beginning.

Chapter 9

It had been another event-filled workday for Governor Atwood but, as always, he felt enriched by new experiences. His energy was as high as it had been eleven hours earlier when he started his usual routine at five in the morning with a rigorous forty-five-minute workout. Afterwards he had showered, read the papers, and been briefed on important issues while he drank his energy shake, made of fresh fruit and lecithin granules.

On the short flight to Shreveport he educated himself with more news and read documents pertinent for the day. After a breakfast meeting with Shreveport's mayor and business leaders, he flew to New Orleans to give the eulogy at the funeral of a former state senator. Following the ceremonies he addressed a group of concerned seniors on health care issues. Before returning to Baton Rouge, he insisted on paying an unscheduled visit to a hospitalized fifteen-year-old who had rescued his two younger siblings from their burning home.

It was almost five o'clock in the afternoon when he arrived back at the Governor's Mansion. As soon as he learned of Angela's presence, he instantly stopped thinking about business matters. The door was ajar and he could see that she was resting. He knocked softly, then went inside and sat next to the chaise lounge.

"Angela?" His voice was tender and loving. Edward smiled when he noticed she had changed her hairstyle and color again. Ten days earlier he had admired her as a stunning brunette with a sleek, elegant upsweep when she gave her final report to the PORTAL Enterprises representatives. Before then, she had surprised her family and friends as a lustrous, raven-haired beauty. Now,

Governor Atwood looked in amusement at the sassy short cut and bright copper color.

Since early childhood, it was obvious that Angela had been blessed with an unusual high intelligence and the rare gift of uncanny awareness and cognition. When it became clear that Angela's intellect was far superior to that of children in her age group, Edward and his wife decided on homeschooling with the finest educators available. Even though they encouraged her to play with children in the neighborhood, Angela preferred the company of people older than herself. The only other child who seemed to hold her attention was Ella's daughter Ebony, three years older than Angela. During their childhood and teenage years, the two girls developed an almost inseparable bond. However, when college and their occupations took them in different directions, they slowly lost contact with each other.

After her graduation, Governor Atwood encouraged Angela to join a committee consisting of public and private partnerships as well as political coalitions to stimulate economic development in blighted areas of Lafayette. As a result of the committee's study, an area in North Lafayette off Simcoe Street was identified.

In addition to housing and commercial enterprises, the revitalized area included a planned Children's Cancer Center. When the shell of the CCC was completed, the corporate sponsorship for the center had shifted from treatment to research and the deal fell through, leaving the project unfinished.

Angela suggested that she would look into opportunities to attract some technology-driven companies to the area, using the unfinished shell as an enticement. She contacted the Office of Economic Development and found that a Southern California-based company, PORTAL Enterprises, had submitted a proposal to set up a human genomic research facility.

When Angela told her father about the Southern California company, there was a strong fire in her eye. The governor remembered his daughter's excitement. "Dad," she had declared then, "this is going to be a slam-dunk! They'll fund 80 percent of the project and it will put Louisiana on the map in terms of medical and scientific research!"

The governor knew that Phillip Portal was one of the wealthiest venture capitalists in the world, with large involvement in the healthcare field. Portal Laboratories, Inc. was a well-known biotechnology consortium in Southern California and a wholly owned subsidiary of PORTAL Enterprises.

A few months after making the contact, Angela's work paid off and brought the first biotechnology company to Lafayette. Her announcement that the unfinished CCC would become Portal Institute for Genome Research (PIGR) immediately drew praise from the public and private sectors, especially when she said the facility would draw millions of dollars, create new jobs, and possibly one day discover cures for cancer and other diseases.

Reflecting, Governor Atwood shook his head in amazement. It did not seem as if eighteen months had gone by already. The once unfinished CCC shell now was a thirty-thousand-square-foot biotechnology research facility. Tomorrow's opening ceremony would be the culmination of Angela's hard work.

As the governor sat next to his daughter, she suddenly stirred, and her face flushed as from a sudden fever. But just as quickly, she calmed again. "What are you dreaming?" Edward asked quietly. He saw her eyelids flutter before they lifted. The unexpected fire of the amethyst in her left eye caught him by surprise and he sat upright in his chair.

"Daddy! It has happened! It happened…finally!"

"What happened, Angela?"

"In my dream I discovered the purpose of my existence. No," she corrected herself, "it wasn't a dream; it was more profound than that. Some powerful force led me away so I could connect with something almost unexplainable." She paused and searched for the right words. "All my life I knew something big was missing and I've been searching for this *something*. Finally, it connected with me!" Angela hesitated. "You look puzzled, Daddy; I don't blame you but I'm having difficulties explaining."

"I'm listening."

"You know I've often told you and Mama that I didn't feel complete—that something was missing in my reality?"

"And you always tried to tell us that we were wrong by diverting your attention whenever the subject came up. But we were selfish then because of our own pain and agony; the loss of your twin sister Anika was so unbearable."

"Daddy!" A glow spread over Angela's face and her voice grew stronger. "Try to imagine the possibility that a part of Anika—think of it as her energy or her soul—never left and today made contact with me." Angela reached toward her father. "Deep inside I knew that something was always next to me, and even though I sensed its guidance, I seemed to be unable to comprehend the awareness. All my life I've been waiting for this lost part of myself to connect and, finally, it came to me." She was talking fast and her dark eyes gleamed; the deep purple color in her left eye was ablaze. "It's as if a powerful missing piece reattached itself to my innermost core." She swallowed at the recognition and nodded. "Yes, there's an existence... *That which is never lost.*"

"I am trying to follow you, sweetie, but I am afraid I don't understand. What existence? What has never been lost?" Governor Atwood looked confused. "Are you talking about your own special qualities and gifts?"

"I know I was different than other children and you and Mama have been more than understanding, patient, and open to my strangeness..."

"It wasn't strangeness, Angela." Edward corrected. "You were born with a special gift that to this day we have difficulty comprehending. It's been challenging, to say the least." He laughed, trying to lighten the conversation.

"Yes! At one point you and Mama believed that Ella's self-declared clairvoyance might've rubbed off on me."

"Your mother and I soon accepted that whatever you were born with was a true rarity—something unique. Just looking at you now with that purple fire in your eye makes me..." He shrugged his shoulders and sighed deeply. "I know I once again will have trouble understanding what you're trying to tell me."

"Until now I've never felt complete, Daddy. I knew I had certain powers, but I didn't understand their true meaning and often abused them. This new information—I mean this vibration—it's so big, so enormous that I can't put it into words." Angela's face lit up more. "This incredible new intelligence might let me help you reach beyond your own sense of perception and understanding."

She took her father's hands into hers. "This awareness is new to me, but I want to share it with you so badly. Please let me try," she said. "Look deeply into my eyes, Daddy. Don't be afraid."

A fantastic sensation took hold of Governor Atwood, something he had never experienced before.

When Angela let go of her father's hands, she hesitated. Then, she asked quietly, "Daddy? Did you receive something?"

"I don't know how to describe what I felt." For the first time in his life Edward couldn't find the right explanation. No word seemed big enough to recapitulate the sensation that still lingered. "Your touch, it relaxed me so—almost as if I'm under heavy sedation," he finally said.

"Was there a message? I've tried to share with you what happened in my sleep. Did you receive that vibration?"

He knew she was trying to open his mind further and it saddened him that he would have to fail her. "No honey. Just…eh…let's say, I'm overcome by this beautiful light…this warmth." He stopped and searched for the right words. "I feel pleasantly paralyzed by some unknown emotion—like I received a guarantee that everything is going to be secure. Is that what you wanted to share with me?"

"Something like that, Daddy," Angela nodded, giving him an encouraging smile.

He knew that she was trying to hide her disappointment, yet there was a distinct clearness in her face. Edward sat silently across from his daughter, mesmerized by the purple aura. He realized that Angela's level of consciousness had been raised to enormous heights—an awakening to a new awareness; it was the cognizance of her unlimited perception. Edward now understood that only a few people would be able to feel those same vibrations and knew he was not one of them.

"Something like that, Daddy," she reassured him again. "We're all part of a very special circle of life. For right now, I distinctly see you, Mama, Ella, and me in this circle. I know there will be others, some of whom we'll never meet, but many who will connect with us. When my mission in this lifetime is finished, this circle will close and give birth to a new one. It always continues."

The governor touched her cheek. "Thank you, Angel. Thank you for trying to let me become part of your experience." He cleared his throat before changing the subject. "Ella said you wanted to have an input in tonight's dinner; she told me she's waiting for you."

Angela looked at her watch and reluctantly let go of the incredible new recognition that would change everything. "I'm sure she's finished most of it by now, but I better make my way to the kitchen." She embraced her father again.

"Promise you will keep your mother and me aware of whatever is going to happen?" Edward asked.

"Whatever is going to take place from now on, I know that I will need your help," Angela whispered. Before she left the room she turned. "After all, Daddy, look at me!" she said and grinned mischievously while pinching her body and shrugging her shoulders. "Look at me. I'm human...after all!"

Governor Atwood listened to her fading footsteps, although her presence seemed to still fill the room. He felt light and peaceful, yet his emotions were a combination of jubilation and sorrow. He remembered that same feeling from twenty-seven years ago when he held his infant daughter in his arms for the first time. His eyes welled up and tears of joy rolled down his cheeks, followed by tears of sadness. He knew he was blessed by Angela's birth and felt grateful for the twenty-seven years during which she had enriched his life. Reluctantly, though, he recognized an emptiness—just as he did almost three decades ago when he had to say good-bye to his other daughter, Angela's twin sister.

Chapter 10

"Ella, I've got to share something very exciting with you."

"Lord Jesus, look at that fire in your eye!" Ella's hands flew to her mouth before she wiped them on her white apron. She took a step forward and whispered, "It's beautiful, but it may scare those folks who don't know you."

"I know, I know. That's why I ran downstairs." Angela motioned her head into the direction of the other kitchen servants. "Let's go outside for a moment, please. I need us to be alone." Still intoxicated, Angela told Ella about the visions in her dreamlike state and the conversation that followed with her father. "I see you're studying my face; you see something, don't you?" she asked excitedly. "With your clairvoyance and intuitive mind, you might be the only one who understands what I'm feeling since I'm unable to express in words what's in here." Angela let her fingers drum against her temples. "My vocabulary is not big enough."

"Child, don't frighten me." Ella looked worried. "I might not be ready for this—I do have limitations."

"I need your help," Angela pleaded. "Somehow I know you're connected; I know you'll understand."

They walked to the far corner of the terrace and sat on chairs across from each other.

"Just relax and find the very depth of my pupils. I'll do the rest." Angela reached across and touched Ella's palms with her own.

As the sun went down, a golden light fell over the pair, encompassing their forms, melting them together.

Only a few seconds passed but an eternity of enlightenment had found its way.

"Holy mother of..." Ella swallowed the rest of her exclamation as she crossed herself.

"Oh Ella, your old, advanced soul understood." She closed her eyes and lifted her head; her face glowing with a grateful smile.

"I've led a very full life with constant high consciousness, 'specially 'round you." Ella rose slowly, steadying herself on Angela. "But *this* I never expected—I never thought *this* was possible." She began to shiver. "I know the growin' goosebumps on my skin are not from the mild evenin' breeze," she said. "This chill is due to the anticipation of the unknown."

"A power was released to me after all these years. I've never felt so complete and yet I'm so uncertain what to do next," Angela pondered. "Could I be right that most of my soul's energy was stored elsewhere?" Then, with fiery intensity she looked at Ella. "Does it mean that somewhere a human being is breathing who is connected to me? Could it be possible that since birth, part of my soul existed in this other living being that should have been my twin sister?" Angela's dark eyes widened and with the ongoing deepening of recognition they began to smile. "Two incarnations are sharing the same spirit; two different physical beings are living the same reality; their time flow has become synchronized."

Ella stared at Angela and nodded. "You and Anika—one old soul in two incarnations—originally were meant to accomplish great things side by side. But then the divine plan changed and Anika had to die! That's it: Anika died and yet, she didn't."

"Ella!" Angela whispered. "You must've felt something twenty-seven years ago when that happened. You were the one suggesting the name Anika because Mama was too distraught losing one of her twin babies. You named her Anika and said the name means Child of God."

"I felt somethin' very mystical—somethin' I couldn' explain. But right before li'l Anika's spirit slipped out of her tiny body, I saw the fire of the amethyst flicker in her right eye. At that moment, somethin' made me look at you. That's when I saw that same phenomenon in your left eye." Ella shrugged her shoulders. "I had no explanation then, but I knew that you were born for a special reason. I felt that one day you would make a difference in many lives." The older woman nodded again. "Yes, there was a divine purpose behind Anika's death and I've never been more convinced that we'll find out soon why tonight all of this is happenin'."

"I agree. Today I was made aware that Anika's powerful spirit never left. *It* was feeling me every day, trying to connect. *It* felt me all along and only now can I feel it as well!" Angela's eyes narrowed in concentration. "There is an existence of a host to Anika's soul—another human being."

Squeezing Ella's hand, Angela continued. "But something bad happened to that individual today. I sense an accident that caused my soul's twin to go into a restful phase for only one reason—to release a very powerful portion of her energy to me." Angela inhaled deeply. "This is why I can see and hear things I never believed possible before."

"Yes, child." Ella's face brightened. "With your transfer of thought, you made me see and feel it myself—*That Which Is Never Lost.* Your true journey is beginnin'."

"Ms. Ella! Ms. Ella?" It was the voice of one of the kitchen helpers.

"I'll be right there," Ella called out from the shadow of the terrace without taking her eyes off Angela. "Listen, Angel. Wherever your journey will be takin' you, you still will live this life and mustn' forget to take a li'l time every day to enjoy what you've been blessed with. Few folks will understand what you've shared with me but they continue to love you. There are many who depend on your love. Help 'em so they can keep smilin' with you."

"I know, Ella. I love this life and the people in it more than you'll ever know." Angela squeezed Ella's hand. "Life has always loved me back and that's why I'm not afraid of whatever will be expected of me."

CHAPTER 11

FORTY-FIVE MINUTES later Angela tapped on her parents' bedroom door. "Are you ready?"

"Precious Angel, you look magnificent." Chantal sat in front of the dressing table and was fastening her pearl necklace. She motioned to her daughter. "Come closer so I can hug and kiss you." Releasing Angela from a long and warm embrace, Chantal said admiringly, "What a pretty dress. Is it new?"

"Yes and no," Angela laughed. "You know how I hate shopping but this dress just yesterday winked at me through a window of a vintage shop. I'm glad you approve."

"Approve? That word doesn't even come close. I adore it, darling! It's so…Audrey Hepburn. You know, lately you look more and more like a modern version of her, except for your unusual hair color."

"Well, I don't know." Angela blushed. "Audrey Hepburn was unique in her looks—much classier than I. She would never dream of messing around with crazy hairstyles and colors as I do." Angela took a step back. "But look at *you*! Smashingly beautiful as always."

Chantal knew that red was a good color for her and had chosen a Valentino-designed light gabardine dress for the evening. Her honey-blonde hair, as always, was perfectly coiffed and her make-up was minimal; she looked her usual elegant self. At fifty-five, her slim figure was the same as it had been at eighteen. Growing up as the daughter of former president Paul Pearson and actress Christine deDroit had afforded Chantal a prestigious education and lifestyle. Her comfort level was at ease even with the highest and mightiest dignitaries. The Louisiana media called her "The Perfect First Lady."

"Chantal, I cannot find my glasses. Did I leave them here?" Governor Atwood asked as he came through the adjoining doors from his dressing room. He wore a dark blue pinstripe suit; the Hermès tie and shirt complemented each other. Even though the cut of his attire was fluid and perfect, there was a hint of his strong shoulders and arms underneath. His full dark hair was slightly graying at the temples, his face reflected intelligence—but mostly, he was a very handsome man at fifty-seven.

Angela looked at her parents and felt an overwhelming desire to tell them how much she loved them. And so she did.

"Let's go downstairs and have a glass of champagne before our guests arrive. I'd like to toast the two most magnificent females in all of Louisiana," Edward said.

They barely finished their drink when Phillip Portal, his wife Miranda, and a few high-ranking corporate officials from PORTAL Enterprises were escorted into the rotunda.

Angela was well acquainted with four of the six guests, having spent long hours with them, their lawyers, and representatives from the state, holding tedious negotiations before signing contracts. Now, in the rotunda of the Governor's Mansion, she again shook the hands of the COO and the CFO. She then welcomed the two VPs, one the executive vice president of research, the other in the executive position of administration. "Nice to see you again," she greeted them warmly and added in a more hushed tone, "especially without all the lawyers!"

"Isn't that a comforting feeling?" the COO responded and laughed with the others.

It surprised Angela when she saw Phillip in person. From the videoconferences she had imagined him taller and larger. Instead, he was slight and rather thin. His sparse brownish hair was strangely parted and the longer thin strands were combed in a circular sweep—an obvious and feeble attempt to cover the bald spot. Despite his enormous power, wealth, and famed intelligence, Phillip seemed uncertain and nervous, hiding behind thick glasses and his taller, statuesque wife. Although the gray suit was undoubtedly of the finest quality, it hung loose and ill-fitting on Phillip's small frame.

"How very exciting to finally meet you in person, Mr. Portal." Angela offered a firm handshake.

"Please call me Phil," he said in a quiet monotone voice. Then he hid farther behind his wife. "May I introduce you to my wife, Miranda."

Miranda was dressed in a bright lavender suit. The collar of the dotted silk blouse was fastened high with a small antique brooch. But despite the hidden designer label, the ensemble made her look dowdy. Miranda's square face, devoid of any makeup, was pleasant and cupped by short, thick, ash-blonde hair. The only indication of the Portals' legendary wealth was reflected in a pair of large and blazing white diamond studs in her ears as well as a platinum ring with a magnificent, fiery, and flawless ten-carat stone on her left ring finger.

The next couple to arrive was Professor Walter Hellmann and his wife, Dr. Sonia Russo. Both taught at Tulane University's medical school and were old friends of the Atwoods. Walter Hellmann had an engrossing personality, and Sonia's sunny disposition could light up the dullest evening.

When Phillip noticed the arrival of two PIGR scientists, he immediately introduced a middle-aged, sturdy-looking man with a receding hairline. "Please meet Dr. Yuri Barsoukov," he said with pride. "PIGR's new brain—freshly imported from St. Petersburg."

The other scientist, older and leaner with sharp lines on his pockmarked face, originally came from Moscow. He bowed and nearly clicked his heels with each introduction. His head bent even lower when he shook Angela's hand. His voice was deep. "Ivan Putin," he said. "No relation to Vladimir," he added and grinned.

The group moved into the drawing room where some of the guests reviewed the outstanding collection of southern art. The rest of them were involved in small talk while sipping champagne from the crystal flutes and enjoying the hors d'œuvres that were passed by professional servers in distinctive livery.

Finally the last two guests arrived.

Dr. Afshin Afshor, at thirty-five, was a tall and swarthy French-Iranian with a neatly trimmed black mustache and cold dark brown eyes.

Angela experienced alarming signs and warning flashes when first introduced to the two Russians and Afshor, but the mere presence of Dr. Hakan Öztürk almost made her lose her balance as she shook his hand. No one noticed the quickening of her breath and the widening of her eyes. No one heard the palpitation of her heart.

Born in Turkey, Hakan was an impressive-looking man. Taller than most of the others, he stood erect and conducted himself with polished etiquette. His jet black hair, thick and slightly unruly, matched his eyebrows and mustache. His brown eyes seemed warm at first glance, yet Angela immediately detected a mixture of boldness, uncertainty, and insolence as she watched him move from person to person, not allowing himself too much time to talk with one individual.

Beneath Hakan's seemingly personable behavior, Angela saw an air of mistrust and ennui. The forced, thin smile never left his lips as he shook the hands of everyone in the room. Even though he tried to portray himself as cordial, he remained aloof; his short sentences were either abrupt or too flowery.

Angela watched this man of contradictions. Every hair on her body stood on end. *This is it,* she said to herself. *This is the person that I'm destined to meet.* Despite the turmoil inside her, she continued the conversation with Barsoukov. Keeping her responses polite and accurate, she kept glancing over the Russian's shoulder, observing Hakan, who was the newly assigned lead scientist at the PIGR facility in Lafayette.

CHAPTER 12

THE SIX-PEDESTAL mahogany dining room banquet table was exquisitely decorated with antique silver place settings framing magnificent French china. Baccarat crystal glasses reflected the light from the twenty flickering candles held in four silver candelabras. The dimmed light from the massive and ornate chandelier above the table and matching wall sconces spread its soft glow throughout the beautiful State Dining Room. The unmistakable sweet fragrance from dozens of Helios roses wafted in the room.

As Chantal asked her guests to take their seats, Angela kept observing the Turkish scientist. Coincidence or not, her mother had placed Angela directly across from Hakan.

When their eyes met, the scientist looked uneasy; there was a nervous twitch in his face. He shifted in the Magnolia chair five feet across from her.

After Governor Atwood gave the welcoming toast, words were exchanged across the table. As expected, most of the dialogue revolved around the opening of PIGR and the new research projects.

Ella produced a six-course feast that started with a sinus-clearing crab cake nestled in swirls of red and white sauce, followed by grilled mayhorn cheese with Beluga caviar and oysters. The next course was a sampler of pasta jambalaya—gulf shrimp, andouille, duck, and chicken tossed with spinach fettuccini. Various fine wines were served to accompany the small but rich and highly tasty courses.

His words at first were inaudible to the rest of the group, but it was obvious that Phillip was saying something as he leaned close over his plate, finishing the last of the jambalaya.

Then, he wiped his mouth and smiled.

"No offense, Miranda," he apologized to his wife, "but this so far is one of my lifetime's most outstanding meals. I can't wait for the next course." He looked at Angela. "Your mother told me earlier that you helped prepare these unusual dishes—tell me, is this Cajun or Creole cooking?"

"It's both and more." Angela explained how Ella had experimented with the recipes, handed down to her and over the years, eventually creating her own modern interpretation of Creole and Cajun dishes. "This is the best of Louisiana cuisine," Angela praised. "Wait until you taste the entrée."

Ella's grilled pompano Napoleon was served on puff pastry and topped with pepper-crushed scallops and a mustard caper sauce. Even the side dishes of flash-fried spinach, pureed butternut squash, herbed gnocchi with green sauce, and fresh, sweet corn disappeared quickly from the silver serving trays as they were passed.

"I can't believe I'm not even full yet," Sonia Russo gushed, looking at her empty plate. "I don't want to sound greedy, but do tell me what's for dessert?"

Chantal shook her head. "No, darlin'. Let it be Ella's surprise. Why don't you give Angela a break and share some of *your* rare stories with our guests." Chantal noticed that Angela—contrary to her usual hearty appetite—had barely touched her food. She had been entertaining the guests with tales of New Orleans and the magic of that city.

"No, please don't stop." Miranda begged Angela. "Listening to your descriptions, I swear I could hear the street musicians around Jackson Square. I saw myself wandering through the lush tropical courtyards and I believe I even could sense the moist air on my skin while walking under those giant oaks dripping with moss."

"Yes, it was fantastic," agreed the COO in an almost dreamlike state. "I don't know what was more delicious, the food or listening and watching you, Angela." He leaned back in his chair, shaking his head. "Fantastic," he repeated.

"Thank you," said Angela. "But now you must excuse me for a moment. I believe I'm needed in the kitchen."

When she returned, her arm was hooked into Ella's. "May I present the genius responsible for everyone's weight gain tonight? The one and only Ms. Ella Laveau."

There were expressions of "Delicious" and "Exquisite," "Thank you so much" and "Nothing will ever compare again." The praise was followed by soft, yet enthusiastic applause.

Ella had left her apron in the kitchen and looked crisp and unruffled. She nodded and mouthed, "Thank you, very kind of you," as her eyes moved from guest to guest.

Miranda sprung out of her chair. "This was so very tasty." She shook Ella's hand and whispered, "I've never seen my husband eat with such a hearty appetite."

As Ella excused herself from the group, she pulled Angela with her. "There are men in there with no good intention," she said with quiet intensity. "There are four people who trigger fear in me. I'm haunted by a vision of a tragedy of great proportion," she warned. "Tell me you're feelin' that too?"

"I do but I'm still having trouble getting used to this new awareness. All my life I considered myself an aberration. But only during the past few hours was I able to exchange those doubtful hindrances with my true self." Angela paused and laughed. "I'm talking like I'm from outer space. Well...maybe I am...but I'm celebrating my new strength, Ella! Everything is becoming so clear and intense that I want to reach behind and grab what I missed. But, impatient as I am, the urge to lunge forward is almost unbearable."

"Control yourself, child. Don't let the wrong people see what's happenin'." Ella put her hands on Angela's shoulders and pulled her close. "Your eyes with all that energy and depth might give away your secret, even to those whose own eyes are dull'n flat. You mustn' let 'em see this. You might scare 'em away—there's a lot at stake."

"Scare them away?" Angela frowned. "I will have to play a whole new role in order to accomplish what lies ahead. I know this might sound conceited but I'll have to use all my powers to make them putty in my hands—especially one of them."

Angela walked behind the cart that carried the desserts. The glossy rich slices of Mississippi mud pies promised a mouth-watering treat, dense hazelnut mousse balls sat provocatively on chocolate-covered filo cookies, and squares of classic bread pudding were surrounded by thin, skillful swirls of golden caramel sauce. Ella's signature dessert was inverted on small crystal plates: Chicory coffee crème brûlée, crowned delicately with fresh whipped cream and chocolate shavings.

The eyes of the guests, mostly the men, lit up as they watched Angela expertly fill their plates. Most of them asked for more than one of the delicacies.

The atmosphere around the table progressively brightened when Angela took turns with Sonia, sharing anecdotes of Louisiana humor with the rest of the group.

"Heh-heh-heh." At first it was an almost suppressed titter. Then, it developed into a high-pitched chuckle. "Hee-hee-hee-hee." Finally he let an uninhibited guffaw escape. "Ha-ha-ha-ha-ha-ha-ha." Phillip kept slapping his thin legs under the table; his head was bobbing back and forth as he kept laughing.

The two VP's, the CFO, and the COO of PORTAL Enterprises looked at each other, disbelieving that the always taciturn Phillip would laugh out loud.

It was after ten o'clock when the group began to break up. PIGR's opening ceremony was less than twelve hours away and some of the men proclaimed they still had work to do.

"You were charming the pants off these stuffy genuflecting deadbeats," Sonia whispered into Angela's ear. "Some of them were so dull, they needed to have some life kicked into them."

"No, it was your stories that made everyone laugh; I laughed the loudest and never get tired hearing them," Angela hugged her mother's dear friend. Looking over Sonia's shoulder, Angela focused on Hakan. She saw him follow her father into the library and watched through the door as the governor showed part of his collection of antique coins to the scientist.

After saying goodbye to the Hellmanns, Angela walked into the library. "Daddy, Miranda and Phil are ready to leave. I'd be happy to explain some of the coins to Dr. Öztürk."

After answering some of Hakan's questions, she leaned over one of the cases and removed two very rare and unevenly shaped Egyptian coins. She could feel the Turkish scientist's eyes moving from the ancient relics to her slightly exposed cleavage.

"Beautiful," he muttered. "I wish I had more time to see the entire collection."

"I have the feeling you have not seen much of anything around here," Angela responded before she closed the case. "Once you're settled in your new home and are comfortable with your new surroundings at PIGR—why don't I show you the rarities of New Orleans? Would you like that?"

Hakan stiffened and swallowed. Then, with barely moving lips he muttered, "Yes, I would like that very, very much."

CHAPTER 13

TEN YEARS EARLIER, Hakan worked at the Pasteur Institute in France, officially heading their Immunology Research Group. Under his leadership, his team did work in immunological approaches to arthritis, but unbeknownst to his superiors, Hakan secretly developed a new recombinant form of the deadly Ebola virus by inserting other genes artificially into the DNA of that strain. He surprised himself when he realized that this new living organism was much more potent, vicious, and faster-acting than anything known to the world of virologists and biologists. He named his brainchild MAX 18, because after infection, the maximum lifespan of any creature would be eighteen hours.

During the same time period, PORTAL Enterprises had introduced a major drug for arthritis. In order to continue and maintain a leadership role in the arthritis market, Phillip Portal started a global search for another senior scientist in the field of immunology. Impressed by Öztürk, who had given presentations on the results of his immunological approaches at a number of major congresses over a three year period, PORTAL Enterprises presented an offer to Hakan to join their U.S. team.

Hakan, who silently led a double life, was a member of an ultra-orthodox Islamic terrorist organization, a group of men who intended to "purify" the world. They had formed a secret organization and called themselves *Al-Saafi*, The Pure.

Hakan discussed PORTAL's offer with his leaders of the group, and it was unanimously agreed that the proposal was a great opportunity to develop a new Al-Saafi cell in the territorial United States.

Building a new research team, Hakan convinced Phillip to hire two additional scientists from the Pasteur Institute: Dr. Afshin Afshor and Dr. Ivan Putin. When Hakan moved his team from California to Louisiana, he requested hiring a third scientist. Shortly after, Dr. Yuri Barsoukov became the last addition to PIGR's crew. Barsoukov and Hakan, years earlier, had met in Iran.

Unbeknownst to anyone other than a few of the pure brethren of their fast-growing international group, all four scientists were members of Al-Saafi.

From the moment he started work at PIGR, Hakan aimed to win Phillip's confidence. It didn't take long before Phillip confessed that he was in the beginning stage of Lou Gehrig's disease. Hakan told his boss that he had experience in the biology and immunology of that disease and offered to do private studies and research for Phillip's illness in addition to the other official research program. That was five years ago and the outcome of Hakan's hard work in all fields was highly admired by his superiors, especially by the trusting Phillip.

CHAPTER 14

AFTER GOVERNOR ATWOOD'S chauffeur had driven the four men back to their hotel in Lafayette, Hakan discussed some important matters with his team. Hakan was the only one as fluent in Russian as he was in Farsi, Arabic, French, English, and Turkish. However, since the Russians spoke no French and the French-Iranian spoke no Russian, their meetings were conducted in English. Sitting in the spacious hotel room, Hakan briefed his three colleagues on the latest communication that had come out of Iran from Al-Saafi. When he finished his report he rose. "Well, I believe there's nothing more to say tonight."

"I don't know," Putin frowned as he tapped his foot. "I still am uncomfortable with the security. How can we be sure that everything is really tight?" he asked in strongly accented English.

"If I secured and tightened things more, you'd be tripping over your own feet," Hakan replied but his sarcasm was lost on the Russian. "You'll just have to take my word for it," he added. With a thin, arrogant smile on his lips, he watched as Barsoukov and Putin left the room. He knew that the Russians' reputation and work in virology and molecular biology were flawless, but at times their cultural differences clashed.

"You need me for anything else?" Afshor asked.

Hakan turned around. "Oh, Afshin," he said, rubbing his forehead. How could he forget Afshor was still in the room? He looked at his watch. "Yes, I'd like you to try and locate Dr. Gottfried Geist in Los Angeles. Get the latest report from him. Then report back to me. I'll be up for a while." He spoke to the French-Iranian man in perfect Farsi.

After Afshor left the room, Hakan double-locked the door and closed the curtains. Hotel rooms never made him feel safe. While undoing his tie, he listened to the few messages on the hotel voice-mail system. Only one important call had come in. The message was in his native language. Paying close attention, he replayed it twice while taking notes—notes that needed to be decoded. Then he erased all his messages and turned on his Sony Notebook. After typing passwords, the machine went through its normal scanning process. Hakan shrugged out of his jacket, letting it fall over the back of the chair. He stared at the screen as his thoughts drifted back to the Governor's Mansion.

Angela Atwood's magnificent face flashed before his eyes and he recalled her captivating voice. "I'll show you the rarities of New Orleans. Would you like that?" she had asked.

Hakan closed his eyes. He remembered his answer, but still was amazed about his response. An unknown pleasure had compelled him to watch her all night and now, sitting in a lonely hotel room in front of his computer, he recalled every sensation that she released in him. He sensed puzzlement and terror when he discovered his desperation to experience love, emotion, lust, and compassion—feelings that he knew existed, but until now had been caged and kept isolated.

Back in his homeland there was a family he tried not to think about. He was in his early twenties when a marriage was arranged to a bride who never stirred any feelings in him. During the act of fathering his two children, he wrestled with irrelevant erotic visions in order to temporarily forget the pressing obligation to spread his seed. Hakan felt no love for his wife or offspring; he only understood the love and total devotion toward his work and the visions created by religious fanatics who had become his true family. Hakan learned to worship Allah and trust no one, but nowhere did he feel more secure than in the cradle of pure science.

Hakan considered himself a highly religious man. For years, prayer and absolute commitment to a cause had replaced the desire for sex and pleasure. Living and working in the United States became a double-edged sword. He was convinced that America represented *Dar-al Harb*, The House of War. The temptations of Western civilization were unsettling, but Hakan continued to fight off the poisonous bait that tarred the evil West. When his financial backers, fanatical men he highly respected, gave him dispensation from *Shari'ah,* he breathed a sigh of relief. Not having to follow the strict Muslim code of laws that included dietary, social, and political rules and restrictions made life easier. Obeying orders to mix and blend into Western society, Hakan resigned himself to the fact that unmitigated obedience and obligation were necessary in order to accomplish the mission. In the beginning, he tried to ignore the provocative allurements by American infidels and found it almost impossible to merge with a world so different from the one in which he was born. Certain foods, lifestyles, and women nauseated him at first, but in the name of religion and his dedication toward the assigned task, he slowly began to move and think more freely. He shaved his beard, bought stylish clothes, and allowed himself the luxury of an expensive watch. With gradually eroding caution, he finally plunged into the stream of Western comfort.

The abundance of sexual decadence was Hakan's last temptation. He convinced himself that even in this decaying society, a man's biological urge needed to be fulfilled. But so far his sexual experiences had only festered in pathetic encounters with offensive whores.

It wasn't until this evening in the Governor's Mansion that something idling in the dark depth of his subconscious came to life. Hardly able to muffle the loud inner voice that kept reminding him to fight the urge, he lusted to enter the sanctuary of feminine mysteries.

He imagined Angela's exquisite, chiseled features with her large black eyes, finely shaped nose, and sculpted moist lips. He tried to blink when he believed he saw her perfect body moving sensually across the seventeen-inch computer screen in front of him.

"Nonsense!" Hakan shook himself out of his stupor and hit the Internet icon. There was important business to be done and nothing, not even Angela Atwood, would distract him. He gulped down some water and with it he tried to swallow his desires; then he wiped his mouth clean.

He quickly typed a cluster of commands into the computer and found what he was looking for. His face moved closer to the screen and he keyboarded another few commands. It took him a while to decode the information before he was able to open the attachments. With intense interest he read the highly secretive message.

Just as he finished reading, the phone rang.

"Hakan? It's Ford."

Ford was the Middle-Eastern Bureau Chief of the CIA; the initials to the name were an abbreviation given many years ago by colleagues who challenged themselves combining job titles with names. During those days, Field Operative Randolph Donner became FORD; the name stuck to him like glue throughout his career in the field of intelligence.

"Listen, I know it's late but I didn't want you to be surprised tomorrow," Ford's deep voice bellowed. "It was decided that during the opening ceremony, there should be an announcement by a spokesman from PIGR that several of their projects *will* be funded by the federal government."

"Really? Is it necessary?"

"Well, since we're going to be in and out of the new facility with certain regularity and spending considerable time with you, we have to somehow explain our presence. Make sense?"

Hakan listened and nodded. "These are your decisions. You must know what you're doing."

He hung up the phone after reassuring himself that the government's statement would be kept superficial, at least for the time being.

What the announcement certainly would not reveal was a new and most important project called *Operation Mayfly*. As one of the CIA's Black Projects, this highly secretive program was one of an unknown number of government-funded scientific research projects, disclosed only to those with the highest possible security clearance. Hakan's contact within the CIA was Ford.

Hakan shook his head, a sarcastic grin on his face. He felt as if he held the CIA in the palm of his hand. "How is it possible," he asked, "that programs such as Operation Mayfly are in fact so secret that even the federal legislative committees overseeing the intelligence service are ignorant of all details except highly aggregated budgetary information?" Hakan was aware the intricate details of such programs were unknown to all but a handful of highly placed agents, each totally and blindly committed to the achievement of project goals at any price—financial or otherwise.

"I'm the puppet master," he laughed. "I'm maneuvering their strings and directing their moves…and my main puppet is Ford."

The phone rang again. It was Afshor.

"I got a hold of Dr. Geist. Everything is going better than expected. The organization in LA has supplied him with a very dedicated and highly trustworthy man. His name is Gary Snow."

Later, during the night, Hakan was caught in a whirl of tempestuous, tormenting dreams in which he experienced delicious sensations and fervent desires. He willingly threw himself over and over again into the intense heat of inextinguishable flames.

His racing heart woke him; he was bathed in his own sweat. Lying on his stomach, his head grotesquely twisted to the right, he felt paralyzed. He tried to swallow, but his tongue was stuck to the dry roof of his open mouth. He heard himself panting heavily as he recalled the exquisite forbidden memory of his dreams. When he finally rolled over slowly, his still-debilitated brain noticed the sticky source of satisfaction on the white sheets.

Los Angeles

...in May

CHAPTER 15

"YESSIR! I UNDERSTAND. I took down the directions and will meet you at eighteen hundred hours sharp." Gary Snow disconnected the call and stared at the receiver before he put it down. He could feel his adrenaline rise, causing a pleasant prickle under his skin. Then, a content smile spread across his angular face. He took another few moments to relish the forecast of his soon-to-be-realized dream.

Still beaming, he walked into the family room of his three-bedroom home and found his two sons engrossed in a video game. He watched the two boys as they sat on the floor, their backs perfectly straight, and he could see that their eager minds and eyes were focused on the execution of their mission on the screen.

"Boys! Did your mother get home yet?"

"Yes, Dad. She's in the bedroom lying down for a minute." Eight-year-old Felix answered politely, but his fingers skillfully still maneuvered the action with the controls.

"She has a stomachache," added seven-year-old Maximilian.

Snow walked down the small, narrow hallway. The door to the bedroom was open and he saw Paula lying on their bed with her eyes closed.

"What's wrong?"

Paula raised her head two inches off the pillow. "Oh, it was nothing. I'm already feeling better, honey," she winked at him. "The monthly nuisance, you know, with the usual cramps and headaches."

"Did you take anything?"

"Yes, that's why I came home a little early; I left my prescription pills. They're the only ones that help." Paula smiled weakly. "As I said, I'm feeling a lot better already, honestly."

"I just was told to attend a meeting tonight. Don't wait for me with dinner. I'll eat when I get back."

Paula sat up. "Everything okay?"

"It couldn't be better!" Snow's smile returned involuntarily. "I've made some great connections. They could prove lucrative for us in the long run," he said, and sat on the edge of the bed.

She flung her arms around his waist and pulled him toward her. "I love when you get that look on your face. Makes me feel really, really good and secure!"

Snow pressed his lips into her light, soft hair and tightened his embrace. He could feel her full, hard breasts pressing against his chest and automatically slid his hands down her back to grab her tight buttocks. "You make me feel really, really good as well. Too bad you're out of commission," he hinted.

"No, I'm not," she protested. "There's one part that is never out of commission, darling." She opened her lips before she kissed his mouth.

Ten minutes later, Snow took a quick shower and shaved for the second time. As he did every day, he made sure that his small mustache was trimmed to perfection. Then, he plucked two long hairs out of his coarse eyebrows and splashed a hint of aftershave onto his slightly tanned skin. He ran his hand over the top of his head; the day before Paula had clipped his and their sons' hair short in a military way. Snow went into the neatly organized closet and removed a pair of khaki trousers and a beige polo shirt. Before he adjusted his thin-rimmed glasses, he made sure they were spotless. Snow glanced one more time into the mirror and was extremely satisfied upon seeing the reflection of his tall, lean body. A month ago he had turned forty-three. "Discipline and clean thoughts have paid off," he said, smiling at his image.

He noticed that Maximilian and Felix had finished their game and were disconnecting the attachments from the television set, after which they put the various parts of the video game in the box and set the same on a shelf in the hallway closet.

"Where are you going, Dad?" the younger child asked.

"I have a very important meeting tonight. I want both of you in bed by nine o'clock. We need to get up early tomorrow morning for our outing."

Snow kissed his sons on the top of their heads and told them to help their mother set the table.

On his way out, he patted the Rottweiler, resting on a mat by the front door. "Good boy, Hero. Be on guard."

CHAPTER 16

SNOW'S CHEVY BLAZER was as tidy as everything else in his life. There was no room for flaws and he liked it that way. He speed-dialed a number on his cell phone and put it on speaker.

"Tom, it's Gary. I just want to make sure that we're still on for six o'clock tomorrow morning."

"Of course," the voice on the other end said. "My boys and I are really looking forward to the next five days. It'll be a great experience for all of us."

"Do me a favor and call the others since I'm on my way to a meeting."

"No problem, Gary. See you bright 'n early tomorrow morning."

As Snow drove toward the northern edge of North Hollywood, he was pleased with the way his life was going. He had initiated the trip with brothers from the Organization of American Aryans. The four fathers agreed this was the year for their children to go to "Outward and Upward," the group's survival camp in the isolated desert between Los Angeles and Palm Springs.

Snow turned at the next stoplight and drove slowly through the North Hollywood section bordering on the industrial area he was looking for. He felt a sense of relief when he left the sight of the neglected homes in this poverty-stricken neighborhood behind him. He glanced at the directions again and soon spotted the narrow, unimportant-looking warehouse in the old industrial complex.

He was a few minutes ahead of schedule. Obeying the instructions, he drove through the alley between the warehouse and another abandoned building and parked his SUV in the rear. He then shut off the engine and waited.

He saw a white compact car pull up behind him at ten minutes past the hour. Snow immediately walked back and offered Dr. Gottfried Geist a firm handshake.

The two men walked to the middle of the alley, where Dr. Geist unlocked a heavy steel door leading into the building. The doctor flicked several switches, lighting up a large empty space. Drained and dented cans of soda pop, broken glass, crumpled-up papers, and other refuse were strewn across the dirty concrete floor. A stale odor hovered in the vast emptiness.

Without speaking, Dr. Geist walked briskly toward a partition, hard-heeled shoes echoing every step. Behind the wall stood a long table with a few folding chairs.

Snow watched the doctor unroll several rolls of paper, carefully taping them to the edges of the table.

Dr. Geist, a fifty-one-year-old German with strong roots in Dresden, was of medium height, neither heavy nor thin; his ash brown hair was precisely parted in a clean line and combed back. His skin tones were pale and his gray eyes seemed too close above his aquiline nose. His lips were thin and colorless. The doctor always wore the same combination of clothing: blue trousers and a white shirt under a gray vest. The only variation came through his nondescript ties. Everything about the scientist seemed unnoticeable until he opened his mouth. With his sharp mind and superior intelligence, he never allowed himself to say anything before he was absolutely certain that his words would have the exact effect he planned to achieve. Dr. Geist was a dedicated neo-Nazi with contacts to the Order of American Aryans. The fact that the German scientist was also a member of Al-Saafi would never be revealed to Snow.

"Let's start with plan A." The doctor's voice was a cold, determined whisper.

For the next hour Snow listened carefully and registered every precise instruction in his head as he eagerly followed the scientist's plan step by step. "Brilliant," he muttered occasionally. "Absolutely brilliant!" Snow was so awestruck by the perfection of the project, he hardly was able to control his anticipation.

"Any questions so far?"

"No, sir! Everything is clear. All I need now is your signal when to start."

"We will get in touch with you. Do you have people lined up and are they ready to go?"

"Yessir!" Snow straightened his lean body. "I have very capable and highly trustworthy men ready to start the build-out. I will see to it that in record speed they'll transform this place into exactly what you have in mind."

"Remember!" Dr. Geist hissed. "You're the only one who knows of the ultimate goal. If there's a leak—if anything goes wrong—your head will be the one to roll."

The scientist's sharp German accent made Snow stand at attention. "No need to be concerned, sir. I'm taking full responsibility."

Dr. Geist put a long black plastic pouch on the table and opened the zipper. "This is the first payment of what we agreed upon. I want you to count it. We will continue payment as we proceed."

Snow felt his Adam's apple bob as he swallowed hard. For a moment he was afraid his excitement was noticed as soon as he saw the money. Cursing himself for a weakness, he had trouble controlling his shaking hands as he counted the neatly arranged stacks amounting to two hundred thousand dollars.

A sudden noise—the rustling of paper followed by an empty can rolling over the cement floor—broke the silence. Startled, both men lifted their heads and looked in the direction of the disturbance.

Dr. Geist's eyes narrowed and the corners of his mouth turned down when he saw a huge rat fearlessly staring at them. In one swift move he withdrew a small handgun, fired, and killed the unsuspecting rodent.

Dr. Geist's mouth turned upward into a satisfied grin. "Did you like that, Snow? Well, soon you'll have the opportunity to get rid of more and bigger rats than that one." He patted his newfound conspirator on the back. "It'll happen just like that." He snapped his fingers.

Tucson

...in June

Chapter 17

Ebony Laveau was not in the best of moods. She had just started her afternoon shift at the Joseph Sugar Neurological Research Institute and found herself confronting chaotic clutter. Because of two emergencies in the early morning hours, the transition from one shift to the other was laced with more than the usual frenzy. Already short of staff, Ebony realized one of her nurses had not punched in nor called.

Ebony usually was admired for her patience and orderly conduct—her soothing and calming voice created symmetry. But today she had no tolerance for the mistakes, moods, or malarkey of her coworkers.

She was tired after having spent another sleepless night waiting for her fiancé Rodney. When he finally returned at five o'clock in the morning, Ebony's trained nose detected expensive booze and cheap women. The few words she had to say to him were followed by a powerful kick to his groin. As soon as Rodney came up for air she gave him another kick, this time in his butt, propelling him out of the door. With her hands on her hips she watched as he gathered his belongings, which she had thrown into the front yard earlier.

"Anyone heard from Caitlin?" Ebony's voice came sharply off-key.

"She just called," Tim Micu, the only male nurse on the ward, responded. "Her baby's throwing up, her five-year-old is having the runs, and her babysitter didn't show. She said she'd be here as soon as her husband gets home from work."

"Cover for Caitlin and start making rounds." She pushed the records for the patients in eight of the fifteen rooms toward Tim and briefed him on the shift reports.

Rosa Lopez, the pile of patient records tightly pressed against her chest, nudged the male nurse. "Let's go, Micu. We're already behind schedule."

"God, what's with her today?"

"I have the feeling it's gotta do with Rodney," Rosa whispered. "My boyfriend works at the Desert Moon Lounge. He saw Rodney last night again buying shots of the best tequila for two *ladies*." Rosa rolled her eyes. "Rodney kept tipping the pretty bartender fifty dollar bills! Can you believe that? Apparently, Rodney was bombed and caused quite a scene. When they threw him out, he needed to be held up by those two peroxided, boob-implanted blondes whom he'd bought drinks for all night long."

Before she turned to enter a patient's room, Rosa frowned. "I feel for Ebony. She wants so badly to be married and start a family. What did she ever see in that loser anyway?"

"I'm so sorry. I got here as soon as I could. Both of my kids are sick and..."

"Oh please!" Ebony replied as she waved the out-of-breath Caitlin away. "I know it's been a crappy day—not just for you. Why don't you find Micu and finish up your rounds. Tell him I need him here."

Moments later, Ebony took a deep breath before she entered the unit manager's room. As the charge nurse, she had all the assignments ready for the month, but there was something else she needed to discuss. Ebony, whom her coworkers called The Pillar of the Ward, was crumbling from yet another disappointing relationship. She felt in need of support and comfort and there was nobody in Tucson who could give her sustenance. She longed to be near her mother. Earlier in the day she had made up her mind—she was going back to Louisiana.

Chapter 18

"I CANNOT DO it! They're arguing and I don't have the courage to fight that bitch. She gives me the creeps," Caitlin complained. She begged Tim to check 319, the room she had purposely left for last.

"Uh-uh, no way," Tim said, shaking his head. "The last time I tried I almost lost my job because I couldn't control my anger. That woman brings out the worst in me."

Ebony emerged from the unit manager's room. "What's the matter? You're afraid of Gloria Prime again?" she asked. "Well, I guess I'll have to deal with her then." Ebony gave the two nurses a disapproving look. "What will you do when I'm not around?"

But before Ebony opened the door, she stopped and leaned against the wall, stealing a glance into the room through the small window in the center of the door.

Gloria Prime was pointing at her husband, Thomas. "When will you realize there is no hope?" Her shrill voice pierced through the closed door. "It's been four weeks with no change and no explanations." She stopped. "What am I saying? I've been looking for an explanation for twenty-seven years. I've been fooled and toyed with ever since I gave birth to her…and now this!" She pointed at the young woman laying motionless in bed. "She's in a permanent vegetative state—neither dead or alive. Don't you and all these ignoramuses get it?"

Gloria's hands gripped the frame at the foot of the bed and started to shake it. "Nothing will wake her up any more. I want her off these support systems so I can finally go on with my life."

"Ssssh, please calm down," Thomas said as Ebony came in.

"Mrs. Prime. I have to ask you to please lower your voice. You, again, are causing disturbances to my patients on this floor."

"Really?" Gloria threw her head back and let out a sarcastic chuckle. "Most of your patients seem to be unable to hear anything anyway. They're all brain-dead, are they not?" She purposely intensified her level of speech. "So what does it matter how loud I talk? Besides, this is between me and my husband and I'd like you to leave us alone."

"Gloria, please! Ebony is right. Why don't you and I leave instead?"

"What?" She shook her husband's hand off her arm and looked at him in disgust. "I'm not leaving until I'm good and ready." She stomped her high-heeled shoe into the floor and continued. "Where is Dr. Berger? I want to speak with him right now!"

"Dr. Berger is presenting a seminar this afternoon. I'll leave him a message so he can get in touch with you tomorrow morning." Ebony tried to keep her composure.

"I want my daughter off these machines. I have waited long enough and I can't stand the suffering anymore." Gloria's voice became even louder as she moved toward the feeding tube.

But Ebony was faster and blocked her way. "If you do anything foolish, I'll call security."

"Spare me your threats. If you call these apparatuses a lifesaver, you're *all* nuts around here." Gloria spat the words at the nurse, then coldly looked at her husband. "We have a lucrative business because we're known for selling *healthy* produce. I'm not prepared to give up my lifestyle because you decided to support the withering fruits and vegetables around here." She glanced at her watch. "There's no sense in staying any longer. I'm late for an appointment already." She diverted her attention to the few crinkles in the ivory-colored silk pants and jacket, ran her hand over the unwanted folds, then lifted her head high and stalked out.

"I...eh...want to apologize for my wife. She has said some terrible things. I think...no, I understand why she is so frustrated and upset."

"I'm sorry, Mr. Prime, but your wife was like that from the moment your daughter was brought here. It's a shame she has no compassion for anyone but herself." Ebony replied, bending over the peacefully resting patient.

"Sleeping Beauty never gets affected by anything, does she? Wherever she is, at times I'd like to trade places with her," Ebony sighed and gingerly touched her patient's arm, staring at the tranquil face. Though only seconds passed, she let herself surrender to a seemingly slow process of quietude-and-truce-transfer.

"I don't know how, but your daughter has the most calming and wonderful effect on me." Ebony finally straightened and looked at Thomas. "I can't say I get the same serenity from any of my other comatose patients."

"I know," Thomas agreed. She's always had that gift. I come here not only to see her, but being near her brings me peace. I just wish she'd come back to us. I miss her spirit and her smile. She's my sunshine; life is so dark and empty without her."

"I think she'll come back. I have a good feeling about it." Ebony patted Thomas's arm. "Just hang in there."

Alone again with his daughter in the antiseptic quiet of the room, Thomas pulled his chair closer to the bed and began to talk. He talked to her every day, about everything; about his pain and fear, his problems and unhappiness. Only in this hospital room did he share his own deep secrets and admitted that he had learned to harden his shell against his wife. He also shared the joys and dilemmas of his employees—people who had known his daughter since she was a little girl. He told her about funny incidents that happened on a daily basis. Thomas did not mind laughing alone.

Even though he knew she could not hear him, the one-sided conversations always gave him atonement; all of the ambiguities, the riddles, and issues of daily life seemed to lift when he sat near her. Even now, as she lay silent, he imagined listening to her advice and pretended he could hear her laughter. He envisioned her endless activities and sensed her powerful presence. The memories put a smile on his face.

"Thank you, Teeba, for helping me keep my faith and honor. You know I'm your ever-grateful and loving father."

As if signing off a letter, he ended his daily ritual. He gave her another long look, knowing there would be no response. Then he gently kissed her brow and left the room.

Her body remained motionless; her peaceful facial expression did not change. But behind the closed lids her large dark eyes were following her father and her inner smile furnished the room with a pristine glow.

What no one at the Joseph Sugar Neurological Research Institute surmised was that Teeba had heard every word that was spoken and had felt every thought that was passed on to her for the past three weeks. She soon would become the foremost interest of one of the most respected experts in the medical field on coma.

CHAPTER 19

AFTER SPENDING FOUR hours at the Millennium Salon and Day Spa on Oracle Road, Gloria Prime reemerged relaxed, released, and rejuvenated. Earlier, an esthetician gave Gloria a luxurious facial while another therapist massaged her feet. Afterwards, Gloria's hair color was touched up, then meticulously blow-dried. Her naturally coarse and curly dark hair now had a silky sheen and hung full and straight just below her shoulders. During a relaxing manicure and pedicure, a makeup artist intensified the highlights, color, and glow on her face. When she looked into the mirror, Gloria felt beautiful.

She changed into a pastel pink summer dress, exposing her tanned shoulders, arms, and legs. The silver jewelry she had chosen for the evening was sparse, but noticeably exquisite. Gloria loved her sexy, new, and very high-heeled sandals, the latest design by Stewart Weitzman. Walking tall, she was aware of her arrogant gait. Swaying her hips and pointing her nose straight ahead, she purred with pleasure as the early evening breeze caressed her glowing skin. She passed by the two restaurants in the Casas Adobes outdoor mall and noticed that the patrons on the terraces turned their heads as she headed for her car. Gloria knew she was beautiful.

She opened the trunk of her white Lexus SC430 and carefully laid down the pantsuit she wore earlier. As she drove out of the shopping center, Gloria was filled with power, pleasure, and pride.

Fifteen minutes later she pulled up in front of the Hacienda del Sol Guest Ranch Resort and instructed the valet to handle her car with extra-special care. Confident that her late arrival would cause a stir, she walked into the restaurant.

About twenty-five women, ranging in ages from thirty-five to sixty, were gathering in one of the private rooms, enjoying their first cocktails.

"Gloria! God, you look wonderful."

"I love that dress. It's so Chanel!"

"Ah, you should wear your hair like this all the time."

"Those shoes...to die for...where did you get them?"

Gloria loved the attention and awarded her admirers with one of her brighter smiles as she air-kissed each of them on both cheeks, producing sounds of "mmmvah" while returning compliments. She finally made her way toward Nadine, the birthday girl, and handed her a beautifully wrapped gift package.

"Happy Birthday, Naddie. I made this especially for you."

Nadine Miller, the wife of the largest landowner and developer in the greater Tucson area, planted a kiss on Gloria's forehead. "If it's what I think it is, I'll absolutely love it. Okay to open it later?" She placed the gift behind her on a table—next to all the other presents—then, turned back to Gloria. "We need a moment alone after the party, so don't rush off," she whispered. "I have a surprise for you." In a louder, more concerned voice, she asked, "How's Teeba?"

A few women close by stopped their conversation in mid-sentence, turning their smiles into pained expressions. "Yes, darling, how is she doing?"

Gloria's happy face changed into a troubled expression. "She's the same. It's not getting any better. Tom and I are prepared for the worst."

"Tz-tz-tz. What a shame," Cyrinda Parker said, shaking her head. In an exaggerated move she grabbed Gloria's hand, almost spilling her wine. "Such a young and beautiful life. What a waste, what a shame."

"Hey, how about a glass of wine? Or would you prefer something more zesty?" Nadine interrupted, pulling Gloria away. "Sorry I asked about Teeba," she whispered. "For the next few hours I promise to do my best to keep your mind busy with more pleasant things." She gave Gloria's hand an encouraging squeeze.

Nadine and Gloria had met only two years before at a social gathering benefiting a promising new local theatre company. Both were forty-seven years old, and both were married to men who had made a prominent name for themselves in and beyond the city of Tucson.

Oscar Miller's wealth was untouchable and his reputation was as ruthless as it was respected. Nadine and Oscar lived in the exclusive gated community of Ventana, where they had built a magnificent modern home, high above Tucson, with spectacular city and mountain views. They had no children. Instead, they doted on their five prize-winning purebred dogs.

As soon as Gloria was introduced to Nadine at the theater benefit, Gloria made it her goal to become better acquainted with the other woman and worked hard on developing the friendship.

Nadine, born, bred and raised a belle in Texas, was not a natural beauty. Her flair, expensive upkeep, and unusual hairstyles, however, only produced an additional tribute to her alabaster allurement. Her ability to be charming and coquettish, demanding and dangerous—often all displayed together—produced the dramatic effect she wanted to achieve.

Gloria was born and raised in Culican, in the state of Sinaloa, Mexico. She was the youngest child and only daughter out of three children. Her father and much older brothers were farmers; many years later Gloria would describe them as behind-the-desk-sitting executives rather than sweating-in-the-fields and hands-on-owners of lettuce-, tomato-, and melon-producing farmland.

Her parents, Juanita and Sergio Perez, as well as her brothers, Carlos and Humberto, took delight in the dainty girl, surrendering to her wishes and demands. They were fascinated, watching her grow and develop into a true beauty. Nothing escaped Gloria's hungry eyes as she observed her two older brothers, male cousins, and all their friends. She did not miss any opportunity to eavesdrop when she heard their laughter and, like a sponge, absorbed the stories young men boast about. She resented the fact that she was protected from the thrills of life as she imagined them, so, sometimes late at night, when their voices woke her from her sleep, she snuck out of the house and went to her secret hiding place from where she could watch rather than just listen to them talk.

She was the envy of most girls in school—not only because of her beauty, but also because her body showed early signs of voluptuous perfection. Studying was not her forte; instead of improving her grade point average, she much rather preferred working on being above average in her femininity.

When her brothers realized that she drew the attention of their male friends, they changed their nightly hangouts to places where Gloria could not follow them. Carlos and Humberto were not prepared for a confrontation with their overprotective father.

The day Gloria turned eighteen, she begged her father and convinced her brothers to let her come along to the annual Cinco de Mayo celebration at a friend's home. It was the day she met Hector Munoz.

In her secret hiding place Gloria had listened to many of the success stories Munoz claimed to have had with the most desirable girls. She also heard the rumors surrounding his family and became aware of their famous but dubious wealth. She knew her father did not approve of his sons' friendship with Munoz. But that, plus the gossip circulating around the Munoz clan and their "dirty" money, became even more of an intrigue to Gloria. Having felt too sheltered from reality and playing host to her vast imagination for too long, she hungered for the truth and needed to quench the thirst of what her mind's eye envisioned.

When she finally met Munoz at the party, he exceeded each of her fantasies. Realizing that her beauty had caught Munoz' attention, she used all of her feminine powers to make his head spin out of control.

At first Gloria managed to hide her infatuation with the sleek and suave Munoz, but soon her fascination grew into uncontrollable passion.

Unaware of the facts, Sergio Perez noticed the overnight metamorphosis in his daughter and only reluctantly accepted his wife's explanation of the natural change from girl into womanhood. Soon, though, he became aware of the steadily growing gossip behind his back, and one day secretly followed his daughter after school to her and Munoz' rendezvous.

Behind the thick walls of the Perez home, Sergio blamed his wife for lacking the necessary motherly instincts. He cursed his sons for their irresponsibility and lack of protection. He threatened to kill Munoz.

"But I love him and he loves me," Gloria had screamed at her father. I'm eighteen and old enough to know what I'm doing."

"You know nothing!" Sergio had thundered back. "What do you know about the Munozes' dirty business? Nothing! All the men in that family not only lust after bucks, booze, and breasts, they also are dangerous criminals."

Sergio put his daughter under strict house arrest. Inside the walls of the Perez home, Gloria learned to hate her father and brothers. She even began to resent her mother, who threw her arms up in resignation and ignored Gloria's pleas for help and understanding.

Feeling abandoned, Gloria came to rely on her own cold and callous calculations. As she did in her childhood days, she again made herself weightless like a little bird and, night after night, unnoticed, flew out of the house when everyone was sound asleep.

For two months Gloria reeled in dizzying ecstasy. Weakened by Munoz's smooth pursuits and sweet promises, she gave herself to him—unconditionally, with pure raw lust and longing.

When she confessed that her need to be with him had become a necessity, he pledged his commitment and they made plans to elope within twenty-four hours.

It was a moonless, rainy night when Gloria escaped her parents' home, carrying only a few of her most precious belongings.

Her father and brothers found her the next day, hiding in the thicket, shivering with anger.

Munoz had never showed up.

Abhorring the idea of living in the same city as Munoz and under the same roof with a family who offered no love or sympathy, Gloria had schemed the other alternative.

Thomas Prime was a produce wholesaler from Tucson and a regular customer of her father. Ten years older than Gloria, he had openly admired her beauty and spunkiness and secretly had fallen in love with her. Gloria hardly paid any attention to the tall and always polite man. She realized that he had a crush on her, but even though he was attractive in a subdued way, he was not her type. Gloria soon discovered that beneath his bravado, Thomas was a shy, sensitive, and serious man.

Plotting her second escape from Culican, Thomas seemed the perfect candidate for her plan. Soon after Munoz's rejection, and to the delight of her parents, Gloria agreed to have dinner with Thomas. She seduced him in his hotel room and within a month agreed to become Mrs. Prime. A hasty, small wedding was planned and during the ceremony, Gloria's lips curled and froze into a victorious, yet mocking smile.

Despite several attempts to abort the child growing in her, Gloria, eight months after her wedding day, gave birth to a healthy baby girl. When the doctor put the precious bundle into her arms, Gloria, with cold indifference, did what was expected of her. She forced herself to kiss the infant. Then, she closed her eyes and cursed the child, fathered by Hector Munoz.

Chapter 20

It was already past ten o'clock when the last guests left the restaurant. Even though Nadine's invitation asked for a contribution to the local animal shelter instead of gifts, most of her friends had eagerly complied by giving a donation, but also had brought a present. Nadine and Gloria watched as the restaurant manager and one of the valets carefully put all the items into the trunk of the cobalt blue Mercedes 600 SL.

"Why don't you and I have a quick nightcap over at Loews?" Nadine suggested, still in a celebratory mood.

The Loews Ventana Canyon Resort lounge was unusually crowded, but the two friends found a small table away from the noise and music.

"I must see what you gave me," Nadine cooed as she carefully unwrapped the gift. "I knew it! It's beautiful. Look at all the details." Nadine turned the handcrafted frame around and around, admiring her friend's skill and delicate artwork. "You're so talented, darlin'; this is absolutely priceless!" she exclaimed, pressing the frame close to her chest. "I think I'll have a mirror put into it rather than a photograph. What do you think?"

Gloria was pleased. She wanted Nadine to admire her work. Gloria had only made six of these pieces and knew that every visitor who ever set eyes on the five in her home expressed a desire to own one. "These are my little treasures of the desert," was the explanation she usually gave, trying to look and sound humble.

This was the first frame she had created for someone else. Guests at her home always were amazed at where Gloria found such odd-shaped stones, crystals, and semi-precious gems. Rare and colorful tiny feathers, wispy branches that resembled filigree, and many other unusual small artifacts were exquisitely combined and crafted together.

Although she never had set foot into the desert, Gloria claimed she carefully and painstakingly found all these gems during her hikes into the mountains or in the dried-out riverbeds. Having told these stories over and over again, she believed them to be true.

The truth was that her daughter, even as a small child, proudly brought home her exquisite finds and over the years had filled several containers. Only seven years old at the time, Teeba created her first frame, into which she placed a photograph of her father and herself. She kept the frame on her nightstand until the day she left for college.

Some time later, Gloria assumed ownership of the contents in the boxes. She prided herself upon her own creativity, ignoring the fact that she had copied her daughter's unusual technique.

The warmth of the after-dinner drink and Nadine's admiration made Gloria tingle with delight. "What is it that you want to talk to me about?" she asked.

"Well, darlin'." Nadine put the frame back into the box and leaned closer. "Oscar told me yesterday that there's no way he can leave the project he's presently workin' on." Nadine's Texas dialect had become more pronounced after several glasses of wine during the course of the night. "At least not now, possibly not at all this summer. So-ho…" she paused for the effect "…I thought it simply would be fantastic if you'd come with me to La Jolla. I'm sure you wouldn't mind leavin' the dreadful Tucson summer heat. I'd show you a real nice time!" She gently pinched Gloria's arm. "How about it, darlin'?"

Gloria managed to hide her instant excitement. Nadine and Oscar Miller always spent the summer months at their palatial estate in California. The home had been featured in several architectural and design magazines, and those lucky enough to receive an invitation came back to Tucson with raving reviews.

"Oh," Gloria sighed. "As good as it sounds, I don't know how I can leave right now."

"Why precious, you deserve to get away. You've been through a lot these past few weeks," Nadine scolded. "Didn't you say it takes a lot out of you when you visit Teeba? I know Tom will understand. I'll talk to him."

"Would you?" Gloria sighed again, this time louder. "Perhaps Thomas would not mind. He never goes away and since business always comes first, he probably wouldn't even miss me." Gloria stared at her hands, folded on her lap.

"You're comin' with me!" Nadine said determinedly and then in a softer tone assured her friend, "And if sweet Teeba's condition should take a turn one way or the other, I'll make sure you'll get back here immediately."

Gloria kept the growing thrill within her under control. No matter what her feelings were, throughout the years she had learned how to disguise them or act the extreme opposite, if needed. She was proud of the achievements and awards that her self-taught acting abilities presented her.

Gloria, though she never finished high school, always had a sharp instinct. The lack of a formal education did not diminish her desire to become rich. Once married to Thomas, her need for recognition and wealth was so concentrated that she made it her calling to expand her husband's business. Soon after the wedding she became an integral part of PRIME PRODUCE.

Prior to his marriage to Gloria, Thomas prided himself on his kindness, integrity, and understanding. He often waited patiently when his customers could not pay bills on time. He treated employees fairly and equally. It did not matter where they came from or what their background was; he admired their hard work and treated them accordingly.

Things changed when Gloria stepped in. With her contempt for everyone but herself and her dictatorial demeanor, bills either had to be paid on time or no new deliveries were made. She reevaluated employees and ranked them according to their accountability, aggressiveness, and accomplishments. Gloria changed the atmosphere within and around PRIME PRODUCE from relaxed to ruthless. Yet the business steadily grew and though longtime workers detested her conduct, Gloria achieved what she had set out for—respect and recognition within the company and the community. Her perseverance turned her husband's business into the largest produce wholesaler in the Tucson area.

At first Thomas was reluctant to accept the changes, but his love for Gloria was so strong, he soon began to openly show his pride. He publicly attributed the success to Gloria's vision and hard work. Her taking charge at work afforded Thomas more time with their daughter—he single-handedly took on all the parenting. "I'm Mr. Mom," he used to laugh, "and I enjoy it very much."

Gloria never told Thomas that he was not Teeba's biological father. She would not reveal her secret to the society circuit where she had become a prominent figure.

The hours she did not spend on business matters were devoted to social and charitable obligations. When Gloria and Thomas appeared together at society functions or dinner parties, Gloria acted out her role to perfection as the loving and caring mother and wife. According to her, the Primes presented the prototype of the perfect family.

As Teeba grew older, it became more painful for Gloria to even look at her daughter. More and more, the young girl began to resemble her biological father, the man Gloria loathed. The child who should have never been was growing into a magnificent beauty of superior intelligence; her big, bottomless black eyes made Gloria feel uncomfortable every time they penetrated hers. Gloria tried to ignore the uneasy feeling that Teeba not only knew of her true parentage, but that she was also able to read her mother like a book. At all costs, Gloria avoided being near the daughter whom she secretly believed was a curse of witchcraft. She celebrated the day when Teeba left for college.

Years later, when Teeba moved back to Tucson, rented a place of her own, and started to teach at Agave High School, Gloria first was infuriated. But since Teeba kept her distance, Gloria ignored the fact that they were living in the same city.

Then it happened. The headlines called it a mystery or a heroic act and, for more than two weeks after the shooting, the newspapers and magazines were printing every detail of Teeba's young life. The reporters and television crews followed Gloria and Thomas everywhere, squeezing them for every bit and piece of information that concerned their daughter. Gloria had to play the role of the distraught and loving mother and hated it. But she also was relieved that the attention remained on Teeba so her own past was never questioned. The arduous hours spent neutralizing her Hispanic accent had paid off—her true origin remained a well-kept secret.

The Agave High School shooting was still under investigation. There were only two silent witnesses—eleven-year-old Timothy Snow, who, because of his autism, was of no help to the investigators, and twenty-seven-year-old Teeba, who remained in a coma.

For more than four agonizing weeks now, Gloria had to pretend that she cared, that she was worried and suffered for her comatose daughter.

Sitting in the lounge that was filled with foot-tapping music and gay laughter, Gloria's spirits finally were lifted by Nadine's invitation to La Jolla. "I have to confess something, Naddie," she said slowly. "Thomas and I are facing a horrible decision. We…" she choked on her words and lowered her head. "We believe it might be in Teeba's best interest to disconnect the feeding tube if her condition does not improve very soon." She managed to produce a tear, enjoying the sensation as it slowly rolled down her cheek. "You might think of me as heartless, but I wish they would just disconnect her without my knowledge and tell me she died peacefully." Gloria looked at Nadine through misty eyes. "You're so right, Naddie, I need a break from all of this and I'm so grateful for your kind invitation."

Chapter 21

After the seminar, Dr. Austin Berger drove back to the institute. He had been there earlier, checking on the conditions and progress of his patients, and even though no emergency called him back to the clinic, he had a thought during the lecture.

"Where's Teeba's chart?"

"I just returned from her room. I wanted to check the equipment again and then decided to give her a massage and a little extra range of motion," Ebony admitted, handing him the chart.

Austin smiled to let Ebony know he was aware of her affection for Teeba. He went into his office where he called his friend and colleague, Dr. Clayton Harris at the Omni Neurological Institute of Southern California in Los Angeles.

"Dr. Harris is out of town and won't be back until next week."

"Is there a number where I can reach him?" Disappointment laced his voice. He saw his second line starting to blink.

"Unless it's an emergency, you'll have to call back tomorrow and speak with Dr. Harris's assistant. She might have a contact number but she's gone for the day," the voice on the other end responded.

"Thanks." Austin cut the connection by depressing the second line. "This is Dr. Berger."

"Uh-oh. Sounds like someone's in a rush or in a foul mood."

"Clay? I don't believe it. I just hung up with ONI trying to get you."

"Really? Well, the tuned brains of two neurologists seem to always awaken the old ESP. What do you know?"

"The tuned brains of the two *finest* neurologists!" Austin corrected him. "Where the hell are you and what brings me the honor?"

"Austin, my man. If you're not already, please sit down. I'm calling for two reasons. First, Maya and I are getting married next year, on the twentieth of February. I want you to be my best man. You may as well block out the entire week because Maya's family is planning pre-and post-wedding parties. Her mother is already going crazy; we're still months away, but she claims she won't have enough time."

"Congratulations and thanks for the honor! I never thought this was going to happen. Who put the pressure on whom?" Austin scratched his chin.

"Pressure? I think common sense is a better term. Further procrastination would eventually have turned me into a lonely and loony old scientist. You should settle down yourself, buddy. Anyone exciting in your life?"

"Nah. There's nothing exciting here in Tucson. How about fixing me up with one of Maya's sexy LA connections?"

"Every time we take that route you leave a river of tears and a trail of misery behind," Clayton teased. "Trying to match you up with someone is impossible. I have more important things to do than console Maya's distraught friends."

"What can I say?" Austin grinned. "I'm committed to my first love—my work. God help the poor soul who might fall for me; she'd be home alone most of the time. Amazing that Maya is willing to tolerate your schedule. Isn't she jealous of all the time you're spending at ONI?"

"I'll have to work on it," Clayton Harris sighed. "Actually, that's also why I'm calling. I let Maya talk me into spending some quality time together at a spa. We arrived yesterday and I'm going crazy already. It started at six this morning with a roadrunner hike up and down the hilly roads. Then I did my usual one-hour run on the treadmill and lifted weights. That's all I can tolerate—the rest of the program here is not for me. Maya and I have hardly seen each other because she's taking advantage of everything on the schedule. So much for quality time together," Clayton sighed. "I need scientific stimulation and with seven more days to go here, I'll be tearing my hair out. You've got to help me, Austin. I won't make a good-looking bald man."

"What makes you think I can prevent you from tearing out your hair?" Austin laughed. "I'm in Tucson and you're in...where the heck are you anyway?"

"I'm at the Canyon Ranch Spa, right here in Tucson."

"No shit!" A big smile spread across Austin's angular, ruddy face. "This is frigging unreal. Wait until you hear why I tried calling you." Austin reached for the Prime chart and leafed through it without looking. "I have an unusual case here. Actually, *intriguing* might be a more alluring word for you." He paused and took a breath. "I very much would like to consult with you on this case. How soon can you be here?"

"It's three o'clock now. As long as I'm back here by seven for dinner...Give me the directions."

Less than thirty minutes later, the two men sat across from each other in Austin's office.

"You look good, man! Really good! It's gotta be due to the regular premarital sex in your life," Austin said. "But since premarital is premature for me, perhaps I should start working on the *regular*," he added with a wide grin.

"Cut the bull, Austin! You've never been able to go longer than two days without it. Knowing you, things have not changed much."

"They have! It's three days now."

For the next fifteen minutes, the two friends continued to reminisce about their college days and intern experiences together.

"Okay." Austin finally said. "Let's get down to business." He pushed Teeba's chart in front of Clayton. "You can leaf through it as I give you the history. Later, I'll copy the whole lot for you, if you wish."

"I'm listening," said Clayton, already turning the pages.

"Five weeks ago this twenty-seven-year-old patient received a gunshot wound at the High School where she was teaching. The bullet nicked her heart and caused bleeding into the pericardium."

"What happened? Who shot her?"

"The case is still open. Nobody really knows what exactly happened or why. The only witness is an eleven-year-old autistic boy, who's been of no help. The investigator calls daily to see if our patient has come out of coma."

"Go on, please." Clayton said, still reading.

"She's had emergency surgery over at University Hospital and was on bypass for six hours. First they had trouble getting her off. Then, everything seemed fine, but she wouldn't wake up in the recovery room. They brought her into ICU when she showed an electrolyte imbalance. There was concern about renal function abnormalities."

"I see that they administered oxygen in ICU, but I question the medicines that were given," Clayton mumbled. "Anyway, it took them twenty-four hours to realize she was in a coma?"

"Correct as usual! As you've probably read already, there had been some edema in the beginning. But the MRI taken fourteen days later proved normal; so did all the other tests." Austin leaned closer. "Since everything seemed fine, they were puzzled over at University. She was transferred to us and now, almost three weeks later...we're puzzled!"

Finally Clayton looked up. "Tell me more about this patient's reaction to stimulation."

"Mmmh. You know that we've been successful here with our treatments on comatose patients through stimulation. We used additional techniques that turned out to be of great value. I think you're looking at those therapies right now."

"Yes, I'm very familiar with your approach. How did she react?"

"When we first noticed that she ever-so-slightly reacted to touch, we performed stimulation through the pathway of vision with flashlights, pictures, and other objects familiar to her. I had her father bring her favorite music; he also bought books on tape he believed she would find challenging. We tried to stimulate the brain by playing the radio every other hour around the clock. In addition, the physical therapists, the nurses, and the staff members talk to her every chance they have. Her father, who comes here daily, always talks to her at great length. We all saw the progress!"

"You also tried stimulating the patient's senses of taste and smell." Clayton tapped his index finger on a page. "How did that go?"

"Great! We placed different odors under her nose and put tastes on her tongue..." Austin shrugged. "She reacted! We were so delighted to see more and more response from this woman. But then, totally unexpected, everything changed. She stopped!"

Clayton looked up. "What happened since then?"

"Her pupils still react to light and all her vital signs are stable. She still pulls away from pain, but refuses to respond to any of the stimulation therapies. The big question remains, why is she still in a coma? It's almost as if she's resisting going any further."

Austin clapped his hands together, then began cracking his knuckles.

"You're still popping your joints."

Austin grinned, then he shrugged. "Look, I'm at the end of my wisdom and admit that I'm perplexed. Since you're the ultimate expert in coma, do I have to tell you how thrilled I am that you're sitting across from me?"

"I must say, I'm intrigued, my friend. Given the circumstances, I'll be more than willing to give it a shot and work with you during the next few days."

"Fantastic! But what about Maya? Won't she be upset?"

"Her schedule is filled with classes and spa treatments. I don't think she'll even miss me during the day. As long as I'm back at night, there should be no problem," Clayton stated, winking at his friend. Then, he turned serious again. "I know you won't be able to be with me all the time, but I need an assistant, someone familiar with the case."

"I've got the perfect person!" Austin got up. "Let me introduce you to Ebony Laveau, the charge nurse. You'll love her!"

Chapter 22

"Omigod!" In an exaggerated gesture Ebony pretended to grab her heart. "I've never seen a more divine-looking creature in my life. I've finally met my brown god." She sank into the chair next to Teeba's hospital bed. Drs. Austin Berger and Clayton Harris had just left the room.

"That voice, those eyes—I wish you could see him...the way his mouth curves...his chiseled features with the high cheekbones..." She stopped and raised her eyebrows. "I wonder if he's married? He didn't wear a ring—first thing I noticed." She slowly rose out of the chair, leaned over the bed and took Teeba's hand. She pressed the limp palm against her chest. "Feel my heart...it flip-flops like it's never done before."

Ebony sat on the edge of the bed and gently placed Teeba's hand back on the white top sheet. She continued with her description.

"He's made up of pure raw physique, like all muscle and strength," she said, and described his dark handsome face with the healthy-looking skin and the baritone voice with the smooth timbre. "I've seen my dream." Gazing at Teeba, Ebony sighed, "You can't talk to me and who knows if you can even hear me—but, as always, I'm feeling as if we're having a conversation." She shook her head and exhaled softly. "It reminds me of years ago, with a very special childhood friend. We seemed to be able to read each other's mind." She touched Teeba's hand again and whispered, "But you're my best friend now. I can talk to you about everything and somehow I believe I can hear your responses." She shook her head. "So strange, it's all so strange."

Later in the evening, Ebony rearranged the schedule for the following week. As soon as some of the nurses realized the changes, they began to protest.

"Nothing I can do guys. Sorry. Dr. Berger brought in a specialist, Dr. Clayton Harris." The minute she said his name, she could see his face and hear his voice in her mind's eye. "I was asked to assist him for the next few days." She gave her coworkers a challenging look and shrugged her shoulders. "Please don't complain—you all owe me big time anyway."

The following morning Clayton arrived promptly at half past eight and found Ebony working on a computer at the nurse's station.

"Good morning," she beamed. "I've got everything prepared for you. So, whenever you're ready…"

"Good morning, Ebony." He shook her hand and held it. "Yellow must be your color—it's very becoming on you."

Ebony felt her knees weaken. She didn't remember the last time a doctor had paid attention to her looks. She knew she was not unattractive, but being the only African-American among the nursing staff, the doctors treated her differently—strictly professional and always with great respect.

"Thank you." She knew she was blushing. "Dr. Berger asked me to page him as soon as you arrived. Why don't you look at some of the tests while I try to locate him? You can use the room over here."

Ten minutes later, Ebony tried to focus on work while stealing glances through the open door as Drs. Harris and Berger discussed the various tests.

He's by far the most attractive, handsome, and nicest man I've ever laid eyes on, she thought after she allowed herself another quick look.

"There you are." His voice startled her and she jumped out of the chair.

"What can I do for you?"

"I would like to repeat some tests for comparison's sake. I'd like another EEG and PET scan. Also, I'd like to order another CAT scan and MRI studies, but want to add a contrast agent for the purpose of enhancement and better visualization."

"Any blood work?"

He smiled. "Yes, absolutely." He handed her the requisitions. "How soon do you think I can have all that?"

"You'll have it in no time. I'll make sure of it."

Later, in Teeba's room, Clayton and Ebony stood by Teeba's bedside. For moments they quietly looked at the patient.

"She's a beautiful young woman. Almost looks too healthy for her condition," Clayton said, breaking the silence. "What do you know about her?"

"I've had long discussions with her father. She's a rare and special individual—very intelligent, insightful, and loving. She was teaching at Agave High School here in Tucson; that's where she got shot. In the beginning there was a never-ending stream of students who came by. They all love her. Now they're coming less and less." Ebony paused to look at Clayton. "I'm sure you'll meet her father today. He's always here and you can ask him any question. He loves to talk about her."

Clayton nodded. "I'll do that. What do you know about the shooting?"

Ebony shrugged. "They're all waiting for her to wake up, hoping she can identify the person who shot her. There's a detective who calls almost every day and stops by occasionally. I can give you his name and phone number, if that'll help you."

"No, actually it's irrelevant." He moved over to the tray table and took the flashlight. "I'd like to repeat some of the stimulation therapies. Let's start with this."

CHAPTER 23

CLAYTON WOULD HAVE intended to stay longer at the Institute if it hadn't been for Maya. She paged him at the hospital and, when he returned the call, she urged him to drive back to the ranch as soon as possible. "I've cancelled my hot stone massage since I met a few interesting people," she said excitedly. "We've decided to hire a driver to take us up the Catalina Highway, to somewhere on Mount Lemmon, to watch the sunset. One of the guests here highly recommended it and the Ranch is preparing a picnic dinner for us to take along. It's supposed to be a spectacular experience."

When he walked into the one-bedroom casita, he found Maya already waiting for him. "You're late, Clayton," she smiled, but her voice had an edge to it.

"I know. I'm sorry, Maya. Give me just a minute to freshen up." When he kissed her, she stiffened in his embrace.

Fifteen minutes later he found himself sitting in a van with six strangers. As Maya introduced him, he noticed that she had changed her pout into a captivating smile.

"Meet Roz and Esther, darling. They're from New York and flew into Tucson on their own jet."

The two ladies owned a small, highly successful investment management company. Both were between their forties and sixties and obviously had been cosmetically enhanced from head to hip.

"These are the Bakers from St. Louis. Peter just sold his business and Emma is pregnant with their first child. Isn't it exciting?"

The Rosenthals, the third couple, were from Toronto. "Miriam and Abe are both physicians. I'm sure you'll find lots to talk about," Maya said cheerfully.

Clayton turned and twisted in the van in order to shake the hands of the various individuals while Maya went to great lengths describing his many accomplishments.

For the rest of the excursion up the winding Catalina Highway, the picnic that followed, and the eventual drive back to Canyon Ranch, Clayton forced himself into conversation, but he could not keep his mind from wandering back into room 319 South at the Institute.

Back in their casita, Maya yelled from the bathroom, "Wasn't it a spectacular evening? These people are so interesting! Gosh, and the Bakers are loaded! He didn't talk about it but I know he was the Chairman of Micro Dynamics." She paused for the impact. "Did you hear that he has children older than his wife?" Maya came out of the bathroom; her skin was still glowing from the herbal wrap and body polish. Wearing a short silvery satin night slip, she combed her shoulder-length hair as she moved closer to him.

Clayton looked up when she took the pen from his hand and pushed the notepad off his lap. "You look beautiful, Maya," he said.

"Not as beautiful as you, you erotically handsome hunk!" Her slip hiked up her hips when she sat astride on his lap. She wore nothing underneath.

Maya Roberts was a very attractive woman. One would not consider her a natural beauty, but her facial features were unique. Her high cheekbones and full lips were the focal points of her face. Her mouth was all embracing, especially when she smiled or laughed. Her hazel eyes were proportionally set above a perfectly reshaped nose.

Maya was the daughter of prominent Hollywood parents, her father being a successful producer, her mother a former actress-turned-director.

For thirty-one years Maya enjoyed the special privileges of famous heritage and high social status. It was only recently that Maya decided she wanted to work and, of course, was immediately accepted into the movie-producing industry. Because of her father's connections, her own success story was just beginning.

"I don't like you working all the time," she breathed as she sat on Clayton's lap. "You were supposed to relax here and pay attention to only me," she whispered, brushing her lips against his.

"My work relaxes me, Maya. But this certainly..." He stopped in mid-sentence when her tongue opened his lips further and her hands slipped inside his clothes.

The next morning Clayton woke up to the sound of Maya's deep breathing. He got up and lowered the air conditioning thermostat, then pulled the sheet over the shapely contours of Maya's naked body. He looked at the digital clock on the nightstand and realized the alarm would wake her within the next few minutes. He knew that despite the extra workout during the night, Maya would not want to miss the early-morning four-mile brisk walk that was part of her spa regimen.

He was brushing his teeth when she came into the bathroom.

"You killed me last night, baby," she said in a low voice, and pressed her naked body against his back. "I believe I'm still dead," she yawned, but grabbed his buttocks.

He turned around and kissed her. "You look too good for a corpse."

"I assume you're getting ready for the walk? It'll be invigorating and wake us up."

"If you don't mind, I'd like to stick to my usual routine. Meet you for breakfast?"

"God, Clay, your usual routines are boring—like eating oatmeal every morning. Try something different, you might actually like it." Her voice rose and she sounded annoyed. "We came here to spend more time together, remember?"

"Maya! You know this is not my thing. I came here because I wanted to be with you but all the classes, the spa stuff...I'm sorry, it's not for me." He put his arms around her. "You love it and that's wonderful. Allow me to do what I like, okay?"

"And what is it that *you* are going to do all day?" she asked suspiciously.

"After breakfast, I'm going to the hospital; I told you about the case last night. Some of the tests will be back and I'd like to continue with my stimulation experiments. I'll be back by five."

"Fine. Suit yourself. Tell your friend Austin he really managed to screw things up for me. Meanwhile I'll have to find excuses when people ask me why you even came here," she pouted.

"You don't have to make excuses, Maya. Tell people the truth. There's nothing dishonorable about the truth."

She finished tying her gym shoes in silence and fastened her hair into a short ponytail. Before she put on her sunglasses, she shot him a killer look. "Have a stimulating day then," she said and slammed the door.

CHAPTER 24

"GOOD MORNING, DR. Harris. If you're looking for Ebony, she's in 319 South," the male nurse informed him as soon as he arrived. The door was open and he saw Ebony talking to a visitor.

"Oh, Dr. Harris! Mr. Prime has been waiting for you. I'll leave you gentlemen alone. Let someone know when you'll need me."

"Dr. Berger told me he was going to consult with another specialist on my daughter's case. I had no idea it'd be so soon." Thomas warmly shook the doctor's hand.

"I happened to be in Tucson on vacation when Dr. Berger called," Clayton explained.

"Some vacation!"

Clayton laughed. "Don't worry, Mr. Prime. I love what I'm doing—it never seems like work to me." He changed the subject. "I've studied the chart thoroughly. Your daughter had no other illnesses as a child other than the chicken pox?"

"No, she's been extremely healthy all her life. I don't even recall her ever having a cold."

"Anything else you can tell me that might be of importance and isn't in the chart?"

"Do you have a few days? It would take forever to talk about the wonderful qualities of my daughter. She's an extraordinary human being. She lights up the whole world with her smile." Thomas Prime talked for awhile about his love for Teeba. "But all that is of no medical interest to you."

Clayton shook his head. "You're wrong. Every piece of information is of value to me. Aside from my medical interest in this case,

I'd like to get a better feeling about your daughter. I understand she was very well liked. Why would anyone want to kill her?"

Thomas glanced over to the bed. "I don't know. The police questioned every single one of her students and the faculty. They all had alibis, but more so, they all loved and admired her."

"What about friends?"

"Teeba has a lot of friends; every person who needs her help becomes her friend. All of the people she's taken care of or has befriended, they're either handicapped, too old, or too young to have made the trip to the school, shoot her, and then disappear without a trace. And what motive would they've had? They're all so fond of her. Believe me, the police checked into everything and are still searching for clues. Only Teeba can solve this case."

"What about male companions?"

"She wasn't dating anyone," Thomas smiled. "I'm sure you're thinking, 'How come such a pretty young lady does not have a boyfriend?' Well, whenever I teased Teeba about it, she told me that the man she was waiting for has yet to step into her circle of life." Thomas shrugged. "Whatever that means."

"Did Ebony tell you I've repeated the tests and scans?"

"Yes. But all of the previous tests were normal. Did you suspect a change for the worse?"

"No, no, no. I just want to make sure. I'll have the results today. Perhaps you and your wife will return later so we can go over the findings together?"

Thomas hesitated. Then he said, "I don't think my wife will be here today. But I'll come back—I'll tell my wife what you said."

Clayton nodded. "That'll be great. I think I'd better get to work now." They shook hands and Thomas kissed his daughter on the forehead before he left the room.

Clayton's eyes focused again on the patient. Ebony had told him about the mother's disinterest in her daughter and the outbursts in the hospital. He wondered why.

Unaware of how long he stood by the bedside, a mysterious fascination took hold of Clayton's thoughts and his mind began to drift. He was startled when he heard Ebony's voice.

"I saw Mr. Prime leave and just wanted to let you know that the scans, the MRI, and blood results came back."

"Oh yes, yes." Clayton felt confused and rubbed the bridge of his nose as he tried to pull himself together.

Ebony watched in silence, then smiled. "I think I know what you're feeling. She has the same impact on me."

Not quite sure what Ebony was trying to say, Clayton cleared his throat. "Let's go and look at the tests."

"Amazing!" he said some time later. "There's absolutely no sign of anything wrong." Clayton studied the films, impressions, and printouts of the tests for the third time. "I was hoping that I could detect something new—but there's nothing. There are no changes." He turned to Ebony. "Let's go back and try a few new things." On his way to 319 South, he stopped at the ice machine and filled a small cup with cubes.

Back in Teeba's room, Ebony busied herself, putting some of the various stimulation therapy objects in order.

"Did her father ever mention what her favorite music is?" Clayton asked.

"Yes, she very much likes Vivaldi's *The Four Seasons*, especially the *Spring Concerto*."

"How coincidental. I very much like Antonio Vivaldi myself. Would you play it please, Ebony?"

As soon as the music from Gil Shaham's violin and the Orpheus orchestra softly emitted from the portable stereo, the notes seemed to become alive as they danced through the sterile-looking hospital room.

"Do you know that Vivaldi wrote poems to his musical score?" Clayton asked as he removed the sheet and lifted the patient's gown.

"Joyful spring has arrived,
The birds welcome it with their happy songs,
And the brooks in the gentle breezes
Flow with a sweet murmur."

Ebony listened to Clayton's poetry recital while she watched him prepare for the stimulation therapy.

"Vengon' coprendo l'aer di nero amanto
E lampi, e tuoni da annuntiarla eletti
Indi tacendo esti, gl'augelletti
Tornan di nuovo al lor canoro ancanto."

The foreign sounds of the words created a brilliant resonance in Ebony's ears. "What does it mean?"

"The sky is covered with a black mantle,
Thunder and lightning announce a storm.
When they are silent, the birds
Take up again their harmonious songs."

"How beautiful," Ebony said and sighed. Then, she watched him take two small ice cubes from the cup and put them gently on Teeba's abdomen. She saw the movement and thought she heard herself gasp, but the gasping sound had come from Teeba.

"Did you see that? Did you hear her?" Ebony whispered, trying to control her excitement.

"Teeba! Can you hear me?" Clayton's voice was controlled and calm. He gently placed his hand to warm the spot from where he had removed the ice cubes.

Ebony remained in a frozen position as they waited. "Please try it again."

Clayton had one ice cube in each hand. Slowly he lowered his hands and gingerly put one under her upper right breast and the other on the lower left side of the abdomen.

This time the sudden movement was strong and there was the unmistakable sound of a loud gasp.

Ebony moved closer to the bed. "May I?" When he nodded she reached out for Teeba's hand and bent over her patient. "Teeba, you're doing great. Please wake up. You can do it. You can do it!"

"Teeba. If you can hear us, try to squeeze Ebony's hand," Clayton said while covering Teeba's torso with the sheet.

"I…Omigod…I think she did it. She squeezed my hand!" Ebony's eyes glistened and she felt her voice cracking. "Teeba, honey, come back to us. We're all waiting for you!"

"I think the black mantle was removed and has cleared the sky. I think the storm is silent and our little bird here will start singing again," Clayton said softly. He took Teeba's left hand. "Yes," he said, "it's time for you to come back."

There was a flutter of Teeba's eyelids followed by a jerky movement of her right leg. Her lips slightly parted and a soft hoarse moan escaped from her throat. Her body trembled for several seconds, then it relaxed and became still.

"Teeba? Don't go back—I'm waiting for you," Clayton's deep voice was filled with enticement.

Teeba's eyelids fluttered again before they slowly opened. For a few seconds her black eyes rolled before she focused straight ahead on the desert landscape painting her father had hung on the wall across from her bed. She made another sound and her mouth twitched into a crooked smile.

Ebony wiped her eyes with the heel of her hand. She saw Clayton move toward the foot of the hospital bed. Ebony let go of Teeba's hand and joined him.

They both held their breath when Teeba made eye contact—first with Clayton, and then her eyes slowly shifted to Ebony.

As the afternoon sun moved farther south, its powerful rays filtered through the half-closed blinds, suffusing the hospital room with a golden glow.

Ebony inhaled sharply and her hand flew over her mouth. Her eyes were still locked on Teeba. "Omigod!" she cried. "Look at her right eye! It's the fire of the amethyst." Ebony's eyes were wide open and her hand seemed glued to her mouth. "How can this be?" she whispered. "It's the same purple fire as in Angela's left eye."

Los Angeles

...in June

CHAPTER 25

THE POUNDING BEAT of drums and the roaring, distorted guitar licks of a band woke him up. He stretched and rolled onto his side, slowly lifting his arm to turn up the volume on the Panasonic Mini System. He lazily looked at the time; it was 6:15 in the morning. He yawned and rolled on his back again, happy to enjoy the luxury of another ten minutes in his comfortable bed. He blinked and let his still sleepy blue eyes wander around the room before he closed them again. A smile of great satisfaction spread across his face. Christopher Snow was very happy.

He had left Tucson a day after graduation, anxiously looking forward to the new life awaiting him in California. Albert Turnquist, a sixty-two-year-old member of the Tucson chapter of the Order of American Aryans, offered to drive Christopher and his few belongings to Los Angeles. The older man had taken a liking to the eager and intelligent young member and, after contacting the LA chapter of OAA, Albert was to introduce Christopher to the group of ninety-three white supremacists in the City of Angels.

Since Albert's cousin was the manager of a Days Inn on Sunset Boulevard, the two hotel rooms were complimentary, and Albert made arrangements for Christopher to remain in one of them until he found a job and different living accommodations.

Two days after their arrival, Albert took Christopher to the LA chapter's monthly meeting. It was a Thursday night in early June when Christopher walked into the large hall. Although the lights were dim and the space was packed with men of all different ages, he immediately spotted the one person who stood out in the crowd—his father, Gary Snow.

"That was only three weeks ago," Christopher said out loud. Still lying in bed on his back, he stared at the white ceiling and kept reflecting on the good fortune that overnight had changed his life.

Christopher recalled the moment when both he and his father were in obvious shock about their surprise confrontation. Then, in an unexpected gesture, his father had opened his arms to embrace him, though he had not seen Christopher in almost a decade. Being pressed against his father put Christopher temporarily in a stupor and he only vaguely remembered the false explanations for the long separation his father gave to the fellow OAA members.

In a soothing trance, Christopher kept listening and heard something about his mother not wanting to leave Tucson and about a bitter and long legal battle in which all of Snow's parental rights were revoked. It was the shark of a Jewish lawyer, Snow lied, who turned his now ex-wife against him.

Christopher remembered hearing one false accusation after another against his mother and the lawyer she never had. Christopher also noticed that there was no mention of Timothy, Snow's autistic son from that marriage.

Stunned by the unexpected encounter with his father, Christopher did not dispute the lies nor defend his mother's innocence. He had dreamt of a better life for so long, he simply ignored the fabricated stories Snow was giving to the sympathetic crowd. That night, the Order celebrated the father-son reunion and several dedicated members immediately extended their willingness to help Christopher in any way they could.

Carlton Hines, who owned real estate around the city, offered a studio apartment on Vineland Avenue in North Hollywood. "No rent, my boy!" he exclaimed happily, slapping Christopher on the back. "I owe your father big time! Finally there's a way I can repay him."

Peter Hines, Carlton's brother, said he would lend Christopher a car from his used-car dealership. "It's only an old Dodge Neon, but it runs just fine," he apologized as he handed the keys to Christopher a few days later.

Roger Browne, the proprietor of Browne Funeral Homes, offered a job to the son of his best friend. “It may not be the liveliest business,” he smirked, slightly pinching Christopher’s cheek, “but the continuous stream of profits have yet to kill me!”

Three weeks later, while enjoying the comfort of his warm soft bed, the smile on Christopher’s face brightened even more when he thought about the recent evening when he had been invited to a BBQ pool party, given by Roger and Cornelia Browne. Their dwelling on Queensbury Drive in Cheviot Hills was opulent, ornate, and overwhelming.

Christopher could not help comparing the Browne’s luxury and extravagance to the misery and suffocating tightness of his mother’s trailer home in Tucson. But when Browne toasted Christopher and pronounced him not only the guest of honor but also sang praises about the newest, youngest, and brightest employee of Browne Funeral Homes, Christopher quickly forgot about his poverty-stricken days in the desert. He felt at home in Los Angeles and immensely comfortable surrounded by and conversing with clean-thinking and proper-looking people. He loved the feeling of his father’s arm around his shoulders and he welcomed the unexpected friendliness of his stepmother, Paula.

Before the BBQ pool party came to an end, Browne took Christopher aside and introduced him to his only child.

Though no raging beauty, Eva Browne looked like an innocent version of Paris Hilton. Her light skin was smooth and without blemishes, her gray eyes were clear and open, and her long baby-blonde hair was fashionably cut. Having just returned from cheerleading practice, she still wore the white and pink pleated skirt with a matching top. Her body was shapely and her legs looked firm. To Christopher, Eva represented the epitome of privileged purity.

Remembering the girls in his high school, he felt appalled by the possibility of still being stuck in Tucson, but decided, right after the BBQ party, to call his best friend Buzz Nolan. “This is a different game here,” he had said, after embellishing his new life in California. “From now on I’ll have to play my cards with care. The opportunities are too great to fuck ’em up.”

While resting on his bed, Christopher grinned. "Amazing," he said. "In just three weeks my life has been turned around completely." He glimpsed at his watch and decided it was time to get up for his daily visit to the gym. His intense workout not only kept his body in top shape, but it also kept his mind sharp so he could focus on the goals he set for himself to excel and stand out as a college student, to become the star of the USC baseball team, and to keep taking full advantage of the opportunities that were offered to him at Browne Funeral Homes on Pico Avenue.

CHAPTER 26

"CHRISSIE?"

"Mom?" With the phone to his ear, Christopher bolted upright. "How did you get this number?"

"Good morning, honey. It's nice to know you're pleasantly surprised to hear from me. I called Buzz, who told me you now have your own apartment." Sugie responded. "How come you never called to share great news? It's been over three weeks since I heard from you."

"Boy, word spreads fast in that hick town, doesn't it? I only called Buzz three days ago," Christopher sneered. "But to answer your question, I've been busy finding a job, getting an apartment, looking for wheels…and now I'm working ten hours a day. I wasn't exactly twiddling my thumbs, Mom!" He climbed out of bed and opened the blinds, blinking at the sun in the hazy blue Los Angeles sky. "Why are you calling so early?"

"I miss you and want to talk with you, but also, I've been dying to share some incredible news with you."

"Like what?"

"Soon after you left, the most amazing thing happened, Chrissie."

Christopher cringed. He hated when his mother called him by that sissy name.

"The newspapers and the TV stations haven't stopped talking about it ever since. Didn't you hear about it in Los Angeles? Didn't Buzz tell you?"

"What the heck are you talking about, Mom?"

"Chris, honey! Are you sitting down?" Sugie paused briefly. "Teeba Prime came out of her coma! It's been the talk of the town for the past three weeks now. It's amazing."

Christopher felt the blood draining from his face and as his knees buckled under him, he stumbled backwards onto the edge of his bed. Cold shivers were chasing down his spine. *This can't be happening,* he thought. *How could I've been so stupid and believe she would simply die one day?*

"How…how is she?" He almost did not dare to ask.

"Oh, she's great. Her recovery is remarkable. Her doctors and specialists from other hospitals are all amazed how she's returned to almost normal health in so short a period of time."

He heard his mother's voice rattle on, and with every new word coming through the receiver, his stomach tightened. He felt waves of nausea.

"Chrissie? Are you there?"

"Yes," he said feebly. "I'm listening."

"Well? Isn't this something? She was your favorite teacher."

Christopher nearly gagged from the pressure in his stomach. "Yeah, yeah, it's good news," he forced himself to say.

"What's wrong? Something is wrong. I can hear it in your voice."

"Nothing, Mom! It's early. You woke me up and you're shrieking like a prom queen into my ear. Let me get my bearings." He experienced dizziness and waited until another wave of nausea passed before he asked, "If she's back to normal…who did she say…" he gagged again, "…tried to kill her?"

"That's the sad part, she doesn't remember. No, no," Sugie corrected herself, "it's not that she doesn't remember; she couldn't recognize the person. Apparently the hallway was dark and she was in a dimly lit classroom. All she saw was the shadowy silhouette of a man—and then she only saw him for a fraction of a second before she lost consciousness."

Christopher, who had been holding his breath, now made small panting sounds. "She…she couldn't see…if he was old…or young?" His head was spinning. "Was he tall or short, fat or thin?"

"Nothing, honey," Sugie said with a sigh. "When the bullet hit her, she fell on Timmy—that's why he was all bloody. But, of course, you know all that—you were still here then. Timmy was covered with Teeba's blood, remember?"

"Are they still investigating?"

"They put her under hypnosis and did all kinds of other things—I forgot what this fancy detective work is called—but her story doesn't change. Teeba says she didn't see the attacker. Since they have nothing else to go by, I assume they will close the case sooner than later. But what do I know…"

Beads of sweat dripped off his forehead and he felt as if every pore of his body was excreting moisture. His heart was still racing and so were his thoughts. His breaths were short and heavy and a strange sensation was paralyzing his brain.

"Chrissie? Did you fall asleep on me?"

"No, Mom, I'm just thinking."

"Oh, honey! How could I be so insensitive? You're probably angry that the bastard got away. We all feel the same around here; everybody still wants to get him."

Even though his mouth was bone dry, Christopher swallowed hard. "What about Tim?"

"That's the next wonderful news. From the moment we visited Teeba after she came out of the coma Timmy's been amazing. He's back to where he was before it all happened. And what's even more exciting, he was accepted into the summer program for disabled children."

Christopher could hear his mother choke with emotion and listened to her sniffle.

"When Teeba was able to communicate again, she made a plea on Timmy's behalf." Sugie stopped talking and blew her nose. "Sorry honey, but I'm so happy! People in town have been extremely generous and made donations into a fund especially created for Timmy. The biggest donor was Teeba's father. Everything is so…" the last words were drowned by Sugie's sobs. "I'm so happy, Chrissie, I'm so happy for your brother."

Before he asked the next question, Christopher could hear the palpitation of his heart in his ears. "Did the police try to find out from Tim about the…the…"

"The shooter?"

"Yes, the shooter."

"Well, they tried. But whenever they approached him Timmy's demeanor changed; he starts to rock and regress as soon as the question comes up."

Christopher managed to get off the bed again, on shaky legs, but his mother's words were beginning to calm his wired nerves. He walked into the bathroom and let the cold water run over his wrists into his hands to splash his face.

"Isn't this all wonderful news, Chris? I've wanted to tell you for so long but had no idea how to reach you. From now on, let's keep in touch more frequently, okay?"

"Yeah, Mom, I promise." He felt a pang of sympathy toward his mother.

"Chrissie? There's something really nice that happened to me as well," Sugie said softly.

Christopher could hear her smile as he looked at his face in the mirror. There were so many physical similarities between himself and his mother. "What's that, Mom?"

"Since Timmy is taken care of all day, I was able to get a full time job as a receptionist in an orthodontist's office. I gave up my night job. Isn't that wonderful? I know that'll please you."

"That's good, Mom; that's really good," Christopher said, staring at his image in the mirror. The paleness that crept under his tanned complexion had turned his skin green. He still didn't feel good.

"I'm like a regular mom now. I pick Timmy up after the program and have time to do things with him before he goes to sleep. Everything has changed. I love my new life and my new job. By the way, the pay and the benefits aren't bad either."

"That's nice, Mom. You deserve it."

"The orthodontist I work for…" she stopped, and Christopher could sense her hesitation.

"Yes?"

"He's got a Down's syndrome daughter. We've got a lot in common and so much to talk about."

Christopher swallowed hard. He didn't like to hear about the retarded and the handicapped. But after his friends had told him he was fucked up when he voiced his opinions about imperfect human beings, he had kept his convictions to himself until he joined the Order of American Aryans. There, he felt comfortable enough to speak his mind. After all, at the OAA they all shared the same viewpoints.

"Why are you telling me this, Mom?"

Sugie giggled like a little girl. "The doctor likes me, Chrissie." More giggles. "He's asked me out several times already. We have a really nice time together. He's a wonderful man and I can't wait for you to meet him. I know you'll like him. His name is Dr. Abraham Levi."

Christopher grabbed the edge of the sink and glared at his mirror image. He wasn't prepared for his mother's last statement; it wasn't what he had hoped for. He felt himself choking on the rising bile in his throat and lowered his head over the toilet bowl. Even when he was done, the bitter taste remained. Not only had his own gentle, pretty mother lowered herself to unacceptable standards by dating a man with a retarded child but worse, that man was a Jew.

New Orleans

...in July

Chapter 27

ANGELA OPENED HER eyes and turned her head. The handsome man next to her was still sound asleep. She inhaled deeply when she felt his warm exhalations.

"I've had a very special time with you," she whispered, "but you're not meant to be in my path of destiny." She kissed his shoulder and traced the contours of his face with her index finger to the curls at the nape of his neck.

They only had known each other since February when she had bumped into Seth Lennon during the Mardi Gras Zulu Parade. He had intended to return to England right after Ash Wednesday, but instead became one of the growing group of residents the locals call *never lefts.* Angela's mystique only added to the mysterious aura of New Orleans and grabbed instant hold of the young British author. He soon developed an idea for a new suspense novel and rented a charming but slightly decayed house not too far from Angela's place.

"How's the love of my life this new morning?" Seth asked, pressing his body closer to hers. He ran his hand over her breasts and kissed them. "Oh yes," he breathed.

Angela slowly rolled on top of him, feeling him writhe in anticipation. Then she straddled his body, her knees pressing firmly against his hips. Her upper body was erect as she took his hands into hers. "I have a surprise for you. Be very still and look deeply into my eyes."

When he saw a magnificent amethyst fire in her left eye, the warmth of a delicious drowsiness trickled through his body. "I've never…" His lips barely moved while his leaden lids lowered.

"...so beautiful." With a smile on his face, he lay stretched on his back—relaxed and at peace—having fallen asleep again.

"We've had a wonderful time together and I thank you for that," Angela said running her fingers through his curls again. "Now I must move on and concentrate on a very important matter. And you need to concentrate on your novel; I know it'll be a bestseller." She kissed him one last time. "Good-bye," she said. "When you wake up you'll believe I only existed in a wonderful dream."

Thirty minutes later, Angela unlocked the door to her Victorian home on First Street in the Garden District. She was the third generation living in the magnificent old residence.

"Good morning, Ms. Atwood," a high-pitched voice sang from the living room. "Your daddy jus' called. I tole him I didn' know where you at. He says he's at the office."

"Thanks, Nel, and good morning to you."

"I decided to give your glass menagerie a cleanin' today," Nel said, motioning toward Angela's collection of Lalique and Daum pieces.

"Anything I can grab on my way up? I'm starving."

"I baked your favorite biscuits. They're on the kitchen counter."

"Yum. I'm going to take a shower and make some calls."

Angela carried the delicious-smelling biscuits and a mug of freshly brewed coffee and chicory upstairs, on a small tray. She took time to enjoy her breakfast while talking to her father.

After her shower, she slipped into her silk robe and dialed the Portal Institute for Genome Research. She asked for Dr. Hakan Öztürk.

He picked up the phone almost immediately. "Ms. Atwood, how nice of you to call." His sandpaper voice had silky undertones.

"I promised to give you time to get settled before I offered myself as your tour guide. Are you ready for some overindulgence?" She heard his nervous cough on the other end.

"I...eh...yes, I'm ready." He tried to suppress another cough. "I've been working too hard these past few weeks. I could use a break."

"Perfect!" Angela chirped. "How about this weekend? I'm going to see my parents on Friday—I could pick you up."

"Uhmm...Friday is not good because there's an early Saturday morning meeting here at PIGR, which should be finished around eleven."

"Okay, would you like me to swing by there on Saturday then?"

"No! May I meet you at the Governor's Mansion? I'll hire a driver."

Angela smiled. She knew that he wanted to avoid the possibility of being seen with her by his colleagues.

She offered to make an overnight reservation at the sedate Pontchartrain Hotel in his name and assured him she would be happy to drive him back to Lafayette late on Sunday. "That'll give me enough time to saturate you with your first impressions. See you Saturday around noon, then."

Lafayette and Baton Rouge

...in July

CHAPTER 28

"IN ORDER TO perform the tests on humans, I demand that each of you put in extra time, starting immediately!" Hakan's voice—cold and callous—overpowered the three scientists in the secured room at PIGR. He controlled the lab with militaristic enthusiasm and his imperious demeanor had a psychological effect on everyone working with him, exactly what he had been ordered to accomplish. "I've been working eighteen hours a day for the past four weeks and I can't say that for any of you. I'm being pressed daily for the progress and from now on I want more from you than you've given so far. We have a goal. We must be on schedule."

"How's the LA project coming along?" Putin asked.

"Good! Very good." Afshor volunteered. "Last weekend Dr. Geist showed me the progress in the Los Angeles warehouse. They'll be ready for us by the middle of August."

"We'll never make it!" Barsoukov shook his head. "I'm still waiting for some data before I can determine if the particular size of the new aerosol dispersant is optimal." He looked at Hakan above his spectacles. "Right now I'm trying different volatile oils. I have it down to two candidates, but need more time for dispersion studies with animals."

"I thought Putin was doing that?" Hakan sounded vexed.

"Well!" Putin grumbled. "It was your sneaky idea that's been keeping me busy. I'm still working on increasing the rate of viral replication in MAX 18 by inserting some enhanced regulatory sequence." He looked at Hakan provocatively. "I'm not exactly working with safe substances here!" The Russian accent intensified in his deep voice. "Even with the level 3 biocontainment lab we really should be going more slowly."

"And now you want us to speed up the process. Talk about pressure," Barsoukov chimed in. "Perhaps we could work three times as fast if you were ready to vaccinate all of us. We're taking a dangerous risk here."

Hakan only smirked.

"Excuse me!" Afshor rose and moved toward Barsoukov. "You know how well the vaccine worked in the animal testing. We're only waiting for our man in LA to let us know when the human test facility there is ready. It's not like we're filing an investigational new drug application with the FDA!" Afshor's mouth turned downward. "We're in the United States of America, Yuri, not in Russia!"

"Actually," Hakan cut in, challenging Putin and Barsoukov, "if you two gentlemen are so eager, why don't you volunteer to be my first two human guinea pigs?"

"*Podonok*!" Barsoukov swore, fully aware that Hakan would understand the nastiness of the word. He turned away and swallowed the rest of his bitter coffee.

"Okay!" Putin waved his hands, attemptimg to ease the tension. "I have no problems working longer hours, but I need my data."

"Here it is." Hakan pushed a thick pile toward him.

Putin acted perplexed. "I didn't expect the data in its entirety."

"I told you, I worked on it day and night," Hakan said while putting some of his personal belongings into his briefcase. Without looking up he added, "I'm tired and I've decided to take this weekend off."

Afshor nodded. "I've already planned on being here for the rest of the day anyway and will be happy to come back tomorrow. You'll have my findings ready and waiting first thing Monday morning." He smiled at Hakan. "I hope you'll enjoy the weekend, Hakan; you certainly deserve a rest."

"What do you want us to do?" Barsoukov grumbled.

Hakan gave detailed instructions. Occasionally he caught himself glancing at his watch. He timed it perfectly, though, and finished a few minutes after eleven o'clock.

He arrived in a taxicab right before noon at the Governor's Mansion in Baton Rouge. It was an unusually hot and humid day, even for that part of Louisiana, and Hakan was neither used to these severe climate changes nor familiar with the feelings that rushed through him. He wished he had not agreed to weekend plans with Angela.

Chantal greeted the slightly disheveled scientist in the foyer. "How nice to see you again, Dr. Öztürk." She noticed his sweating face.

"The cab…it was very hot in there. I am sorry. I must look terrible."

"You poor dear. Please, feel free to freshen up. Angela is not ready yet either." Chantal showed the scientist to a large, cool bathroom.

When he returned a few minutes later, he looked restored. He quickly put his dopp kit into the side pocket of his hanging bag and stood in the foyer until Chantal appeared a few minutes later.

"There you are." She took his arm and led him into the library. "I understand the heat is dreadful. I've not been outside at all today. Would you believe my husband decided to play golf in this weather? He's an elephant of a man," she laughed. "By the way, he apologizes for not being here and hopes you'll visit us soon again." She motioned him to take a seat. "Lemonade? Iced tea? What may I offer you?"

"Iced tea will be great." Hakan watched Chantal as she poured the tea into a tall glass and walked toward him. At that moment he believed he had never seen a more graceful and attractive woman. Her skin reminded him of porcelain and her shiny hair of liquid gold. Her body was slender and her movements seemed fluently choreographed. Her legs appeared long in the white cotton pants and the short-sleeved red blouse gave her light skin a rosy shimmer.

"Wonderful," he said, and realized that his statement had a double meaning. "The iced tea is just wonderful. Thank you."

"So, I understand Angela has been able to tear you away from your hard work?" Chantal took another packet of Stevia sweetener from the crystal bowl and with a long delicate silver spoon stirred its powdery contents into her lemonade. "You will enjoy New Orleans—no other city is like this anywhere. Did you know I was born and raised there until my father was elected president? But when I met my husband, I was thrilled to return home to New Orleans." She smiled. "I've visited many countries and experienced many cultures, but nowhere do I enjoy myself more than right here in Louisiana."

"I agree," Angela said as she entered the room. "New Orleans once was the most exotic stop for the great riverboats; they called this pleasure-filled island the Paris of the Americas."

Hakan, just having sipped on his tea, almost choked on a piece of ice and unsteadily put the glass down before he rose.

"Darlin'...don't you look lovely." Chantal rushed toward her daughter and embraced her. "What do you say, Dr. Öztürk, doesn't she look lovely?"

"Indeed, yes!" To his horror Hakan heard his own voice two octaves higher. He cleared his throat, then shook Angela's hand and was magnetized by her laughing dark eyes. "You changed your color...your hair...it's longer," he stammered—grateful for having found his normal voice. But being at a loss for words, he touched his own hair in order to indicate what he was trying to say.

"You like it?" Angela's throaty laugh was enticing. "I've had fun during my experimental phase for the past year, but now I'm ready to get back to basics." She ran her fingers through a few golden blonde strands. "Obviously I needed some temporary help from my friendly stylist, but give it another four weeks and it'll be all natural once again!" She faced her mother. "I finally realized that I want to look as beautiful as you, Mama." She planted a kiss on her mother's cheek. Then, she clapped her hands. "So, Dr. Ö, are you ready for some excitement?"

He felt himself blushing when she took his arm. "Yes," he said and nodded.

"We'll start with the very basics of Southern Comfort 101," she teased, and in an assuring gesture patted his arm. "Don't worry, you'll soon find out that I'm a very good and patient teacher. Shall we go?"

Hakan unsteadily followed Angela, who, even in a simple pair of black shorts, white blouse, and gym shoes, looked stunning.

Chapter 29

Angela drove faster than anyone else on Interstate 10. She realized that with her jovial chatter she was able to loosen up her fellow passenger and engage him in animated conversation, but also noticed that his hands were tightly clasped around his knees and that his knuckles were white. It was obvious that Hakan never before sat in a sports car traveling at high speed.

"You can relax. We're almost there." Angela smiled at him. With her right hand, she patted his white knuckles. "Relax," she said again. "I've never had an accident—you're perfectly safe. After all, I have big plans with you."

The Pontchartrain Hotel was a longtime local landmark. Even though it was a little worn at the edges, it still provided old-world gentility and plenty of elegance.

"I hope you have a weakness for faded grandeur," Angela laughed when she dropped him in front of the hotel. "But I think you'll find this hotel as charming as I do. The Pontchartrain has lured dignitaries from all over for years; you'll be in good company."

"How soon will I have to be ready?" Hakan handed his lightweight bag to the porter.

"I don't live far. I'll drop off my car and swing by in a taxi in fifteen minutes. I hope you're hungry because I'm starving!"

The late-lunch crowd at Tujague's was still in full swing when they arrived. As with most of her favorite places, Angela didn't need a reservation. The chef rushed over as soon as he heard she was there. "Angela, *ma chère,* I almost did not recognize you; another new hair color, another new style. You're full of surprises. *Mais,* as always very becoming and *très chic.*"

After Angela introduced Hakan she pointed at her stomach. "This needs some serious filling up. What can you do about it, Gaspard?"

During the next hour Angela successfully encouraged the skeptical Hakan to help her feast on fried crawfish tails, oysters, gumbo, baked garlic, and *Bonne Femme* chicken. She talked about her friendship with many of the local restaurateurs, her strong connection to the various blues and jazz artists in the clubs, and her fascination about the multitude of writers in New Orleans. Even though she was not a writer, she often got invited to literary meetings or readings by captivating new authors.

"For centuries New Orleans has been a mecca for writers and their work," she explained.

"William Faulkner, F. Scott Fitzgerald, Tennessee Williams, Truman Capote, and many more...they've all lived and worked here." She saw that Hakan was hanging onto her every word. "Some of our native authors have made it to stardom with their novels. Have you read Anne Rice, Chris Wiltz, Nancy Lemann...?" She stopped when she saw him blush and shake his head.

"I'm sorry, Ms. Atwood. I've only heard about some of these famous people. I'm ashamed to admit, I never took the time to read anything other than material related to my research, studies, and work." His eyes shifted to his plate and he poked at the last few pieces of food. "Perhaps I've been too dedicated to only one cause."

"Look, you're a brilliant scientist and you have your own agenda. Most people wouldn't be able to follow your line of work, nor would they understand your intense ambition."

"What do you mean?"

"Your research is so sophisticated and uncertain. The majority of people only become intrigued when the results are ready to be put to use. They're not interested in the tedious years of studies, but always are grateful when a cure for another disease is found."

She saw him staring at her and held his gaze. She wanted to grab his hand to get the full benefit of his innermost thoughts, but for now she was content with what she sensed.

The subject of conversation became lighter again after a taste of the chef's famous bread pudding.

It was almost four in the afternoon when they left the restaurant. They started a walking tour through the French Quarter with Bourbon Street. Angela did not care much for the many T-shirt stores and early drunks who came swaying out of the rows of bars, but she allowed plenty of time when she saw Hakan's fascination, especially in the bustling activity at Jackson Square. They stopped and listened to every musician, laughed with the crowd during the entertainment from street performers, smiled with the mimes, marveled at the peculiar "living statues," and paid compliments to the artists while admiring their drawings or paintings. Angela could see that Hakan's hard shell had started to soften.

They walked by the expensive antique shops on Royal Street and looked into other interesting stores on Chartres and Decatur streets. Angela gave a running commentary of the origin of the historic buildings, the Cathedral, and the memorials in The Quarter before finally taking a break at the Central Grocery. They sat on the riverbank, finishing their ice-cold drinks.

When Angela saw Hakan wiping his damp face with his cotton handkerchief, she said, "The summer turns this city into a gigantic steam bath—very hydrating for the skin." She was used to the heat and humidity. "Look at me. My hair got liberated and went from the confines of styled straightness to its natural unruliness of curls and waves." She saw the desire in his eyes and took his hand so his fingers could touch her soft hair. "It's just another mystery of this city." She smiled when she saw his face redden.

After walking through the French Market, Angela suggested a stroll through Woldenberg's Riverfront Park. As Hakan admired the greenery in the heart of the city, they stopped on the Moonwalk at the Mississippi and sat on a bench to watch the busy port of New Orleans.

On the way back to the hotel, Hakan thanked Angela. "I have not once thought about my work at PIGR," he admitted. "This is a whole new world for me."

"It's only the beginning." Angela promised. "I'll pick you up at nine tonight. That'll give you enough time to freshen up, rest your feet, and build a new appetite for something really special."

She watched as he slowly walked toward the hotel entrance. He turned around three times, smiled, and waved his hand.

"There'll be a rocky road ahead for both of us." Her lips barely moved as she saw him disappear through the door. Even though her visions had become much clearer during the day, there still was vagueness—almost as if she were looking through an out-of-focus lens. Despite knowing of his deadly intentions, she felt sorry for him and his destiny. "You're going to be held captive by besotted love," she sighed, stepping on the gas pedal. "It's the only way you will open up to me; it's the only way to prevent the ultimate tragedy."

CHAPTER 30

HAKAN COUNTED THE minutes until nine o'clock. After showering and shaving he stared at his image in the mirror and realized that never before had he looked at himself so critically. With a small pair of scissors and his razor, he meticulously began to trim his mustache and eyebrows. He was glad he had a haircut two days previously, because the image that smiled back at him from the mirror was a different face. His eyes looked larger and his pallid face tones had disappeared. The hot New Orleans sun had quickly painted his skin shades darker. He saw a healthier, younger version of himself.

He had packed a lightweight gray pair of trousers and was happy to see that they'd survived the short trip wrinkle free. The soft cotton fabric of his crisp white shirt felt smooth against his tingling skin. He looked critically at the blue tie with the thin silver stripes, the only one he had packed. He assured himself one more time that there was no dust on his black loafers before taking his midnight blue blazer off the hanger.

Downstairs he spotted a quiet corner in the discreet ambiance of the lobby, where he admired the old furnishings. He looked at his watch. Another ten minutes, he thought, and wondered what had happened to him. *Why,* he asked himself, *have I started to pay attention to things that never seemed important before?* He realized he'd probably missed out on many pleasurable parts of life in restricting himself to his medical research, Operation Mayfly, and his religion. The latter thought brought a sudden feeling of enormous guilt. He shuddered when he heard the familiar voice threatening him not to venture off his path. He felt torn between the desire to stay where he was and the urge to get up and retrace his steps back into his laboratory. But the voice inside him was shut out when he saw Angela walking toward him. With every stride that brought her closer, he sensed the uncertainties ebbing further away. He felt weightless as he rose out of the plush chair.

Angela's honey-blonde hair was swept back and held up by a small ornate clasp; a few thin strands casually fell down the sides of her face and onto her forehead. She wore minimal makeup; her long black lashes enhanced her dark eyes and the faint pink lip gloss on her lips harmonized with her face. She wore an above-the-knee, fitted black halter dress, exposing her shoulders and a good portion of her back. Her toned legs looked smooth and, like the rest of her skin, glowed with a golden tan.

Hakan took her hand and bowed his head; his lips never touched her skin.

"Dr. Öztürk, you're quite the gentleman."

As they walked toward the exit, she hooked her arm into his and felt him stiffen. She leaned closer, "You look very handsome tonight."

When they arrived at Commander's Palace, the maitre d' greeted Angela with enthusiasm. The restaurant was housed in an 1880s Victorian house with many different-sized dining rooms. Angela and Hakan soon were seated in one of the smaller, more intimate chambers.

One of the waitstaff brought a bottle of fine wine. "Compliments of the house," said the wine steward, and after filling their glasses, another waiter took the order. By the time they finished the restaurant's famous turtle soup laced with sherry, they already were sipping their second glass of wine. Since he rarely allowed himself the indulgence of alcohol, Hakan felt the effect almost immediately. He liked it and raised his glass.

"Thank you for spending so much of your valuable time with me, Ms. Atwood." He took a sip and put the glass down. "I hope you don't mind, but I would like to ask you a very personal question."

"First of all," she grinned, "it's Angela—no more Ms. Atwood, please." She bent closer across the small table. "And second, go ahead, ask anything you want. I don't mind at all."

Hakan noticed the roundness of her breasts and smelled the faint fragrance of her perfume. He took another sip of wine. "You're so beautiful, so entertaining, and so very intelligent…how come you're here with me on a Saturday night and not with a husband or a boyfriend?" he asked.

"I'm a free spirit and a free thinker. I guess I've been too busy working, enjoying life, and having fun." With a twinkle in her eye she asked, "Perhaps speeding down life's fast lane is a reason that no one could catch me…yet?" Angela let the wine roll in her mouth. "I'm certain the moment is not too far off when destiny will put me on the same path with whomever is willing to walk to the end of that path with me. Do you believe in destiny, Dr. Öztürk?"

"I…eh…I never…" Hakan stammered. "You're catching me off guard." He felt the pounding heart in his throat as the unanswered inquiry lingered above their table in the romantic chamber.

After they shared the carpaccio salad with roasted eggplant and nibbled on homemade biscuits, they ordered another bottle of wine.

Hakan had never felt so free before. He started to talk about his accomplishments in Europe and the United States. But as the wine loosened his tongue, he had to remind himself to be careful not to reveal certain details about his life. He experienced a strong urge to talk about everything, yet his inner voice ridiculed that desire and demanded control. Too much was at stake.

He wanted to say, *Having you next to me me all day and now this evening has been the highlight of my life,* but instead he complimented, "I very much appreciate the introduction to a whole different way of life. I truly enjoy your company."

Hakan had ordered the mixed grill, lamb, rabbit, and sausage, but he wasn't hungry. He preferred watching her as she ate the boned Mississippi roasted quail stuffed with Creole crawfish sausage. He would have been satisfied simply feasting his eyes on her. But when she offered a taste of her food, he couldn't resist. For desert they shared the chocolate molten soufflé.

Angela suggested a few of her favorite nightspots. First they went to the Palm Court Jazz Café to listen to classic jazz. Later, she introduced him to a more authentic club experience at the Mid City Lanes Rock'n'Roll Bowl to listen to Zydeco. The place was crowded and the humidity level almost unbearable. But Hakan did not mind the mass of people or the sticky air. At times Angela's body was so close to his that he thought he could feel her firm breasts against his back and smell her vanilla breath. He closed his eyes, shut out the noise, and envisioned himself alone with her—naked.

Not until the taxi returned them to the hotel did Hakan feel his exhaustion from the heat and the humidity as well as from the hot emotions that had zigzagged through his mind and body all night. Now, at this early morning hour, he could feel Angela steal glimpses of him and he could sense her smile. Despite his fatigue, he did not want the night to end nor did he want to be alone. But he lacked the courage and the experience of a suitor.

"I could be at your hotel around eleven for breakfast or later for lunch. Will that give you enough sleep after our long outing?" Angela asked as the taxi came to a stop.

Hakan's heart began to race. He wanted to force himself to offer a nightcap or an espresso to her; instead, all he could say was, "The earlier you arrive the better."

Angela touched his hand as she leaned over, and for a second her gaze held his. Then, she pressed her full lips against his cheek. He heard her say, "Thanks for a wonderful evening." In a stupor, he clumsily left the cab.

As soon as he covered his naked body with a cool sheet, he closed his eyes and willed the experience of his previous dream about her to return. As he created the first tingle of pleasure with his hand, he abandoned his lifelong vows. He shut out his father's rough voice, he snubbed his mother's frightening threats of punishment from Allah, and forgot about clandestine meetings and pressing assignments. The dizzying pirouette in his brain spun away all of the past and allowed him to live only in the moment. He gasped as his imagination carried him from unknown territories into heavenly celestial spheres. When the pleasure turned into a tidal wave of uncontrollable force, he could not stop himself. "Angela," he cried out loud as his lust erupted. "Angela, oh Angela," he whispered and with every spasm he kept repeating her name.

CHAPTER 31

LATE THE NEXT morning Angela appeared in the coffee shop of the Pontchartrain Hotel. "Good morning. You look like you had a good night's rest," she said.

Because I dreamt about you, Hakan thought as he kissed her hand, but said, "It's wonderful to see you again."

"I have more surprises for you today," she said cheerfully. "But first we need some food." She sat across from him. "Today, I'll let you make the decisions about what to order. I'm starving again. What do you think we should eat?"

Hakan could feel his heartbeat increase as he imagined other possibilities to her question. He buried his flushed face in the menu.

"You're a quick study. This is my favorite dish here," Angela said after the server brought the crabmeat au gratin omelette.

He saw her reaching for another blueberry muffin. "How can you stay so slim?"

Angela shrugged. "Genes and a fabulously engineered metabolism, I guess."

She was wearing a pair of tight jeans, which flared slightly at the bottom. A white tank top stopped right above her navel, exposing a sliver of tanned skin. She did not wear a bra, and the cool air inside the restaurant made the thin fabric of the cotton top ripple above her breasts.

Hakan couldn't help but stare at her and tried to control his heavy breaths.

"Listen," she said, "I know I'm outspoken, but would you mind if I called you by your first name?"

"I'm sorry," he stammered, scraping for words. "I should have offered since I ought to be used to the American customs by now. It's…" He swallowed hard. "Please do."

"Okay, then…Hakan." She grinned. "Since you asked me some personal questions last night, it now is my turn." She smoothed her hair behind her ear. Hanging on to one strand, she twirled it around her finger, letting the ends tickle her lip. "Hakan," she said, as the fine hair fluttered from her breath, "I know you're forty-three years old—how come you're still single?" She released the strand of hair, crossed her elbows on the table, and leaned closer. "Or are you hiding a wife and children in Turkey?"

"No!" he answered sharply. "There is no wife. There are no children…in Turkey."

I'm telling the truth. I have no family in Turkey, he thought and lowered his eyes, afraid she would see the lie in them.

"Ah!" she said, raising her eyebrows. "Does that mean you and I are free to do whatever we want?"

Hakan set his cup into the saucer too fast, creating a clanking noise. He took the napkin and pretended to dab away some drops of tea. Instead, he dried the perspiration that had formed on his upper lip under his mustache. He could only nod.

"Okay then, let's start." Angela rose and stretched her hand toward him. "I hope you're ready for the first thrill."

With the top down on her convertible Porsche, she raced toward Bayou Segnette in Westwego. Her car flowed as smoothly across the pavement as the Great Mississippi streamed through its wide riverbed.

Hakan felt more relaxed. He liked how the warm fast wind grabbed his face and played with his hair. His head was turned slightly to the left and through half-closed eyes, behind dark glasses, he watched Angela as she sang along to a Cajun tune that sounded loudly from the CD player.

Away from the town, Angela wound the Porsche over unpaved roads and finally stopped at a hidden cottage.

"Cyrus!" She jumped out of the car and ran toward an old Cajun man, who offered an almost-toothless smile in a sun-weathered face full of deep wrinkles. They hugged and talked rapidly in a foreign tongue.

"This is Cyrus Guilbeau." Angela took the eccentric-looking character by the hand and led him toward Hakan. "You're in for the treat of a lifetime, because Cyrus knows the bayous like the back of his hand."

Over the next two hours the Cajun captain made strange sounds and calls to lure the alligators close to the boat.

Hakan stood safely two feet behind the rail, his arms tightly linked behind his back, as he watched Cyrus and Angela feed chunks of chicken meat to the gators.

"You want to try?" Angela asked.

"No, thanks, I'm afraid these monsters might mistake my hands for chicken legs." Hakan had not intended to sound funny but Angela's throaty laugh was music to his ears. He kept watching the young woman whose enthusiasm never stopped.

Captain Guilbeau maneuvered his boat into secret holes of the bayou and, in the silence of nature, the three of them got glimpses of herons, ospreys, otters, and other wildlife.

"This was indeed a rare treat," Hakan admitted on their way back to the city. "I'm in awe of what I've seen."

"If you give me the time, there'll be more," Angela said, and took him to visit St. Louis Cemetery No. 1 where she showed Hakan the reputed grave of Marie Laveau.

"You met Ella," she reminded him. "She claims she's a direct descendent of New Orleans' famous Voodoo Queen."

"I know little about Voodoo," Hakan admitted, staring at the site. "But I did appreciate your cook's witchcraft. She certainly had me under her spell with her magic food."

"Voodoo is not witchcraft," Angela corrected. "And Ella is much more than a cook. Her wisdom has been an inspiration to me all my life."

Later, during a stroll through City Park, Angela answered Hakan's inquiries about the origin and the misunderstood practices of Voodoo.

They sat down on a bench, and Angela could see the exhaustion in Hakan's face. "How about some ice cream?" She pointed to a nearby vendor.

He declined.

"Mmmh," said Angela when she returned to the bench, "this is delicious. You don't know what you're missing."

He eyed the ice cream suspiciously and then moved away as a bee began to buzz around the cone.

When Angela swooped the insect away, it flew in Hakan's direction. He jumped and kept swooshing his handkerchief.

"What's the matter?"

"I'm sorry. I must look ridiculous," he said out of breath. "But I'm highly allergic to bee stings. It has put me into anaphylactic shock before. I have to be very careful." He spoke fast and sounded neurotic.

"Let's go. I think you've had enough for today. We'll have dinner at my house. You can rest while I cook."

CHAPTER 32

HAKAN WELCOMED THE coolness inside the old Victorian home. He had never seen such beautiful furnishings, artwork, and unusual artifacts. "Magnificent," he complimented as he walked around the house and admired the expanse of the luscious garden. "It reflects your ethereal distinction." He asked if he could be of help to Angela in the kitchen.

"No, thanks. Make yourself comfortable in the library," she said.

The sounds of pots and pans and the chopping of a knife against a wooden surface, together with the first delightful aromas coming out of the nearby kitchen, had a calming effect on him, and soon the Sunday paper rustled to the floor and he was fast asleep.

He woke to her voice and the scent of cinnamon candles. He looked around the room and saw her standing in the doorway. Angela had changed into a rose-colored, short summer dress; its fabric was thin and from the faint light behind her, he could detect the outlines of her long legs as she stood in the doorway between the library and the dining room.

"I'm ready when you are," she said.

Hakan slowly got up and walked toward her. "You're beautiful," he said in a raspy voice. "I don't understand why I'm so lucky to have met you."

"It's not luck—it's fate," she replied, looking into his eyes.

He mistook the shimmer of sadness in her dark eyes for sensuality and pressed her body against his. "Yes, it's destiny," he breathed.

She pulled away, but took his hand and led him to the candlelit table.

At first he thought he was not hungry for food—all he desired was to satisfy his craving for her—but the delicate red wine and the tangy shrimp and avocado salad triggered his appetite.

In the background he heard gentle piano music. "What is it?" he asked. "It's so beautiful."

"It's a local jazz musician playing his own rendition of Vivaldi's The Four Seasons. The Spring Concerto is my favorite." She took a deep breath. "This artist's flawless instrumental technique, pure tone quality, and brilliant sense of phrasing is awesome; it brings a sensuality to an already great work." She put her finger over her lips. "Sssh," she whispered, closing her eyes. "Whenever I hear this I like to listen to my soul."

"Joyful spring has arrived,
The birds welcome it with their happy songs,
And the brooks in the gentle breezes
Flow with a sweet murmur.
The sky is..."

Unable to grasp the profundity of Angela's state of mind, Hakan only paid attention to her beauty as he watched her sitting across the table from him. Her dreamy voice caused his imagination to see her nipples rising under the thin fabric of her dress, and he visualized tasting them with his tongue.

He blinked back into reality when he felt a stirring in his groin. Still oblivious to her meditative state, he reached for the decanter. "May I pour you another glass of wine?"

Without opening her eyes, she nodded.

For most of the meal he respected her silence and her desire to absorb herself in the music.

"Is there anything you don't do well?" he finally asked, after glimpsing at the dessert—ice cream and fresh berries over a double chocolate brownie.

"There'll be a time when you can answer that question yourself."

Hakan did not know when or how it happened but, as if in a dream, he felt himself swaying next to her as they listened to the piano orchestration. In slow rhythm, surrounded by the dancing notes of sweet melodies, they twirled into another room. Through drowsy, half-closed eyes, he spotted an oversized chaise lounge that magnetically drew him closer. Holding Angela tightly in his arms, he felt his cheeks getting painted with pleasure.

He briefly let go of Angela so he could look at her in the candlelight. Then, his touch on her skin pushed the straps of her dress off her shoulders. Like a snake, the garment slithered off her body, revealing the most perfect creation Hakan had ever dreamt of.

His voice thickened as if liquid caramel lined his throat. "You're the most beautiful woman in the universe." His eyes feverishly feasted on her naked body. "Your parents chose the perfect name. You're an angel. My angel." He panted in anticipation, believing his fast-racing heart was ready to explode. He came closer, but controlled his desire to greedily grab her breasts.

Shakily, he peeled away his shirt. Soon after, with increasing excitement, he removed the rest of his clothes. In his nakedness he could detect his own body's musky odor, reminding him of overripe dates. Then, in slow motion, he knew he was descending, and with a groan he softly lowered himself on top of her curvaceous glowing body.

To him, her skin emitted deliciously demonic fragrances, and he let himself drown with sighs of delight as he opened her like a predatory posy.

Nothing, not even his wildest fantasies, had prepared him for what was happening to his head and his body. Endless explosions simultaneously sizzled through him and, when he thought he could not endure another one of the delicious thrills, the heavenly creature—sometimes below, other times above him—made him cry out for more.

Before he sank into quiescence, he whispered, "Angela, my angel. You're my damnation—but my descent to hell will be a heavenly trip."

Slowly she allowed herself to enter this world's reality again. The music had stopped and the dying candles were flickering fast, trying to brighten up the last minutes of their short waxen lives. Her black eyes—the fire of the amethyst brightly shining in one of them—pierced the dimness of the room in which she had just discovered the magnitude of her mission. A sad sigh escaped her when she felt the heat from the body of the man next to her. She turned her head and watched his chest rise and fall. Her spiritual being had become even more aware that her physical body needed to be the main instrument of her mission, namely to win the total attention and attraction of the man who had become her destiny.

Unbeknownst to him, she had extracted his every thought, miscreant intentions, and confused intellect with her advanced intelligence. Enlightenment had shown her that this was the beginning; insightfulness allowed her to foresee the end. It was the in-between that would require her to stop a terrible tragedy. She knew of the pain and danger ahead but, being above fear, she was at peace. She sensed the guidance that blessed her ability to finish the difficult task ahead.

When the last candle faded away and the room turned dark, she closed her eyes and let herself be guided toward the magnificent light in another dimension.

CHAPTER 33

ELLA ARRIVED EARLY at Louis Armstrong International Airport. She walked to the nearest P.J.'s coffee shop and ordered a tall latte and a vanilla almond biscotti. Near the monitors, she found an empty seat, smoothed her dress before she sat down, and waited for the American Airlines flight from Dallas. Ebony had left Tucson late that morning, had connected in Dallas, and was on her way to New Orleans. Ella glanced at the monitor again and saw she had another twenty minutes before going to the arriving baggage area.

Ella took a bite of the biscotti and enjoyed the first sip of coffee. She liked her own brew better but this would have to do. She felt good in the new outfit, a beige cotton piqué sleeveless dress with a matching wing-collar jacket. Ella especially liked the contrasting appliquéd detailing and the scalloped hem. She had spent more money than anticipated on it, but was happy with her choice. She ran her fingers over the turquoise and blue topaz cross, pinned on the collar of the jacket, to make sure it was still there. The cross pin, the matching earrings, and the bracelet had been a gift from Governor and Mrs. Atwood for her last birthday. She enjoyed wearing the three magnificent pieces together, but fancied the cross and wore it almost every day.

Finishing the biscotti, Ella discarded the rest of the coffee. As she walked toward the baggage area she noticed the glances of people rushing by her. Even though she considered herself past the prime of her life, she still walked erect and steady, always looking proud and immaculate and never without a smile on her lips.

"Momma!"

Ella had not seen Ebony in two years. With a broad smile, exposing two rows of white, even teeth, Ella pulled her into a warm, long embrace.

"You look good, child. Real good!" Ella took a step back and looked at her pretty daughter.

"You think so, Momma? I know I've gotten chunky, but you should've seen me four weeks ago. Since then I've lost fifteen pounds with some more to go." She patted her hips before slipping her hands into the pockets of the tunic that hung loosely over matching pale yellow clamdiggers.

"I said you look good, Ebony. Pretty as ever! Gotta give your daddy credit for the one and only thing he did well: sharing his good looks with you. Let's find your luggage."

Ebony stopped walking and took her mother's hand. "Momma, there is no luggage. I only brought my carry-on."

"So you've changed your mind—you're not plannin' on movin' back here," Ella sighed. "I had a feelin'."

"I can't move back to New Orleans. There's much I have to tell you; there's confusion in me and I need your help. But I know for sure that I can't stay here; I must go back to Tucson."

As they waited in line for a taxi, Ella linked her arm with her daughter's. They stood in silence, enjoying the warmth that passed between them.

"We're not goin' home tonight," Ella said, breaking the quiet several minutes into the taxi ride. "Angela begged me to convince you to spend your first evening with her. She's lookin' forward to the three of us bein' together."

"That's amazing," Ebony exclaimed. "The reason I changed my mind about not moving back to New Orleans—the metamorphosis that has taken place within me—I believe very much involves Angela. Besides wanting to be with you, Momma, she's the main reason I came here." She looked at her mother. "You of all people will understand what I came to share: I think there's a supernatural connection between someone in Tucson and Angela."

"Don't tell me now, child," Ella hushed, and motioned her head toward the taxi driver. "This is not the place to talk."

Angela shrieked with delight when she opened the door and with both hands pulled Ella and Ebony into the house. She threw her arms around Ebony. “I’ve missed you so much, Ebbie.”

“You look…incredible,” was all Ebony could say.

Angela wore a sleeveless sand-colored shirt tucked into a pair of matching shorts. Her hair was slicked back into a short ponytail and not a trace of makeup could be found on her flawless face. Her exposed skin looked luminous as she danced barefoot around her guests.

“You have not changed,” Ebony said admiringly.

“Uh-uh, you missed all the changes,” Ella mocked. “Angela changed somethin’ almost every month for years. Only lately she looks like herself again,” Ella teased.

Angela brought them into the kitchen and poured three glasses of champagne. “Here’s to our long-overdue reunion.” The resonance of the clinking glasses vibrated through the air like musical tones.

“Remember our old vow? ‘We solemnly pledge to always be together until…’” Ebony started, and smiled as she saw Angela nod and chime into their childhood promise.

“…until the day we die; only to be reunited in other lives again and again and again and again,” they said in unison.

“Mmmh,” Ella was sniffing. “Smells good ’round here. What you cookin’?”

“It’s not a surprise, Ella. You should recognize the aroma. It’s your recipe.”

Ella smiled. “I was kiddin.’ I’ll be ready for that good-tastin’ étouffée whenever it’s done.”

“Let’s just catch up on missed times and enjoy the champagne before I put the finishing touches on our dinner.” Angela led the way into the living room. For the next two hours the three women reminisced about the past twenty years. They laughed until they cried, and after they dried their tears, they found more to laugh and cry over again.

It wasn’t until they finished their dinner, and after exchanging their daytime clothes for comfortable sleepwear, that they relaxed in the upstairs sitting parlor.

Ebony cleared her throat. "I came here for one reason, but don't know where to start. There's a lot that I need to share with both of you; some of it I don't know how to explain."

"Start at the beginning, child. Always at the beginning," Ella suggested.

Ebony began to talk slowly, trying to put the facts of the past seven weeks into order. As soon as she finished telling about her last disappointing relationship with Rodney and her desire to move back to New Orleans, she began to talk with fast precision.

She told of her care for the young woman in a coma and her fascination with the case—the serenity she experienced whenever she was alone with that patient. She talked about the young woman's loving father, and referred to the mother as a jar of snake-filled venom.

Ebony blushed and paused when she retold of when she met Dr. Harris and the impact the handsome doctor from California had on her. She shared the details of the time she had spent with him at the Institute in Tucson.

"Even though I now know he's engaged to an LA socialite, I can't shake the feeling that I will know him for the rest of my life," Ebony sighed. There was a moment of stillness, then she searched Angela's eyes, and seconds later she found her mother's.

"That man's not the only reason why you came here, Ebony." Ella frowned. "There's more than the man that you want to talk about. I can see it." Aware that a purple shimmer was brightening the diffused light of the room, Ella turned to Angela. "You see it too, don't you?"

Angela nodded and said in a soft and low voice, "I can feel a strong tie between that doctor and you, Ebbie, but the true connection to him is coming via another person—someone who is truly rare."

"Yes," Ebony breathed. "There is indeed. It's the patient I've been telling you about. She's the true reason why I'm here and only you two can understand what I have to say." Ebony's face brightened as she looked at Angela. "This woman, her name is Teeba Prime, has the same impact you've always had on me. But what's more amazing, you and she share something so unique that I immediately sensed a connection." Ebony's voice was now only a whisper, but it cracked with emotion. "Ever since we were kids, I've been mesmerized by the purple fire in your left eye, Angela. I always believed that the fire of the amethyst shone only in you, like one of a kind. But then I saw it again. The same unbelievable fire is in Teeba's right eye."

There was silence in the room. Ebony moved closer to Angela. "I know it sounds weird but you have to believe me. I can sense the linking, but I can't find words to explain it."

"I do believe you, Ebbie. You don't have to say any more. Let me take your hand and let me read the rest through your eyes."

Tears flowed down Angela's cheeks as she surrendered to a never-before-experienced physical emotion. "Ebbie," she finally managed to say, "you're the messenger I've been waiting for. Oh, my sweet, sweet friend."

Angela hugged Ebony tightly. "I'm beginning to feel lighter and lighter from a new level of illumination. You've discovered my missing piece...you've located the existence...that which is never lost."

Los Angeles

...in July

CHAPTER 34

"CONGRATULATIONS, CLAY!" DR. Austin Berger's excited voice came through the phone. "This is great news. How long have we talked about working side by side? Good thing we've maintained our licenses in California and Arizona."

In Los Angeles, Clayton leaned back into his chair with his eyes closed. There never was a question in his mind that the offer from the Joseph Sugar Neurological Research Institute in Tucson was a rare opportunity for more than one reason. But negotiations and details needed to be worked out before he was able to make the full commitment.

"Hey, are you still there? I hope you're not battling second thoughts."

"No second thoughts. Just thinking how much my life is about to change."

"I guess so, but only for the better as far as your career is concerned. I'm not so sure about your personal life, though, with Maya being a true California gal. What was her reaction?"

"That's the problem. I haven't been able to reach her all day." The relaxed expression on Clayton's face was replaced by a frown.

As soon as he finished his phone conversation, Clayton dialed his parents' number.

"Dad, how are you?"

"Son! What a coincidence! Earlier, I was reading an article on biologic genetics in the Lancet in which your piece in the New England Journal of Medicine was quoted. How come..."

"Darn!" Clayton interrupted. "I was going to give you a summary of the paper before presentation but I've had so many things on my mind lately that I forgot...I'm really sorry, Dad."

"Don't worry. I just finished reading it in NEJM via the Internet and I must say I'm very pleased and impressed with the scope of research and the breakthrough that you and your team accomplished. I must say I'm fascinated by your research on the etiology of amyotrophic lateral sclerosis."

Clayton could hear the pride and admiration in his father's voice. "Thanks, Dad. I'm very proud of the results on ALS, but it's always nice to be complimented by a great man like you."

After more talk about the article, Clayton changed the subject. "Listen, Dad, I'm still at ONI, but I'd like to swing by to discuss some private matters with you and Mom. Will both of you be home within the next hour?"

"Uh-oh...Do I hear concern in your voice? Are you all right, son?"

"Of course, I'm better than all right, but what I want to share with you and Mom needs to be done face-to-face."

"Your mother went for her daily walk on the beach. She's been gone a while. She should be back any moment now. Why don't you head on over, son? Will you be staying for dinner?"

"No, thanks Dad, I'll be having dinner with Maya tonight."

As Clayton drove into Malibu, he wondered how soon he would see his parents again. Although Tucson was less than two hours of flight time away from Los Angeles, something deep inside was telling him that his visits back home would be rare in the foreseeable future.

Clayton was the only son of Dr. Aaron Harris—a recently retired, well-known geneticist—and Emma Lisboa, who had won international acclaim with her poetic, imaginative novels.

Aaron Harris grew up in housing projects and his earliest memories were those of screams and pain. His drug-addicted mother showed no responsibility toward her four children from three different fathers. He heard about his mother's death when he was seven years old and did not see his half-siblings again until many years later because they spent most of their young lives separated from each other in foster homes. Aaron never knew his father, but in his longing for a better life and vivid imagination he created a fantasy of a caring, loving man with high hopes for his only son. Eager to please, Aaron made it his life's goal to become a productive and preeminent personality. He studied day and night as he worked toward his goals.

Emma Lisboa, a native of Brazil, was the offspring of progressively intermixed ethnic groups. Her ancestry went back to the earliest days of Brazil's colonial history when the Portuguese mixed with Indians and Africans who were brought to work in mines and on plantations. Emma's family had grown prosperous and sent their talented, strong-willed, and beautiful daughter to study in the United States. There she met Aaron, and began to write novels. Whenever she did readings, she appeared in native clothes, some woven from llama wool, others from cotton. The outfits, with their original patterns and bright colors, and the various ornaments in her braided hair all complemented her stories about American Indians. She never offered an explanation about the strange looking marks she often painted on her smooth coffee-cream skin, but she prided herself on anecdotes about the ancient pelts and animal scalps, an inheritance from her ancestors.

As Clayton drove up the winding road toward his parents' home, overlooking the Pacific Ocean, he experienced the usual fond feeling that took hold of him whenever he reentered the coziness of his childhood.

They sat in the shaded part of the terrace. Located high above the Pacific Coast Highway, they could not see the cars that whizzed by below them and were oblivious to their steady hum; instead, their eyes rested on the immense body of water that glistened like a giant aquamarine in the late afternoon sun.

Emma had poured three glasses of her own organic concoction of fruit iced tea; its color was a shade of brilliant purple. Her husband suspiciously looked at the drink, then smiled and shrugged. "Let's give it a try, I've seen stranger tints before."

"It's delicious, Mom. What is it?"

"You wouldn't know the difference between a checkerberry and a red currant, Claytonio," she teased. "But as long as you like it, let me keep my little secrets and surprises." Emma wore a long, gauzy caftan of sapphire blue. Her hair, once black as ebony and now the color of mother-of-pearl, was pulled straight back into a chignon. Over the years her skin had remained smooth and supple. Emma, now in her sixties, still was an eye-filling, effervescent woman.

Clayton felt his mother watching him with a hint of a mischievous smile on her lips. "What are you thinking, Mom? Are you trying to read my thoughts again?"

"Trying?" Emma shook her head. "My darling, I know you like I know myself. You remind me of the day when I told my parents I wanted to study in the United States, but deep inside knew I was saying goodbye to my homeland."

Clayton grinned. "I don't believe it. That's exactly why I'm here." He paused and looked from his mother to his father. "I'm not leaving my homeland, but I'm leaving LA to take advantage of a great opportunity in Arizona." He grinned at his mother. "I'm not as adventurous as you, Mom. I need to stay in this country and fairly close to both of you."

He then told his parents about his consult on the patient at the Institute in Tucson, his success with Teeba's case, and his fascination with her fast and unexplainable recovery.

"I was approached to take over the Research and Development Department at JSNRI," Clayton's voice rose. "The offer includes appropriate funding, plus I can have a consultant's practice and house staff." He saw his father's nod of approval. "It's a chance of a lifetime to be in charge of the R & D at a prestigious neurological institute—something I couldn't refuse. Plus, I get to work with my old buddy Austin Berger again. That's another bonus."

"Well," said his father, "I think you're making a wise decision. You've got my blessings, son. But what about Maya—how's she dealing with this choice of yours?"

"I'm not sure she's taken my negotiations seriously. I've been keeping her apprised of the developments, but know she's only lent me half an ear so far and I didn't have a chance to tell her of today's news. I'll break it to her over dinner tonight. I'm a little nervous, but if she loves me the way she says she does, how could she not be happy for me?" He looked at his mother with uncertainty.

"She will not understand," Emma said, her smile disappearing. "She will not be supportive, nor will she be willing to leave Los Angeles." She moved closer to her son and looked him straight in the eyes. "But, you must not let anyone stop you, because you'll be sacrificing amazing experiences." Her gaze increased in intensity. "You're doing the right thing, Claytonio. Don't let Maya's reaction sway you." Her Portuguese accent was strong and there was passion and urgency in her low voice.

"Oh, Emma," Aaron scolded. "Are you trying to use your Brazilian ritual magic and clairvoyance again? Clayton is perfectly able to handle the situation."

Emma got up and stood behind her husband, kissing his graying, short-cropped curls. "You always doubt my predictions and then look at me in surprise when they prove true. In all the years you've known me, you have yet to learn and trust this part of me." With her hands on Aaron's shoulders, she said to Clayton, "Try to analyze the feeling when your instincts told you to accept this opportunity, Claytonio. Soon, you will discover the meaningful reason behind this important decision. I sense an unknown happiness waiting for you. You're about to enter a rare adventure."

Clayton heard his mother's words, but he couldn't take his eyes away from the glass she held in her hand. At sunset, the last rays of the sun reached into the now half-shaded area. They pierced the bright purple tea, reminding him of the amazing fire of the amethyst he had seen in Teeba's eye.

CHAPTER 35

EVEN THOUGH THE traffic was sluggish, it still made the long drive from Malibu into Beverly Hills too short. Wanting more time, Clayton didn't look forward to the next few hours. He had the uncomfortable feeling that his mother's words would ring true. He waited for the oncoming cars to pass before he turned left by the Beverly Hills Hotel, then slowly drove west three miles into Holmby Hills, finally turning turn into a quiet cul-de-sac. He lowered his window and pressed the combination to open the heavy iron gate.

Maya Roberts still lived with her parents; there had been no reason to move. The estate was the largest in the Bel Air/Holmby Hills area and Maya had her own sizable house on the grounds. The legendary mansion on four acres of parkland was once owned by a famous silent movie star and had been gutted, rebuilt, and enhanced by Maya's father.

Clayton looked at the pile of papers on the passenger seat—work that needed to be done tonight—but decided to leave it where it was. He heard the white gravel crunch under his shoes and heard his deep breaths before he opened the door.

Maya was on the phone. In rapid talk she ridiculed and gave explanations and orders to someone on the other end. Her raised voice stopped only briefly, apparently being interrupted, before she cut in with a shrill, "No way! This is not what we've negotiated! Tell your hotshot partner that he's got no spine and that I'll do the project by myself if he tries to change things now." She banged her fist into an oversized pillow on the Holly Hunt sofa. "There'll be no deal if you guys are trying to screw around with me. You should know better by now."

Clayton stood in the doorway and watched Maya as she paced back and forth through two rooms. Her expression was angry, her cheeks flushed, and her movements determined.

After an abrupt and cold, "I demand an answer tonight," she disconnected and turned around. Then, like a chameleon, changed colors. "Darling! How long have you been here?" She threw her arms around his neck and pulled him close; she wet her lips and nuzzled his ear. "Mmmh, so good. You've arrived just at the right time. What a day I've had." She kissed his mouth and looked at him seductively. She tried to pull him toward the Mies van der Rohe nutmeg-leather daybed.

Clayton gently took her shoulders and looked her in the eyes. "I have some wonderful news that I need to share with you. Let's have some wine and sit down."

She pouted and purred, "It better be more wonderful than what I had in mind."

After he poured two glasses of Chassagne-Montrachet, he sat next to her and took her hand. Clayton told her the news he shared with his parents hours before.

She remained dead silent and never changed her posture or facial expression. But the color had drained from her face. She looked like one of the antique porcelain dolls in two airtight, custom-built display cases across the room.

"Are you done?" Maya finally asked, pulling her hand out of his. Her voice was cold and her eyes still held the contact. "May I ask why you didn't bother to ever mention a word about this to me before?"

"I've talked to you about this, but you've been too wrapped up with the wedding and your own work. You're rarely interested in what I have to say or when I try to share my professional life with you." He tried to caress her arm, but she inched away. "I've really been trying to get you interested but you usually claim you don't understand my medical jargon. I realize we have different interests, and I've been paying a lot of attention to yours, but..."

"Well, you're right," she interrupted. "I don't remember you ever mentioning a word about this. I've had more important things to concentrate on. Plus, I never imagined you'd seriously want to leave LA and ONI for some second-class institute in a hick town like Tucson." She gulped her wine and looked at him with cold eyes. "You cannot be serious." She put the glass down hard. "Well, it's just not going to happen. It's as simple as that!"

"It is Maya. I've accepted, and after ironing out some details, I'll start as soon as possible. The board scheduled a meeting with me this week and I'd love you to come along." He wondered if she was listening. "I want you to see how impressive the Institute is and introduce you to some fine scientists. Austin offered to show you around the city. I'm told there are beautiful homes tucked away in the mountains." He tried to take her hand again. "I will make it right for us, Maya, I promise!"

She laughed a short, dismissive laugh. "You must have lost your mind. There is no way I'll move to Tucson and neither will you. We're going to be married in a few months and we will live right here in LA. No fucking way am I moving to some shitty, dusty town in the godforsaken desert with you or anybody." She shot him another killer look and refilled her glass.

Clayton sat in silence. He did not like to argue and rarely had disagreed with Maya's suggestions. He easily gave into her demands. He had his own opinions, but since Maya filled most of his free time with personal and social obligations, he let her have her way. She was the one who had pursued their relationship after they were introduced less than a year ago and was the one to suggest they should get married. She made the plans, the decisions, and ran their social lives. Clayton had welcomed the change, but now he saw Maya in a different light—a much darker one.

"Why don't I give you some time to get used to the idea? I'm prepared to shuttle back and forth. I could come to LA every weekend until you're ready to make the move."

"You must've lost your mind," she hissed. "You mean to tell me that you're willing to sacrifice the fabulous life I've introduced you to? Are you expecting me to go to social functions by myself while you're away?" She stood and put her hands on her narrow hips. "What is happening to you? Who or what turned *your* brain into mush?"

He shook his head. "You said you were proud of my accomplishments and that you would go to the end of the world with me. You should be more proud of me now since this offer is a great honor and important to my career. I don't understand why you refuse to share my excitement." Clayton paused when he heard her sharp breaths. "Yes," he continued softly, "adjustments will have to be made and our lives will change, but I believe it can only get better."

She tapped her manicured fingernails against the crystal glass of the table. "*Your* career, huh? Well, what about mine? I can't imagine working anywhere but right here. This is the only city where things are happening in the movie industry. Not in Shitville, Arizona, where no-class-no-talent cowboys ride pickup trucks instead of horses." She mocked a laugh.

"We won't be far from LA. You could shuttle or work part-time," Clayton reasoned. "What's wrong with not working at all? I would love to start a family. We certainly…"

"Not working? Family?" she hissed and kicked the horsehair ottoman that separated her from Clayton. "Are you mentally masturbating?" Maya's chest heaved. "Damn you! I should've listened to my father. He tried to tell me you were not what he had in mind for me." She eyed him with disgust, her lips curling down. "He doesn't believe in mixed-race marriages but I let myself fall for your *different* looks. You were a challenge then; now, I'm sorry." She slapped her forehead. "I must've been stupid, not hearing my father's warning. He and I always think alike."

Clayton stood in stunned silence. Why had he never seen this side of her before? How could he have been so wrong? He froze when he realized that Maya mistook his silence for a change of mind as she walked around the ottoman and touched his arm.

"I'm sorry if I overreacted," she said. "Can't you see that you belong right here with me, darling? We look good together; we've been the talk of LA," she purred. "You've given me many thrills and I know I've made you happy too. We don't want to lose this, do we?" Her long fingers stroked his arm.

Clayton stepped away. "I don't belong here, Maya. I have to follow my instincts and they are telling me that I must move on in my career." He looked her straight in the eye. "I believed you when you said you loved me. Now you can prove it by coming with me. If you do, I will forget the hurtful things you just said."

He walked to the door. The crystal glass missed his head by two inches as it broke into a million pieces when it hit the marbleized wall.

Swan Valley

...in July

Chapter 36

Hakan did not care for being on small planes, no matter how private and luxurious. As a matter of fact, his main neurosis was fear of flying. No matter how many times he tried to focus on something different, his hands ended up in tight fists; his knuckles white.

"Dr. Öztürk, kindly fasten your seatbelt. We'll be landing shortly."

He nodded toward the long-legged, frizzy-haired female attendant who had been reserved with words but generous with smiles throughout the entire flight that originated in Lafayette. Even though he knew the food on board would be first class, he declined and, instead, asked her to steep his own tea during the long trip. "Too late to have another one?" he questioned and handed her the mug. A few minutes later, without words but still smiling, she put a fresh cup in front of him. As always, the sweet, steaming, maroon-colored liquid calmed his nerves, especially as the Gulfstream G-3 began its descent into the Swan Valley, located between Jackson Hole and Idaho Falls. He wondered if what he was seeing below was already part of Phillip Portal's enormous ranch: thousands of acres of private property with roaming hills, trees, and a river coursing through the secluded nature. When he spotted the private runway carved into wilderness, he knew they had arrived at one of Phillip Portal's many hideaways.

As soon as the plane doors opened, Hakan felt immense relief standing on solid ground and welcomed the fresh clean air and sunshine. A Land Rover waited nearby; a tall muscular man in western gear tipped a cowboy hat.

"Dr. Oster? I'm Doug."

Hakan did not bother to correct him and entered the vehicle.

"Welcome to Clearwater Ranch." Doug placed the carry-on on the backseat. "Why don't ya sit in front? Our roads are a li'l rough; might get slightly bumpy on the ride."

They passed by grazing cattle, sheep, and hay fields. When they crossed the Snake River, Doug stopped the car and pointed to a herd of elk in the distance. As they approached the compound, Hakan noticed the stable hands doing various chores around the stables. Among the men he saw two teenage girls grooming their horses. The girls looked up and waved as they saw the Land Rover approach. Hakan smiled back and lifted his hand.

"The blonde gal on the left—the thin one—is Katie Portal. The other one's a friend. Nice kids," Doug said matter-of-factly.

The Portals' picturesque sanctuary contained several log-style homes. The largest structure was impressively enhanced by glass and steel, yet perfectly integrated into nature; it was the one occupied only by the family. Two smaller guest houses were nestled between tall trees and a short distance from the main house. The remaining buildings—still farther away—housed the staff.

Hakan followed Doug into the two-bedroom log house.

"You've some time to freshen up and relax. The other gentleman from D.C. has not arrived yet," Doug drawled while glimpsing at his watch. "I'll be pickin' him up in a li'l while. Mr. Portal expects y'all for lunch at the main house. I'll come'n git ya then." Doug tipped his cowboy hat and left.

Hakan stood in the middle of the living room and looked around the room. He did not know that the bowls on top of the rustic armoire were those of Hopi, Pueblo, and Navajo tribes. He stared at the Plains Indian headdress that rested on the mantle and the pairs of Shoshone and Kiowa moccasins hanging from a painted New Mexican kitchen *trestero* that now housed a fax machine, computer, and phone. When Hakan bent down to smell the leather-covered sofa, the Navajo blanket slipped off and landed on his shoes. He was quick in picking it up and draped it over the sofa again. He looked around to see if someone was watching even though he knew he was the only one in this house. He shook his head and opened the door to the shaded porch. He sat down on a comfortable wicker chair and listened to the whispering aspen above, the gentle flow of water nearby, and the echo of wildlife in the distance.

But even in the stillness, Hakan could not silence the thundering voices of his financial backers and religious leaders that were peppered with anti-American bile and kept reminding him of the ultimate goal—to destabilize the U.S. government.

Hakan liked the important role he played in the web of intrigue, but never before was he more confused. His new lifestyle, as well as the generosity and kindness of people he had met, played havoc with his mind. He compared the poverty and suffering, neglect and carelessness, and deceit and corruption in his native land to the carefree culture and lavish way of life that surrounded him. He longed to live this life to the fullest and without care, but a tormentor kept visiting him in nightmares, pointing to the masses of good people left behind in the grime, waiting to be rescued. Hakan reminded himself over and over that all of mankind was vulnerable whether living in cages or in mansions. Over the years his teachers had convinced him that the Day of Judgment would only fall upon the greedy and opulent. The day was near when Allah's word would do justice; the infidel would lose and the faithful would be rewarded.

Hakan still considered himself blessed. He had been born into the prosperous Khatami family in Iran, a family that once prided itself on a fine reputation dating back to times when the country was still known as Persia. However, his father, Parviz Khatami—a respected physician—ruined the family's rank and dignity with his thirst for control and influence. First, he pursued misguided ideals as a subordinate to men who toppled the Shah during the revolution. Soon, the Islamic fundamentalists killed Parviz' idealistic desire for prominence and power, but by then it was too late. With the family's fortune gone and under the watchful eyes of the Mullahs, there was no escape. Parviz had sold himself and his family to the new devilish antagonist. In his confused state of mind he betrayed the new regime—a mistake that would cost him his life.

Hakan tried to forget the horrifying and miserable days when he carried a different name. His life only turned better when he was whisked away by Al-Saafi, a secretive, hard-line revolutionary group, allied with Iran's ruling clerics and financially backed by wealthy Saudi fanatics.

The group in its infant stages consisted of disciples from several different Middle Eastern nations, all united in their belief that worldwide acceptance of Islam could only occur after the deaths of Israel and the Great Satan, the United States. Over the years the movement grew rapidly by successfully recruiting bright and willing men, not only from the Muslim world, but also from European nations, Indonesia, Asia, North Africa, and even from within the United States.

It was in the early days of Al-Saafi that the group's greatest hope and pride was Dr. Sattar Khatami, a brilliant scientist fresh out of medical school. But when the young man's father smeared the family's good name throughout Iran with double-tongued crimes, Al-Saafi decided to give the son a clean beginning.

Al-Saafi's fanatical operatives were in luck when they spotted a Turkish student at Johns Hopkins University; his name was Hakan Öztürk and he resembled Sattar Khatami. The terrorists showed no compunction in brutally killing the unsuspecting Hakan and then making certain that his parents in Turkey were silenced as well. A temporary clerk in the registrar's office, planted by Al-Saafi, changed the murdered Turkish student's records at the university, thus giving birth to the new Hakan Öztürk.

Hakan took to his new life as quickly as to his newfound obsession for the fall of Western civilization and the world's purification through Islamic jihad. Because of Al-Saafi's relentless pressure, Hakan soon suppressed the memory of thirty-two-year-old Sattar Khatami, whose identity and past in Iran had been meticulously wiped out with hard cash.

His rebirth with a false undergraduate degree in biochemistry from Harvard and graduate work at Johns Hopkins allowed Hakan's career to soar when he became part of the virology department at the Pasteur Institute in Paris.

As Sattar Khatami, he once dreamt of the Nobel Prize—he certainly was blessed with superior intelligence, strong ambition, and many theories—but Al-Saafi had another prize in mind for Hakan; it was a prize with rewards far bigger than the would-be Nobelist ever imagined.

Now grown into a sizeable organization, Al-Saafi had vowed not to strike until its first deadly plan was perfected.

A magnificent butterfly slowly approached and fluttered before his eyes, causing Hakan to blink his thoughts into the present. The insect landed on his lap and expanded its strikingly colored wings. Fixing his gaze on this wondrous creation of nature, Hakan welcomed the mental vision of Angela. He longingly thought of the previous night with the woman who led him to mysterious places he'd never explored before. He indulged in the reverie of still tasting her nectarous fluids on his tongue. He swallowed.

The mere thought of her once again turned him into quivering jelly as he felt his sex grow beneath the butterfly. Hakan held his breath and resigned himself to the fact that he was blinded in her presence and lovesick when apart.

He ignored the guilt that tried to creep between him and the woman who had turned him from an impetuous male who regarded females as lugubrious objects into a gentle lover who now prided himself on his stamina. With his guilt pushed aside, he told himself that certain practices, as required by the Qur'án, were ignored in many of the Islamic countries. He knew different interpretations were applied everywhere; observances were executed when suitable, and devotion and duty atoned when appropriate. So, Hakan comforted himself with the fact that he was not committing a breach of Islamic law.

"Dr. Oster? Hello! Dr. Oster?"

Doug's booming voice startled Hakan. Embarrassed he brushed the butterfly off his lap. For a second he watched it glide away into the wilderness.

"I'm out here," he answered. He stuck his head into the house. "I must have dozed off. Please wait in the car, I'll hurry and freshen up."

Chapter 37

Fifteen minutes later, Doug led Hakan over a pathway marked by boulders. Walls of granite and stone extended from outside into the interior of the main house. Panoramic windows were framed by a palette of dark-bronzed copper panels that had taken on their natural patina in deep shades of green. He followed Doug through the labyrinth of rooms, galleries, and landscaped atria. There were only a few solid walls between the many floor-to-ceiling tinted-glass panels. The boulders, waterfalls, natural stone floors, and landscaped plantings created an outdoor illusion. The two men walked upstairs and through another pavilion before Doug opened a massive, sculpted door that led into high-tech office quarters.

"The boss'll be right with ya. Please take a seat." He tipped his cowboy hat.

A whizzing sound made Hakan turn around, and in amazement he watched a granite and stone wall open. He stood up when he saw the chairman and CEO of PORTAL Enterprises beckon him into the spacious office.

"Welcome to my self-imposed isolation," Phillip said dryly from behind his desk. "I hope your trip was pleasant." He got up and shook Hakan's hand. "Doug is fetching Ford. As soon as he gets here, we'll start. We'll have a bite to eat while we're conducting business. Hope you don't mind waiting a bit longer."

Through the wall-to-wall window panels, Hakan could see the rich vistas of the Swan Valley surrounded by the majestic Rocky Mountains in the far distance.

"You picked a beautiful spot, Phil," Hakan said, but he also heard an inner voice screaming: *This infidel has more money than soul. Don't be lead astray by the wealth of demons.* Hakan's teeth tugged nervously on his lower lip and he could feel his heart as it thudded hard against his ribs. *Quiet,* he warned his inner voice. *You must quiet down.*

Phillip motioned his guest closer to the window. "See that pool below? It was built into a swale and we kept the existing stone and boulders. We took every step possible to preserve the native vegetation." There was sincere softness in his eyes. "I couldn't imagine anyone wanting to disturb this natural setting."

Hakan saw two boys diving off the rocks; he could neither hear the splashes nor their excited shrieks. The insulation was perfect and the glass was bulletproof, as it was all throughout the house.

"My son, Lincoln, and his buddy Eli," Phillip said while nodding in the boys' direction. "Our children, Katie and Linc, are encouraged to invite different friends every two weeks. Otherwise it gets too lonely up here." The slim man smiled as he watched the boys in their play.

A faint chime sounded.

"Aha, that must be Ford."

The wall opened again for the Middle Eastern Bureau Chief of the CIA.

"What a magnificent hideaway. I've never seen a more beautiful display of nature before," Ford exclaimed as he shook the chairman's hand. "I'm retiring next year. Mind if I become your neighbor?"

Ford's retirement was actually overdue; he had planned to find his own Shangri-La by now but his plans were put on hold when the CIA learned of an unidentified terrorist group with possible headquarters in Iran. Since Ford was an expert on biological warfare and terrorism, he was asked to postpone his retirement. That was almost two years ago, a frustratingly long time for a man who was more than ready to assure his wife, two children, and three grandchildren that no danger could possibly lurk in the waters that he was planning to tread for the last phase of his life. Aside from spending more time with his family, his biggest dream was to stand in waders with his feet forty inches below the surface of sparkling clean rivers and whistle his line back and forth, sending it to fly upstream toward the trout that were hiding in the ripples.

Ford sighed as he stood between Phillip, the man who had a perfect river for fly-fishing running through his vast property, and Hakan, who two years ago had stopped him from executing his retirement plan by becoming the informer of bad news to the CIA.

"Gentlemen!" Phillip gestured his guests to follow him into an adjoining room. Unlike the rest of the house, there were no windows in this richly paneled chamber, but hidden lighting mimicked bright daylight. A conference table, large enough to seat ten people, was framed with four equally distanced upholstered chairs. On the table were four wooden trays, each containing a plate with a thick grilled chicken sandwich on crusty seven-grain bread, a glass plate with a few slices of tomatoes—topped with fresh mozzarella cheese and basil leaves—as well as an oversized mug filled with wild mushroom soup. Since the soup was steaming and the chicken warm, it was obvious that someone had served the food through a hidden door just seconds before they entered. Aside from the shiny conference table and the chairs, there was not another piece of furniture in the room.

"You won't find any distraction here," Phillip said in an assuring tone of voice. "I prefer to strictly concentrate on business during my meetings, and I find that everyone reacts faster and more efficiently in this type of environment." He motioned his guests to take a seat. "Today I'll excuse a necessary slight distraction." Phillip gestured toward the trays.

"Who's the fourth?" Ford pointed at the empty chair.

"My wife, Miranda. She now is CEO of PORTAL Enterprises. I remain the chairman."

As they were taking their seats, the granite and stone wall opened in Phillip's office and Miranda entered, casually dressed in a pair of blue jeans and a white button-down shirt. The heavy wall in the office whizzed shut behind her and, as soon as she entered the windowless room, a wood panel automatically closed, sealing the four people into temporary confinement.

Hakan felt his chest tightening. He did not like the feeling of enclosures. He prayed he would make it through the ordeal and forced a thin smile at Miranda when he greeted her. He noticed his shaking hand when he reached for the water pitcher to fill his glass.

The water was ice cold and he longingly wished for his hot and sweet maroon-colored tea. Mechanically, he took a bite of his sandwich. Without realizing, he stirred the hot soup and poked at the sliced tomato, separating it from the cheese and the green leaves. He still was not hungry—airplanes and closed quarters had that effect on him. He tried to concentrate on Phillip's monotonous voice as his boss gave Miranda a preliminary rundown for the record.

Hakan took the napkin and wiped his mouth. He hoped nobody noticed that he also dabbed cold sweat off his forehead.

"So," said Phillip, looking at Ford. "What we know is that Al-Saafi exists with cells in various countries. We also know that by now Al-Saafi allegedly has a hierarchy of international fanatics, but we still don't know who they are, where they're hiding, what they want, and when, where, or on whom they will use their ghastly weapon first." Though there was anger in his voice, behind his thick glasses, there was worry in his eyes.

"Yes," Ford responded. "We also know a terrorist cell is small, moves very fast, and has the capability of multiplying even faster." Despite his great girth and formidable presence, Ford had the ability to sound like a lamb, but his words had the chilling effect of a ferocious animal. "Yes," he nodded with narrowed eyes, "since we know so little, we're wrestling a hungry lion with both hands tied behind our backs." In a demonstrative move, he clasped his oversized hands behind his back and shrugged wide shoulders that could be the envy of any NFL linebacker.

"What about the informant, the man that gave Hakan the lead and the original strain of MAX 18?" Miranda asked. "He must know more." She expectantly looked at Ford.

"Yes, Dr. Yousef Khan. He *was* our only contact. He also was part of one of Al-Saafi's cells." Ford's mouth went into a straight thin line. "We thought we had him sealed into our plans when we offered a new identity and a safe haven here in the U.S. in return for exclusive information. Khan was interested in our proposal, but refused to reveal any more than what he already had told us as long as he was still abroad. He was over-anxious to get out of Pakistan and agreed to all our terms just a month ago. But no sooner than everything was arranged...he vanished." Ford took a deep breath and turned his head toward Hakan. "Why don't you tell Miranda what you know?'

Hakan was caught off guard. "I...eh...I can't be sure, but two Pakistani colleagues here in this country heard through the grapevine that Khan died of a mysterious and very fast-acting disease. I can only assume that someone within Al-Saafi found out that Khan acted as a double agent and killed him with this new recombinant form of Ebola, known to us as MAX 18," he said shakily and dabbed his forehead again.

Calm down, he again urged himself, knowing this lie had brought him satisfaction before. He hastened to recall the deep antipathy he felt toward Khan, the traitor who had tried to take credit for Hakan's original idea and almost succeeded in an attempt to corrupt the entire plan.

Khan had been a fine scientist and was one of the few people aware of Hakan's findings. Khan vowed to obey Al-Saafi's strict orders and agreed to stay in the background and solely deal with Hakan. But Khan became greedy when he detected a shortcut to sudden wealth and fame offered by the infidel. He chose to become too friendly with the CIA by pretending to have more information than qualification.

When Al-Saafi learned that Khan agreed to seek asylum in the United States, Hakan gave the order; Khan became the first human to die an inexorable but agonizing death from an injection that contained MAX 18.

Hakan stared at his half-eaten sandwich while these unpleasant memories rushed through his head. For a moment he forgot where he was.

"You all right?" Ford asked.

"What? Yes, I'm fine," Hakan responded quickly. He felt the blood rushing in his ears and thought his eyesight was weakening, but willed the sudden dizziness to pass. He needed to get a hold of himself; he could not afford to cause any suspicion. He drank some cold water. "I've just worked long hours lately and the pressure is getting to me."

"I can understand your predicament," Miranda agreed. "I'm still a little in the dark, though. Since Phil encouraged me to ask questions, I'd like you to detail MAX 18 for me. First of all, how did you even get a hold of it?"

Still sweating, Hakan looked around the table and cleared his throat. He told himself it was time to perform and become the puppet master again. Without realizing it, he briefly closed his eyes while his mouth turned upward into an involuntary grin. Then, he straightened his posture, assumed his set-in-stone facial expression, and addressed Miranda by nodding in her direction.

"To answer your question, I made Dr. Khan's acquaintance at several congresses over a period of years," he lied. "Somehow I must have won his trust because he began to confide in me. I learned he was part of a group of scientists working on a secret and deadly weapon. Khan supplied me with a small cryo-preserved vial that contained the actual engineered virus." As he spoke, Hakan began to enjoy directing his game again. When he imagined the restless unease of the others in the room, he felt his confidence returning. "I frankly didn't believe this was real, so I sequenced the genome of the sample and compared it to the wild type."

Phillip cut in. "That's when Hakan discovered that these extra and very dangerous genes had in fact been inserted. We now know that Al-Saafi's scientists took the DNA of Ebola and artificially inserted other genes. Via this recombination, or insertion of genes, Al-Saafi's biologists were able to change aspects of living organisms at the genetic level."

Hakan ignored Phillip's intrusion. Hakan wanted to glare at his boss, but instead he rearranged his face and looked at Miranda. He immediately wished he had not done so. Her soft eyes seemed harder and bore into his. He felt as if she were looking into his brain. He looked away. "Unfortunately Al-Saafi now has the capability to disperse this new strain in an aerosol form, so it can be spread effectively through the air, especially in an HVAC system. On a more targeted note, they also can simply inject it into an individual," Hakan explained and inhaled. "We all know that Ebola is very fast acting; however, this new strain will kill within twelve, maximum eighteen hours. That's why I named it MAX 18." He paused and then, as if to lighten the severity with positive aspects, added, "The only good thing about MAX 18 so far is that it's self-limiting and will become incapable of infection after thirty minutes of exposure to oxygen."

"I hardly consider that a good thing," Ford contradicted. "From what I understand, the short infectious life is in fact one of the aspects of the virus that makes it viable as a weapon. Any terrorist organization would most likely prefer an infectious agent of highly limited duration. That way the terrorists could target the pathogen much more effectively. The short infectious life may delimit the impact of individual exposures, but it makes the weapon much more controllable and encourages its use against a highly targeted population. It's also likely it could be used more than once."

"What about transmission from person to person?" Miranda frowned.

"The terrorists thought of that angle, too," Hakan cut in. "We are certain it cannot be communicated from human to human. We know this because our sequencing work detected a gene insert that limits its infectivity to a single victim. So, while it's certain that an individual directly exposed will die a horrible death, it becomes impossible for that person to infect others." Hakan swallowed and reluctantly glanced at Miranda. "If the virus could be communicated from person to person, a single attack could set a pandemic—a chain reaction that could spread it around the world, ultimately threatening the terrorists themselves and the societies which they imagine they are championing. You will recall that anthrax has been the natural pathogen of choice for terrorists until now. This is precisely because it cannot be spread directly from human to human. By engineering the short infectious life and lack of communicability into MAX 18, Al-Saafi's scientists combined two of the three most important elements of control with one of the most lethal organisms known."

"Two of the three most important elements?" asked Miranda. "What is the third?"

"The incubation period—the time period during which an infected person shows no symptoms," replied Hakan. "This third factor is crucially important only if Al-Saafi's objective is to spread the disease from human to human. In such a case, they would desire a long incubation period so as to maximize the potential for communicating the virus while the host is still apparently healthy. In the case of MAX 18, however, this factor is somewhat moot since Al-Saafi clearly is not planning for its attack to generate a pandemic. In fact, the incubation period is extremely short."

Phillip spoke up from the head of the table, "Thank you, Hakan. We certainly have learned quite a bit." Turning to Ford he asked, "How would you analyze the available facts?"

Ford shifted his weight in the chair and looked around the room. "All these facts taken together tell us some important things. First, it is clear that Al-Saafi understands what it is doing, biologically speaking. This means it has access to highly trained, sophisticated scientists. It also suggests that Al-Saafi is extremely well funded. Second, the fact that the weapon is highly controllable, with little potential for blowback, tells me that Al-Saafi and its cronies are anything but suicidal. In fact, the steps they have taken prove they would prefer to survive so they can reap the rewards of their attack. Third, the short incubation period means that they probably intend a single massive attack or an intensive series of attacks over a relatively short time frame."

"How do you conclude that?" Miranda asked.

"The short incubation period will allow epidemiologists to rapidly identify the source of exposure by tracing back the recent activities of those infected. So, after only a couple of attacks, the odds of finding the attackers will increase dramatically. Since these terrorists have planned carefully so as to survive the attack, we can be sure that they have taken every measure of not being caught. Therefore, I believe it is relatively safe to conclude they intend a single massive attack or a very brief flurry of highly targeted attacks."

Impressed by Ford's analysis, Hakan could barely suppress his surprise. But he felt enormous pride and pleasure as he witnessed the three people's reaction.

Ford looked disgusted. His huge arms were crossed; his triangular face was grim. Miranda Portal kept shaking her head. For a moment there was deep concern written all over her face, but as soon as she noticed the worry in her husband's eyes, she sent an encouraging smile across the table toward him. The temper in the room had definitely grown very fractious.

They have no idea where this is leading, Hakan thought with glee. *I'm holding all the trump cards. They're losing their game.*

CHAPTER 38

HARD AS POURED concrete, Ford's voice broke the silence in the isolated chamber. "I came here today to talk about the vaccine Hakan has developed." He made eye contact. "Phil, I know that you are being informed daily and so am I. But my superiors have questions about the efficacy of the vaccine, what the cost estimates look like versus the budget we gave you, and, finally, when it's going to be available." Ford turned to Hakan. "What can I bring back to my superiors?"

"Excuse me, Ford," Phillip's thin voice interrupted. "In order for Miranda to understand the entire development, let Hakan start from the beginning."

Hakan removed three sets of documents from his briefcase and handed them around the room.

"Where are your copies?" Ford asked.

"Miranda has mine. I didn't know she would be here. Anyway, I don't need a copy." He pointed to his head. "It's all in here."

He then led them through his findings, saying he decided to develop a subfactor vaccine rather than using a weakened or killed form of the whole virus. Hakan reasoned that by using a subfactor vaccine, the concept would be sufficiently safe, if given a chance, of being approved for even limited human use without extensive testing.

"Also," Hakan said, "since the subfactor vaccine contains only a part of the actual virus, the chances of the vaccine accidentally causing the disease is theoretically zero. This is not the case with the whole virus vaccine."

"Am I understanding correctly that by using a surface protein vaccine, you've made a good choice for a vaccine constituent since this is the part of the virus normally seen by the body's immune system?" Miranda asked.

"Definitely," Hakan answered, hiding his surprise. Obviously the woman was smarter and better informed than he thought. "By using the surface protein we train the immune system to recognize and defend against the virus without actually exposing the recipient to the virus itself. That's why such a vaccine is so much safer than a whole virus vaccine."

Phillip looked up from the sheets of paper in front of him and addressed his wife. "We know there are several effective viral vaccines on the market that use surface proteins."

"Absolutely. A good example is Recombivax, a vaccine against hepatitis B," Miranda agreed.

Hakan nodded and gave a detailed explanation of the makings of the vaccine, the production of proteins, and the insertion of genes into the DNA of a good production organism such as yeast or *E. coli.*

"I understand all of that," Miranda interrupted. "I believe you should tell us about your experiments.

Hakan gave Miranda a disapproving look; he could not accept being ordered by a woman about what to do next when it came to his medical research.

"Very well," he said after clearing his throat. "Let me preface my remarks by saying that our in vitro results strongly suggest that the vaccine will confer an active immunity against MAX 18. But interestingly enough, our in vitro studies also revealed that MAX 18 had been engineered by Al-Saafi's scientists to affect mice and rats, suggesting that whoever developed it really knew the immunology business." He paused. The hot coal of the secret was burning his tongue; he found it difficult to give false credit to nonexistent scientists while referring to his own brilliant work. He inhaled and said, "Yes, they really knew their business because by making mice and rats susceptible, they had a ready-made testing regime in nonhuman species."

"I presume you've studied your own colonies of mice and rats?" Miranda asked.

"Of course," he chuffed back without looking at her. "For our in vivo studies, we accumulated a colony of fifteen mice and fifteen rats, which we separated into three groups. Only Group One was injected with the vaccine but all three groups were exposed to MAX 18. Group Two and Three immediately began to show symptoms peculiar to MAX 18. As soon as the symptoms began and within three hours, Group Two was injected with the antidote."

"You did this just recently, am I correct?" Ford asked.

"Yes," Hakan replied sharply and shifted in his chair. He was not happy about being interrupted again. "Within less than eighteen hours, the animals in Group Three all died. But, as of now—one week later—Group One still is showing no symptoms of the disease and Group Two is showing continuing withdrawal from MAX 18 symptoms." Hakan leaned back in his chair, obviously pleased. "In summary, it appears that we have a vaccination and an antidote that are both working."

He shifted his gaze to Ford. "That answers your earlier specific question. Namely, that based on the small number of studies we've performed, the tests appear to be working. As to your other two questions, we're within the budget you've given us and the timing is now."

"Yep. That certainly answers my questions." Ford showed a toothy grin.

"I'm still a little uncomfortable that this particular sample size of animal studies is sufficient to unequivocally say that we have a viable product," Phillip added with a frown while scribbling notes on a pad.

"I concur," Ford agreed in his Dr. Henry Kissinger-like voice, "but because of the project's secrecy, we need to be careful. We want to avoid the trials becoming so large that they might attract attention beyond the small group of authorized people."

"I've given this a lot of thought," Hakan cut in. "I suggest that we consider doing another small in vivo trial, but this time with chimps since they most closely resemble the genetic makeup of humans." He tried to sound determined, fervently hoping his suggestions would get their approval; he needed to buy time to perform secret testing on unsuspecting humans in Los Angeles.

"Chimps?" Miranda frowned. "Here at PIGR?" She shook her head. "PIGR limits itself to testing with mice and rabbits. Any further testing is always sent to outside labs that specialize in other animals."

"I know," Hakan agreed hastily. "But because of the secrecy of this project, I've already done some checking and have identified an opportunity for us to get two chimps." He directed his attention toward Phillip. Hakan did not like the look in the woman's eyes; they seemed ancient and all-knowing and reminded him of something he couldn't identify. He inwardly shivered.

"Actually, that sounds good to me," Phillip said, nodding in Hakan's direction before looking at his wife. "Since we've already built a dedicated facility for Hakan and his group adjacent to our main research park, we should be able to move the animals in and out with discretion."

Turning to Ford, Phillip commanded, "But, I suggest your company pay for the acquisition of the chimps. I refuse to have the purchase show on PIGR's financial records."

"Phi-hil?" Miranda quizzically looked at her husband. "I'm not quite sure I'm in favor of what is being planned right here."

"Look Miranda, Operation Mayfly needs to go forward. Without further studies, we'll never get the proper results."

"Well, don't worry about PIGR's financial records," Ford boomed. "Let me get back to what Hakan was trying to say just minutes ago." Ford shifted his weight in the chair. "It's my understanding that the use of chimps as lab animals is highly regulated. Also, getting the test animals is extremely difficult, expensive, and closely supervised by animal rights groups. I know the company will agree to provide the chimps. After all, we do realize the urgency of this project. Hakan, how long will it take to get the results of this phase of the testing?"

Hakan shrugged, twisting his head from side to side. He rapidly calculated, directing his scheming to the human testing rather than animals. "I think..." he paused, quickly reevaluating his computation before he continued, "I can say with certainty that the project can be completed within three months."

"Good." Phillip's voice rose. "Sounds like we've identified what needs to be done to complete the next phase of this project." He glimpsed at his electronic date book. "Three months will take us close to the holidays in the November-December time frame. I suggest we have our next follow-up meeting in early January, unless something develops. Is there anything else we need to discuss before we adjourn this meeting?"

"Yes," Hakan said, almost raising his hand. "I've discussed the possibility of this next clinical phase with my team. As scientists we hesitate to give an unequivocal thumbs up on the project completion unless we have done some human testing."

"Human testing?" Miranda looked aghast. "That's out of the question. You know that can't legally be done in the U.S. without FDA approval."

"Except…the confidence between me and my team about the efficiency of this product is so strong that Putin, Afshor, and Barsoukov volunteered to receive the vaccine and be exposed to MAX 18 once the in vivo trial with the chimps is completed."

"Good grief," Miranda exhaled. "It still would be illegal." She cocked her head. "What about you, Hakan? Aren't you part of the volunteer group?"

He lowered his head and shook it. "In the past I've had problems with anaphylactic shock. Over the years I've developed some severe allergic reactions." He shivered inwardly again at the thought of these past experiences. "I must admit I'm afraid to take the risk. The vaccine might kill me for reasons that have nothing to do with the vaccine itself."

"If the product proves safe with the two chimps and then the three human volunteers, perhaps there'll be others within our organization who might volunteer for the sake of science and the safety of our country," Phillip said. "What do you think, Miranda?"

"Right now I'm against it. It sounds unsafe and barbaric to me. But most of all, it's illegal."

"Miranda, Phil…I personally like Hakan's plan," Ford's voice interjected softly, but rose again when he turned to Hakan. "However, *you* must understand that the company would never formally approve this kind of human testing, even if it's by free choice. So, if you do it, I suggest you have no documentation and I personally will disclaim any knowledge." His lips tightened as he paused. "On the other hand, I must admit it sure would make my job easier to convince my superiors that we have a good test. It certainly would later eliminate the concern about injecting it into the people who run our government."

"I hear what you're saying, Ford." Phillip nodded. "But Miranda is right. We also have to consider the potential liability for ourselves and our company if anything goes wrong."

"Gentlemen, Miranda..." Hakan, whose teeth had been tugging nervously on his lower lip, interjected. "I'm not surprised by your reaction; I've anticipated these comments. I've already decided that I will take total responsibility—even to the extent of signing an acknowledgment that I received a letter from both of you not to test on human volunteers. This should prevent any blame going to either one of you, PIGR or the CIA."

Twenty minutes later Phillip adjourned the meeting. The wood-paneled wall opened silently and Hakan breathed a long sigh of relief, not only because the late afternoon sunlight finally spread into the claustrophobic conference room, but also because he was more than grateful that the entire meeting had gone according to his plan. Al-Saafi would be very pleased.

In Phillip's office, Miranda took a phone call, speaking in a low voice.

Standing near the window, Phillip turned to Hakan. "So, you prefer not to stay the night, Hakan?"

"No, thanks Phil. If it's at all possible, I much rather would fly back to Lafayette right away. I could use a full day tomorrow in the lab." Hakan tried to sound and look sincere. He didn't like the thought of being cooped up in another closed environment for the next few hours. But the idea of being near Angela, possibly later tonight, would make the flight worthwhile. She was the only person who made him forget about all pressing issues; in her presence he felt relaxed and ceased to remember who he truly was.

"I call that dedication," Phillip replied. "Let me just confirm with the crew." He pressed a key on his cell phone and spoke briefly. Then he turned toward Hakan. "Doug is waiting outside to take you to the plane."

"Oh, I forgot my briefcase," Hakan gasped as he slapped his forehead.

Phillip pressed a button and the panel to the conference room opened again. Hakan hurried to retrieve his belongings. He left the room quickly; somehow he feared to be sealed in again. But he allowed himself another look over his shoulder and realized that everything in the chamber had been cleaned. The dishes were gone, as were the discarded papers and pens. Ten chairs, instead of four, were perfectly arranged around the conference table. Hakan shivered again; whoever had come had vanished like a magician's rabbit.

"Please excuse my hasty departure to your wife. I don't want to disturb her on the phone," Hakan apologized. He shook hands and with relief heard the granite and stone wall close behind him.

"Well, Phil, since it's too late for my military pickup today, you're stuck with me overnight," Ford said, grinning from ear to ear. "Why don't I take advantage of this rare opportunity and do some fly-fishing right now and first thing in the morning? I assume you've got some gear for me?"

"Of course," Phillip answered without changing his expression. "How about if I join you tomorrow? I always go fly-fishing on Saturday mornings."

CHAPTER 39

AFTER MIRANDA FINISHED her long conversation on the phone, she found herself alone in her husband's office, but knew he would return to discuss the meeting. She sat behind his desk and gazed outside at the sights of nature, bathed in the late-afternoon sun.

Miranda had first run into Phillip when she was seventeen at the Public Library in Sacramento; they both reached for the same book, *The Philosophy of Right; The Philosophy of History* by Georg Wilhelm Friedrich Hegel. "Go ahead," he had said and turned on his heel. Some time later, Miranda spotted the thin, intense youth again, deeply concentrating on a text in front of him. She walked over and whispered, "I'm done. Thanks for letting me take the book."

The following day she was surprised when she noticed him during lunch at her local high school; she knew she had never seen him there before. He was sitting by himself, slowly eating a sandwich, his nose stuck in a thick book. He did not notice when she noisily put her books on the table and sat across from him. He finally looked up when she began to talk.

That very day, Miranda not only found out that Phillip was new to the school—his father had just been transferred to Sacramento—but also that they had a few things in common. Discovering a shared interest in the same literature, they agreed they had never before found someone in their age group willing to listen to their thoughts and able to give a stimulating, inspiring response. They each admitted they were aroused by the other's powerful intellect.

The friendship intensified during their junior and senior years; as a matter of fact, they had no need for other friends. Because of their intense yearning for learning and desire to inspire, they knew the majority of the student body stamped them as nerdy and weird, but they easily shrugged off the shallowness of others. The night of the high school prom, they only followed the formal dress code in order to please their parents, never intending to participate in what they considered a mindless circus. Instead, they found a friendly late-night café where they sat for hours. While slurping on teas and munching crunchy cookies, they philosophized and heatedly debated the issues that were of interest to them.

Their paths divided after high school. Years later, after Miranda graduated summa cum laude from Yale, she swiftly worked her way up the ladder in the business world. Meanwhile, Phillip's legendary business success story often brought a smile to her face whenever she read an article or heard discussions about her old high school friend. Miranda's thoughts never lingered on him because her quick climb up the career ladder absorbed all of her time. When she turned thirty-seven she was promoted to director of strategic planning at Jones & Jordan, a New Jersey-based giant in the health care industry. She remembered the day when she gave a paper with a supporting slide show on "Product Development Opportunities, Based on Recent DNA Breakthroughs" at a congress in Seattle.

The research vice president of PORTAL Enterprises heard her presentation and reported it to his chairman and CEO, stating how impressed he was by her knowledge. He believed she would be a great addition to PORTAL Enterprises' senior management team.

The next day, Miranda, still in Seattle, received a call from Phillip. He had flown in from California and asked her to have dinner with him. That evening he overcame his shyness and let her know that in all the years gone by, he never again felt as comfortable and as intrigued by any other woman as he had felt with her during their last two years of high school. Miranda blushed when she heard him admit to something that was repressed, but alive in her own feelings.

They were married two months later in a very small and private ceremony, followed by a honeymoon on a secluded island in the Caribbean whose owner was Phillip Portal.

Their first child was born nine months later. Katie, even as an infant, was the spitting image of her father. Two years later Miranda gave birth to Lincoln, a plump boy whose resemblance to his mother was uncanny.

As Miranda reflected on her privileged existence, she realized that even in the calmness of their Idaho compound, jeopardy had followed them. She picked up a remote control. After entering a three-digit combination, the brilliant Rocky Mountain nature scene—displayed on the large plasma screen against the natural stone wall—changed into a blank blue screen. Miranda pressed rewind and waited for the beginning of the earlier meeting that had been videotaped.

Taking the remote control with her, she rose from behind the desk and took a seat in one of the more comfortable chairs closer to the screen. She leaned her back into the soft cushion and rested her feet on the ottoman. Miranda only wanted to focus on Hakan Öztürk, the man who had caused fear in her since the first time she laid eyes on him.

She did not hear her husband return to the office and jumped when she felt his hands on her shoulders. She stopped the tape, freezing Hakan's face—eyes narrowed, his mouth in a grimacing smile—on the screen.

"I didn't mean to scare you, my dear," Phillip apologized. He walked around the chair and sat next to his wife. "Interesting meeting, wasn't it?"

"And very scary as well."

"Scary? You seemed comfortable with almost everything. You also were quite impressive in your new role as CEO."

"I'm not talking about my position, Phil. What bothers me are my strange feelings about Hakan."

"Really?" Phillip looked surprised. "My experience, as you know, has been very positive considering the impact that the compounds he developed have had on my illness. And since he's not betrayed our confidence and kept silent about my condition, I think he can be trusted."

"Oh, Phil," Miranda sighed, and clasped her husband's hand with both of hers. "Granted, he's a brilliant scientist and I'm grateful for what he's accomplished to improve your health, but I can't help the feeling that he's hiding something." She paused and pursed her lips in thought. "You know, from the beginning I never liked the idea of PIGR's corroboration with the CIA's black project *Operation Mayfly*, especially since the whole thing started via Hakan." She shivered.

"I know that you've been uncomfortable with it, but again, what if you're wrong? What if Hakan's research, just like all his other findings, proves to be a blessing? Many lives will be saved."

Miranda offered no response; she simply took a deep breath.

"Look dear, you always say there never are any guarantees. If my condition worsens, then your participation in all of these projects will increase dramatically." Phillip produced an encouraging smile. "Let's continue for now, but if you receive any specific proof to support your feelings, let me know right away." He changed the subject. "Who kept you on the phone so long?"

"It was Sarah Epstein. Her father's Alzheimer's condition worsened, and she asked if Eli could stay another week so she and her husband can drive to Palm Springs and move her father into their house. They don't want him to be in a nursing home."

"How admirable. I like the Epsteins. Good people. I'm sure you told Sarah that Eli was welcome to stay."

She nodded and smiled. "Of course I did. You know Jamal Shakir will arrive in another two days."

"Usually I only like Linc to have one guest at a time, but given the circumstances and the fact that the three guys are such good friends...they'll have a good time together."

Miranda looked at Phillip with loving eyes. "You're wonderful; always trying to make someone's life a little easier."

"You are the force behind me, dear. Without you there wouldn't be private schools around the country with the finest education available—not only for privileged children like Katie and Linc, but also for the many less advantaged children. Without you there wouldn't be global health care programs, focusing on child vaccines." He put his arm around her shoulder. "Whereas I prefer to partake in our family's charitable work from behind the scenes, you and the children favor to be hands-on."

Miranda leaned closer. "You're a good man, Phil, and I'm a lucky woman." She kissed him on the cheek. Then, her expression changed again as her eyes drifted back to the wall where Hakan's twisted image was still frozen on the large screen. Using the remote control, she quickly replaced it with the peaceful Rocky Mountains winter scene.

"While I was on the phone, I couldn't help but overhear some of your conversation with Ford after Hakan left. Did Ford tell you that Hakan is dating Angela Atwood?"

"I was unaware of it myself until today." Phillip's face brightened. "How about that? Angela not only is a beautiful and intelligent young woman, but her father is the governor of Louisiana and her mother the daughter of a past United States president. If Angela considers Hakan worthwhile, he can't be all that bad, don't you agree?"

"I don't understand it. I get such different vibes from both of them; they seem to be worlds apart." She closed her eyes. "I don't know if I've ever met anyone like Angela before. That young woman had me spellbound. Not only because of her charming personality…there was something so deep and meaningful within her. Did you get the same impression?"

"You always seem to discover more about people than I do, dear. But I must agree, Angela was magnetically fascinating."

"Yes. Where she's open and free-spirited, Hakan seems locked into some sort of confinement." She shook her head. "What does she ever see in him?"

Phillip grinned sheepishly. "Now dear, look at me." He stood up, pointed at his sparse hair, his thick glasses, and his thin frame. "What did you ever see in me?"

Tucson

… in July

CHAPTER 40

THE LAST FEW days of July were extremely hot and there had been no rain in eight months. Almost every person in Tucson longed for the arrival of the monsoon season, which would bring relief from the heat. But Dr. Clayton Harris was unaffected by the swelter of the desert summer; as a matter of fact, he felt exhilarated by his own heat of excitement. The past couple of days had been filled with meetings at the Institute where he had been introduced to the board, met new colleagues, and been shown the facility in its entirety. He was more than anxious and could hardly wait for his first official workday.

In three days Clayton was to fly back to Los Angeles, finalize his work at ONI, and deal with the sale of his condominium. He still had to find a house in Tucson. A realtor was to pick him up in another hour, giving him enough time to try and connect with Teeba Prime.

His friend Austin had insisted that Clayton stay with him until he found a place of his own and, for the past couple of days, the two friends enjoyed every free moment to celebrate their friendship and the déjà vu of their roommate days.

In the afternoon, Clayton left the Institute early in order to accomplish two more important matters. The first one had been on his mind before he even arrived in Tucson. From Austin's kitchen he dialed the only number he found in Teeba's chart, her father's office.

"Mr. Prime? This is Clayton Harris, I don't know if you remember me. I was..."

"Dr. Harris!" Thomas' voice sparkled with delight. "How can I forget you? If it hadn't been for you, my Teeba might still be...no, I'd rather not even think about it. How delightful to hear from you. What brings me the honor?"

"I've accepted a position here in Tucson at JSNRI..."

"Yes, I heard. I ran into Dr. Berger. Welcome to Tucson."

"Thank you. I understand your daughter is doing remarkably well. I'd like to see for myself with a follow-up exam," Clayton blushed. "But I don't have her number."

"I'm sure Teeba will be delighted to hear from you. Wait until you see her. She looks better than ever before, and there are no signs she ever was sick."

Clayton wrote down the number, thanked Thomas, and disconnected the call. He stared at the piece of paper in front of him and hesitated before he slowly began to dial. He heard it ringing five times and he expected a voicemail to kick in. After the tenth ring, he wondered if she was in the shower or backyard. He urged out loud, "Pick it up, pick it up, please, pick up the phone." After the twentieth ring he reluctantly put down the receiver and sighed. He would try again later. He had to see her.

The realtor, a middle-aged, robust-looking woman with hips as wide as Wyoming, proved to be exactly what Austin had promised. Clayton only had spoken once on the phone to Wanda Wiley to give her a vague idea of what he envisioned in a house and what his needs were. Somehow the woman must have read his mind better than the description he remembered giving her because he fell in love with the first house she showed him. The three-bedroom ranch on Paseo Bocoancos was five years old and in prime condition. Its location was very private and had beautiful views from the spacious wraparound decks. As the house had been on the market several months, the owners were overanxious to sell and Clayton's offer was promptly accepted. The realtor offered to organize the necessary inspections, and the parties agreed the closing should be as soon as possible.

It was shortly past six o'clock in the evening when Wanda stopped in front of Austin's house on Tanuri Drive. "Congratulations," she said. "You've purchased a beautiful home—big enough to start a family," she winked. "It's been a pleasure doing business with you, Dr. Harris." She shook his hands. "I wish all my clients were so easy to please."

Austin would not be home for at least another two hours; he was visiting relatives in Scottsdale. Clayton went into the kitchen and poured a tall glass of cold water. The piece of paper with Teeba's number was still in the same spot on the counter. For a few moments he stared at it, then picked up the phone and dialed. He felt his heart flutter when she answered.

"Teeba, this is Clayton Harris. I hope I'm not disturbing you." He experienced a calming sensation as soon as he heard her voice.

"Dr. Clayton Harris." She spoke the name slowly. She paused. "I've been expecting your call."

"Your father must have told you that I'm in Tucson and would like to see you...for a follow-up exam." He scolded himself for sounding too businesslike. "I heard you're doing remarkably well and, speaking not only as an interested physician but also as a friend, I'd very much like it if you'd spare some time for us to get together."

"I didn't talk with my father today and was unaware you spoke with him but...I knew you'd call. I myself would very much like to see the man who awakened me from my deep sleep so I can thank him again."

"This might be presumptuous...but in case you haven't had dinner...perhaps you might care to join me tonight? I truly would enjoy your company."

"I rarely go to restaurants. But it would be my pleasure to invite you to my home if you don't mind a simple meal."

He had no trouble finding her house on Camino de la Cumbre; it seemed as if a magnet attracted him toward it. He parked his rental car on the quiet street. As he slowly walked toward the house, he noticed that the sapphire blue sky was changing to indigo blue; further west, the purplish tint was already dipping into the red fire that glowed low above the horizon.

Bougainvillea vines covered the small adobe brick house, and a nearly white Labrador lazily rested in the open, bottle green front door, his soft furry head stretched over his paws. The dog's warm brown eyes calmly greeted Clayton like they would an old friend.

Clayton stood and admired the setting that reminded him of a Norman Rockwell painting. Then, he patted the animal's shiny coat. "Are you guarding your mistress?" he asked. The dog rose slowly and led the way into the small hallway.

"Hello? Teeba?" Not wanting to go past the door, he knocked. The dog stopped and looked at him with eyes that seemed to say, "It's okay. Just follow me."

Then he saw her. A shimmer spread through the room and, in his mind's eye, a spiral of images began to spin fast—impressions he could not explain.

"Dr. Harris." Her voice was warm and inviting as she came toward him. Her dark, glossy hair draped voluminously over her shoulders and her olive skin was bronzed by the summer sun. Her delicate physiognomy reminded him of what he admired in old quill portraits. Long-legged for her rather small frame, she looked unconsciously elegant in a short, white cotton shift as she greeted him with a mysterious Mona Lisa-like smile.

"Teeba." As he reached for her hand, he caught a last dancing sunray trying to escape through her fingers. "I'm so happy to see you again."

Chapter 41

Sʜᴇ ᴛᴏᴏᴋ ʜɪs hand and let the warmth of her smile comfort him as she guided him out onto the deck. "Let's not miss a spectacular display of nature. I try to watch the sunset every evening and never tire of it," she said.

The horizon was once again painted in glorious colors of amber, red, and purple. They stood motionless side by side, mesmerized by the spell of the moment.

As the sky turned darker, they found themselves bathed in the soft glow of a full moon that hung above the edge of night.

"I'm glad you're here to share this with me." Her soft voice broke the silence and she looked up to the taller Clayton. Teeba knew this was only the first of more of the desert's wondrous sunsets they would share; only another beginning—they had been there before but Clayton was still unaware of it. *Soon you will know,* she thought. *Soon you will accept the knowledge to recognize why we had to meet.*

Their eyes locked. *I will help you understand why some force released sparks of energy within us and pulled us together so we could bond,* Teeba thought. *Our feelings and images will become one.* She knew the fire of the amethyst was shining brightly from her right eye. *Soon,* she silently said again, *it has to be soon because time is of the essence.* She pressed his hand, letting him know that a pact had been made.

"Your eyes…they're like big reservoirs the millennia filled with sageness and sentiment." He took a breath. "Your eyes seem to hypnotize me; through them I sense an awareness of familiarity." He hesitated. "No, it's so much deeper and harder to explain in words, but I've never experienced a more profound feeling than this."

Teeba knew his confusion was slowly being replaced by recognition. "Good. Very good," she said.

They walked back into the house and Teeba asked if he would mind lighting the candles and setting the table. While checking the butternut squash in the oven and adding various herbs to the chicken and potatoes on the outside grill, she took frequent glances at Clayton. He obviously enjoyed being of help. As she tossed the salad, she saw him moving around with the virile handsomeness of a young athlete; there was precision and control in the flow of his motion. When he finished his chores, she saw him looking around the cozy candlelit space with its comfortable and colorful Southwestern furnishings. He looked pleased.

"Feel free to look at the rest of my little house," Teeba suggested.

"I'd rather watch you," he said, sitting on a turquoise-lacquered kitchen stool at the mosaic counter. "After all, I came here to see for myself how well you're doing."

"I've been waiting for your professional judgment," she teased. "What do you think?"

"You look amazingly well and vivacious. As a matter of fact, I can't hide my medical curiosity. Have there been any problems related to your injury and the coma?"

"No," she laughed. "My body and mind must have needed the long sleep. There's something to be said for a rest that takes you into different dimensions."

They sat on the deck, overlooking the sparkling city lights in the distance, while talking and enjoying the meal.

"Sitting next to you and listening to your voice, I swear I hear music gliding through the summery air," Clayton said finally. "My mother predicted I'd be very happy here." He looked at Teeba. "It's amazing but I feel I know you from somewhere before." He moved the lightweight wooden chair close to hers and smiled. "It feels as if the soft fuzz of hair on your arm is tickling my skin—or is the desert's wind teasing my imagination?"

Teeba laid her small hand on his, threading their fingers together, letting the warmth of the moment take over.

"Oh," she whispered and stretched her neck. She lifted her head and let her nose rise to take small whiffs of air. "There…it's arriving," she murmured almost to herself. Then, she turned to Clayton. "I know you've never seen celestial fireworks light up the desert. You're in for a treat. Look to the right."

There was a bolt of lightning in the distance, followed by the low grumble of thunder. Soon after, the battle of the clouds began and the skies lit up with quick intermittency from every direction. Fierce thunderclaps applauded the bright flashes. As the white bolts brilliantly shot out of the black sky, sometimes four or five together, they produced a kaleidoscopic vision.

The onset of rain came with a soft swoosh. But soon the endless fine strings, made from countless tiny drops, changed into solid sheets of water.

They sat sheltered under the overhang inhaling the sudden dampness in the air. For fifteen minutes they watched the spectacular show of nature until the sheet of rain thinned and stopped. The frequent bursts of lightning lessened as well. A final bolt zigzagged weakly in the distance and the last hollow growl of thunder sounded as if it were coming from a fatigued bear retreating into the depth of his cave. The night turned quiet again.

"This is magic," Clayton said. He lifted his hand, still entwined with Teeba's fingers, and brushed his lips against each of her fingertips. "Thank you for allowing me to be with you."

They rose and their bodies trembled as their mouths met. First, there were small fast kisses, hasty and uncertain like hummingbird pecks, then soft gasps each time their lips brushed against each other. Although they sensed their own hesitancy, they both longed for more. Slowly, the power of nature took over and with soft, sensitive desire they opened each other's lips, permitting themselves to explore and travel to the destination of a distant dream in the kiss of kisses.

"I remember now; I've tasted you before," Clayton breathed against her mouth. "And I've been searching for you…ever since."

A purple film spread over Teeba's dark eyes and then, the fire of the amethyst sparkled. "And I've been waiting for you…a long time."

Chapter 42

THE MONSOONS SOAKED the desert throughout the night and the rain did not stop until early in the afternoon of the next day. Mostly gray skies crowded overhead, but in the southern distance patches of blue already were visible as the sun pried through the remnants of drained clouds. An arc of a circle in concentric bands showed the colors of the spectrum.

Teeba watched the glittering array, embracing another phenomenon of the endless vibrations and pulses of nature. She smiled at the faraway rainbow.

After she filled two backpacks with necessities for the outing and after placing them into her old Jeep, she crouched next to Troy, her Labrador. She scratched on his belly and behind the ear. "I'll be back," she whispered and pressed her face into the fur.

Fifteen minutes later she pulled the Jeep into Austin's driveway and saw Clayton waiting by the door. His face lit up when he saw her.

"I was afraid our outing might be cancelled due to weather; I thought the rain would never stop." He closed his eyes and embraced her.

"There was no need for worry. We won't see rain for a while." She stepped back and looked him over. "For a big city boy you look like a seasoned hiker. I'm impressed." She leaned close to him again and said softly, "We both will enjoy this excursion."

Teeba parked the Jeep in the parking lot at the foot of Sabino Canyon and helped Clayton with the straps of the heavier pack. When they reached the Phoneline trailhead, she took the lead on the narrow, rugged path.

They climbed steadily for the first twenty minutes and Teeba could hear Clayton's heavy breathing.

"Just a little higher. It will get easier after this," she promised.

"Piece o' cake," he joked. "Nothing better than feeling the sweat run down my back under this heavy backpack."

When they reached the top, they paused for a water break.

"I can feel my heartbeat slowly returning to normal," he grinned. "I'm envious how you climbed effortlessly despite the heavy load on your back." He wiped his forehead with a small towel. "It really is remarkable," he said. "Having witnessed your condition just a few weeks ago, motionless in a hospital bed, your progress is simply amazing."

"Life is amazing. Every day brings something new. By tomorrow, you and I will have more wisdom and understanding about many things, especially about us," she replied, her dark eyes shining at him. "There is much I need to share with you."

For the next two hours they enjoyed the views of the valleys, Kino Peak, Cathedral Rock, and Mount Lemmon. From the Saguaro Palo Verde community to the riparian zone, all the vegetation thirstily had soaked up the earlier heavy rains. The previous year and the recent spring had brought a double period of rainfall so the desert landscape was sprinkled with showy wildflowers. Perennial brittlebush tinted the hillsides, giving the appearance of a mass of gold. Bees collected the oil from the magenta range rhatany, and the lemon yellow heads of biennial desert marigold framed the sides of the trail as if they were mirroring the sun. Some of the sky blue flowers of blue flax were dropping their shiny petals while sporadic patches of annual summer poppies flowered in bright bursts of apricot.

As if for the benefit of the two hikers, nature coordinated the hum of insects, the swoosh of gentle winds, and the rushing water in Sabino Creek, creating musical simplicity.

Throughout the hike Teeba shared her knowledge of the Catalina Mountains and the Sonoran desert with Clayton. She gave detailed explanations of the many varieties in vegetation and wildlife.

At times they stopped to drink water and listened to the drowsy silence in the heat.

Finally they reached their destination. Hutch's pools were filled from ample rain and the soft splashes of water, falling over huge boulders, brought a refreshing sound to the hikers. Tall cottonwood and sycamore trees provided shade and cool comfort as the late afternoon sun sent its last energy to the desert.

Clayton loosened the straps around his waist and shed the weighty bulk off his back.

"We've not seen one person on this hike. Are we the only ones in this paradise?" He took off his shoes and hung his long legs over the rim of a boulder. He sighed as the cool water seized his heels.

"Paradise is infinite," Teeba replied. "During the summer there are areas that are more desirable in higher altitudes with cooler temperatures, but since you have to go back to Los Angeles tomorrow, this was the shortest hike to one tiny spot in paradise." She had begun to unpack but stopped for a moment to watch Clayton, who remained sitting on the boulder, his toes forming circles on the surface of the water.

Aware of their short precious future together, Teeba couldn't imagine a purer happiness on this golden late afternoon.

"I'm wondering if you've ever slept outdoors before?"

"Never!" He pulled his feet out of the soothing water. "But I can't begin to tell you how much I look forward to everything new you'll introduce me to." He crouched next to her and took her hands into his. "Let me help you, please."

On a sandy, soft patch of soil she showed him how to pitch the tent. Nearby, they created a fire circle from river rocks, then put branches and small logs in the middle of the wheel.

"I had no idea how delightful this kind of experience could be," Clayton said. "I feel like I'm experiencing a time reversal: I've arrived from the future wondering how to survive. Thank God I have my cavewoman to teach me everything she knows." He took her head into his hands and found her mouth.

Chapter 43

Nightfall brought a full moon that lit the clear dark skies. Flames flickered in the fire circle and only the occasional loud pop of crackling wood split the quiet.

Teeba and Clayton sat side by side by the fire, their eyes following the sparks flying toward the twinkling stars.

They had feasted on a simple meal of rice and beans, raw vegetables, guacamole, and cheese. While eating, they began to share tidbits from their past. Though the reserved exchange was informative, both acknowledged that there was more to be told.

"Why can I suddenly feel this amazing consciousness?" Clayton whispered. "I don't recall ever experiencing such joy. Where does it come from?" He shook his head. "My mind is pulsing, yearning for more recognition. I have feelings that I imagined existed only in books. Where does it come from?" he asked again. "It's you, isn't it? Ever since you opened your eyes and looked at me in that hospital room, I could feel the metamorphosis. Everything I've believed in has turned toward a different form of understanding. It's you," he repeated.

"It's us—together. You and I are causing the changes you're seeing." She caressed his cheeks. "In this life, as in every lifetime, everybody is given the possibility to complete a personal mission. You and I had to meet in order to accomplish that."

In the moonlit deep blue of the night, Clayton saw Teeba's delicate features enhanced by the fire's glow. Her large black eyes not only mirrored the flames, but reflected the flying sparks. Her satiny skin glistened and there was an unbroken smile on her lips that reminded him of a Botticelli angel. She sat in a half lotus pose, holding her back as straight as a candle. She looked peaceful and serene.

"I've never viewed life this way before; I've never given thought to more than one lifetime," Clayton said. "I'm benumbed by your symmetry and balance."

"I may seem unique to you, but everyone is given the knowledge to recognize why we're here; only a few of us truly listen to our instincts." She moved closer. "It may be strange for you to hear this, but it takes multiple lifetimes to reach the level where universal knowledge begins to make sense. Deep in your core you always knew there was more, and now that your eyes have been opened, you're getting your first glimpses at timeless wisdom."

"Does that mean I've been here before?"

She nodded slightly. "Yes. And you and I have met before."

"If my eyes are fully opened, why do I still feel blinded?"

"You have the ability to see and understand; the time has come to let the possibilities unfold." She traced his long fingers and placed her palms into his. "Hold onto me."

CHAPTER 44

INSPIRED AND DESIROUS, Clayton encircled her hands and moved his face so close he could feel the moisture of her breath on his skin. Entranced, he heard her voice in an unknown remoteness of his head.

"I'm going to transfer some of my universal knowledge, stemming from supreme principles only entrusted to the wisest," he heard her say.

The soothing sound encouraged him to relax.

Then, the fire of the amethyst shot from Teeba's right pupil. Clayton had never seen anything more beautiful and let himself sink into the depth of it, only to be lifted by its luminance to an unknown sphere. Surrounded by a brilliant light, he felt weightless.

"Are we having an out-of-body experience?" he asked when he saw himself sitting by the fire with Teeba. He realized his lips were not moving; his voice came from within.

"You now are in one of many dimensions. Only here will you understand what I'm about to transfer to you."

Clayton saw Teeba's face and heard her voice without physically seeing or hearing her.

I came into this physical world long before books were written. Countless times throughout the centuries I had to cross the Great Sea of Knowledge and the High Sea of Learning before I was allowed to pass under the Archway of Outer Surrounding Gleam and enter the Door of Inner Filling Light.

There, the golden brightness fills me with strength and permeates my powers, allowing me to keep coming back into this physical world.

My wisdom is great and my knowledge is beyond speech and words. My extra sense detects events before they happen. My visions see what eyes cannot.

I am a very old soul.

As Clayton listened to the vibrations of Teeba's voice, he was able to follow her to the earliest of days.

My missions throughout time have been many. I have rescued nations and prevented unnecessary bloodshed and torture. Over and over I was celebrated and crowned for my visionary leadership and accomplishments. But over and over I also have been tortured and put to death because the misguided have been afraid of me and do not understand my divine perceptions and apocalyptic prophecies. I have worn manifold robes and have carried countless names—many of which have been mentioned in books throughout history.

Oh, Clayton sensed himself say. *I see it now; everything is clear: I wrote about your suffering; in another life I shared your joy. But then your soul was chosen to advance and I had to wait for many lifetimes. Share with me your knowledge and show me where you've been.*

I have always followed my callings and applied myself as a simple healer by giving hope to the hopeless, clarity to the agnostics, and love to the lost, therefore establishing the balance between the past and the future. My ultimate mission has always been to open the eyes and the hearts of mankind so optimal vision could be achieved.

From the beginning, the lesson has been the same: through hope and love there is ample time to ascend toward life's true potential. Losing fear of the unknown will create the understanding of infinity.

Every lifetime has strengthened my power and given me more wisdom; however, my true growth takes place between physical lives. That is when I receive the Upper Light, when I reseed and grow buds, when I begin to bloom.

I am only one of countless old souls. Many others are far more developed and far more divine, but the mission is the same. The soul always lives in hope!

As life on this planet quickened, the deputation of the advanced and powerful souls became more urgent in the recent history of time. Even though these souls are multitudinous, the Law of Rebirth *was rewritten. Time between physical lives has grown shorter and a new calling has become a necessity. Each old soul was to divide in order to accomplish the ultimate goal.*

For the first time, I had to go into two incarnations. Now, two different physical beings are sharing the same reality; their time flow has become synchronized.

My Desire to Receive has been told of my new assignment; its purpose will reveal itself in actuality.

The revelation came through illumination when I received the Light That Extends and once more the seed of the revelation enriched me with more wisdom. The knowledge I obtained is a gift that comes from a world beyond human reality.

When this lifetime's mission is fulfilled, the Light That Extends will again extend into The Endless and be carried anew to recipients born on earth.

And so it continues. It is the law of Continuum.

The brilliant light faded as Clayton experienced his spiritual descent. When he opened his eyes, he sat by the fire circle, his hands still holding Teeba's. Even though he felt as if millennia had gone by, only seconds had passed.

CHAPTER 45

NOTHING STIRRED IN the desert's night calm. It was as if the wild inhabitants respected the importance of Teeba's powerful transmission, like they understood they were simply a tiny fragment of a multidimensional existence—beyond mankind's comprehension.

In the hushed silence, Clayton's half-asleep gaze hung onto the slowly dimming amethyst fire in Teeba's eye. A stream of familiar images flashed through his head as if propelled by a powerful projector, but now the mental pictures decreased in speed. A rhythm took hold; through the rhyme of logic he heard the vibrations and fluctuations of life. They came as beautiful melodies, gifting him with the true elements of existence.

"How can I thank you?" His voice trembled and a mist clouded his vision. He blinked himself back into reality. "I'm only beginning to understand that words will never be enough to describe what just took place." He pulled Teeba close and held onto her tightly.

"I needed you to understand," she said softly. "All my life I've waited to share this part of me. And even though I've met people who came into this world with soulful wisdom, they either were unaware of their gift or ignorant of their capabilities."

"If it wasn't for you, I'd still be one of them."

She shook her head. "No, something in you was already open because you heard the music when you were determined to wake me." She leaned her cheek against his. "Every soul is like a Stradivarius violin in perfect tune. But in order to hear the full potential of the melody, we not only have to open our ears, but also allow our minds to unlock so we can hear the sweet sound that continuously echoes through life."

"I'm beginning to understand the concept. You showed me how to hear without a word being spoken. You made me see what eyes cannot." Clayton cupped her face. "I have so many questions, though; questions that should be answered in words." He brushed his lips against hers. "But I'll wait," he whispered. "Sometime later, I will ask my questions." His fingers traced along her neck, collarbone, and shoulders.

"Later," she murmured in between his kisses and smiled, "later, I will answer. Later you'll find out everything you must know."

Their embrace and kisses intensified; their bodies merged into a single shape as the currents of the ancient river of time floated them toward their destination.

He finger-combed the dark hair that draped over the pillow of white sand below her, kissed her slender body, and slid his hands beneath her hips, lifting her toward him.

With her eyes closed, yet wide open, she stroked his brown smooth skin.

Together they sighed as they reawakened their desire. They gasped with joy when their bodies fused, and as they recognized their eternal love. As one, they tumbled and experienced the extraordinary journey of timeless passion.

They did not hear the sounds of nocturnal animals that had come to life again. They did not see the thousands of stars reflected in the dark mountain pools, nor did they smell the woody odor of the mesquite trees whose leaves waved their blessings at the two bodies below.

They only smelled, tasted and listened to each other. The fever of passion flushed their cheeks and intoxicated their brains. They took pleasure in everything they had held back for too long. Like the moon and the stars mirroring themselves in the dark water nearby, Teeba and Clayton began their swim in the deep and mysterious sea of love.

CHAPTER 46

THEY DID NOT remember sleeping that night and only drifted off occasionally for short periods of time. They woke as soon as they felt a part of their bodies relaxing and slipping away from one another. The night seemed too short for their longings and their lovemaking intensified as the sun again rose above the horizon.

"After waiting for you forever, this is the beginning of a new beginning." Clayton inhaled, expanding his lungs in the fresh mountain air. He had never before breathed more freely. He welcomed the metamorphosis that had taken hold of him and accepted the sweetness of the mystery. He knew he finally had found his life's path. He exhaled slowly and blinked into the early morning sun. Gingerly he rose and lifted her light body. "We'll never be apart again. I'll never allow you to leave me for so long," he said, and kissed her neck and breasts.

She leaned her face against his chest. "If ever I must leave you, it won't be for long. I promise you that."

"What does that mean? What do you know that you're not sharing with me?"

"I will share everything with you in due time. I might have the vision, but I don't know the details or the outcome; I flow with my perception," she said. "You're part of the calling and together we will have to accept whatever lies ahead." She looked up to him and smiled. "Let me kiss your worry away. I know last night we created a new beginning."

CHAPTER 47

EVEN THOUGH IT was only seven o'clock, it was already obvious the day ahead would be hot. As they packed their gear, Clayton wiped perspiration off his forehead, squinting at the already powerful morning sun rising in the cloudless blue sky. He did not want to leave and could not imagine being away from Teeba, even if just for a few days, but understood that a life beyond last night's revelation was waiting to go on. He sensed Teeba's look and knew she could feel his thoughts.

"Let's cool off before we hike back to town," she suggested. She took his hand and pulled him toward the nearest boulder. Together they jumped into the mountain pool.

"You know what amazes me?" Clayton asked as they started on their way back. "Here I feel I've seen the light and gained the knowledge of something utterly profound, and yet there are things I'm still in the dark about; things that you'll have to help me understand."

"Might one of your many questions be who and why somebody wanted to shoot me?" Her dark eyes twinkled at him.

"Yes, my little mind-reader," he grimaced and shook his head. "I guess from now on I have to be careful what I think," he teased. "What happened that day?"

"He didn't mean to shoot me. His intention was to kill my young pupil, Timothy Snow."

"So you know who he is."

"It was Timmy's older brother, Christopher."

"But you told the police you didn't see him."

"I didn't, but I felt his anger and turmoil for hours before. By the time he approached the classroom, I instinctively knew what needed to be done before he pulled the trigger." She sighed, but the peaceful expression on her face never changed. "I can't always interfere in events to happen—they'll happen for a reason. Christopher soon will face the consequences of his radical thinking. But before then, he unfortunately will cause even more harm." She saw the confusion in Clayton's face and continued. "You see, from beginning to end, each life becomes part of a circle. There are many players involved in the circle that forms our assignment. Christopher is only one of them but he connects with the rest of the players, including us." She stopped and gazed at nature's scene below as it lazily awakened when the sun lifted a transparent veil. "Christopher's disorientation will lead to the next misguided person and so on. Before the circle closes, Christopher, as well as others, will have written their own destiny."

"Who are the others? What do you know of them?"

"Most of them I've not met or might never meet. Very few of them present positive forces, but there also are strong, negative forces involved. Their good or misguided ways of thought and belief will eventually connect us for the reason why we're here." She picked up the rhythm of her pace as she continued on the uneven, rock-strewn path.

Clayton, still unsure of this newfound perception, talked hesitantly—almost to himself. "So, all of us volunteered to be here to live this tempting and exciting life but some need to outsmart the others and by doing so, forget their original intention." He realized Teeba was agreeing and continued. "Is that because self-esteem turns into self-doubt?" He knew he'd asked a question, but also realized the answer was right there and he affirmed his thought. "We're all constantly tested, but we're given an equal and free choice in anything we do. But those who decide to build on sand instead of rock will lose touch with their true worth."

"Ask your next question—the one that's mostly on your mind."

Clayton laughed. "I'm glad I have questions left. For a moment I was beginning to get overconfident." They stopped for a water break at a rare shaded spot and sat down, leaning against cool rock.

Clayton thirstily drank from a full bottle, then poured the rest of the water over his head.

"I don't even know how to ask the next question because the concept is so mind-boggling to me." He took a small towel from Teeba and dabbed his head dry. As he handed the cloth back to her, he held onto her hand. "You provided me with an awesome awareness, the Continuum of Souls." He closed his eyes in concentration. "You shared with me some of your wisdom and made me aware that for the first time one soul went into two incarnations for reasons still unknown to me." He opened his eyes again and searched hers. "If you hold one part of that soul, what happened to the other?"

"Twenty-seven years ago, my soul split for the very first time. It was supposed to go into twin infants who together during their lifetime would be able to execute an awesome task. But for some reason—a purpose yet to unfold—one of the twins had to die during birth and my part of the soul had to enter another baby born at the same moment." She smiled at his perplexed expression. "I know this is strange, but I also know that soon you will fully understand why and what this is all about."

"Do you know who you were supposed to be and who your soul's twin is?"

"I don't know who she is or where she lives. But there isn't a moment when I don't feel the connection." Despite being in the shade, a brilliance lit up her face. "It's the epitome of oneness," Teeba breathed. "But until recently only I was aware of the linking since I had been gifted with the more powerful part." She lifted her head and looked at the skies. "The day of the shooting, when I went into my self-inflicted coma, I knew I had to release the energy. From that day on, my soul's twin, whoever she is, needed the strength, the power and the understanding more than I. She soon will have to master a much bigger task than I."

"If you know that, then what quest do you have to accomplish as a player in the circle you've been talking about?"

"My revelation came when you stepped into the circle. Our assignment has already begun." She looked into his eyes. "As time goes by you will recognize the importance."

"Tell me about your parents," he said later, after they resumed their hike. "How did they deal with having such an exceptional child?"

"They never fully understood. My father more than once told me that the day I was born, as he held me for the first time in his arms, he knew I was special for more reasons than one. To this day he calls me his gift from heaven. He's been the most loving and caring parent—my only parent."

"What do you mean" What about your mother?"

"My mother tried to kill the growing life inside her many times before my soul slipped into its body. She didn't want the child she conceived and she had no use for me as I grew up. She couldn't believe all the attempts to rid herself of the baby had been futile. And when I arrived in perfect health and with what she believed were dangerously dark eyes that seemed to know her secrets, she experienced fear and felt damned. She cursed my heritage and named me Tituba."

"Tituba?" Clayton asked incredulously. "Wasn't that the name of a black woman from Barbados who was persecuted in the Salem witch trials of the 1600s? She was mentioned in Arthur Miller's play *The Crucible*."

Teeba nodded. "My father soon realized the origin of that unusual name and abbreviated it, believing it would protect me. Actually, my mother wanted to hurt me by naming me after someone she believed was a witch. Instead, she paid homage to the kind and strong Tituba, who was an admirable woman with tremendous compassion for others. Throughout her life she was a healer, helping many others in need." Teeba sighed. "Tituba had courage and great wisdom. And for that she was punished. She was an old soul—even then."

Clayton was silent as he walked side by side with Teeba on the last stretch of the hike. He thought of his own parents and the extraordinary loving relationship he had with both his mother and father. He could not imagine life without their nourishing and insightful upbringing. "Will I ever meet your mother?"

"No," said Teeba. "Even though she's part of our circle, she will only touch us again indirectly. For years, my mother knowingly hurt many people. She's about to cause great injury to herself."

La Jolla

. . . in August

CHAPTER 48

GLORIA PRIME WAS in her element. This was day twenty-two of her visit in the Miller mansion in Lower Hermosa on Camino de la Costa, the Street of Dreams. The twelve million dollar home was right on the ocean and was bigger and more exquisite than anything that Gloria had ever envisioned.

From the first day of her visit, Nadine Miller had spoiled Gloria with her generous hospitality. "You deserve every moment of luxury and pampering after what you've been through, darlin'," Nadine had exclaimed after welcoming Gloria and instructing the various household staff to cater to every whim of her guest.

Luxuriating in the attention given to her, Gloria played her part well—the one of an emotionally exhausted, but ever so euphoric mother.

She met many of Nadine and Oscar's friends at almost nightly invitations to their splendid homes. She enjoyed the ladies' luncheons at the private clubs and frolicked with socialites on their shopping sprees, at golf courses, and on tennis courts. She even swallowed her dislike for playing bridge and found some enjoyment in what she had believed to be a waste of time. Whenever the topic of Teeba's return to health came up, Gloria—despite her fury about Teeba's survival—acted her role better than Julie Andrews' prototype mom performance in *The Sound of Music.*

As if in a silky-warm and fragrant bubble bath, she daily saturated herself with the attentiveness, constant courtesy, and exclusive exorbitance that surrounded her in La Jolla. Gloria believed she had found her true belonging; with her still growing lust for luxury, she finally recognized how she should live her life to its full potential.

She did not miss Tucson or her imperial role at Prime Produce. She hardly ever thought of her husband and never wasted a fraction of a second on her daughter. Instead, she enjoyed every minute and dreaded the day when her blissful stay on the Street of Dreams would come to an end. But since Oscar was not expected for at least another two weeks, Gloria thrived on Nadine's attention.

Sunday morning, Gloria had planned to play two rounds of tennis with Nadine and her friends at the racquet club, followed by a luncheon. But the night before, during a birthday party at another mansion two blocks away, the high heel of Gloria's new René Mancini red satin sandal got caught in a small crack in the otherwise perfect deck around the pool, causing a light sprain in her ankle. After the ice packs were applied, she enjoyed the massaging hands of a few of the handsome gentlemen whose wives were either too busy talking about their cosmetic surgeries or too tipsy to care about their husband's activities.

As on most Sundays, the Millers only employed one servant during the morning hours. Rosa, the young Hispanic woman, had served Gloria a late poolside breakfast. After changing the linens on the beds, the towels in the bathrooms, and the flowers in the crystal vases, Rosa spent another two hours catering to the animals. Nadine had brought two of their five dogs to La Jolla. The three larger dogs would arrive with Oscar.

Elvis, the hyperactive black cocker spaniel, rocked the quiet house with choppy rhythmic barks each time the phone rang. Fleur, the apricot poodle, was too laid-back to bark and spent most of her time on her dog chaise lounge while the television ran around the clock for her entertainment. Lollie, the gold and blue macaw, whistled and screeched obscenities each time Elvis barked or Fleur pranced by.

After Rosa had walked the dogs, brushed their coats, and cooked their meals, she cleaned the parrot's fancy cage until it sparkled and provided the big bird with fresh food as well.

Gloria did not care for either of the spoiled dogs or the nasty parrot. The feeling seemed to be mutual because neither of the animals paid any attention to her either. As a matter of fact, the dogs avoided her and only Lollie occasionally croaked something disrespectful at the sight of her.

"Anything you would want me to do before I leave?" Rosa asked.

"No. I'm perfectly fine. Have a nice day." Gloria was resting comfortably in the shade, leafing through the latest issue of *Vogue*. She did not bother to even look at the young woman.

Ten minutes later Gloria heard the car pull away. Her ankle was already feeling better—not good enough to have played tennis, but certainly good enough to plan on spending the evening with Nadine. They were going to a brand new restaurant whose reputation in other cities for food was as high rated as the killer martinis at its popular bar that served the in-crowd before and after dinner. Gloria looked forward to another exciting evening.

She put the magazine aside and walked into the house. Feeling the thrill of having the Millers' palace all to herself, she moved slowly from room to room, admiring the furnishings, paintings, and other details. Remembering that Nadine said Oscar was the genius behind the interior design and had single-handedly put together both of their outstanding homes, Gloria looked at everything again in awe. She could not envision Oscar having such extraordinary taste. She knew he was a prominent and successful land developer, but somehow he looked the opposite of most men who made interior design their specialty. Gloria realized how little she knew about Oscar other than his accomplishments. While slowly moving from room to room, it occurred to her that she was still in the dark about Nadine's past as well.

"Strange," she mumbled as she flipped through a photo album of the Millers' prize-winning dogs. "Both Nadine and Oscar always cleverly change the subject or claim privacy whenever anyone tries to question them about their early or formative years." Another photo album was filled with more pictures from another Best in Show contest. By opening albums and cabinets, Gloria thought she would discover what she sensed might explain the Millers' evasiveness about their past. She wondered why no rumors ever circulated in the elite groups they socialized with or why there was no gossip whispered behind their backs. Instead, Nadine and Oscar were admired in the society circles without them sharing anything about their past.

Gloria had always been a pitiless critic of those who used their social status and influence to reach out to the next-higher level. She knew the Millers did not fit that category, but was oblivious in noticing the trait in herself. She was equally blind and deaf to the fact that her eyes widened with anticipation and her ears opened with delight whenever she found out about other people's misery.

She stood in front of a magnificent old painting in Oscar's den and lightly ran her fingers over the delicate brushstrokes. She did not know who the artist was—her knowledge of fine art was limited—but suspected the piece to be worth a lot of money. She touched the wide ornate frame and wondered if it was made from real gold. To her, it certainly looked like it. She expected the painting to be protected against theft and searched for the wiring between the frame and the wall. She stiffened when her fingers hit a sensor and, with a loud gasp, she jumped as not only the painting, but also the part of the wall it was hanging on, opened to expose a large shiny vault. She stared and wondered what was behind the heavy steel door.

"Expensive secrets," she whispered. "Everybody has secrets." She turned around and addressed a painted portrait of Nadine and Oscar on the opposite wall. "I know you guys *must* have secrets, too."

Trying to avoid the pressure on her left ankle, she slowly walked up the wide marble staircase, but instead of turning toward the guest wing, she turned right and without hesitation opened the massive, ornate doors to the master bedroom suite. She had been allowed to see this part of the house before, but only when Nadine offered a tour shortly after Gloria's arrival.

The clicking noise of her low heels on the marble floor made her aware of her intrusion and she quickly stepped out of her sandals. As before, she was stunned by the beauty of the rooms and wondered what it was like to live like this. She had always been proud of her own home in Tucson, knowing it was impressive in size and tastefully decorated, but it certainly did not compare to either of the Miller estates. She felt a quick stab of jealousy as she moved from the enormous bedroom through the large walk-in closets, opening more drawers and cabinets in her effort to discover the owners' history and hidden habits.

Both Oscar and Nadine had designed their home so they could enjoy their own grand baths and dressing areas, each one being the size of a luxury hotel room. Crossing the vast space, Gloria opened another door. She hesitated and did not remember seeing this room on the tour through the house before. It was a study—obviously Nadine's—complete with a lounging area and a fully stocked bar below the audio/video equipment in the handcrafted armoire.

Gloria lowered herself into the soft ivory leather chair behind the curved wood desk and looked around the room. She opened the top drawer of Nadine's desk and stared at twenty identical gold pens, a bunch of perfectly sharpened pencils, plus ten even-sized ivory boxes, stacked with paper clips, notepads, post-its, scissors, Scotch tape, and keys on a silver Gucci key ring. Everything was aligned and arranged in meticulous order. Gloria carefully closed the drawer, hoping no pen or paper clip would shift from its place. She bent down and tried to open the right desk cabinet, but it was locked. She remembered the keys in the drawer and slowly opened it again, her eyes memorizing the arrangement. She estimated that the medium-sized key might fit the lock of the cabinet.

"Bingo," she said and smiled triumphantly. In the cabinet was a good-sized leather case, also locked. She tried two other keys and the third one opened the box. "Bingo, bingo," she said again.

The leather case had three dividers. In the top divider was a charm bracelet, loaded with various tiny symbols; Gloria wondered about their meaning and origins. She looked at a child's necklace with a small cross dangling from a thin chain. Her eyes moved from a dried, pressed white rose and an empty perfume bottle to a man's white handkerchief with stains of mascara; "OSM" were the three hand-stitched initials on the neatly folded handkerchief.

"Mmmh," said Gloria, and stared at several powder blue envelopes, addressed to Nadia Melamed; the envelopes were empty and the postal stamps all dated back to different days of April, 1971.

She assumed that OSM were Oscar's initials on the mascara-stained handkerchief. "But who is Nadia Melamed?" Gloria wondered. "And why does Nadine keep these things in here?" She gave a last look at the unexplained memorabilia. "Secrets, secrets, secrets," she said. "I'm dying to know what they're all about."

She lifted the top divider and gently put it on the unblemished desk's surface. The second tier of the case had only one item sitting in the middle of it, a small jewelry gift box. Gloria removed its lid and held her breath as she looked at a magnificent ring with a ruby so big, she could not even begin to estimate its units of weight. She had to squint in order to read the tiny engraved words: You are mine and I am yours, FOREVER ❤ OSM ❤ April 21, 1971.

"If OSM represents Oscar's initials, he must have given this ring to Naddie," Gloria said out loud. "Why the heck is she hiding it in this case of old souvenirs?" Gloria stared at the piece of jewelry before she lifted the middle divider.

"I knew it. I think I've hit the jackpot!" She removed the diary, bound in soft ivory leather, and opened it. Recognizing Nadine's handwriting, Gloria giggled like a victorious schoolgirl.

She looked at her watch and leaned back into the chair when she realized she had at least another hour alone.

The first entry in the diary was made when Nadine was only thirteen years old. She wrote of a secret crush on a young man, eleven years older. For the period of one year, the diary writings revealed Nadine's angst that her parents would forever separate her from her lover should they discover her secret.

"Today IT happened and it was magic." Gloria snickered when she read about the details of what her friend called magic. "We've got a lot in common, Naddie," Gloria said under her breath. "We both had secret lovers, but you beat me by losing your virginity at fourteen. You certainly were way ahead of me." Then, Gloria stared at the date of the entry: *April 21, 1971*. It was the same date engraved in the ring.

As Gloria flipped through the pages, she found that Nadine's relationship with her parents deteriorated over the next two years, mainly because Nadine was hopelessly in love with her secret beau, who had moved to another city. Nadine's parents worried when their daughter grew increasingly quiet and depressed. They unsuccessfully tried to cheer her up with expensive gifts and introductions to eligible sons of wealthy Texans.

The following page had only three sentences: *"June 15, 1973. I'm pregnant with our baby, but for obvious reasons we decided to go through with the abortion. I'm so devastated and frightened. What if I might never be given the chance to have a baby again?"*

"She was only sixteen," Gloria mumbled and turned the page to the first of several newspaper clippings from successive dates later in July of 1973. The articles described a head-on collision on I-45 where Sarah and Jacob Melamed, parents of Nadia and Oren, were killed.

Gloria's eyes froze on the names. Her mind raced. Her heart pounded as she turned another page. There she found the answer.

Beneath the extensive obituary with pictures of Sarah and Jacob Melamed was Nadine's last entry: *"What have I done? What have WE done? They died the day they found out about us. Both of us forever will have to take the blame. Did our love for each other kill our wonderful parents?"*

"Por dios mio! No lo puedo creer!" Gloria was unaware that for the first time in many years she was speaking Spanish. She slapped her forehead. "It's so obvious: Nadia changed into Nadine and Oren became Oscar. Together, they turned Melamed into Miller." Gloria closed the book slowly and whistled softly. "What do you know? She married her brother."

Chapter 49

THE CHIC, GRAND-style restaurant was packed to capacity. Everybody of name and rank in the San Diego area had eagerly looked forward to the by-invitation-only extravaganzas during opening week.

This latest culinary child of Lorenzo Estrada was the eleventh creation in the Estrada establishment; all the eateries were in important locations throughout the United States and Mexico.

On the last day of opening week, family members, close friends, and longtime patrons flew in for a private sit-down dinner that would mark the official beginning of the new Estrada restaurant on Prospect Street in La Jolla.

For years Nadine and Oscar had been loyal and enthusiastic patrons. Wherever they traveled and there was an Estrada restaurant in the city, they chose to eat only there. "Why bother looking for something better when you already know where the true food heaven is?" Nadine laughed, after explaining to Gloria how long they had been faithful to Estrada and his extraordinary chefs.

As Gloria and Nadine were shown to their table, Gloria breathed a sigh of relief. Her injured ankle throbbed fiercely, and her feet hurt from standing and making small talk with the socialites in the large crowd. But she would rather endure pain than not wear her favorite Manolo Blahnik ankle-strapped sandals. Earlier, she had given special attention to her appearance and her carefully selected attire. Her pink Marc Jacob dress hugged her curves and revealed plenty of cleavage. Gloria also was high, partially from the champagne and the excitement of being part of the group, but more so from discovering Nadine and Oscar's secret.

"So, Naddie," she said, grinning. "It was you and Oscar who got invited to this divine opening. Thanks for taking me instead of him. I know I don't even come close to being a replacement for the love of your life."

Nadine looked puzzled. "Don't be silly. Actually, he doesn't care much for grand openings."

"How lucky can I be?" Gloria lifted her glass. "Here's to Oscar." Then, she leaned closer. "Would he be jealous if he knew how many men were trying to get your attention tonight?" Gloria's eyes widened.

"On the contrary, my precious," Nadine cooed and touched Gloria's arm. "Can I tell you a secret?"

Gloria held her breath.

"Oscar likes it when I flirt. He says it turns him on because he knows in the end I leave the gentlemen panting while he's the one who gets the trophy." Nadine giggled. "I can probably flirt better than anyone else, but there's no man in the world that I adore more and love as much as my Oscar."

Gloria didn't let her disappointment show. "How long have you felt like this?" she asked.

"Forever, darlin'. Oscar and I have something very special."

You bet you do, Gloria thought. She wanted to ask more questions, but Nadine cut her off.

"Don't turn around. There's an extremely handsome gentleman behind you toward your right. He's sitting with three other men and a rather trashy-looking young lady. He's trying to get a better look at you." Nadine shook her head. "Nah, forget it, why bother? We both shouldn't be interested in other men. I've got my treasure and you've got your own *prime* of a guy. How befitting for Tommie's last name to be Prime."

Gloria turned cold at the mention of her husband. *Perhaps if I shock her with something in my life—maybe she'll tell me about hers,* she thought. "You don't know him, Naddie," she said glumly. "There's a whole other side to him."

"What do you mean, sweetness?" Nadine's forehead crinkled in surprise.

"Thomas doesn't care for me; he hasn't for many years." Gloria lowered her head and tried to look misty-eyed. "When Teeba was born, I was demoted to second fiddle. As she grew up, Thomas treated Teeba better than a king treats his queen while I got the status of a Cinderella."

"Oh, baby, that sounds impossible. Not Tommie..." Nadine shook her head. "Not that gentle sweetheart of a man. I can't believe I'm hearing this."

Gloria smiled but her mouth wasn't radiating any warmth. "Yes, they both have treated me with cold indifference for years." She dabbed at her dry eyes. "I've been pretending for a long time by playing the role of loving wife and mother. Thank God I was able to drown myself in my work." She dabbed at her eyes again. "And even at work my accomplishments were not fully appreciated." With a sigh, she took the freshly filled champagne glass and stared at the tiny bubbles. "To tell you the truth, it feels okay to stay away from home without feeling guilty since I'm not missed by either of them."

"You sweet, poor thing." Nadine's Texas drawl thickened. "I had no idea."

"It's okay, Naddie. I've been wanting to tell you for a long time." Gloria gestured weakly. "I often think of leaving Thomas—freeing him from a mate he doesn't love or care to be with." She produced a weak smile. "Thanks for listening. I'm feeling much better already."

"I'm concerned, darlin'. Do you want to leave? Perhaps you need to let it all hang out in a more private surrounding? We could go home."

"Are you kidding? I finally feel alive again, being away from the family that has no use for me." Gloria worried she might have overplayed her role. "Look, I've talked enough about my problems for tonight. You know, misery always needs company; I don't suppose there's something in your life that you want to share?"

"There's nothing to tell, baby. My life's like a delicious pie, so-o-o creamy and rich; I wish I could give you a big slice of it. I tell you one thing, though," she said. "On a lighter note, that handsome hunk behind you is still stealing glances. He even changed seats to get a better view of you."

"How are you two beautiful ladies enjoying yourself?" Estrada interrupted.

"Oh Lorenzo darlin', here you are! Let me introduce you to my friend, Gloria Prime."

After Estrada and Nadine exchanged small talk, Nadine gestured for him to come closer. "Who's that man back there? The one who looks like he just jumped out of GQ."

"I honestly don't know, Nadine. But I can find out. We have a list of all our guests."

Less then ten minutes later he returned. "The gentleman in question is a regular in our Mexico City restaurant. His name is Hector Munoz."

CHAPTER 50

GLORIA'S HEAD WHIPPED around, drawn by a seemingly magnetic force. Her knees went weak and butterflies fluttered in her stomach when Munoz flashed her a smile.

"I feel faint," she whispered.

"Gloria? What in the world is happening?" Nadine reached out to calm her.

Feeling Nadine's hand on her arm, Gloria's lips trembled, but she was unable to speak. She watched Munoz rise from his chair and felt her heart going into a fast drumroll as he approached their table.

"Gloria! *Que milagro*! I thought I'd never see you again. You look absolutely beautiful—you have not changed a bit." He spoke in English with a strong Hispanic accent.

His voice reminded her of sugary, soft ice cream. But instead of remembering the ice cream's chilling density, it recaptivated her as it had three decades previously.

"Hector?" she asked, and swallowed hard. The sudden touch of his hand on her bare shoulder had a deliciously hypnotizing effect on her, but she pulled herself together. "This is Nadine Miller, my best friend," she forced herself to say. Her body trembled and despite the intense heat rushing through her, she realized that her skin was covered with goose bumps and her nipples had hardened under the delicate fabric of her dress.

"Hector Munoz," he said, and bent to kiss Nadine's outstretched hand. "Charmed to meet you."

"Well, the pleasure's all mine! From the way you kept looking at my beautiful friend here, I should've realized you know each other." She motioned a server to bring a third chair.

"It seems like only yesterday when I last saw you," Munoz said, then took Gloria's hand in his. He turned to Nadine. "We grew up together and have known each other since we were children. Our families were very close."

Gloria wanted to wake her numbed brain and untie her heavy tongue, but felt pleasantly paralyzed in Munoz's presence. She couldn't take her eyes from him while he answered Nadine's questions. Through a fog she heard his lies about the closeness of their families and couldn't stop him from revealing her carefully hidden Mexican origin. She knew she would not have a problem explaining and appropriately embellishing her Mexican heritage to Nadine the next day. But for the moment, Gloria simply wanted to listen to the only man who had gifted her with the ultimate in passion and pleasure. Oblivious to the lethality of this love, she again was blinded by the perverse attraction of nostalgia. As if applied with Crazy Glue, Munoz still was attached to her heart. Like before, she didn't see the waving red flags that surrounded him. Instead, she realized she wanted to forget that Munoz left her pregnant with his child thirty years previously, forcing her to marry a man she never loved. Weakened by long-denied feelings of desire, Gloria willingly fell under his spell again and lowered the barriers she had created over the years.

Later, Munoz joined them at Estrada's bar where he regaled them with anecdotes of his life, career, and accomplishments.

"What a great connection," Nadine exclaimed when she heard he imported and exported precious stones. "My husband loves to buy diamonds, sapphires, and rubies. Since our anniversary is coming up soon, may he call you?"

"By all means," Munoz responded, flashing a big smile. He handed Nadine a business card. "Please have your husband call me at any time. It'll be my pleasure to help him find something rare and very special."

Munoz tried his best to sound sincere when he told the ladies about his import and export business of precious goods. Inwardly he grinned as he thought of his other, more lucrative line of work in illegal drugs. He enjoyed living a life of half-truths. He liked living two lives: one as the legitimate businessman and the other as the sly racketeer. He almost laughed out loud when he handed Nadine his business card, knowing it wasn't diamonds and sapphires that had made him a wealthy man. Instead, his acquired fortune had come through dark but juicy drug deals in Mexico and South America.

Munoz smiled at Gloria and lifted her hand to his lips. "I'm so happy we met again," he said, counting it a good omen that he had run into her at Estrada. She was perfect for his upcoming plans, and he had no doubt that he could win her over; her eyes told him everything. He had seen that look many years before.

"We have to spend more time together," he whispered, knowing he could use Gloria in more ways than one. She certainly was different from the much younger women he normally surrounded himself with, but he admitted being fascinated by her great looks. As a matter of fact, her elegant style, well-chosen words, and the sight of her full breasts had caused a stirring in his groin.

As the crowd thinned out, Munoz invited Gloria and Nadine for another glass of champagne at the Whaling Bar in the La Valencia Hotel. "I'm having such a wonderful time," he said. "It would be a shame for us to part, especially since the night's still so young."

"I would love to join you but I want to be home when my sweetie calls to get his goodnight kiss over the phone," Nadine said. "But why don't the two of you continue to celebrate your unexpected reunion?" She winked at Gloria. "I'll have my driver take me home now. What time shall I tell him to come and pick you up?"

"That won't be necessary," Munoz cut in. "I'll be happy to drive Gloria to your home whenever she's had her fill." He laughed and put his arm around Gloria. "All she has to do is let me know when."

Later that night, he made sure Gloria didn't leave the La Valencia Hotel.

Los Angeles

...in September

CHAPTER 51

"*PHANTASTISCH!*" DR. GOTTFRIED Geist said under his breath. He had walked from room to room and now stood in the main office and watched as Gary Snow showed him the efficiency of the electronic equipment that monitored every room inside the finished warehouse. From the hidden cameras installed on the shabby-looking exterior of the building in the abandoned industrial park to the newest innovations in technology on the inside, nothing seemed to be amiss. Dr. Geist could smell the success of his mission as he watched Snow demonstrate the sensitive equipment.

Dr. Geist finally let his eyes wander away from the screens. What only recently had been a gray, dirty, and neglected space was now a fine-looking research facility. "*Erstklassige Arbeit,*" he muttered. Then he turned and slapped Snow on the back. "First-class work, Snow. First class."

"Thank you, Dr. Geist. I must admit I am proud of it myself. My men worked fast and hard for their money," Snow replied.

"Speaking of which…" Dr. Geist's face hardened again. "Were there any questions asked or did any suspicions arise amongst your workers?"

"No, sir. I told them a private laboratory was planning on doing research on sleep patterns. They had no reason to doubt what I told them. They were happy with the extra work and the generous pay."

"I'm still uncomfortable with the idea that there are people walking around who know of this facility. I hope they keep their mouths shut and don't pay a surprise visit when we're in the midst of our experiments."

"Don't worry, sir. All the workers belong to OAA—they're trustworthy and will keep quiet. By the way, I told them the research would not start until next February, and by then this place will only be a burnt-out ruin."

"I hope you're right, Snow. There's a lot at stake here," Dr. Geist hissed. He saw Snow's face redden and Adam's apple bob. The German enjoyed causing emotions in others, especially fear.

"I will vouch for my workers' silence, I promise you that."

"Good, then," Dr. Geist grunted, and took a seat. "Sit down, Snow. I have another proposition for you." He could see the curiosity in Snow's eyes. "You made some good money with this project, *ja?*"

"Yessir. It paid for remodeling my wife's business and bought new furnishings and equipment."

"I thought you wanted to build an addition to your home."

"Yes, but Paula and I decided that her salon needed the overhaul. Our house will have to wait a while."

"Well, perhaps you won't have to wait much longer. You know that we need bodies for our research, *ja?* We also need someone trustworthy to *select the patients*." He grinned as he pronounced the last three words. "We originally had two men in mind, but they're still occupied with another project in South America." Dr. Geist's thin lips curled a smile as he noticed Snow's Adam's apple bob again, this time with anticipation. "Anyway," he continued, "I recommended you for this job. It'll pay extremely well."

"How much are we talking about?"

"We need twelve to fifteen subjects—we'd like them in groups of no more than three at a time—and we're prepared to pay..." He paused and watched Snow squirming. "How does twenty thousand dollars per head sound to you?" When Dr. Geist saw Snow's reaction, he cackled, hearing the sound echo through the sterile space. He raised his hand, indicating he was not finished. "And since a smooth execution of this project is extremely important to us, we're also prepared to pay generously for the proper disposal of the bodies; we're thinking another ten thousand per corpse."

"I'll do it," Snow blurted out.

Dr. Geist turned stone-faced again. "I thought you would," he said, then explained what would be expected of Snow. "Any questions?" the German asked.

"I don't think so." Snow coughed nervously. "I...eh...I believe I might need someone to help me, though."

"You've got someone in mind who you can trust?"

"Yes, my son Christopher."

CHAPTER 52

THEY MET AT Morton's Steak House. He had never been there before, but since the meeting with Dr. Geist, Snow had been in a celebratory mood.

"You look nice, son," Snow admitted after bear-hugging Christopher. "I've never seen you wear anything but jeans."

"You told me to dress nice, Dad. This seems like a fancy place." Christopher glanced at the menu. "Wow! Did you check these prices? I'm afraid to order anything here."

"Son, order yourself the biggest steak on the menu or even lobster tail; maybe both, like surf 'n' turf. Don't be shy."

After making his selections, Christopher asked. "What's the occasion, Dad?"

"I'll tell you after dinner, son. I think you'll like what I have to say. It'll be your dessert."

It was past ten o'clock when Snow parked his SUV by a public park, a few blocks away from his son's apartment building. He kept the engine running and the windows rolled up.

"I've been working with a group of people on a very secret project." Snow said. "They're not exactly members of OAA, but there's been a crossover—a link, you might say—with another organization." He stopped, realizing that he did not know the name of the group, nor Dr. Geist's role in it. "These guys could've picked anyone from within the OAA but they chose me for the job."

"Who are they?"

"I'm not at liberty to go into detail about what I know," Snow said, feeling adrenaline pumping power to his brain. "But I can tell you their goal is a *cleansing* one and the end results are going to be *pure* and gratifying."

Snow described his recent project in converting the warehouse into a high-tech research facility. "Wait until you see what I did; it's fantastic." Recalling Dr. Geist's words, he added, "It's first-class work."

Christopher suppressed a yawn. "Sounds cool, Dad, but if it's finished, what do you need me for?"

"You and I are going to select the subjects—the impure, the undesirables, the scum—for this first phase of the research, my boy." Snow's icy blue eyes shined in the dark vehicle. "Let me tell you how you and I are going to start the cleanup process."

"Youwantmetodowhat?" Christopher blurted out minutes later. "Liveamongstthehomeless?" He stared at his father. "I wouldn't know how to act and live with a disgusting pack o' rats. Plus, there's no guarantee that anyone will follow me to some unknown sleep research project for a few lousy dollars," Christopher protested. "I don't think I can do that, Dad."

"You *will* do it, son," Snow demanded. "It's payback time. You owe the organization and you owe me."

"But Dad," Christopher objected. "I just started college. I have a shitload of studying to do and Mr. Browne expects me to put time and effort into my work at the Funeral Homes." He blinked fast. "Plus, coach is already putting demands on the team, even though we're months away from the season. There's no time left."

"You will *have to make* the time, Christopher," Snow ordered. "We'll do it on the weekends. We need no more than four or five weeks to finish the job. You'll not only have to make the time, but you'll *want to make the time* when I tell you how much money I'm prepared to pay you per scumbag."

"You'd pay me for it?" Christopher asked, and started to rock in his seat. "How much?"

Snow felt a foamy lightness in his chest as he thought of the rewards. As the elation began to bubble in his throat, he exclaimed, "I'm going to give you half of what I'm getting paid—one thousand dollars per head. Multiply that by ten to fourteen bodies...not too shabby for four weekends, huh?" Snow experienced no shame deceiving his son; he grinned when he saw Christopher's reaction.

"Wow, that's a ton of money."

"That's not all," Snow added as he leaned closer. "More of the green stuff will be coming our way after we dispose of the bodies. I already talked to Roger Browne and he offered to let us use his crematorium." He winked. "You know what I mean?" Feeling like a financial wizard, he added, "I'll pay Roger a good amount of money, of course."

"Jeez, the thought of what I'll have to do gives me the creeps," Christopher mumbled. "How *am* I gonna do this? Where will I find these people?"

"It's already taken care of. I researched what needs to be done." Snow reached for his briefcase on the back seat. He took out a folder and handed it to his son. "Read it over and start rehearsing for your role as a homeless drug addict and alcoholic. And don't let anybody see this folder. Burn it the minute you know what to do."

Christopher leafed through the pages. "If I'm going to do this despicable work, I need to know why. What do these people want to accomplish with their experiments? Who are they after?"

Snow eyed his son and grinned. "Good question. I'm convinced that the ultimate goal is to cleanse the world from all scum and to finally finish Adolf Hitler's dream," he said, envisioning his own version of the final solution; the sensation gave him a medicated rest, almost as if he had swallowed a Demerol with shots of tequila.

A long silence followed Snow's last statement. With a sigh, he started the engine and drove a few blocks before dropping off his son. "By the way, I understand you and Eva Browne are dating. How is it going?"

Already out of the door, Christopher leaned back into the SUV. "I don't know, Dad. Eva's beginning to bore me. Her conversational skills are limited to clothes, hairstyles, makeup, and the lifestyles of Hollywood stars. Lately, I'm trying to avoid her."

"Don't ruin a good thing, Christopher," Snow warned. "Eva is the perfect girl for you. You must play your cards right. I can see the day in the future where Browne Funeral Homes will become Browne & Snow or, better yet, Browne & Son."

CHAPTER 53

WITH ONLY ONE week of preparation behind him, Christopher did not feel ready for what lay ahead. Anxiety had caused his stomach to feel raw and his taut nerves were like over-tensioned guitar strings.

It was late afternoon on Friday when his father dropped him at the MTA bus station in a rundown area of downtown Los Angeles. Christopher dreaded the next two days and nights as he walked the remaining distance toward Santa Fe Street. He realized he was no eyesore in this part of town; nobody would feel pity for the filthy young man who obviously had chosen booze and drugs over trying to make an honest living.

He put the two sacks filled with meaningless belongings on the ground and wiped an angry tear out of his eye. Then he pulled the fraying knit cap deeper onto his head. *No money in the world is worth going through this shit,* he thought. *Why the fuck did I agree to do this?*

The temperatures were in the nineties and he was sweating profusely under the two layers of rags he was wearing. He gagged again at the thought of his own stench, which would greet him after this nightmarish weekend.

When he reached his destination, he walked along the old railroad lines. As soon as he passed by the first, few apprehensive-looking men in grungy clothes, he lowered his head. But out of the corner of his eye he could see they watched his every step. The stink in the air was a mixture of raw sewage, decaying waste, and bodies that were in need of water and soap. The foul odor made Christopher heave, and he tried to camouflage his nausea by coughing and spitting. He passed by other small groups of vagrants and didn't stop until he found a shady and sheltered spot. He quickly looked around. Hoping he was not invading some other derelict's territory, he took two worn blankets out of one of the plastic bags, doubled them up, and curled onto them. He was determined not to get hungry for the duration of his first assignment and was glad he had enjoyed a hearty meal in clean and appetizing surroundings. He hoped he could fall asleep and wished that he would survive this weekend without breaking down.

His body jerked and he bolted up when he felt hot breath on his cheek. He almost collided with the lumpy-faced man bending over him.

"Never seen you b'fore 'round here," the man drawled. His lips were hidden beneath the long hair of an uneven mustache streaked with gray. Liver spots dotted his face and hands. Despite the warmth of the Los Angeles summer night, he wore several layers of clothes; his worn-out gym shoes were of different style and color. "Where you come from?" The man's breath was putrid.

"None of your fucking business," Christopher spat as he sat against the wall.

"You too nervous, man. I'm jus' checkin' out the newcomers." A big smile parted the hair over his lips, revealing brown, rotten-looking teeth. "Ever'body call me Daddy 'round here 'cause I been here b'fore an'body else show up. I take care o' things, 'specially new kids like you'self." As he started to smile again, the lines around his brown eyes crinkled like crunched parchment paper. "I'm ever'body's sugar daddy 'cause I take care o' things. If you want, Daddy'll take care o' you, too." His eyes fell on Christopher's sacks and he moved closer. "Got some sauce fo' Daddy in them bags?"

"You fucking stay away from me," Christopher hissed. His palms were sweating and the fine hair on the back of his neck was bristling. Like a frightened dog he growled, "Just stay away from me."

"Hey Gertie," Daddy called out to someone Christopher could not see. "Come o'er here. Gimme some help."

A short, round woman with a weathered brown face and stringy gray hair came shuffling around the corner. The long, buttoned brown coat gave her a Yoda-like appearance. She carried a bottle of booze in her hand. "Who'th thith? Thomeone new?" she lisped.

"He's afraid o' Daddy. Tell 'im Daddy's harmless."

"Thath right. We all friendth 'round here, but Daddy'th the betht. You can trutht Daddy." She nodded and took a big swig from her bottle. Then she held it toward Christopher. "How 'bout a welcome drink."

"Thanks," Christopher said, barely audible. His mouth had gone as dry as a saltine cracker and, despite his disgust for the situation, he thought of the reason why he was sitting between the two derelicts. "I got my own shit," he grumbled, and pulled a plastic bottle of Smirnoff from underneath his jacket. He hated what he would have to do next.

During his high school years he had always prided himself as being different from his drinking and drug-abusing buddies. He despised their incoherence when under the influence and swore that he would never weaken to their standard. Temporarily ignoring his principles, he unscrewed the cap of the fresh bottle and lifted it toward his lips.

"Ah...what the fuck," Christopher said when he saw the lusty thirst in Daddy's bloodshot eyes. He handed the bottle to the addict. "I got another one." He untied the heavy sack and pulled out two more plastic bottles.

"Shit, man," Daddy swore, grinning at the bottles as he huddled closer to Christopher. "You my nigger! You 'n' me gonna git 'long jus' fine."

During the night, Christopher met others by one of the fires. He shared his alcohol with every new scurvy drunk and junkie, trying to melt into their existence. He hoped to win their trust and friendship through liquor and speedballs. He prayed that soon they would ask questions and he would be able to tell them about the sleep clinic and the benefits that sustained his own alcohol and drug needs. Pretending to drink and pop drugs, he realized during the hours of the first night that he would be able to survive the next three to four weekends. He looked at the drunk, wasted parasites around the fire, trying not to be too selective. He finally decided to move closer to Gertie, the lisping pariah who was talking and laughing hysterically by herself.

"Whath crackin', thweetie?" She sucked on her cigarette and exhaled more noxious fumes into the already stench-filled air. "Come thit down. How 'bout sharing thome of your thauthe with ole Gertie?"

Christopher crouched at her level. When he handed her his bottle, he felt himself stepping into the shoes of his first victim.

BATON ROUGE

...in October

CHAPTER 54

"AIN'T NO SUNSHINE when she's gone
It's not warm when she's away..."

She softly sang the lyrics along with the Neville Brothers, moving her head and body to the rhythm of the music. Her hair flew in the warm autumn wind as her car sped over I-10.

"Ain't no sunshine when she's gone
And she's always gone too long
any time she goes away."

Angela Atwood loved Bill Withers' song. Her mother had been singing it to her for years, always indicating she could not envision her life without her daughter.

"Wonder this time where she's gone
Wonder if she's gone to stay
Ain't no sunshine when she's gone
And this house just ain't no home
Any time she goes away."

Her eyes became misty when she thought of what soon would become brutal reality for her parents. So much had happened since May when the transfer of spiritual power permitted her to recognize the true purpose of her existence. The biggest challenge still lay ahead. She did not fear her final hour; in her reality there was no end, only infinity. But her physical body hurt for the people she would have to leave behind. She could feel their love, their loss, and their pain when that day would come. For a fraction of a second, she wished she could freeze time or have the authority to alter imminent events.

Shortly after PIGR opened in Lafayette, Portal Industries had hired Angela as a lobbyist to look out for their interests. With the current administration led by Angela's father as the governor of Louisiana, this was very favorable to Portal Industries; it also gave the company a resource who reported on the progress and the development of the technology park.

Since the day in May when Angela awakened to her special awareness, she welcomed the new job opportunity at PIGR because of her interest in Dr. Hakan Öztürk. It wasn't physical attraction or love in the sense of a woman for a man—her love had many shades and her interest in people varied. Her reason for the attention she was giving the angry and troubled Turkish scientist was because of his deadly goals.

Because Hakan didn't recognize Angela's powers, it was easy for her to tap into his brain and read his twisted thoughts. She had learned about the gruesome plan he and his radical co-conspirators had in store. The blueprint was ingenious, but calamitous.

Soon after she made his acquaintance, Angela realized that Hakan transformed into someone different in her presence. She had found their common denominator and it was none other than the ancient attraction between man and woman. But where physical lust turned him into a panting dog, she had always been alpha. Where Hakan believed he would scientifically reshape the world, Angela already knew that the road he was paving could lead to his own inferno.

"Ain't no sunshine when she's gone
Only darkness every day
Ain't no sunshine when she's gone
And this house just ain't no home
Any time she goes away."

Angela finished singing and allowed human emotions to take hold of her as she pulled into the driveway leading to the Governor's Mansion.

Lafayette

...in November

CHAPTER 55

"HE WAS HERE?" Hakan's face was ashen. "Why didn't anybody try to get hold of me?" He put his lab coat on without realizing it was inside out.

"We tried the entire weekend," Dr. Ivan Putin grumbled, keeping his attention on the computer screen in front of him. "Ms. Atwood's bedroom walls must be soundproof for you not to have heard the constant ringing of your cell phone."

"Maybe your cell phone exploded from all the messages we left," Dr. Yuri Barsoukov suggested. "It was embarrassing for us to explain your absence at a crucial time like this."

"Gentlemen, please." Dr. Afshin Afshor interjected. His hard and cold brown eyes were shifting back and forth between the two Russians. He turned to Hakan and shrugged. "Don't worry," he scoffed. "The situation was uncomfortable but we managed. We walked Farouk al-Fatah through every phase so far, and I believe he understood most of it."

"Nonsense!" Putin contradicted, thrusting his chair behind him. "Al-Fatah has no clue about our work. He understood shit," he bellowed. "That man is only interested in two things: How soon are we ready and how he will get us out of here."

"You're absolutely correct, Ivan," Barsoukov agreed. "Farouk al-Fatah might be a genius in planning and performing his plots, but he doesn't know the first thing about science. *My* only interest is to keep him happy because I need him to keep putting the rest of the money in my account so he can get me the hell out of this country—the sooner the better." He faced Hakan. "I think you have some explaining to do. Your disappearance did not sit right with your Saudi taskmaster. After all, the reason for his visit was to see and speak to you."

During the interchange of obvious hostilities, Hakan's expression had turned from shock to grim as a crocodile. With flaring nostrils he looked at Barsoukov. "First of all, stop looking at my windpipe as if you'd like to use it as a straw." Then he turned to Putin. "Secondly, I owe neither one of you an explanation. Period!" He was fumbling to button his inside-out lab coat before he realized the problem. "You two never seem to get it," he spat. He pointed at Afshor. "You come with me. I need to see you in my office…alone!"

As soon as the door closed, Barsoukov threw a pen against it. "*Idi k chortu*! I can't stand the double-faced bastard. He's been playing a game with us ever since we got here. They all have." He sat on a stool, supporting his elbows on the table behind him. His right heel tapped the sterile white floor in rapid speed. "He's never told us the truth; he's just been using us." Speaking in his native tongue, he sounded even more outraged. "Hakan would rather pass a kidney stone than pass information."

"Come on, comrade." Putin said. "We both signed on for our own reasons. We'll soon have what we've always dreamed of—lots of money and recognition."

"You don't know what I know," Barsoukov rasped. "While we were frantically trying to get hold of the Turk, Afshor—the slimeball who never knows whether his French head is cooking or his Iranian ass is burning—left the door open to Dr. Ö's *forbidden chamber*." Barsoukov leaned closer; both of his heels were tapping the floor. "What do you think I found?"

"His spiral notebook?"

Barsoukov nodded. "Yep, the one that he protects like the crown jewels of England." Didn't you ever wonder why a man who has codes and scanners on everything electronic meticulously records all our work *plus more* in his spiral notebook, like a schoolboy in the olden days?" He shook his head. "Well, he made a childish mistake because I was able to read everything! Just imagine, our multilingual leader recorded the whole thing in *English*, yet!" He scraped the stool closer to Putin. "You won't believe what I found out," Barsoukov whispered. "They're actually planning to kill the entire current U.S. administration, president and all." Barsoukov's head bobbed forth and back like a chicken running from a predator.

"Impossible. How do they think they can pull that one off?"

"I don't know the details but I plan to find out. But what I do know, there's a plan to soon kill a few, isolated U.S. hotshots with MAX 18. That'll create a panic among the higher-ups in this country and will make it necessary..."

"...to vaccinate against MAX 18," Putin finished the sentence. "If they want to kill the administration, but vaccinate against MAX 18, where's the catch?"

"They're planning to make a last-minute switch. They're going to exchange the vaccine for the *"privileged"* by replacing it with the actual virus. So, instead of *saving* the U.S. government, they're actually going to eliminate it in one clean sweep. It's fucking ingenious and what's even more cunning...I think they're going to be successful."

"I'm trying to compute this fantastic information that has such devastating possibilities," Putin grumbled. "Do you think Hakan worked himself into the governor's daughter's pants in order to win the respectability of the American government for that reason? I understand her father is a very good friend of the U.S. president." He paused. "How clever! If what I think is happening, I'm taking a rare, but impressed Russian bow."

"Don't be impressed," Barsoukov spat. "All I know is that we purposely were kept in the dark. We've worked our asses off; we were supposed to be a team."

"Look, we fooled them as well. We made them believe we converted to Islam." Putin grinned from ear to ear. "You and I are the only ones who know that we both don't give a shit." The older Russian laughed and slapped his knees. "The minute we're safe, Hakan and friends will know that we didn't give a flying fuck about Allah or any religion." He stopped laughing. "We just have to play along for a bit longer. Before fucking Al-Saafi accomplishes the mission, we'll disappear with our own, privately arranged, guaranteed new identities. You and I can look forward to a rather luxurious, new life in old Mother Russia."

While Putin and Barsoukov finished their conversation in the sealed lab, they had no idea their voices were secretly taped. Neither Portal Industries nor the CIA had any involvement in this particular installation of listening devices nor would they ever find out about it. Instead, Hakan and Farouk al-Fatah were to become the only recipients of this fatal information.

CHAPTER 56

"YOU SHOULD HAVE given me her address or phone number." Afshor spoke in his characteristically precise Farsi. "I looked everywhere, including your office. I know you don't approve of my being in here alone, but this was an emergency. I almost called the Governor's Mansion but was afraid it might cause alarm."

"You did all you could. It was my fault for forgetting my cell phone." In his private office, Hakan had regained his confidence. He reached in the pocket of a lab coat behind the door and took out his cell phone. He stared at the device and shook his head. Of all weekends, he thought, the Saudi had to pick this one. Hakan activated the cell phone, typed his personal codes, and saw there were more than forty messages.

"I talked to al-Fatah Wednesday when he called from Germany. He didn't say a word about coming here." Hakan took a deep breath. "Did he give you a reason for his surprise visit?"

"Of course not; has Farouk ever explained his actions to *me*?" Afshor asked, eyebrows raised. "But he did say that he was on his way to Los Angeles. You're to call him as soon as possible."

Hakan's eyes grew wide. "If that's the case, he might want me there with him." His head felt tight and he began to massage his temples. "The experiments in LA usually start on Mondays and are finished by Wednesday. This coming Thursday is Thanksgiving and I'm invited by Governor and Mrs. Atwood. I was really looking forward to that evening."

"I certainly understand, especially since there's a prettier bird other than the turkey waiting to be...?"

Hakan shot him an angry look. "Be careful, Afshin."

"I'm sorry." Afshor said and bowed. "I'd better go. I know you have work to do."

Hakan—his mind temporarily blank—stood staring at the door after it hissed shut behind his assistant. Then, without warning, he realized Afshor had accessed his confidential territory during his absence.

What if Afshor was watched? Could it be possible someone else might have let himself into my office? Hakan wondered.

His white lab coat flapped like a bedsheet drying in the wind as he rushed across his office. With trembling hands he fumbled for his keys and unlocked the door to an adjacent room. Hidden behind a panel were the listening devices that monitored the labs and the offices of his assistants. He looked at the dates on the apparatus and rewound the tape. Outside of normal routine noises and work-related discussion in the labs, he detected nothing suspicious.

He fast-forwarded the tape and stopped breathing when he heard Barsoukov's voice. When it was finished, Hakan stood motionless. He could hear his heart pounding.

"I knew it," he whispered. "I knew they couldn't be trusted." Filled with anger and thoughts of revenge, he walked back to his desk. He needed to contact Farouk al-Fatah immediately. Together, they would have to work on a cure to rid themselves of the Russian malignancies.

CHAPTER 57

HE LEFT THE lab earlier than on most working days. As soon as he came home, he started to prepare material for Farouk al-Fatah. When the phone rang, Hakan answered immediately. "Angela?" His surprise was genuine. "I…eh…I was expecting another call."

"I can call you back if the call you're waiting for is important."

"You're more important."

"You sound distracted."

"No, but I'm pleasantly surprised you called me at home," Hakan admitted.

"Listen, I'm at my parents' and I'd like to get together."

"On a Monday? We never meet privately during the week. Anything wrong?"

"Absolutely nothing. I just want to have dinner and talk with you. I know the perfect place in Lafayette."

Oh," he said softly. He could feel himself melting under her spell again. "I would love that; I've had a rough day." He hesitated before he continued. "But you'll have a long ride ahead of you."

"It's only sixty miles, and the way I drive…" she laughed. "I'll meet you at seven at Prejean's."

When Hakan arrived at the crowded family restaurant, his eyes searched for her. Oblivious to the live Cajun music in the seafood emporium, he remained near the entrance. When he saw her waving her hand, his face brightened.

"I arrived early and ordered an appetizer already. I was starving," she said.

As always, he watched her as she ate with the enthusiasm of a true connoisseur. She had ordered eggplant pirogue—a hollowed out eggplant, breaded, fried, and stuffed with shrimp, crawfish, and crab. He smiled when she let out little sounds of pleasure with each bite.

"This is better than ever before," she exclaimed. "How's yours? Can I taste your Catfish Catoula?"

Hakan watched her in total fascination and amazement. "Why am I so lucky? You drove all the way here just to be with me? I'm flattered."

"I came here tonight because I won't see you next weekend," Angela said as she folded her napkin and put it beside her empty plate. "I have to go away on business."

He almost choked on a piece of catfish. He quickly drank some water and cleared his throat. "Something came up for me as well. I'll have to be out of town over Thanksgiving. I'm leaving tomorrow." He shifted uneasily. "Phillip Portal called. He wants me to meet with some visiting scientists in Los Angeles. I won't be able to spend Thanksgiving with you and your parents."

When she leaned closer over the table, he felt her hand touching his. He looked into her eyes and experienced a sudden fatigue. Through a strange mist, he believed he saw a purple fire. He tried to blink the apparition away.

"I'm sorry," he finally stammered, and rubbed his eyes. "I feel lightheaded in a strange way. Maybe the wine…"

"I wish I could change your mind," she said in a low voice.

He reached for her hand again, oblivious to the chill of her palm. "Did you tell me why you're going out of town?"

"I have something important to do in Tucson."

Los Angeles

. . . in November

CHAPTER 58

THEY MET AT Ali Baba, a Middle-Eastern restaurant on Melrose, and picked a table where they could talk in private with their faces hidden, worried someone might be able to read their lips. Otherwise, the two clean, nice-looking men, dressed in casual attire, did not stand out from the rest of the dinner crowd.

"You've changed since I last saw you," said Farouk al-Fatah. The forty-nine-year-old Saudi Arabian looked older than his age. He was balding and no matter how often or how close he shaved, the outline of new stubborn hair was ever-present, as if it were tattooed across the lower part of his face. It made him look daring and somewhat powerful for being rather stout and short.

"The last time we met, you looked pale and pasty," the Saudi said matter-of-factly in high-class Arabic. His dark brown eyes revealed nothing, but his wide nose twitched with nervous regularity. The vague indications of jowls vibrated each time he spoke.

"You look different yourself," Hakan responded. The last time I saw you, you had more hair."

"Today I may be bald, but tomorrow I might have abundant hair, appear taller, and look perfectly Western…I am a master of disguises; necessary in my line of work," al-Fatah said, studying the menu in front of him. Without lifting his head he shot Hakan a look. "Never let appearances fool you. Does anyone know you're in Los Angeles?"

"Afshin knows I'm here with you, but the Russians are under the assumption I'm on holiday break. A lot of people at PIGR are taking a few days off over Thanksgiving."

"What about the governor's daughter?"

Hakan felt his face redden. "She's out of town herself; she went to Arizona." He stared at a glistening olive, then put it in his mouth. "I have to talk to you about the Russians," he said, diverting the focus from Angela.

Al-Fatah nodded, spreading more hummus on a piece of pita bread.

"They know what we're up to."

Farouk swallowed and wiped his mouth. "How so?"

Hakan told the Saudi what he had learned from the tapes.

"But how did Barsoukov get into your office? You assured me it was the most secure place on the premises."

"He spied on Afshin and somehow got the codes."

"That sounds impossible considering that the codes change weekly."

"Of course I change them weekly," Hakan replied, trying to hide his discomfort. "But what's the difference now? The snake broke in, slithered around, and told Putin. Both of them are dangerous, not worthy to be part of our cause. They're infidels and don't deserve to fight or die for Allah." Hakan shivered from the painful prickle under his skin as his throat thickened from the venom. "When you hear their poisonous voices on the tape, they sound as if their mouths are filled with maggots." He swallowed the bitter taste. "They're trying to diminish our ideals—our life's work. You must talk with them, or better yet, they must go."

Al-Fatah added some more sauce to his falafel and without looking up, said, "I agree, but this is not the time to do anything irrational. First, I must visit PIGR again next week. I hope this time you'll be present. Then, I will have a talk with them. I will compliment them on their fine and dedicated work, and promise them more money—much more money—for the many extra hours they have worked. In return they will guarantee their total commitment and absolute silence." He put the fork down and turned his hand over. "They will eat out of this palm because that's where they smell and taste the money." He paused and rubbed his abdomen. "This is excellent falafel. Do you mind if I have the last few?"

Hakan shook his head. His stomach was too tight. He had barely eaten anything.

"You still need the Russians' help," al-Fatah continued. "There's much left to do. This is not the time to bring in new people, nor will you or Afshor be able to handle the work yourselves." He inhaled deeply. "Let us relax and block the door where the wind comes through." After swallowing the last bite of his food, he licked his lips. "Mmmh, that was very tasty." Taking his eyes off the empty plate, he faced Hakan. "Within the next three months we will meet our goal. But before you execute our plan, I shall execute the Russians."

Hakan's shoulders lowered in relief. "How will you do it? They're alert and extremely suspicious of anything out of the ordinary."

"Does the wind tell the yellow camel in the desert a sandstorm is coming? Sometimes even the sturdiest of camels is not supposed to survive nature's unpredictable forces." Al-Fatah raised his index finger. "Allah directs all the natural forces; Allah is nature." He waved to one of the waitstaff. "I understand you have excellent baklava."

Chapter 59

They sat in silence in the backseat of an old Oldsmobile, a faded gray car that would not attract anyone's attention as they approached the warehouse. The driver, a young, stoic-looking man, was silent as well.

Hakan was still digesting the information he'd received in the past twelve hours. Farouk al-Fatah had told him about the rapid growth of Al-Saafi. In an apparent evolution of a crossover, Islamic fundamentalists, white supremacists and neo-Nazis, and groups that formed after the collapse of the Soviet Union were teaming up with South American freedom fighters as well as a strange assortment of U.S. citizens who had opted to convert to Islam. These forces shared the same ideology, and their common goal was to erode Western dominance in the world. The various groups were operating not only within their own countries, but they also had found a very fertile breeding ground along the border of Paraguay, Brazil, and Argentina, known as Triple Border.

"Why?" Hakan asked again. "Blood never mixes with water. How can we trust strangers?"

"You cannot clap with one hand alone," Farouk replied with raised eyebrows.

Things were happening too fast. Hakan felt his head spinning. He leaned closer to al-Fatah and whispered, "I know that the planned attack on the U.S. government with MAX 18 is only the first of many strikes, but I don't like to hear that my life's work soon will be shared with other organizations."

Farouk al-Fatah looked at Hakan through narrowed eyes. "You're a scientist; you don't understand that we need their help," he hissed. "We must share MAX 18 in return for fake European and U.S. passports. Right now I'm negotiating to get ahold of some of the enormous stockpile of cold-war-era weapons."

As much as he tried to understand, Hakan felt betrayed by Al-Saafi. With painful reluctance, he realized it was too late to undo the twist of events. Unable to control his frustration, he began to shiver.

"Stop trembling like a timid woman," Farouk al-Fatah said. "I know what you're thinking, but your thoughts are foolish. Your scientific genius is well appreciated. Once you return home, you will be able to bathe in the admiration of your superiors until the day you greet Allah." The Saudi put his fleshy hand on Hakan's thigh. "In the meantime, always remember that wisdom is beautiful; foolishness is ugly."

Hakan nodded but Farouk's comments calmed him only slightly. *I must hit the iron while it's still hot, even if my hand gets burned,* he thought. But instead of the pain in his palm, he knew he would forever feel the anguish in his heart as his mind spun around Angela. His heart ached as he thought of the many years, days, hours, and seconds that would come and go without ever being with her again. He felt his eyes mist over and swallowed hard. "Yes," he said out loud. "The day won't come soon enough when I shall return to the bosom of Islam."

Chapter 60

RAMY RIBELLI PRETENDED to be concentrating on the traffic. He was proud of his ability to scour large areas without moving his head or, as in this case through the rearview mirror, observing every move of the two men in the backseat of the Oldsmobile. He did so by blinking his dark eyes quickly and often, mimicking a nervous habit. Ribelli, despite his Argentinean background, understood Arabic fairly well and caught the important parts of Hakan and al-Fatah's conversation.

Twenty-eight years earlier Ribelli's parents had left Argentina for the United States. His father, a disgruntled city employee in Puerto Iguazú who rarely got paid because of misappropriation of funds by the corrupt city officials, had promised his Lebanese wife a safe and secure life. A year after their arrival in Los Angeles, Ribelli let out his first cry in a small and dingy apartment shared by his father's relatives. For twelve years he listened to his mother's complaints about the injustices and horrors in the United States. He heard her endless pleas to return to Argentina, where she longed to reunite with the honest, hardworking community of Lebanese people who had fled the civil war in their country to make new beginnings at Triple Border. But his Argentinean father was stubborn, always reminding his family of the corruption and crime now ravaginging the country of his birth.

Ribelli had turned thirteen when he witnessed his father's death, caused by a stray bullet. Soon after the funeral, his mother grabbed her meager belongings and returned her three children to Argentina.

Ribelli never knew of luxury until his father's cousins introduced him at the age of sixteen to drug trafficking. He soon advanced to being an expert in money laundering. Before he turned eighteen, he moved to Ciudad del Este, the Paraguayan city at Triple Border. He drove a late-model BMW and provided his unsuspecting, proud mother and two younger sisters the comfort of life that until then they had been unable to imagine.

Ribelli was slight, but managed to look impressive by walking tall and holding his head high. His dark eyes matched his ink black hair; his protruding cheekbones arched over a wide mouth, and his strong white teeth almost looked out of proportion compared to the rest of his dark features. The unexpected turn from hopeless poverty to promising opulence had made him very hungry and, like a famished crocodile, he turned insatiable. He did not miss any opportunity to make new connections or explore the thriving black market of goods crossing Triple Border. Since he was in legal possession of a United States passport and had relatives in Los Angeles, he soon was chosen to make many trips to America to unload large amounts of drugs. Aware that his frequent trips might soon become a red flag to customs officials, he needed to reestablish himself in the United States.

On one of his flights he met Tufan Keshishian, the owner of Sultan's Oriental Rug Palace. The established businessman had large, impressive stores in all the major cities along the West Coast. He specialized in antique, old, and contemporary rugs, tapestries and kilim of exceptional quality and beauty.

Ribelli was aware of the rumors about Keshishian that circulated not only in Ciudad del Este, but also in Foz do Iguaçú, Brazil. Both cities were in the area of Triple Border. Ribelli found out that the quiet and robust-looking businessman was a major player in a highly secretive organization that was recruiting Islamic young men, training them in camps on the Brazilian-Paraguayan border, and paying huge sums of money to the brightest and best of them.

Being the son of a devout Shiite Muslim mother, Ribelli had always been respectful of his mother's conviction. But without his mother's knowledge, he joined the radical forces and was more than eager to help blow up the United States and kill all Jews.

His manipulative ploy worked and for the previous two years, Ribelli had been working for Keshishian. Officially, he was the general manager of Sultan's Oriental Rug Palace; unofficially, he maintained a base of operations for Al-Saafi as logistics co-coordinator in Los Angeles. Secretively, though, he remained active in the illegal drug business and already had several rather healthy bank accounts in various countries. But he was hungry for much more. And he knew that soon he would be able to satisfy his ravenous appetite.

The warehouse was eerily bathed in the pale moonlight. As Ribelli pulled the car around the back, he took another quick look at the rearview mirror. The two men were still quietly talking.

"We're here," Ribelli said in English. "Unless it has been changed again, I was given today's code."

"Then proceed," said Farouk al-Fatah.

Ribelli punched four digits into the remote control. The middle of three large doors rose slowly. Inside, to the left and to the right, were several parked cars. Only one spot was available next to the Oldsmobile. Ribelli shut off the engine and got out of the car to open the doors for the two men. "I was told to wait for you here," he said.

Farouk al-Fatah nodded. "We'll be approximately two hours, maybe less."

"Take your time. I can use a nap," Ribelli smiled. He heard a door open and saw a middle-aged man of medium height appear in the entrance.

"Gottfried Geist," the man said in a strong German accent. "You must be Dr. Öztürk. I'm extremely pleased to finally meet you." He ushered the two visitors through the door.

Before the door closed, Ribelli cringed as he heard ear-piercing screams and long, agonizing wails coming from deep inside the building.

CHAPTER 61

THE SOUND OF slamming doors and loud voices woke him up. Ribelli blinked and looked at his watch; he had slept for over an hour. In the dimly lit garage he saw that a steel gray van had pulled up next to the Oldsmobile. Two men were busy helping three badly clothed people out of the van.

"Easy, easy," said the middle-aged man in a white lab coat, trying to steady two black men while their heads bobbed back and forth. A wrinkled, older white woman wore a mindless toothless grin as she swayed toward another much younger man, also dressed in rags.

"Where's the bed?" The woman sank to the concrete floor like a deflated plastic doll. "You tole me I could sleep in a bed."

"Relax, you'll sleep plenty," the younger man with the knit cap said, helping her back to her feet.

The door opened and two male lab technicians in crisp white uniforms took charge of the swaying threesome. "Disgusting," said one of the technicians. "This is truly disgusting. Let's get them sanitized before I throw up."

The garage was silent again, but Ribelli still held his breath; his mind was working feverishly. He was trying to assemble the bits and pieces of the Arabic conversation that he heard earlier. Slowly, a satisfied smile spread across his face. He laughed out loud but stopped when he heard the lab door open again. He slid further down in his seat, but only enough to still see what was happening. One after the other, three body bags were carried out and heaved into the rear of the van.

The middle-aged man slammed the back doors shut and brushed his white lab coat. "Good work, Christopher. We're some team, huh?" he laughed. "Now that we're experts, this is almost fun. Nothing better than knowing these outcasts have seen the bright and the dark side of the moon for the last time." He laughed louder. "Why don't you clean up while I go back into the lab. I won't be too long." The man went inside and closed the door behind him.

The young man pulled off his knit cap, exposing short clipped blond hair that became almost invisible in the sallow light. He stripped off three layers of bad-looking clothes, then tossed them into an oversized duffle bag. At the other end of the garage he opened the door to a bathroom. Ten minutes later a much cleaner version of the blond youngster reappeared. Tucking a crisp white T-shirt into a clean pair of jeans, he looked up and froze.

"Whothefuckareyou?" Christopher bellowed nervously. "Whatinhellareyoudoinghere?"

"Hey man, take it easy," Ribelli soothed. He was leaning against the Oldsmobile, holding his hands up in mock resignation. "I'm legit. You guys woke me up with your ruckus."

Christopher's blue eyes widened. "Ruckus, my ass. What business do you have here and who the fuck are you?"

"I'm Ramy Ribelli—Tufan Keshishian's right hand."

"Ramy-shit-face? Tufan who? I never heard of either one of you."

"Really?" Ribelli gave Christopher a wide, big-teeth smile. "Well, perhaps you're interested in knowing that Mr. Keshishian is *the* boss—the main man who happily funds your dirty work with nice clean money."

"Yeah?" Christopher looked at the shabby car that Ribelli leaned against. "If you're this guy's right hand, why are you driving such a stinkpot?"

"Mmmh let me think." Ribelli rolled his eyes toward the ceiling. "Could it be that a Bentley or Rolls Royce might draw unnecessary attention in this area?" He smiled at the still-frowning younger man. "Relax. I told you I'm legit. I'm also fully aware of the role you play in all of this, Christopher." Ribelli was happy he remembered the name the other man had called this feisty youngster.

"If you know so much, then what is my role?" Christopher asked.

"Let me see. You must be the one who finds the bums on the streets for the tests. Awful task, isn't it? I give you a lot of credit, kid." Ribelli nodded and gave a thumbs-up, hoping his quick calculations had hit the nail on the head.

Christopher relaxed somewhat and eyed the much shorter man. "To be honest, it's disgusting," he grunted. "Only three more weeks though, maybe two if I'm lucky. I can't wait to be done with this." He took a step closer. "But you're right, I do get paid pretty nicely. The other man you saw is my father. He's splitting with me, fifty-fifty. I get one thousand per scumbag."

Ribelli's eyes narrowed as he quickly calculated again. He realized the enormous amount the father was keeping for himself. "Unbelievable," he muttered. He thought of how the same thing was done to him by a man he vehemently despised and almost choked from excitement when an idea popped in his head. "What do you do with the corpses?" He casually motioned toward the van. "I forgot how you dispose of them."

"We cremate them at Browne's Funeral Homes. I work there part time and Mr. Browne is a member of OAA. My father still hasn't gotten paid for it. Do you know how much this Mr. Tufon-whatever-his-name-is is gonna cough up for this?"

"I don't think they've agreed on a price yet, but I'm sure your father will soon find out," Ribelli said quickly. His mind was racing. The information Christopher had just provided was perfect. "Listen," he said, pulling Christopher behind the van. "I might have someone in a couple of weeks for you; someone for the tests," Ribelli whispered. "Less scumbags for you to recruit," he grinned. "I know of a couple of *undesirables*." He reached in his pocket. "Here, write down your number and I'll call you if it works out."

"Great." Christopher scribbled the information on the piece of paper. "Thanks a lot. That would be great."

"Uh-oh, they're coming. Let's split." Like lightning, Ribelli shot away from the van and ducked into the Oldsmobile, gently pulling the door shut.

Christopher came around the van. "Dad? You ready to go?"

"One moment, son," answered Snow without looking in Christopher's direction. Snow was busy shaking hands with Farouk al-Fatah and Hakan. "It's been a great honor to meet both of you," he said and bowed.

"Mr. Ribelli, are you awake?" Al-Fatah knocked against the window.

"Oh, so sorry, sir. I must've dozed off." Ribelli jumped out of the Oldsmobile to open the doors.

As soon as he pulled the car out of the garage, the two men in the backseat quietly began to speak in Arabic again. This time, though, Ribelli did not listen. In two weeks or less he would be free; he would be his own boss. He would eliminate one of the biggest players in the drug cartel. He would rid himself of the man who for years had treated him with disrespect and took loyalty and honesty for granted, continuously shortchanging his hardworking people on the immense drug profits.

His smile widened as he drove the two men toward Keshishian's mansion in Beverly Hills. Ribelli's pulse quickened with the thought that in two weeks he himself would disappear; his new identity was waiting for him in Argentina.

"In two weeks I'll crown myself like Napoleon; I'll be *the* fucking kingpin!" Ribelli said in Spanish, grinning from ear to ear.

"Did you say something?" Farouk al-Fatah leaned forward.

"Sorry, sir. I was talking to myself—the traffic is really terrible tonight." Ribelli glimpsed in the rearview mirror; the two men already were engaged in their quiet conversation again.

Still smiling, Ribelli hissed, "*In two weeks you're finished! Adios, Señor Hector Munoz. Ya estas muerto.*"

TUCSON

....in November

CHAPTER 62

TEEBA WAS AWARE that Yasmine Abbasi was waiting for the eight other students to leave the classroom. The last three to go through the door were still engrossed in a heated debate, continuing the challenging subject that had just been discussed in their weekly extra-curriculum class at Agave High School.

The seventeen-year-old girl with the shiny dark hair, neatly pulled back in a long ponytail, pressed her books tightly against her chest. Her head was lowered and through thick black lashes, she peered at Teeba.

"Ms. Prime?" She bent her head even lower, her face red. "I'm sorry, I meant to say Mrs. Harris." She took a step forward. "Can I speak with you for a moment, please?"

"Of course, Yasmine. How can I help you?"

Teeba closed the classroom door. "Let's sit by the window while it's still light outside.

You were quiet today, Yasmine. You usually have so much to offer in our current events debate group. I really missed hearing your point of view."

"I'm in trouble Ms. Pri..." she shook her head in embarrassment. "I'm sorry; I know it's been Mrs. Harris since before school started but I still can't get used to it. I'm sorry." Her eyes filled with tears. "You're the only one who can help me—you've always helped me. You're the reason I'll graduate early and because of you I'm getting a scholarship at UA. I don't know where I'd be without you. But today I need your advice more than ever before."

"Thank you, Yasmine, but I don't deserve the credit. You alone made these things possible. You're a rising star and I am so very proud of you."

"The rising star has crashed—there's no light left in it anymore—and you won't be proud once you hear about the predicament I've gotten myself into." Yasmine took two tissues from the box and dabbed at her eyes. "I'm pregnant, Mrs. Harris, and I'm only seventeen years old. Do you know what that means?" she sobbed. "If I have this baby, I won't be able to follow my dream; there'll be no future. But what's worse than anything: I've let my family down. I've betrayed them, our religion, and our tradition. They will disown me."

Neither one spoke until the girl's sobs softened and she looked up. "I'm seriously thinking of having an abortion without letting my parents know, but something tells me that decision would only worsen my betrayal and shatter everyone and everything that I believe in. I don't know how I'll be able to go on." She took a few more tissues.

"You once shared with me that you knew you were destined to be with only one man for the rest of your life. I assume Bari al-Bashani is the father." Teeba said. "He is an extraordinary young man."

"Yes." For a fraction of a second there was a glimmer in Yasmine's eyes. "He wants us to get married right away. He's told his parents that we're pregnant. And even though the family is of the Islamic faith as well, they took our irresponsible action rather calmly." She dried her eyes and nose. "Bari's family has lived in America for two generations; they're more tolerant about many things. My family only came to the States ten years ago; my father will never accept this breach of trust." Yasmine brushed her hands against her stomach. "How can I abort something that was created by two people who love each other more than words can explain?" She began to cry again. "Somehow we were unable to control ourselves. But still, we made a mistake and now I don't know what to do."

"Yes, you do, Yasmine." Teeba touched the girl's wet cheek. "There are things in life that happen for a reason. The life that is growing inside of you is not a mistake."

"It's amazing but you always seem to read my mind." For a moment she was lost in thought. "My father taught us an old religious saying: *'What hits you could not have missed you, and what misses you was not meant to hit you.'* If he believes in that and if this is my destiny, why am I so terrified of his reaction?" She shook her head. "If only I could verbalize what I feel deep inside of me..."

"I've told you many times before that you're very special, Yasmine. You're blessed with gifts that in due time you're supposed to discover yourself," Teeba's voice soothed. "However, time is of essence. In order for you not to make any irreparable decision, I must help you discover why you're here." She placed her palms on those of her student's and allowed the fire of the amethyst to do the rest.

"Oooh." The girl exhaled with the sound of soft, warm air. "Please don't stop. I want to see and learn more. Please let me go back there," Yasmine pleaded. Still entranced, she closed her eyes. "Please don't stop, not yet."

Teeba folded the girl's hands. "You have allowed me to open your senses. You now understand who you are and why your baby has been conceived. From this moment on, your knowledge will guide you and give you the confidence to do the rest."

Yasmine's small frame seemed to grow from inner strength. "Yes," she exclaimed. "I see now what needs to be done. I know I'll be able to make my father understand. After all, it was he who gave me profundity." The girl put her arms around Teeba. "Mrs. Harris, how long have you known...I mean, when did you recognize that I was...?" She stopped in mid-sentence, her eyes brimming with tears.

Teeba smiled. "That you are an old soul?" She patted Yasmine's hand. "It takes one to recognize one."

CHAPTER 63

WHEN DR. CLAYTON Harris left his office at the Institute, he glanced at his watch and quickened his pace. It was already past seven o'clock in the evening. Ten hours had again raced by; each day never was long enough to accomplish everything. Although Clayton loved his work, nothing could surpass what he felt for the woman he was rushing home to, the woman he had wed four months ago.

When he saw her twenty minutes later, he stood still, inhaling her presence with long breaths. In the unusually balmy air for a late November night, Teeba again reminded him of a rare painting as she sat, straight as a candle, in a peaceful half-lotus pose on the wooden deck that hung over the moonlit desert. Long dark ringlets and corkscrew curls rolled over her shoulders and came to rest on her uncurved spine.

He thought of a quote by Paul Tillich from *The Eternal Now*: *One cannot be strong without love. For love is not an irrelevant emotion; it is the blood of life, the power of reunion of the separated.* "I pray I'll never have to separate from you again," he whispered, and quietly left.

While he took a shower, he marveled about the intensity of his feelings and counted his blessings to be able to comprehend this new awareness. He would never cease to remember the magic of the summer night they spent at Hutch's pools. It was the night Teeba opened his senses; it was the night they both created new life.

They were married in August. A judge performed the civil ceremony and aside from Clayton's parents and Teeba's father, only a few close friends were invited to witness the union. Gloria remained in La Jolla with a summer influenza that she claimed kept her bedridden.

Immediately after the wedding, Teeba, together with her dog Troy, moved less than a closetful of clothes and other personal things into the house Clayton had purchased on Paseo Bocoancos.

Lost in the thoughts of the recent past, Clayton didn't hear the door open while he was shaving. When he felt her warm arms around his waist, he turned and looked at her as if for the first time.

"I've missed you all day," she said.

He lifted her off the floor and held her tight. "Not as much as I've missed you."

CHAPTER 64

"DELICIOUS," CLAYTON SAID. "I still could eat more but there's no room left."

"You could *not* eat more," Teeba laughed. "You've eaten it all." She loved experimenting with food, creating new recipes and naming them. "I must admit my Mellow Mushroom Medley and Pasta del Sol wasn't bad," she said, stroking her belly. "Even I ate more than normally."

"I should hope so—after all, you've got more than one tummy to fill." He lit the logs in the fireplace and pulled her onto the soft rug next to him. "By the way, I don't want to repeat myself, but do you have any idea how happy I am?"

"Please keep repeating, I'll always love hearing it," she said, and leaned her head against his shoulder. She told him of her day and the awakening of her student, Yasmine. "When doctors and nurses deliver babies, they claim they never tire of the miracle of birth. I feel the same way when I recognize an old soul."

"Who is she? Did I ever meet her?" Clayton asked.

"Yes, I recently introduced her to you when we met her and her boyfriend at the farmer's market."

"Of course," Clayton exclaimed. "She's very pretty and so polite. Her boyfriend is one of my interns; Bari al-Bashami is a genius despite his young age." He paused. "Why do I get the feeling these two young people are meant to cross our path? Are they part of our circle?"

"Not directly, at least not yet. But when their baby is born, a new circle already will have formed in which some of us are going to play a very important role." She placed his hands on her belly, which had begun to round.

"I feel tiny soft taps and flutters from inside against my palm. Is this another Morse code?" he asked, and lowered his ear to her belly. "It says...get ready...only five more months."

Teeba caressed his hair. "Have you run into Ebony Laveau lately?"

"Yes, funny you should ask." He sat up. "She recently changed shifts and now I see her daily. But for the past few days she's been on vacation." He kissed Teeba's cheek. "Ebony's lost a lot of weight. I bet you wouldn't recognize her. She's a very pretty lady."

"She's always been beautiful. I've felt her symmetry long before she and you woke me from my coma." Teeba snuggled and turned to face him.

The purple flicker in Teeba's eye caught Clayton by surprise. "Amazing," he said soon after. "I know only seconds have passed but visions, sensations, and the ever-growing expression of thought once again speeds me forward into the future."

Teeba smiled as Clayton continued to explore the bottomless chasm of the amethyst. She knew that he sensed a strong connection to Ebony—a higher purpose for having met her.

Later, sitting in the afterglow of the purple fire, Clayton whispered, "I wonder why."

CHAPTER 65

IT WAS AFTER eight o'clock in the evening when Ebony emptied the last box and put it on top of the others in an empty closet. Wiping her hands on her jeans, she looked around her new spacious dwelling.

"Omigod, I love it," she said, clapping her hands while beginning to twirl. With every more-dizzying turn she belted out, "I love it, I love it, I love it," until she fell on the sofa and laughed as the room spun. "I'm so lucky," she giggled, and kicked her legs in the air while throwing hand kisses toward the ceiling. Out of breath, she let her arms and legs fall onto the soft cushions. Like a rag doll, she remained in that position.

She had made the decision to move from her one-bedroom apartment on River Road to a townhouse in the gated community of La Paloma in a split second. The harassing calls and threatening letters from her ex-fiancé Rodney and his bar-boozing buddies and relatives had finally gotten to her. She was not afraid of Rodney—he was spending time in jail for killing an elderly man while driving under the influence with a blood alcohol level of 0.2 percent. Ebony was simply annoyed by the nightly disturbance of the pestering calls and bothersome letters.

By coincidence she heard of the availability of the townhouse, took one look at the bright airy space, and without giving it another thought signed the lease. The rent was much higher than what she had been paying, but she decided she was worthy of a little more luxury. After all, she worked hard, saved her money, invested wisely, and rarely indulged herself in any kind of excessiveness.

She'd decided to move less than a week previously and took a few days off from work to make the necessary arrangements.

Ebony did not tell anyone at the Institute about her move, planning to inform them when she returned to work. But before she cancelled her old telephone number, she called her mother in Louisiana. Not knowing when her new unlisted phone number would be in service, Ebony gave her mother the new address.

Still lying on the sofa, Ebony pondered over her serendipity, enjoying the quiet of her new environment. It startled her when the doorbell rang, and her first instinct was not to open the door. But then she bolted into a sitting position, cocked her head, and listened. Was her mind playing games or did she hear a familiar voice?

There was another ring, followed by a knock on the door. "Ebbie?"

Ebony raced barefooted over the cream-colored tiles and, before she yanked the door open, screamed, "Angela!" She stared in disbelief at her dearest childhood friend, who stood in the entrance with a small suitcase in hand.

"I hate to do this to you, Ebbie, but no one could get a hold of you." Angela dropped her case and flung her arms around Ebony.

"How in the world did you find me? How did you even get past the gate? The guards never let unannounced guests come through."

"Oh...I have my ways. Even though I promised myself to stop abusing my abilities, I don't think the nice man at the gate even remembers my coming through," Angela said. "Okay to leave my rental car in front?"

Ebony held onto Angela's hand as she dragged her through the house, proudly showing what she had accomplished in only two days.

"I knew it would just be a matter of time before you'd make your way to Tucson," Ebony said. She poured two glasses of wine. "You came here to meet my former patient—the one I told you about when I visited you in New Orleans. That *is* the reason you're here, isn't it?"

Angela nodded. "Because of you I found out about my soul's twin. The time has come that I have to meet her, but I'm also here because you play an important part in this whole circle of our existence."

"I don't understand," Ebony frowned. "You know I don't have your gifts and insights—I don't even think I've inherited any of my mother's clairvoyance."

"You certainly have, Ebbie. As children we were best friends because of it. But for your own reason you stopped sharpening your instincts and trusting your foreknowledge. It's time to tune in again, my sweet friend." Angela raised her glass. "It's so good to be with you. Together we have much to accomplish."

CHAPTER 66

CLAYTON STIRRED. "WHY are you up so early?" His early morning voice was three octaves deeper. "It's Saturday. No work for either of us." He drew her close and kissed the nape of her neck.

"This is going to be a special day," Teeba said.

"I have the feeling you've learned something during the night."

She nodded. "While my physical body rested peacefully next to you, my spiritual being was illuminated by the Upper Light. When morning came and the rising sun sifted through this bedroom, I didn't need to blink the sleep away. I was wide awake with the knowledge something wonderful will happen."

"Will I be part of it?" Clayton asked, finger-combing her hair.

"I couldn't do it without you."

After breakfast, Clayton took several medical journals from the stack on his desk and joined Teeba on the wooden deck. "I'm not complaining, but is it normal for the weather to be so warm in late November?" He pulled a lounge chair into a shaded spot.

"Just like life, the desert is unpredictable. What's normal today may be hard to accept tomorrow," Teeba said, while putting a new canvas on the easel.

For the next two hours, Clayton was absorbed by his scientific publications. He was still reading when a sweet sound made him lift his head. He saw two mockingbirds sitting on top of a tall saguaro cactus. Clayton put the journal aside to watch and listen to the long-tailed birds' melody; he did not want their song to end.

"Stay," he begged the female who flew skyward, waving goodbye with her white-patched wings. "Go follow," he silently urged the bird left behind on the cactus. But the male remained perched on the saguaro; his tiny head was pointed upward as he continued to serenade his mate. Clayton sighed and let his eyes drift toward Teeba.

She stood barefoot in front of the easel. Bathed in sunshine, he could see her nude contours under the short white gown whose gauzy fabric had fallen off her left shoulder. He watched her dip the brush into the range of colors on the palette. Then, she took a step back and with soft strokes transferred the paint onto the canvas. She swayed from side to side while adding more brushstrokes from different angles. While painting, she never looked at the canvas; her eyes focused on something beyond the landscape in front of her.

Clayton quietly rose and stepped behind Teeba. The composition on the canvas had no resemblance to the Sonoran desert; instead, violet waves crested in pastel pink foam before rolling onto ivory beaches. The luminous sand was covered with soft lilac flower petals and shaded by tall, mysterious emerald green plants.

The magic of the painting captured Clayton's warm brown eyes and he felt goose bumps forming on his arms as the scene on the canvas seemed to become reality. He believed he heard the sound of the sea and could feel the mist on his skin. He listened to the rustling of palms wavering in the wind and with a deep breath wanted to inhale the fragrance of perfumed floral leaves.

"Where is this?" he whispered. "Can you take me there?"

"When the time comes, you'll always find me in your own beautiful creation of worlds." She leaned her cheek against his chest.

"That's good," he said, trying to understand. "But for now, the most beautiful world is here on Earth with you."

CHAPTER 67

LATER IN THE afternoon, Teeba and Clayton read passages from their favorite classics to each other. They exchanged views on age-old rituals and the sageness of ancient gods; they talked about the freethinkers and visionaries throughout the centuries. They laughed about the strange characteristics of narcissistic monarchs and consoled each other when they remembered thousands of years of innocent suffering and lost lives caused by the hands of soulless persecutors. They only fell silent when the the telephone rang, suspending their unity of thought.

"Let's hope there's not an emergency at the Institute," Clayton said before he went inside. He returned a few minutes later. "It's for you. It's Ebony Laveau."

Clayton felt the air ripple and noticed an incandescence before Teeba finished her short phone conversation. As she stood in the doorway, the emission of light caressed her skin and she again reminded Clayton of a rare painting by an unknown artist from the Florentine school. "Ebony must've given you good news; it's written all over your beautiful face."

Teeba pulled him toward her. The fire of the amethyst sparkled in its brightest colors. "It is here—finally! You are about to witness something never seen before."

Clayton's heart skipped beats when he heard the sound of crunching rocks caused by tires rolling down the driveway. He opened the gate for the white compact car and closed it again after the vehicle came to a stop under the carport. Before he could help, two women had already emerged from the car.

"Dr. Harris, this is my friend Angela Atwood."

Clayton noticed that Ebony's voice shook and her rose-colored lips trembled. He realized that Ebony's natural almond-shaped eyes were now as round as walnuts.

"Dr. Clayton Harris," Angela crooned; her voice was like velvet. "I must admit it's strange and yet so wonderful to stand in front of a man who, through the miraculous transfer of energy, I seem to know so well already." The fire of the amethyst in Angela's left eye started to build as she took his hand.

He nodded, searching for words. "This vibration…I can only feel it with one other person." He exhaled. "Teeba is waiting for you."

As soon as Angela turned to face the entrance of the house, Teeba appeared in the doorway. The two young women, in what appeared to Clayton to be slow motion, walked toward each other.

"Omigod," Ebony said. "This is supernatural…like a dream." Her voice quivered.

"Sssh," Clayton took her hand. "This is real."

The soft late afternoon breeze ceased and the swaying Queen Anne palms stilled; the leaves on the mesquite trees stopped fluttering. All natural sounds hushed.

Clayton knew Teeba wasn't speaking, yet he could hear her voice.

Twenty-seven years ago, one soul went into two incarnations. Two different physical beings started to share the same reality; two hearts became a direct expression of one soul. Our time flow became synchronized. Energy seeded wisdom and understanding took form so the purpose of our mission would reveal itself in actuality. Together, we are the epitome of oneness—That Which Is Never Lost.

Two flashes of purple fire connected; their combined energy was so powerful that Clayton believed he felt the earth quiver. He sensed that two parts connected and one soul took a journey to where there is no end, only infinity. In its speed of flight, the amethyst fire brilliantly colored the sun and sky in translucent shades of amber, pink, and violet. As the potent flash returned, Clayton saw how the mountain ranges draped themselves in purple robes. Like a waterfall, the color spread over the desert. Slowly, the flash dimmed before it returned to where it had originated. Clayton felt the ground steadying and watched as the sun parted the remaining violet clouds for dominance again.

"Omig…" Ebony stopped before the word even left her throat. "I know I just witnessed the greatest phenomenon," she whispered. "I'm filled with a recognition way beyond anything I've ever known."

Clayton linked his fingers tightly with hers. He saw that she was unable to take her eyes off Teeba and Angela who, in their embrace, appeared to have become one being.

"You saw what I saw, you felt what I felt," Clayton said. "Together, we now understand that prior to our modest way of thinking there existed a pattern—there is a reality that has been guiding us and from now on will direct every one of our thoughts."

Washington, D.C.

...in November

CHAPTER 68

FORD WENT TO the nearest house phone in the lobby of the Watergate Hotel and asked the operator to connect him with Ariel Cohen.

"Ariel, old boy. Welcome to D.C. I'm in the lobby," he boomed.

"Randolph? I've lost track of time and am not quite ready. Please come up."

Ford grinned. Aside from his wife, very few people addressed him by his birth name. Colleagues had conveniently abbreviated it in his early days with the CIA. Even after all those years, it still rang funny to be called Randolph.

Ariel was an agent for Mossad, the Israeli Institute for Intelligence and Special Tasks. Ford met him during the 1970s after Mossad eliminated several Arabs connected with the Black September terrorist group. Since then, they not only exchanged valuable information, but they also had grown to become good friends.

The two men bear-hugged and slapped each other on the back.

"Good to see you, Randolph. You're looking well," The Israeli was lean but as tall as Ford. "Flying through time zones always gets the best of me. I fell asleep as soon as I saw the bed in this room; if it wasn't for you. I'd still be snoring." He spoke English without a trace of an accent.

"I'm glad you rested. How long before you'll be ready? We've got important matters to discuss."

While Ariel took a shower, Ford powered the television just in time to catch the nightly news. He was still staring at the screen when Ariel joined him.

"I heard some people talking about this at the reception when I checked in," Ariel said, buttoning his shirt. "What happened?"

Ford shrugged. "They're saying there's never been an earthquake of this magnitude before in Arizona, yet the National Earthquake Information Center can't confirm any data on the occurrence. Despite severe tremors, nothing registered. Apparently the shocks were only felt in Tucson, which they think was the epicenter."

The two men watched the footage and listened to a few of the many eyewitness reports in the area. All of them gave the same portrayal: while the earth seemed to rumble, people experienced no fear; rather they felt pleasantly paralyzed and calmly captivated from witnessing a natural phenomenon.

"Amazing!" Ariel shook his head. "We're hoping to prevent tragedies that are caused by the misfits of our species, and then there is nature with its unpredictable forces and mindblowing miracles."

"Indeed," Ford replied. His eyes were looking past the screen as if searching for an explanation that would substantiate the strange vision of two faces merging—someone he had met before. He couldn't shake the notion that the mission he was working on, in some bizarre way, was connected to the happenings in Arizona.

"I don't know about you, but I'm starving," Ariel said. "Where should we have a bite to eat before we get serious?"

Ford turned off the television set and rubbed his eyes. "I'm going to show you my new house. Did I tell you that we moved from Bethesda to McLean?"

"When?"

"Just recently," Ford replied. We downsized and I'm within a stone's throw from work. But, if you ask Ginny, she'll say she bought the house because of the state-of-the-art kitchen. By the way, she's cooking your favorite dish."

"Pot roast! I can smell it!" Ariel exclaimed and embraced Virginia Donner. "I've been salivating since the last time you made it for me."

After they sat down at the table, Ginny asked, "Have you heard what's going on in Tucson? I was so fascinated, I almost ruined our dinner."

"Thank heavens you didn't," Ariel laughed.

"Speaking of heavens...the skies over Tucson were like purple velvet. Maybe more like pink satin? I can't even describe the colors," Ginny said. "The whole thing was fantastic and yet frightening with the earth vibrating like that. I had to call my friend in Tucson right away to see if he was okay."

"Who's your friend?" Ford questioned.

"Randolph," she scolded. "You met him at my thirty-fifth high school reunion last year in Albuquerque. Don't you remember?"

"With all those people there, how could I possibly remember?" Ford asked with raised eyebrows.

"You talked to Thomas Prime at great length," she protested. "You even told me how much you enjoyed your conversation with his daughter." Ginny shook her head. "Anyway, I was glad to hear that Thomas is okay. He sounded strangely elated and called whatever happened there a miracle and an awakening."

"Miracles in the Arizona desert?" Ariel laughed. "Like the burning bush or the parting sea? I thought that only happened in our neck of the desert."

"I remember him now." Ford's face lit up, holding a forkful of meat in midair. "Thomas Prime, the produce king. Instead of his wife, he brought his daughter."

"That's right. You talked with her all night," Ginny nodded. "Thank God he brought Teeba instead of his wife. I don't know why he's still married to that monster."

"Teeba Prime," Ford said, and laid the fork with the food down. "I've never met anyone like her before."

CHAPTER 69

AFTER DINNER, VIRGINIA excused herself for a game of bridge with some of her friends in the neighborhood. "Don't be a stranger and come back soon," she said as she hugged Ariel. "The next time I'll make you my killer meatloaf."

"With your special mashed potatoes?"

"Plus the glazed chocolate fudge cake for dessert," she winked. "Everything non-dairy, of course." She kissed him on the cheek.

"Oy gevolt! I'll end up looking like the Michelin man in clothes. You're the best, Ginny."

Ford and Ariel crossed the kitchen and went into the pantry. Behind the shelves was a hidden door leading into the safe room that served as Ford's home office. It was a good-sized, cozy room, equipped with three computers, two telephones, and every technical device he needed in his line of work.

"Cognac, cigar?"

"Some cognac, thanks." Ariel sat down in one of the leather chairs.

"Put your legs on the ottoman; that's what it's for," Ford said as he handed Ariel a brandy snifter. "Make yourself comfortable." Ford sank into a chair and lit a cigar. "You said you have information for me. I can't wait to hear what you have to say. Shoot."

"When you first alerted Mossad we had nothing whatsoever on Al-Saafi. Like you, we directed case officers at our stations around the world to have agents do sneak-and-peek routines. We came up with nothing." Ariel swirled the liquid in his glass and took a sip. He smiled. "Good stuff."

"Don't keep me panting. What'd you find out?"

"Well, two weeks ago, and by total coincidence, one of our moles sniffed out someone interesting at Triple Border."

"Triple Border? We've been monitoring Al-Qaeda over there since 1999 but we had a breakdown in relations with Argentina's intelligence. Our operation didn't pick up steam again until after 9-11." Ford adjusted his weight as if to stand up, but changed his mind and sank deeper into the chair. "We now have a lot of interest there and rediscovered Triple Border all over again. But we've yet to hear anything relating to Al-Saafi."

"Have you ever come across the names Tufan Keshishian or Ramy Ribelli?" Ariel asked. When Ford shook his head, Ariel continued. "Keshishian is the owner of Sultan's Oriental Rug Palace in Los Angeles. But that's just for show; what he doesn't tell is his big-time involvement with various crossover terrorist organizations." He took a breath. "Keshishian is an expert in soliciting. He knows who's got the money and who's willing to support the unified ultimate goal—changing the world to their fanatic beliefs."

Ford stood up. "I knew I wanted to be in intelligence before I was thirteen. I've never regretted that decision." He walked back and forth. "But I can't get used to this kind of war where men hide under the cloak of religion while *hate* is the only faith they ever knew." Ford stopped pacing. "Please go on. I know there's more."

"Much more," admitted Ariel. "But I brought you a gift." He took a disk out of his pocket. "This'll be your bedtime story."

"How'd you know I love to read bedtime stories?" Ford teased. "What about the other guy you mentioned, this Ramy Ribelli?"

"Keshishian has enough money to finance any kind of attack imaginable; Ribelli does the dirty work. Ribelli travels on five different passports, Keshishian travels on even more." The Israeli pointed to the disk. "Everything you need to know is on there, pictures and all." Ariel emptied his glass. "May I have a refill? Once in a while it feels good to numb."

After Ford handed the glass back to his friend, he glanced at the cigar in the ashtray but decided against relighting it. "We'll check out Keshishian and Ribelli." Ford sat down, clasping his long fingers between his knees. "Now, what do you need from me?"

"I'll take whatever you're willing to share on Operation Mayfly," Ariel replied. Squinting his eyes, he added, "I'd also like to know more about the PIGR scientist."

"Dr. Hakan Öztürk?" Ford looked surprised. "We've checked him left and right—he's got a spotless record."

"No offense," Ariel grinned. "But you know us Israelis; we need to check everything. You know we only trust ourselves."

Los Angeles

...in November

Chapter 70

Angela looked at the sprawling city below her as the Boeing 737 took off for Los Angeles. "Good-bye Tucson," she whispered. "Yesterday's occurrence made you famous, but many more extraordinary things are yet to happen." She put on her sunglasses and closed her eyes. Soon the steady hum of the engines lulled her into a welcome, meditative state of mind.

At LAX airport, she spotted Miranda Portal below at the bottom of the escalator.

"I can't thank you enough for coming to Los Angeles." Miranda embraced Angela. "When I made the call I was prepared to meet you in Louisiana."

"I got your message while I was in Tucson and since it's so close, I just booked the flight. It seemed quicker and easier."

"Tucson! The media hasn't stopped talking about it. You were there during that phenomenon, weren't you?"

"I certainly was." Angela smiled.

"No chauffeur today," Miranda explained as they walked toward the car. "I seldom get the opportunity to sneak off on my own. Phil is always so overprotective."

During the twenty-minute ride to the Royal Beverly Hotel, Miranda talked about the damage to their Malibu house caused by recent wildfires. "Phil and I are still deciding whether to rebuild or not. He wants to sell the property; he prefers our home in Montecito." Miranda shrugged. "I still find it necessary to be in LA once a week because of my role as CEO. In the meantime, the hotel keeps me quite comfortable."

They took the elevator to the luxuriously appointed presidential suite where English High Tea was waiting for them on fine china.

"Look at these delicate tea sandwiches," Angela said. "Let's start with this one." She reached for one from the cucumber mint tea variety. She lightly pushed the tray toward Miranda. "How about you?" she asked. "Have one before I eat them all. They're absolutely wonderful."

Miranda shook her head. "Not yet, maybe later. I'm too nervous about why I asked you here."

"You shouldn't be," Angela said and moved closer to Miranda. "I've been expecting your call for some time now." She saw Miranda's bewilderment. "Let me explain," she continued. "We met for a very specific reason; something much bigger than my work involvement with PIGR connects you and me."

"It's..." Miranda hesitated. "My need to speak with you privately has to do with Dr. Hakan Öztürk."

"The reason you wanted to see me is because you're quite concerned about some of Hakan's research."

"So you know already?" Miranda exclaimed. "He's not supposed to talk to anyone about it—it's top secret work." She seemed undecided on how to proceed, but then continued. "I know the two of you have been seeing each other privately, but even so, I'm surprised that he spoke to you about this."

"He hasn't told me anything in words. However, I know about the sinister reason that's behind his research at PIGR."

"Now I'm really lost. If he didn't talk to you about it...how could you possibly know then?"

"As I said earlier, you and I were meant to meet for a reason. I'll help you understand," Angela offered. "At birth you received a special gift. Up until now you've only glanced at the beautiful package without ever trying to unwrap it and see what's inside." Angela took Miranda's hand into hers. "Because time is of the essence, I'm here today to help you open this package and make you discover the gift." She held Miranda's other hand. "Please look into my eyes. I have a lot to tell you."

Tears rolled down Miranda's flushed cheeks. "I was not meant to open that box before today," Miranda mused. "Without you, I would've never understood its significance." She put her arms around Angela. "You opened my third eye and showed me beauty beyond speech and sight and yet…" she pulled away and searched Angela's eyes again, "…and yet there's a dark cloud hovering over this divine symmetry."

"That's life," Angela said. "It's always been this way—I've witnessed it countless times." Her face lit up. "My mission is to try and break up another dark cloud."

"Where do I fit in? I'm not as evolved as you. I understand so little. Do you know the outcome? Do you know how to stop it?"

"No. Even if I knew, I would not be allowed to interfere until all the pieces of the puzzle and the players in the circle have connected. But what I *do* know is that you and I were meant to join hands." Angela smiled assuringly.

Full of emotion, Miranda sighed. "Something doesn't make sense," she said. "Hakan has developed a deadly weapon to be used against mankind, but on the other hand, he's already helped countless others with his arthritis research and might help thousands more once his Lou Gehrig's treatment is approved. His research has stopped Phil's disease from progressing." She shook her head. "Does it make sense for good and evil to be housed in one body?"

"Throughout history, it was brilliant people who caused much devastation—their fear and misguidance turned them blind and deaf to the true importance of life." Angela hugged Miranda tightly. "In time you will understand that old souls keep returning, trying to bring back the balance between the past and the future."

As the hours of the afternoon passed, Angela further opened Miranda's awareness toward the purpose of their mission. Eventually, Angela looked at her watch. "I've only a little more than an hour before I have to leave for the airport."

"No chance you could leave tomorrow? There's so much more I need to know."

"I want to be home with my parents for Turkey Day," Angela said, knowing it would be the last time she would celebrate Thanksgiving with her mother and father.

"Can I have the restaurant prepare something for you before you leave?" Miranda asked when she saw Angela look at the empty tray.

"Food is always a good idea. Let's go downstairs and see what's on the menu."

"No room service? It'll be much more private."

"No." Angela shook her head. "I sense I'm supposed to meet someone—people who are linked to our circle."

Chapter 71

In the van, parked across the street from the Royal Beverly Hotel, Ribelli looked at his watch. "In exactly twenty minutes, go into the bar and hang around long enough so you can get a good look at them," he instructed. "Once you see me leave, follow me into the bathroom. That's where I'll give you further instructions." After a quick check in the mirror, Ribelli flipped back the visor and faced the younger man next to him. "Any questions?"

"Shit, I've never been in a fancy place like this," Christopher said, staring at the hotel. "What if they ask for my ID in the bar?" He looked at Ribelli. "Worse yet, I don't even like alcohol."

"You'll do fine. You look older than eighteen. Show 'em your new driver's license or passport; the perfect fakes I gave you prove you're twenty-two. Act your age and order a fucking drink." Ribelli buttoned his jacket. "I know little boys like you love their milk and chocolate, so slurp on a White Russian or have a chocolate martini," he cackled. "Just keep thinking about the *muchas dolares* that will be coming your way." Before he slammed the door, Ribelli clicked his fingernail against the crystal of his Rolex. "Be on time, *muchacho*!"

Even though they were tucked away in the corner, Ribelli immediately spotted the two men. "Hey, Hector. You're looking great, man," he said, patting the man's shoulder. "Fine leather jacket; wish I had your classy taste." He turned to shake hands with the other man. "Long time no see, Gustavo. What's up?"

For the next twenty minutes the three men conversed quietly in Spanish. Occasionally they nibbled on the nuts and black olives, and separated only once from their huddle to order another round of drinks.

Finally, Ribelli leaned back in his chair. "*Gracias señores,*" he said, raising his glass. "You'll never regret making this deal." Looking sincere while toasting with the two men, Ribelli quietly thought of his plan. *You fuckers won't be able to regret your final deal; you've screwed me long enough,* he thought.

"*Ay carumba,*" Munoz interjected. "*Mira esta mamacita! Que cuepaso.*" He elbowed Damian.

No matter how hard he tried, Gustavo Damian looked disheveled despite dressing only in the finest designer clothes. His dark hair was too long and greasy; his skin was pockmarked and his crooked, stubby nose showed signs of being broken more than once. A razor-thin scar sliced from his right ear to the corner of his mouth and his left jowl was visibly more developed than the right. Despite his fine Armani suit and newly capped teeth, he looked like a bullmastiff in heat.

"*Ay-ay-ay,*" Damian grunted. "*Esta muy buena.*"

Ribelli turned and spotted Christopher, hesitantly standing in the entrance, next to the woman who had activated Munoz and Damian's hunting hormones.

Find a seat already, you useless worm, Ribelli silently urged, and exhaled in relief when he saw Christopher walk toward the bar.

How convenient, Ribelli thought, when the attractive young woman and her female friend took the only other two empty seats next to his innocent young partner. Ribelli knew that either Munoz or Damian would soon make an advance.

CHAPTER 72

CHRISTOPHER HAD NEVER felt so out of place as he did when he stiffly sat on the edge of the chair, staring at the bartender who seemed at great ease despite the crowd that kept him busy.

"What can I get you?" the man asked, only briefly looking up.

Christopher lifted his chin and deepened his voice. "I'll have a beer—Corona Light." He pressed his sweaty palms against the fabric of the only pair of dress pants he owned. Out of the corner of his eye he noticed a pretty woman sitting down next to him. He heard her ask for the bar menu.

After forcing himself to swallow some beer, Christopher scanned the room. He spotted Ribelli in the far corner with two middle-aged men. Christopher felt extremely uncomfortable in this place that was filled with elegance and wealth but, at least he had spotted the two men who soon were to become his targets.

Christopher got lost in thought recalling his first encounter with Ribelli in the garage of the warehouse. The prospect of getting fast and extra cash without his father having knowledge of it had enticed Christopher to follow up with the Argentinean. Originally, Ribelli had said that Christopher only had to drive two drugged subjects to the warehouse. When Ribelli changed the plan, Christopher almost threw in the towel. But when he heard the Argentinean's offer to pay him twenty thousand dollars to help dispose of the bodies, Christopher abated.

Suddenly a magnetic force seemed to turn his head against his will and he found himself looking at the most magnificent woman he had ever seen. He gulped when he saw a purple fire in her eye; his spine straightened as a strange sensation surged through him.

When Teeba's image took hold of his mind, he gasped for air like an asthmatic. Fear gripped his body and he tried to turn his head away, but he remained powerless.

The junction only took seconds, but Christopher felt as if his life's energy was slowly extracted. When he regained control, he found himself gaping at the chiseled silhouette of the woman on his left. His body slackened from sudden exhaustion and perspiration dotted his lip and brow. Did he experience a blackout? He couldn't remember anything. His throat felt dry, as if it were lined with parchment paper. He lifted the glass and in one long gulp emptied the contents.

"Ladies, excuse me, but my friend and I would like to have the pleasure of buying you a glass of champagne," an accented male voice crooned.

Christopher realized the man making a pass at the women next to him was Hector Munoz; Ribelli had described him perfectly. Christopher shifted his weight and scanned the room. He noticed Gustavo Damian approaching and saw Ribelli leaving.

As Christopher paid the tab, he took another look at the two Hispanic men. Slowly he strolled out of the bar toward the men's lounge.

"You were so close, you must've seen the wax buildup in their ears," Ribelli cackled.

Christopher nodded. Ribelli's humor had started to irritate him.

"Okay, here's the deal. Hector's staying at this hotel. For some reason he hasn't checked in yet—says he's waiting for some chick to arrive. I guess she's the one carrying the goods," Ribelli droned while washing his hands. "Stick around the lobby. When you see Hector, follow him and find out his room number." Ribelli checked his teeth in the mirror. "As soon as you know, call my cell and leave the info." Satisfied with his appearance, Ribelli faced Christopher. "Meet me at 11:30. You remember the address of the motel and the room number?"

Christopher nodded again.

"Well muchacho, let's do it then. We only have to endure their stink a little longer. Once you fry the pompous bastards, their stench won't be gone soon enough." Ribelli's cackle bounced off the marble walls. He slapped Christopher on the back. "And tomorrow, my young friend, you'll get your well-deserved reward. Let me know how it feels when you walk around with a big bulge in your pants." He cackled again. "Remember, *muchas dolares* always excite the *mamacitas*."

Left behind in the lounge, Christopher leaned against the cool wall and closed his eyes. *After tomorrow, I'll never have to listen to this asshole again,* he thought, before walking into the hotel lobby to wait for Hector Munoz.

CHAPTER 73

"STUCK-UP BITCHES," Damian slurred. "Who cares anyway? There was only one hot number. The other one..." He pointed his thumbs down.

"I would've loved to taste her. She was *magnifico*. Her eyes..." Munoz mumbled. He yawned. "I don't know why I'm so tired and light-headed. Did I drink that much?" The picture of the woman at the bar flashed in his mind again and his eyelids drooped further. He wondered if it was his imagination or if he actually had seen a purple fire in her eye. Munoz scratched his head. Everything was foggy.

"It's getting late. Do you suppose your other love interest has arrived yet?" Damian's voice brought Munoz back into reality.

He walked to the nearest house phone. "Has Mrs. Gloria Prime checked in yet? Good. Connect me to her room." He needed to pull himself together. He blinked his eyes a few times and slapped his cheeks gently with his left hand.

"Gloria, *mi amor*, you're finally here," he purred, forcing excitement into his voice. "What's the suite number? I'll be up in less than a minute."

"*Bueno*," said Damian. "I'll wait for you in the bar. Try and hurry, we have to be at the motel in one hour."

"Hold the door."

Hearing the voice, Munoz put his foot between the closing elevator doors.

"Thanks."

Munoz looked at a clean-looking young man with a blond crew cut and ice blue eyes.

"What floor?" he asked.

"You've pressed it already; same floor."

Leaving the elevator, Munoz tried to focus on his next encounter. Before he knocked on the door to his suite, he heard a voice coming from behind him. He turned around and saw the young man from the elevator fumbling with the lock.

"Damn! This key card isn't working. Now I've gotta go back down."

Munoz watched the long-legged young man sprint toward the elevator.

He raised his hand to knock at the door again when it opened. Gloria stood there, looking radiant.

"*Mi vida,*" Munoz said as he pressed his torso against hers. "You look absolutely stunning." The low-scooped tight cashmere sweater revealed her firm bosom and when he bent down to kiss the luscious mounds, he thought of two ripe cantaloupes.

"I've missed you so much, mi amor," Gloria whispered. Her breath was hot against his ear and when he felt her fingers against his crotch, he was surprised by his immediate reaction.

"Not now, *loquita,*" he snickered, sounding hoarse. He extracted himself from the embrace. "Unfortunately, I must leave again—but just for a little while. I have a late business meeting." When he saw her disappointed face, he pulled her closer. "You know I'm never interested in quickies. When I make love to you, I want it to last for hours." He ran his tongue over the exposed skin of her breasts. "Where are the cases?" he breathed into her cleavage.

She pointed to the closet behind her.

"*Delicioso.*" Munoz licked his lips. Inside the closet were four Louis Vuitton suitcases. He envisioned the neatly stacked twenty-dollar bills amounting to 250 thousand dollars in each one.

"I myself brought two large pieces of luggage—I've packed more than I needed—but arriving with six expensive pieces made me feel really weird," Gloria said while kissing his neck. "No, actually, it made me feel like a celebrity." Her breath was still hot.

"You're *my* celebrity. And you certainly look like a movie star."

Gloria giggled, snuggling closer. "I assume it's jewelry you brought again in those cases," Gloria said, clinging to him like dead weight. "You promised you'd show me the gems this time so I could take my pick. Can't we do it now?"

"We'll do everything." He wagged his finger. "But you must be patient, little girl." He pulled two of the cases out of the closet, explaining that he needed to show some of the gems to a jewelry wholesaler who was passing through Los Angeles. Before he left, he grabbed her buttocks. "Meanwhile, don't let anyone come near you or the rest of my other precious cargo. Keep the doors locked." He leaned her against the wall and pressed his pelvis hard against her. "I'll be back within two hours," he rasped. Halfway out of the door, he kissed her again and said seductively, "*Prepare te! Te quiero mucho.*"

He actually looked forward to spending the night with Gloria. Even though she was much older than he preferred, he could not deny the sensuality that seeped out of her and gratified his appetite. Ever since he ran into her at the opening of Estrada's in La Jolla, he praised the encounter. After all these years, Gloria not only lusted after him, she also was the perfect cover-up for his ploy. They had met several times since July and on each occasion Gloria obligingly made the hotel reservation in her name and paid with her own credit card. He, of course, always reimbursed her—not only with cash but also with false enthusiasm about their renewed love. She was clueless that she was loved only because she had become Munoz' convenient carrier of illegal goods. The suitcases she brought to the various fancy hotel suites were stuffed with either high-grade heroin or enormous amounts of money.

As the elevator door opened, Munoz stepped into the lobby and grinned like a victorious gladiator. One million dollars would soon change hands and Ribelli in return would deliver twenty kilos of black tar heroin. Munoz had to control his desire to laugh out loud, thinking about the enormous profit. The street value for the twenty kilos would be somewhere around fifteen million dollars.

CHAPTER 74

THE COZY NOOK Motel was located off Sunset Boulevard in West Hollywood. It was one of the cheaper places where desperate young men and women often prostituted themselves for bargain prices.

Ribelli had changed into garish clothes, adorned himself with an equally flashy fedora, and donned sunglasses that would have brought joy to Elton John in his younger years.

The thin man behind the desk in the badly lit reception area pursed his lips when Ribelli pranced toward him.

Ribelli raised his voice and lisped sweetly, "There's a reservation for eight rooms, all next to each other; it was made under the name…Dick Hunter." He pointed into the direction of one of the shorter buildings of the E-shaped motel. "I assume the accommodations over there are still available?"

"I've been waiting for you and your group," the receptionist said. "By the way, I like your name." He smacked his lips. "It's been a slow night—at least until now. Where's the rest of your group?"

"The other gentlemen won't get here until later. They're still partying at the Pony Club." Ribelli smiled sweetly, sugarcoating his words. Then, he paid in cash, twenty-nine dollars for each of the rooms. A basement bargain price for the gigantic payoff, he thought as he took the keys.

He parked his rental car in front of the one-story building where he had rented every room. Then, one by one, he went into each of the seedy rooms, closed the vinyl curtains, and tuned each television set to one of several different pornographic stations. He ripped off the stained bedspreads and messed up the yellowed sheets and pillows. In some rooms he flipped a chair or a lamp; in others he left empty bottles of various brands of alcohol, as well as half-full or crumpled packs of cigarettes, butts, and ashes. He even went as far as leaving used condom boxes, empty vials, and other assorted party paraphernalia.

After he finished messing up the rooms, he went to the last one at the end of the building. Before entering, he removed the light bulb above the door.

Then he waited.

"Is this number 36? The fucking light is out; I can't see," Munoz complained.

"It's gotta be," said Damian as he turned the doorknob.

The two men stepped inside the dark room.

"Hey Ribelli. You here?" Munoz fumbled for the light switch on the wall.

"Maybe we've got the wrong ro...?" Damian sank to his knees from a hard blow.

Munoz turned. "What the..." A blow keeled him over as well.

Ten minutes later the strong smell of ammonia made them cough and open their eyes. They were bound and gagged. Their eyes widened when they saw Ribelli in the dimly lit room.

"*Buenas noches, señores. Cómo están ustedes?*" When he heard them grunt, he wiped the smile off his face and replaced it with a grim look. "Did you believe you could fuck me over again, you bastards?" Ribelli spat at Munoz. "You think I'm stupid, huh? You think I have no idea what I'm really worth?" He kicked Hector in the groin. "Two years I've smuggled the finest *chiva* and *coca* all over the world for you." Ribelli tapped his index finger on his chest. "I was the one who came up with the idea how to hide your shit in Keshishian's imported rugs. While you led *la vida loca,* I was the risk taker." He took a step back. "Did I ever get caught? No! Did I ever leave a suspicious trail behind? No, again! Did you ever show me your appreciation about keeping your fucking names clean? No, no, no!" Ribelli frothed and spat toward Damian. "In me you found your genius. But instead of rewarding me with my well-deserved fair share, you gave me handouts like you would a beggar," Ribelli hissed. "You didn't think I knew that you cheated me out of hundreds of thousands of dollars, did you?" He looked at the two Louis Vuitton cases. "Let me see what you brought me this time."

He found the keys to the luggage in Munoz's pants and unlocked the cases. "Uuui!" Ribelli whistled. "Looks like you did bring half of the *dinero.* Very good! I assume the rest of the money is in your hotel room. I'll get that later."

Two OD green duffle bags sat on the bed. Ribelli opened one and took out a plastic-wrapped kilo of black tar heroin that resembled a huge Tootsie Roll. He sniffed around its edges like a food connoisseur. "Mmmh, this shit is rare, pure, and so very good." He lifted the bag and displayed it like a trophy. "Just think, had you behaved yourselves this would've been all yours." He tossed the plastic pouch back into the duffle bag. "Instead, it's good old Ramy now who's in the possession of twenty keys of chiva. You guys have been in the business long enough to know how much this'll be worth. From now on, Ramy is no longer the mule…I'm the man!" Laughter shook his whole body when he heard their guttural, unarticulated sounds that could have been curses.

"What? I can't hear you. Speak louder," he cackled and forcefully kicked each man in the groin again.

"Oh, but before you'll rot in hell, let me send you two hard-ass motherfuckers one more time to heaven." He reached into the side pocket of one of the stuffed bags and took out two syringes. "I've prepared a very special cocktail for you." Ribelli grimaced when he saw Munoz's angry expression turn into pale horror as he writhed vehemently in the chair.

"This'll make you feel really, really good, *patron,*" Ribelli said and then jammed the needle into Munoz's vein. "I knew you'd love it," he cackled and pinched Munoz's cheek. Ribelli turned to Damian. "Don't worry, scarface, I haven't forgotten about you."

He hoped they would not die when he was through with them. After all, his gruesome plan of execution was not over. He looked at the listless bodies and spat at them one more time.

At exactly 11:30 there was a knock on the door.

"Ready?" Christopher asked.

"Yeah. Let's get them into the van."

"Holyshitthey'restillalive." Christopher jumped back.

"Calm down."

"I can't cremate them alive!"

"Why not? They're as good as dead. They're nodding out—even the heat won't wake them," Ribelli cackled.

Once the two drugged-out men were thrown into the back of the van, Ribelli returned to the motel room and removed any possible evidence of his presence. With a satisfied grunt he carried the two Louis Vuitton suitcases and duffle bags out of the dingy motel room. He was extremely pleased with himself. Knowing that for the next few hours Christopher would be in charge at Browne's Funeral Homes, Ribelli relaxed and dozed off in the car.

CHAPTER 75

WHILE MUNOZ'S 178-pound body was being reduced to several pounds of bone fragments and ashes by the intense heat and flames, Gloria woke up feeling scared.

The awful nightmare still immobilized her and she stared into the room without seeing anything. She tried to convince herself that it was only a figment of her imagination, but the ghostly illusion of her lover lying in a pool of blood, crying out for Teeba—the daughter he had never seen—still was much too vivid in Gloria's head. She looked at the digital clock radio and froze. It was almost two o'clock in the morning; Munoz still had not returned.

What if he was in an accident? Recalling her dream, she started to worry. She saw him lying in the pool of blood again.

Despite the hour, she poured herself a glass of champagne. "Please not an accident," she whispered. "But why is he so late? Maybe he's with another woman?" Gloria stopped in front a mirror. "What shall I do? Where will I begin to look for him?" she asked, staring at her reflective twin, dressed in the latest seductive ensemble from Frederick's of Hollywood. Her mind began to play havoc with her emotions. Tidbits and flashes from her past mixed with the present. She longed for the long-gone days of teenage passion in Culican, but cringed at the memory of Munoz's cool reaction when she spoke of her desire to be with him forever.

Gloria was beginning to feel trapped, but her gaze fell on the open closet and the two locked remaining cases with the LV initials. Her pounding heart slowed down. "He'll be back," she said to her mirror image. "If not for me, he'll be back for his other precious cargo."

Three soft knocks at the door startled her.

"Hector?" Even though she knew it had to be him, she remembered his warning to be aware of intruders.

"Mi amor." The male voice was muffled. "It's me, Hector."

As soon as she unlocked the door, she was slammed against the wall. The pain made her cry out, but a strong hand stifled the scream.

"Be quiet and nothing is going to happen to you," rasped the stranger in Spanish as he pulled a blindfold over her eyes and snapped handcuffs on her wrists. "Where's the rest of the dinero?"

"You knew Hector's name. What happened to him? Where is he?" Gloria demanded. Despite her fear, she tried to sound strong.

"Hector? He went on a lo-o-ong journey," the voice cackled as hands pushed her against the wall again. "Where's the dinero?"

"What money? I don't know what you're talking ab…" The blow to her face came unexpectedly and she doubled over. "I don't understand," she sobbed. Panic filled every cell of her body.

"Listen carefully, bitch. If you value your life, you better tell me now." Gloria felt something sharp against her throat.

"I swear, I don't know of any money." She sensed drool running down her chin, but her throat was dry. It pained her to swallow. "He only brought four cases with jewelry," she sputtered. Then, she began to shiver uncontrollably.

The man threw her on the bed and attached the handcuffs to the bedposts. Sprawled helplessly on the sheets, Gloria realized that her skimpy lingerie now revealed every intimate spot that she'd meant to be seen only by Hector. But in her situation, she did not care. Her whole body convulsed.

She heard the man wrestle the cases out of the closet.

"*Fantástico!* This is a better sight than the bitch on the bed," the voice cackled.

After a while, the broken laughter and rustling sounds stopped. Without warning, Gloria felt putrid breath near her mouth. "Tonight I looked at a million pretty green pieces, but I must admit I can't resist a piece of you!"

During the next two hours her body became a playground for Ribelli. Gloria, after unwillingly having her first encounter with heroin, was turned into a helpless sex object whose occasional screams were silenced by Ribelli's various body parts. Eventually a cloth gag was put into her mouth.

Stripped, drugged, and discarded, Gloria did not hear Ribelli when he left at six o'clock on the rainy November morning. She could not see that he looked like a respectable hotel guest. Clad in Munoz's tan Burberry with a hat pulled low into his face to protect him from the rain, he rolled his luggage through the lobby and fetched a taxi.

The unsuspecting uniformed housekeeper screamed and almost passed out after entering the suite on the ninth floor at nine o'clock in the morning.

CHAPTER 76

"FOR THE NINETY-ninth time, I'm telling you that I didn't know the man. He broke in here, doped me up, and brutally raped me," Gloria cried. Her pale face was streaked with mascara, her long black hair dull and messy; some strands were knotted together by a sticky substance. She still shivered even though someone earlier had dressed her in a thick, clean white robe. Somebody handed her another Styrofoam cup with steaming coffee as she sat hunched in the chair like a heap of bad luck, looking ten years older than the night before.

"So, you checked into the hotel all by yourself a day before Thanksgiving. No family?" The BHPD detective queried.

"No, my husband doesn't know I'm here. He and I have recently separated. My daughter and I don't talk." Despite the horror of the situation, Gloria already was growing impatient. "I came here," she glared at the man across from her, "to rest and spend a few days by myself."

"Well," Detective Bart Moody probed, "the hotel telephone records show you received a call last night at 9:30. Who called?"

"A childhood friend. He was here on business and came up to my room for ten minutes to say hello. Then he left again."

"Could it have been he that came back and did this to you?"

"God no!" Gloria again wondered about Hector's whereabouts. Her desire to be with him had turned into doubt. Since he abandoned her once before, she struggled with the idea that he was capable of doing it again. She wiped tears with the back of her hand and sniffled. "All I remember about the intruder was that he was short and stout. He wore a dark hat and ridiculous sunglasses. I was beaten, blindfolded, and handcuffed right away."

"It would be helpful and in your own interest if we could question your friend who visited you. What's his name and address?"

Gloria's chest rose and fell fast under the thick fabric of the robe. "I'm sorry. I don't know where he's at." She shook her head. "Even if I knew, I couldn't tell you. He's a happily married man and...and his wife has always been jealous of his friendship with me. I...I just can't do that." She wasn't sure if her hasty response was plausible, but was relieved when the detective moved to the next question.

"According to the valet, he brought up six pieces of luggage. Only two are left in this room." Moody raised his eyebrows.

"The beast that molested me must have taken the others. How would I know? I was unconscious."

"Mrs. Prime," Moody's voice softened. "I realize you've been through a lot in the past ten hours, but in order for me to help you, you must help me first. May I ask you what was in the cases that would make your attacker want them?"

"Only my unpacked clothes and some other personal belongings," Gloria sobbed and thought quickly. "I packed a lot of stuff because I wasn't sure if I ever would go back to my husband," she lied. "We had a big fight—that's why I left home."

"I'm sorry to hear that, Mrs. Prime." Moody walked to the closet where he picked up a dark duffle bag. "We found this in the closet. Does it belong to you?"

"No-o-o," she scowled.

He sat the bag next to Gloria and unzipped it. He took out a plastic bag. "You wouldn't happen to know how this heroin got here, would you?"

Gloria shrugged. "I've never seen this duffle bag before in my life. And I wouldn't know heroin from a pound of chocolate."

"Well, it's just strange that an alleged rapist and thief prefers to take two suitcases full of women's clothes when he could've bought a fleet of Hummers from the proceeds of this heroin." Moody winked at the other detective in the room. "Unless, of course, he happens to be a cross-dresser."

"The stupid duffle bag was not here before. Why don't you dust if for fingerprints? You'll find out that mine won't be on it," Gloria snapped. She put the Styrofoam cup down and stood up. "When will I be able to clean myself from this nightmare? I need to shower now," she demanded.

The detective ignored her demand. "Then how do you explain your flight tags from Tucson to LA on this bag?" He held up an airline ticket and a wallet. "These items were in the bag as well—they're yours."

"What?" Her shrill voice made the other detective in the suite spin around. "That's impossible!" Her mind worked feverishly. "I was drugged—someone's trying to frame me."

"I'm afraid you'll have to come with us for further questioning, Mrs. Prime."

"No!" In a sudden outburst of hysteria, Gloria grabbed Moody and pounded on his chest.

"I've nothing to do with this bag. I was beaten, drugged, and raped. I'm in need of medical help and you're trying to arrest me?" Her knees turned jellylike and she sank to the floor. "I want to make a call. Please!"

With shaky hands she dialed the number. She did not expect *him* to answer the phone.

"Oscar? It's Gloria." She tried to steady her voice. "I have to speak with Nadine, please."

"She's working at the animal shelter, Gloria. She's out for the day," Oscar's deep voice resounded through the receiver.

Gloria could feel her mind tick like a time bomb. "Oscar? Did Naddie tell you about my problems with Thomas and Teeba?"

"Yes, sort of. Why?" Oscar sounded uncomfortable. "Thomas is a good friend of mine. I would rather have you discuss your marital problems with a lawyer than with us."

"Oscar, listen to me. I don't want to talk about my marital problems. I need your help right now." Gloria spoke softly. She had always been good in fabricating stories; she knew that this time she had to be better than ever before. In a fast whisper she shared her plight and embellished the mental abuse by her husband and daughter, hoping the BHPD detectives would not hear her.

"I was so distraught, Oscar. I ran away for a few days and checked into the Royal Beverly Hotel to get away from everything." In a continued low voice she told him of the intruder, underlining each short phrase with sobs. "Someone framed me with this bag of heroin and now the police want to take me in. They're even talking about FBI involvement!" She added a quiver to her already desperate voice. "I know you have a lot of influential connections here in LA, Oscar. You must do something right away. Please."

What a horrible story, Gloria," Oscar Miller said. "Look, I truly want to help you, but I can't do anything until you call and tell your husband."

"Never!" She regretted that she blurted the word out too quickly and harshly; she softened her tone again. "It's over between Thomas and me...we're finished. Don't you understand?"

"But you're still married to him—plus he's my friend. I can only be comfortable in helping you once he's aware of what's going on." There was a pause again. "Why don't I call Thomas and explain the situation," he offered. "Together we'll figure out the fastest and best way to get you back home."

"Oscar, do not call Thomas," Gloria hissed. "Either you'll help me now or I'll make sure your and Nadine's reputation won't be so pure and lily-white anymore."

"Excuse me?" Oscar Miller sounded baffled.

"You heard me! I happen to know *your* dirty little secret."

"And what might that be?"

"How about incest, Oscar? How about marrying your baby sister?"

There was silence on the other end.

Gloria's confidence grew. "Well, how about it, Oscar? You gonna help me now or not?"

"So you sniffed around in very private quarters and found Naddie's diary while you were a guest in our home in La Jolla. Unbelievable." He paused and breathed hard. "You...Pathetic... Stupid...Woman!"

Gloria glared at the wall in front of her. "You better watch your language and think fast, Oscar."

"Let me give it to you plainly in my language then. I'm my father's son and Nadine is her mother's daughter. My father married her mother when Nadine was two years old. There's no blood relation whatsoever." Before he hung up the phone, he said, "May God have mercy on you."

LAFAYETTE

…in December

Chapter 77

Christmas Day fell on a Friday, making it a long holiday weekend for most of the workforce in the country. At PIGR, many of the employees would leave early on Thursday, either to finish last-minute shopping or rush home to their families.

Hakan did not celebrate Christmas, but felt privileged to be invited to the Governor's Mansion for their family celebration. What excited him most was to be close to Angela; he had not seen her in almost two weeks. He knew that being near her would take his mind off difficult matters at PIGR; she would make him feel better.

As he cleaned up his desk, he welcomed the idea of being able to focus on something more pleasant. Work morale had sunk to a new low. He wanted to hold only the thought of the upcoming evening, yet could not help but recall recent developments.

After Al-Saafi's secretive human experiments were finalized in the Los Angeles warehouse lab, Barsoukov and Putin volunteered to receive the vaccine against MAX 18. Afshor, still hesitant despite the accomplishments, only agreed to be vaccinated after the two Russians showed no side-effects.

The three official vaccinations to be performed on PIGR volunteers were loudly protested by Miranda Portal, but under the pressure from her husband and Ford, she reluctantly agreed to them. Each one of the three vaccinations was monitored, documented, and witnessed by Miranda, Phillip, and Ford.

Everything had been going as planned until Farouk al-Fatah, in yet another disguise, appeared in Lafayette for an unexpected one-on-one meeting with Hakan; he hadn't felt well since.

Two new operatives of Al-Saafi had been killed in a small hotel room in Moscow, the Saudi had told Hakan. The new cells had made several distress phone calls to which one housekeeper, the hotel manager, and a physician responded. All of them died of the same mysterious symptoms within eighteen hours. The Russian investigators hushed up the incident, but sources close to al-Fatah detected an eerie resemblance to the peculiarities of MAX 18.

"How could that be?" Hakan had asked. "The way these people in Moscow died could've only been caused by the aerosol form of MAX 18. Only I and my three assistants have knowledge of the components or access to the substance."

"What about our test lab in LA? They've used the aerosol form."

"Yes, they did, but I personally gave it in precisely measured, very small amounts to the two scientists. They barely had enough for their own experiments; there's no way they could have given some of it to anyone else." Hakan then reminded al-Fatah that MAX 18 was self-limiting and that the aerosol would dissipate as soon as the area was exposed to fresh air for a short period of time.

"Is it possible the LA scientists produced their own?"

"Impossible!" Hakan objected. "It was a long and tedious process for us to develop the aerosol here at PIGR. Nobody could reverse-engineer and reformulate the aerosol in the short time they had available for the tests in the warehouse."

"Then the production must have taken place here in Lafayette."

Like al-Fatah's words had wounded him, he stared at the Saudi in disbelief. "You're not accusing me, I hope. I also put my hand into the fire to rule out Afshor because he's not capable of plotting anything of this magnitude on his own." Hakan shook his head. "If additional production took place here in Lafayette, then it had to be done by Putin and Barsoukov." He frowned. "Why?"

"Because of money," al-Fatah replied matter of factly. "The deceased Al-Saafi cells in Moscow most likely were not targets; we have reason to believe they might have accidentally released MAX 18. It has come to our attention that, without our knowledge, they were planning something on their own."

"I don't understand."

"They were newly recruited operatives in training. They tried to use us for their own greedy motive; they were parasites, not worthy to be part of our pure cause. Allah justified their death," al-Fatah said.

Reflecting on the incident in Moscow, Hakan turned angrier. It had become quite clear to him that his colleagues at PIGR were double-crossers, working strictly for their own interests. Hakan decided that the only thing to justify Putin and Barsoukov's audacity would be death. Hakan hoped al-Fatah would act soon and arrange their permanent disappearance.

Hakan's cell phone buzzed, indicating that he had a message waiting. He immediately recognized the accented voice that spoke in English.

"Hakan! It's me, your old friend Feroz. I bet you're surprised." Laughter. *"Listen! I'm in Metairie visiting my cousin Majeed al-Siddi. If you're not busy, you must spend the day with us tomorrow because I have to leave and attend an important business meeting on the twenty-sixth. Come for breakfast. This way we'll have all day together and you can see the whole family. They're equally anxious to see and talk with you. No need to call me back; you would never get through. Majeed only has one phone line and his children are on the phone all day."* More laughter. *"I must finish now. See you on Saturday, my friend."*

Hakan moaned. He listened to the message two more times, taking notes. The call was a coded message from al-Fatah; Feroz was one of his many aliases.

According to the message, Hakan was to meet al-Fatah at the Al Nur Mosque in Metairie on Christmas Day to discuss a matter that was to be carried out on December 26. Hakan was to appear early because other members of Al-Saafi would be present and many things needed to be discussed. He was warned not to make any incriminating phone calls because U.S. officials were actively intercepting phone conversations. "*I must finish now*" stood for "I now have a date for termination."

Hakan felt his stomach twisting and searched for another antacid in his trouser pocket. With weak knees he walked into the bathroom and found a bottle of Tums. He drank some water and swooshed it around his mouth to get rid of the taste.

Things were going to happen fast now—perhaps too fast for him. If al-Fatah eliminated Putin and Barsoukov, Hakan worried not only about the reaction from the Portals and Ford, but also feared possible confrontation with local authorities. Hakan desperately hoped that al-Fatah's plan was foolproof.

"Everything is going to change drastically when Al-Saafi makes its first big statement by killing the delegation of traveling U.S. officials with MAX 18," he muttered to himself and shivered, feeling feverish.

Nobody knows you're the creator of the virus, he heard an inner voice say. *As soon as the first MAX 18 attack is executed, everybody will turn to you for help. You're the inventor of the vaccine. Everyone will be concerned about the country's utmost priority: to protect the president of the United States and his administration.*

Hakan straightened and looked at his flushed face in the mirror. "You're right," he said. "I'll have to be convincing. I'll have to give my best performance. I alone hold the trump cards when the surgeon general will recommend protection against MAX 18 for the current administration." He opened a bottle of aspirin, took three, and drank more water.

That's right, the inner voice said. *But instead of saving them, you'll kill them all.*

Hakan shuddered as he stared at his pale face. He pointed the finger at himself. "You are chosen to do this great task. Only *you* are capable of switching the vaccine with the actual virus of MAX 18."

Despite the reassurance, Hakan felt weak. He leaned his hot forehead against the mirror and closed his eyes. He knew that as soon as the fatal symptoms became evident, he would be on a private plane to South America where he was to receive a new face and identity. Soon after, he would set foot onto Iranian soil again, where the wife he never loved and the grown children he never cared to know had been waiting for him for many years.

His wristwatch alarm reminded him he was expected at the Governor's Mansion. He looked at the tormented face in the mirror. "Why," he cried, "did I have to meet Angela and learn about true love and pleasure, kindness and charity?"

Fool, the inner voice screamed. *Allah alone represents true love and offers you pleasure. Don't let the infidels and their brainwashing techniques mislead you.*

"Stop," Hakan cried, banging his fist against his chest. "Why do you keep testing me? Why did you show me this other side of life? What if I weaken?"

Baton Rouge

...in December

Chapter 78

THERE WERE FEWER people around the dinner table than in previous years. Age and health reasons kept Governor Atwood's father and mother in Palm Springs. And Chantal's parents, former U.S. President Paul Pearson, and his wife, Christine, were stranded in their Maine home; all airports in the East were closed because of a severe winter storm.

Ella, who originally had planned to spend the holidays in Tucson with Ebony, had at the last minute decided to stay in Baton Rouge.

When Governor Atwood lifted his glass and proposed a toast, Angela saw how Ella's gaze took in the Atwood family, but as soon as her eyes moved to Hakan, the happiness drained from her face. Aware that Ella's senses detected evil spirits all around him, Angela smiled her understanding toward her old friend.

Keeping the tradition, Angela had prepared the meal. A pumpkin soup preceded the fennel, spinach, and watercress salad with pecans. The entrée was a crisp, golden roast goose stuffed with apples and onions, accompanied by wild rice with roasted chestnuts and cranberries.

Hakan folded his napkin and took Angela's hand. "How delicious," he said. "But I'm not surprised. Everything you do is perfect." He air-kissed her hand before he bowed toward the Governor and Chantal. "Thank you for including me in your family tradition."

For a moment there was silence at the table. Then, Governor Atwood took a deep breath. "I was going to wait until tomorrow—

still hoping that it'll stop snowing in the East so Grandpa and Grandma Pearson can hear what I'm dying to share," he boomed. Winking at his wife and daughter he continued. "But I'm bursting at the seams—not only from stuffing myself with these superb dishes, but more so from a phone call I received earlier this morning."

"Well, looking at your face, it must be very important," Chantal said.

"The president called and invited us to ring in the New Year at Camp David. It'll be just our two families—very intimate."

Chantal clapped her hands together. "How exciting, darling. It's been years since I've been to Camp David," she beamed. "I know you and the president are good friends, but this comes so unexpectedly. Any special reason?"

"Mmmh, let me guess," Angela cut in, mimicking concentration. "Since this is the president's second term, might it be that he asked the Governor of Louisiana to run for the presidency of the United States?"

Governor Atwood grinned from ear to ear. "Well, after talking with him this morning, you've once again hit the nail right on the head, Angela."

"Darling! How dare you you keep this from me all day long?" Chantal complained with a smile on her face.

Angela rejoiced in her parents' elation, but her heart ached when she felt a strong vibration coming from Hakan. She slowly turned her face toward him; she would only need a second to read his thoughts.

While Hakan seemed to be listening with interest at the exchange of information, Angela could feel him cringe at every word that was spoken. She sensed the mixed messages and troubling emotions that rummaged through his brain, some trying to alter his deadly course while others warned him to defy his newfound *joie de vivre.*

She saw him sitting at the festive table, applauding the hopeful future of her family, while his dark side laughingly mocked their naïveté.

She knew that six months earlier Al-Saafi's goals were Hakan's prime ambition. But as soon as he met her, his ideals were interrupted. Despite the inner turmoil and confusion Angela was causing him, she was well aware he was preprogrammed to proceed with the hellish plan.

They don't know you'll be the terminator, Angela heard Hakan's inner voice hiss. *Judgment Day will soon put an end to anybody involved in the Jewish conspiracy to dominate the world. Glory to* Dar al-Islam, *Glory to...*

His thought pattern suddenly stopped. Angela knew her purple radiance had caused Hakan to lose focus. She saw him rub his eyes, attempting to wipe away the powerful glow.

Unaware of his daughter's extraction, Governor Atwood broke the momentary stillness. "I don't know though. The country might be ready for a younger president. I'll be sixty in three years."

Angela turned away from Hakan to face her father. "This nation will continue to encounter many challenges; it will be in need of a great leader. With your famous diplomacy you'll make a wonderful president, a much beloved one," she said.

"Listen to you," the governor laughed. "Who is giving you that guarantee, my smart beauty?"

"The angels," Ella whispered into her napkin. "The angels are telling her everything."

Chantal looked at her daughter. "You're coming with us to Camp David, darlin', won't you?"

"Of course, Mama. I wouldn't miss it."

"Will you be joining us as her escort, Dr. Öztürk?"

"No!" Angela cut in. "He already has made other plans."

Hakan, still in a daze, looked at Angela in surprise. "What plans?" he asked, still blinking rapidly.

Angela let the fire of the amethyst pierce him again. She needed to cause his mind to go blank, his body to feel fatigued.

"I'm sorry for leaving so soon, but I feel rather exhausted—I worked long hours lately," Hakan stammered shortly after.

His face was flushed when he leaned his cheek against Angela's cool skin. "When will I see you again?" he rasped into her ear.

"I'll call you," she said as she watched him walk slowly toward the waiting limousine.

"I wasn't going to do this again, but I've never been more certain why I have the ability to erase people's memory or extract their thoughts," she whispered as the car pulled away. "Even though it pains my physical being—I have a mission to accomplish. You are my mission, my destiny."

CHAPTER 79

"WHAT WAS THAT all about?" Chantal asked when Angela returned to the table. "Have you grown tired of Dr. Öztürk?" She moved closer to her daughter. "Forgive me for interfering but I've been trying to understand your fascination with him. You two are so different, darlin'."

"It's not fascination, Mama. It's a form of gravity that pulled me toward him for reasons quite different from love and affection. I was the one who seduced him. I had to do it because I know him to be my fate." She caressed her mother with her gaze. "There's a divine justification behind everything that happens in life, Mama."

"That man should've never been born—there's a malignancy all 'round him," Ella grumbled behind gritted teeth.

"Oh Ella, don't be angry," Angela said. "Try to listen to the forces of the universe—they direct the world of action." She shook her head. "I'm not making excuses for Hakan, but unfortunate circumstances threw him off balance in his early life. He was never taught how to see, what to hear, or when to feel. He could never develop the pure good that all of us are given at birth."

"The man had enough drive in him to become a famous scientist. He used his brain about all kinds of good stuff," Ella said. "Why did he choose to forget about his true self and purpose?"

"Hakan is only one of many throughout history who ceased to remember who they are. Because of people like him, there has been and there'll always be unrest in this world," Angela responded.

"I know, I know," Ella admitted. "I've learned so much from you and I'm still tryin' to learn, but I'm havin' trouble dealin' with folks who are hateful and evil."

"Unfortunately, as long as people hate, there will be violence."

Ella forced a smile. "What's unfortunate is that only a few chosen folks understand the true depth of this; I'm afraid I'm not one of 'em," she sighed. "You're one of the few, Angel; you've made me see farther, hear better, and feel stronger. You're my teacher."

"What are you two talking about?" Chantal asked.

Angela sat on the floor in front of her parents. She took one of each of their hands into hers. "You both know that I've always been different," she said. "But I was born into this family for a very specific reason and only in the past six months has that true purpose revealed itself."

"I know you were born with a gift that has nothing to do with inherited genes," Chantal said after a long pause. "I've known it for twenty-seven years, but I'm still asking myself where it came from, always looking for an explanation."

"I can see awesome possibilities—events that have not been actualized yet. I am what you would call a visionary."

"Angela." Chantal cupped her daughter's face with her hands. "We've never talked about this before, but your father and I have long understood that we're not in your league. We realize we might never comprehend the actual guiding principle of it all, but we're prepared to listen to whatever you're willing to share." She pressed her lips against Angela's forehead. "We're ready now, but please be patient with us."

Angela slowly began to talk about their circle of life and the roles of the people in it. She described the ultimate goal of teaching life's true potential, the understanding of love and hope.

She defined how every lifetime had strengthened her power and wisdom and explained how true growth took place between physical lives. She unfolded the advancements of being able to lose fear of the unknown, thus understanding infinity.

Angela chronicled her own life since birth and the reason behind the loss of her twin sister. She told of Ebony Laveau crossing paths with Teeba Prime in a hospital room in Tucson. She untangled the phenomenon that took place when Angela and

Teeba's physical incarnations met for the first time in the beauty of the Sonoran Desert.

It was that night when Angela revealed the secret of her old soul.

McLean

...in December

CHAPTER 80

FORD STOOD IN the doorway next to his wife and waved to his children and grandchildren as the cars pulled out of the driveway. Virginia Donner inisted on exchanging gifts on Christmas Eve; it was their long-standing tradition.

"What a great night," Ford said, and drew his wife closer. "I'm a lucky man."

"Let's go back inside. It's cold out here." Virginia pulled her husband into the warmth of the now-quiet house and locked the door. "We're all lucky to have each other," she smiled, looking up at him.

"Need any help?" Ford asked as she started to put the dishes away.

"No, silly!" she teased. "For the past couple of hours you've been aching to hole up in your office. You can't fool me. I've been watching you." She gave him a gentle push into the direction of the safe room. "Nothing serious, I hope."

He kissed her on the forehead. "Nothing for you to worry about."

He secured the door behind him and lit a cigar. He took a disk out of an envelope, inserted it into the computer, and began to read. An hour later he glanced at his watch and calculated the early morning hour in Israel. He dialed the fourteen-digit number on the secure phone line.

"Randolph? I can't believe it! I just had the strongest urge to call *you*," Ariel exclaimed. "The only thing that stopped me was respect for your holiday and the late hour."

"Thanks. You're a better person than I am. Did I ever hesitate to interrupt you in the midst of your high holidays?"

"Hey, what are friends for?" The Mossad agent laughed. "Can't wait to hear why you're calling me."

Ford leaned back into the chair. "Because of your pointers, I've made great progress." He added that he was sending coded information via the Internet and briefed the Israeli on how to decode the text.

"In the meantime," Ford continued, "let me tell you that due to your tip on Keshishian, we've been able to uncover a whole slew of possible connections."

"Connections to Al-Saafi, I assume?"

"Yes indeedy. Just like Al-Qaeda, Al-Saafi has countless cells and like bad flies they seem to be in every country, including both of ours." He exhaled the cigar smoke. "Since you told me of Keshishian's aliases, we've been able to follow his every step. We recently spotted him in Teheran with someone very interesting."

"And who might that be?"

"None other than Farouk al-Fatah."

"I hope you're not pulling my pisser. We lost track of him years ago. We thought he was either dead or slowly wasting away in some remote cave."

"Well…he hid all right after vanishing with large amounts of Al-Qaeda's money," Ford grunted. "We think he holed up in secluded hunting lodges near the Pakistani border that once belonged to the Shah. Wherever he was, he took his time and only resurfaced after transforming into a chameleon."

"Double damn him!"

"He became so good in disguising himself that he managed to blend in with any Joe Sixpack on our soil. I'm sure he'd even go unnoticed sitting next to a Benny Bagel in your country."

"I get the picture," Ariel snickered. "No matter how serious the issue, food always seems to be on your mind."

"Kidding aside. Just when I thought we were on al-Fatah's heels, we lost him," Ford admitted. "But I'm confident we're gonna get our hands on the bastard real soon. I can't wait for him to lead us to the drones of Al-Saafi."

"What about Keshishian? Do you have enough evidence to grab that parasite and squeeze the juice out of him?"

"Yes and no. Currently we're in an 'After you, Gaston' routine with the FBI."

"How's that?"

"You told me about Keshishian's errand boy, Ramy Ribelli. Turns out the FBI was already on his tail for drug trafficking. It seems he used Keshishian's rugs for smuggling huge amounts of coke and heroin."

"And where is Ribelli now?"

"Gone with the wind." Ford sighed. "At least for the moment." Typing commands into the computer, he watched as the picture of Ribelli and Christopher appeared on the screen.

Ford told Ariel of the FBI involvement in a drug-related arrest at the Royal Beverly Hotel in Los Angeles and explained that the apprehended woman broke down after several days of interrogation. "She ended up singing like a nightingale and her song revealed the names of her lover and his associate; both of them wanted drug lords who mysteriously disappeared."

"I assume you're going to tell me names that I know."

"Before I tell you, I have to marvel at coincidences and remind myself that we live in a very small world," Ford said. "The raped and beaten woman—her name is Gloria Prime—happens to be the estranged wife of a good friend of my wife's from Tucson."

"No shit! I actually remember you guys talking about her the night I had dinner in your house."

"Yep. From what I understand, she wasn't a very nice person, but whatever happened to her in that hotel room, it seems she was framed by someone and is unable to identify the intruder." Ford paused and took a breath. "And here's where it gets exciting. We got a match from the fingerprints on the planted duffle bag in the hotel room. We also got a match from the sperm swab they took from Gloria Prime for DNA." Ford purposely stopped and waited.

"Okay, Randolph. I give up. Who's the match?"

"None other than Ramy Ribelli." Ford described how, after showing pictures of Ribelli to the hotel personnel, one of the doormen had no problem remembering the Argentinean.

"The doorman remembers seeing Ribelli with a younger man earlier that night in a parked van across from the hotel," Ford said.

"The doorman prided himself for having an eye for suspicious characters and took down the license plate number. We later traced it to Peter Hines, a used car dealer and member of the Order of American Aryans."

Ford also told the Israeli what first was believed to be an unrelated report. "A citizen on Pico Avenue kept calling the police department about a suspicious van that, with weekend regularity in the middle of the night, pulled up behind Browne's Funeral Homes. Two men unloaded what looked like body bags. Turns out the owner of the funeral business is a member of the OAA, and the license plate of the van checked out the same as the one recalled by the Regent Beverley Wilshire doorman," Ford said.

"I have the feeling that's not all; there must be more."

"Further investigation led us to a young college student by the name of Christopher Snow, who was noticed in the bar of the Royal Beverly Hotel the night of Gloria Prime's rape. A housekeeper insisted she saw the young, clean-looking blond man running down the hallway of the ninth floor toward the elevator on that night. And a member of the bar staff recalled serving drinks to Ribelli and the now missing drug lords." Ford stopped to take a breath. "Last but not least, Christopher Snow, as well as his father, are also OAA adherents," Ford said. "Whether it's related or not, would you believe that young Christopher was a student of Teeba Prime, the daughter of the woman who got raped?"

"That's going full circle," Ariel said. "But why do I get the feeling that you think there's a connection between Al-Saafi and the OAA?"

"I don't know. It's one of my gut feelings again," Ford grumbled. "Anyway, the FBI is going to follow up on Snow in Tucson and we were given authority to concentrate on some folks in the OAA."

For a moment—just like the ocean that separated them—silence interspaced the two men.

"You're always right when it comes to your gut feelings, and I've had my share of good luck when it comes to my strong hunches. But, I've not found anything on Dr. Hakan Öztürk—at least not yet," Ariel finally said. "Strangely enough, I was briefed today on something that should be of great interest to you, unless you're ahead of me already."

"I've said all I know."

"My man in Moscow got wind of five recent and rather uncanny deaths in a hotel. The Russian doctors are still in the dark about what these people died of, but from what I've learned, the symptoms are definitely those of MAX 18."

"What?" Ford scooted forward in his chair. "MAX 18? That's almost impossible. There's been no chatter and there's been no warning or threat from Al-Saafi. Nor have there been any claims. Who the heck were the targets and why didn't *we* learn of this?"

"You're right. So far, no organization has claimed responsibility," Ariel said. "The two dead men were Russians; we suspect they were Al-Saafi cells that caused their own deaths accidentally. The other three were hotel employees—the first ones to enter the room. The autopsies all revealed that the virus entered through the respiratory tracts. But whoever came in touch with the bodies later did not catch the virus. It appears MAX 18 was airborne but did not survive for long."

"Are you thinking aerosol?" Ford asked. "I know the only ones capable of developing the aerosol form of MAX 18 are the PIGR scientists."

"Well either somebody is much brighter than your famous Turkish academic believes possible or..." Ariel swallowed the rest of the sentence. "I know you've done a thorough background check on the PIGR scientists involved in Operation Mayfly, but might I suggest concentrating on Putin and Barsoukov again? It wouldn't surprise me if you found a few overlooked glitches in their past."

"Ariel, don't do this to me. What else do you have?"

In three short sentences the Mossad agent restated his suspicions.

"Your gut feeling smells rotten! Anything fishier than that can only be found in rusty old cans of sardines," Ford said. "If this proves true, I'm not sure the Portals are gonna be able to digest this foul piece of evidence."

"Do me a favor. When you bring this to the attention of the Portals and their PIGR scientists, I'd be interested to hear about Dr. Öztürk's reaction."

TUCSON

...in December

CHAPTER 81

TEEBA AND CLAYTON Harris had dedicated the week of winter break to sharing their good fortunes with needy people of all ages. One of the smaller warehouses at Prime Produce was emptied and decorated for the holiday season, encompassing people of any religion and belief. For eight days, from eleven in the morning until seven in the evening, they fed the needy at a sumptuous buffet. The Agave High School Chorus enticed everybody to partake in a sing-along. Elderly volunteers sat in overstuffed chairs and read stories to young children, while others initiated games. People who stepped through the door with uncertainty in their eyes left with smiles on their faces and with gifts in their hands. The adults received generous food packages from Prime Produce and each child was given a toy and clothing.

After Teeba first spoke of the idea to her husband and father in October, the word spread fast. Ebony became Teeba's most enthusiastic co-organizer. Nadine, Sugie, and Teeba's student Yasmine became a tight-knit, hardworking team. The big corps of other volunteers ranged from Agave High School students to women and men from Tucson's social register. Thomas Prime and Oscar Miller funded the entire production.

On the last day of December, Nadine and Oscar hosted an open house for all the volunteers. Among the last few people to leave were Sugie with her new husband, Dr. Abraham Levi, and their two children.

Timothy had grown since May, not only in inches but in his mental progress too, which astounded most people in the field of autism. Abraham's handicapped daughter Mandy also showed significant improvement under Teeba's care in the special ed program.

"Please stay a while longer," Nadine begged the remaining four guests after the Levis left. "I haven't had a chance to talk to any of you."

"Okay, but only for a little while," Thomas agreed and sank into a comfortable chair. He looked at his daughter, son-in-law, and Ebony. "I don't know about you young folks, but I'm exhausted."

"So am I," agreed Clayton, "but it's a wonderful exhaustion. I feel so fulfilled being able to bring a little happiness into so many people's lives."

"We must do this every year." Nadine chimed in. "Perhaps even twice a year. We don't need a holiday season—this kind of charity is worthy of our effort any time."

"Then we should do it," Oscar said matter-of-factly. He sealed his promise with a kiss on his wife's cheek. "Count me in."

The discussion that followed livened up Thomas's spirits, but he saw his daughter was quiet. "What's the matter, sweetheart? Are you all right?"

Teeba nodded. Her dark eyes glistened, yet her face radiated serene symmetry. "I'm well, Dad. My thoughts were about you."

"Why, honey? You're not worried about me, are you?"

Nadine stopped the animated conversation she was having with the others and turned.

"I couldn't help but hear," she apologized to Thomas. "However, I've been worried about you as well—you're not the same ever since…"

"Ever since Gloria left me? Is that what you're saying?" Thomas inhaled sharply and nodded. "You're right, I haven't been the same. I may be more quiet, but I certainly feel better than in many years." He looked at his daughter. "You must know how I feel. After all, you know me better than I do myself."

Oscar was the last to sit down. "You're my best friend, Tom. I hope you don't mind my saying so, but it was time for you to rid yourself of that accursed woman." He turned to Teeba. "I'm sorry, honey, but I had to get this off my chest."

"It's okay, Oscar. It's time for all of us to air our minds," Teeba agreed. "As a matter of fact, I'd like to be the first one to speak." She looked at everyone, her eyes radiating warmth. "My mother never wanted me and tried everything possible to kill the baby in her womb, but there was a purpose for my coming into this world. No matter how many times Gloria attempted to abort, she had no control over the power of nature."

"She fooled us all, didn't she?" Nadine shook her head. "How could I've been so blind? All these years I thought of you as a happy family."

"My father and I *were* very happy," Teeba said.

Thomas straightened in the chair. But before he began to speak, tears rolled down his cheeks. He reached out for his daughter. "You've read my inner thoughts countless times. It wouldn't surprise me if you already know what I'm about to say, but I need to disclose what should've been done many years ago."

"The rest of us can leave," Ebony offered. "This sounds very personal."

Thomas waved his hand. "No, please stay. I'd like all of you to hear this." He took a deep breath before he continued. "Because of an illness during my adolescence, I knew I would never be able to father children. When Gloria agreed to marry me, I didn't have the guts to tell her. I really loved her and didn't want to lose her." He paused and swallowed. "And then, less than two months after the wedding, she told me I was going to be a father." Thomas smiled through his tears. "As in many other instances, Gloria never came forward with the truth, but I've always known that I'm not Teeba's biological father."

Silence followed Thomas's disclosure. Like a long overdue rain, washing the dirt of the roads, the stillness in the room felt cleansing and refreshing.

Teeba's gentle voice broke the quiet. "But you were the one meant to be my father. Without you in my life, the order of events to happen could not have taken place." Being aware that her father and the Millers were unable to fully grasp her higher purpose of life, Teeba chose her words carefully and described in detail the miracle of her existence. She gave examples of why each person in the room had become an integral part of her life. She defined why events first needed to happen for others to receive justice. She revealed the guiding principle behind the connection to her soul sister in New Orleans.

"Once the circle is ready to close, our mission is done," she concluded.

"But the circle isn't closing yet, is it?" Thomas asked.

Teeba saw the concern in his face and stroked his hand. "There'll be many years before your mission is finished."

"I'm overwhelmed." Oscar's deep voice cracked with emotion. "If I perceived everything correctly then Nadine and I were drawn into this circle by Gloria." He shuddered. "Could anything have changed her? Couldn't you have changed her and made her see?" he asked Teeba.

"I only have visions for what I was meant to foresee. With that capability I can try to halt a possible disaster. But there are things I have no control over; I'm unable to cure a sick person."

Thomas wiped his eyes again. "I know you can't, honey. But you began healing me from the moment you were put into my arms. You've grounded me all my life while I seemed to be unable to make your mother see the miracle she had given birth to," he said, his voice filled with passion. "Because I blindfolded myself all these years, I couldn't protect you from Gloria's evil ways."

"What you gave me surpassed all the dreadful things she's ever done to me, Dad. "Ultimately, it's unconditional love that counts—and that's what you gave me over and over again."

Thomas smiled through his tears. "Thank you," he whispered. "Your words again are like a beautiful melody."

"I really shouldn't care...but does anyone know what happened to Gloria?" Nadine asked.

Thomas nodded. "During the interrogation in Los Angeles, Gloria broke down. I don't know the details, but it's no secret that this summer she hooked up with a man from her past—Teeba's biological father. His name is Hector Munoz."

"That's unbelievable," Nadine cried, her eyes as round as saucers. "I've met that man through Gloria in La Jolla. He dealt in fine jewelry; he gave me his card."

Thomas shook his head. "Hector's a big drug dealer, Naddie. Nobody knows what happened to him; he disappeared after Gloria's arrest." Thomas took a deep breath. "Anyway," he continued, "when Gloria was cleared of the charges in Los Angeles, she didn't come back to Tucson. The embarrassment was too much for her. I've shipped her belongings and wired her fair share of the business to an address in New Mexico." He tilted his head to the side and shrugged. "And yet, after all she's put us through, I do feel sorry for her. She's wasted what could've been a wonderful life."

Lafayette

...in January

CHAPTER 82

HAKAN LOOKED PALE as he darted toward the laboratory building. The separate PIGR structure had not only been created for his official research, but also for the Operation Mayfly secret project. In the small foyer he tried to steady his shaky hand before he punched in seven letters. A red light flashed and a robotic female voice pronounced that the password was incorrect. Confused, he stared at the blinking red dot before realizing he had used yesterday's password. Nervously he fumbled for his Palm Pilot and, after keying in commands, found the security clearance for the day.

He rushed toward his office, only to stop in front of the door, trying to remember his own new code. He cursed himself in Farsi and closed his eyes. He tried to take a deep breath, but instead, his inhales were quick and choppy. Fearing hyperventilation, he sensed every pulsating fiber of his body. His head buzzed as if under attack from a swarm of Africanized bees. He leaned against the wall and began to pant.

"*Mon Dieu!* Hakan, are you all right?" Afshor's high-pitched voice spoke in French. "You look as if you ran a marathon through a million nightmares."

"I gave you the code to my lab earlier—punch it in," Hakan ordered weakly in Farsi. He disliked whenever his assistant took on his French personality.

Hakan teetered toward the bathroom and pulled the door shut behind him. He fumbled for the extra rolls of toilet paper in the cabinet and extracted a hidden jar of Xanax. He rarely resorted to medication of any kind, but the developments of the past week had changed his aversion into an addiction.

He swallowed the pill and immediately drank a second glass of water. He splashed his face until he sensed it cooling down and stared at his pale, drawn image. He put a few drops of Visine in each of his eyes and with still unsteady hands combed his unruly hair.

There was a knock. "Are you okay?" This time Afshor spoke in Farsi.

Hakan opened the door. "Can you brew a cup of my tea? It'll make me feel better."

"We don't have much time. I'm sure they're waiting for us already. Okay if I put the tea in a large Styrofoam cup to go?"

Hakan nodded while unlocking the Fire King file cabinet. He removed three thick folders, put them in a briefcase, and sat down at his desk. He sighed with relief as he felt the first calming wave from the Xanax.

"Ready?" Afshor stuck his head through the door, holding the Styrofoam cup high. He watched as Hakan took careful sips from the steaming maroon-colored liquid.

They drove in one of PIGR's golf carts to the main building, signed in at the reception desk and, after passing various ID scanners, took a private elevator to a small conference room on the top floor.

"You look like a sick dog," Ford said as he shook Hakan's hand.

"I've had better days," Hakan muttered and shot Ford an irritated look.

Miranda rose from behind the table. "My husband could not make the trip. He'll be joining us in a few minutes." She pointed at the screen. "He's very disturbed about the recent developments." She peered above her round reading glasses at the two scientists and added, "Needless to say, so am I."

"You think we've been celebrating?" Afshor sneered, his French accent stronger than usual. "We've been through hell and back trying to figure out how any of this could have happened."

"Sorry I'm late," another man apologized as he stepped into the room. "A long distance call…" he pointed at his tiny cell phone.

"No problem," Ford assured him and patted the man on the back. "Dr. Afshor and Dr. Öztürk just arrived as well." He faced the two scientists. "May I introduce Ariel Cohen, my friend and colleague from Mossad in Israel?"

Both Hakan and Afshor visibly stiffened.

"Agent Cohen was the first to find out about the MAX 18 attack on the two men in Russia," Ford explained. "With Miranda and Phillip Portal's permission, it was decided to let Mr. Cohen in on future developments."

Hakan cringed. He hoped his and Afshor's objectionable reaction wasn't noticed by anyone.

"In case you don't know," Ford continued, "most intelligence agencies around the world work closely, especially when it comes to international terrorism. Ariel and I have enjoyed a long working relationship."

Hakan exchanged a quick glance with his assistant. He could tell Afshor was as appalled as he; neither of them expected sitting next to a Jew at this meeting.

"I think Phil is ready to join us," Miranda said, and clicked a button.

"Miranda, gentlemen..." the soft voice was heard before Phillip Portal's face appeared on the screen.

"Let's talk about the latest, most devastating development first—the unfortunate deaths of Drs. Barsoukov and Putin," Miranda began. "Ford and I had a long meeting with the local police earlier. We found out they still don't know the cause of the explosion. So far, all evidence points to the possibility of a faulty gas line. Once they clear away the rubble from the apartment complex, they hope to get to the bottom of it." She shook her head and sighed. "With two more women dying today, twelve people now have lost their lives and several are still in critical condition."

"Tragic," Hakan said.

"Tragic indeed," echoed Afshor.

"Who notified Putin's and Barsoukov's families?" Hakan asked with a grave expression on his face.

"Miranda and I called Dr. Putin's ex-wife. She gave us the phone numbers of their children in Moscow." Phillip spoke from the screen. "As you know, Dr. Barsoukov wasn't married, but we were able to reach his parents in St. Petersburg."

"And PIGR already has established memorial funds for Dr. Barsoukov and Dr. Putin. Their families in Russia will be well taken care of," Miranda added.

"When did you see your colleagues last?" Ford asked, turning to face the two scientists. "The accident occurred on a weekday afternoon. From what I understand, they never before left PIGR that early; they usually worked quite late into the evening, isn't that right?"

Afshor looked at Hakan and shrugged. "I didn't see them at all that day. I was preoccupied in the BL 3 Biocontainment facility and did not leave until after nine o'clock in the evening." He spoke hurriedly and his eyes shifted fast from one person in the room to the next. "I was waiting for them the next morning to go over some data, but they never showed up."

Hakan nodded. "I had a meeting with Ivan and Yuri around noon. Afterwards they went back to their lab and I worked on my computer for the rest of the afternoon. When I left—it must've been around seven—I noticed their cars were gone. I didn't think anything of it." He spoke slowly, blessing the calming effect of the medication. But he didn't notice that his right foot was rapidly tapping the carpet. Ignoring the Israeli, Hakan looked at Miranda and then at Ford. "Dr. Afshor and I both gave our statements to the police as soon as we were informed of what happened."

"I'm aware of that," Ford grumbled as he rubbed his ear. "I'm just puzzled by the fact that both of them left early and went home—it's so unlike their routine." Addressing both Hakan and Afshor, he asked, "Since you're the only people who got to know them better than anyone else in this country, did they ever mention any personal contacts?"

Afshor shook his head. "No," he said quickly. "They never talked to me about anything other than our scientific projects."

"I don't recall any dialogue of that sort either," Hakan added. His mouth had gone dry and his tongue felt heavy as lead. He took the Styrofoam cup and drank the rest of the now-cold tea. "They never spoke about their personal affairs—they seemed to live only for their work," he lied.

"They were of the Islamic faith, just like you," Ariel said, smiling thinly. "Did you gentlemen ever attend prayer sessions at a mosque together? Would you know of any other acquaintances your colleagues may have made within your religious group?"

"None!" Hakan had trouble looking at the Israeli. "The four of us barely had time to finish our research every day. I can't speak for Dr. Afshor or Drs. Putin and Barsoukov, but for the past year I was only able to observe my religion by praying in the privacy of my surroundings." He lifted the cup to his mouth again and let the last drop of tea roll onto his dry tongue. "May I have some water, please?" He now was aware of his right leg shaking below the table and tried to will a halt to the movement.

Miranda dangled her reading glasses in front of her and turned to Ford. "Even though the local authorities are focusing on a faulty gas line, you earlier implied the explosion might not have been an accident."

"We can't rule anything out. After all, Putin and Barsoukov worked on a highly secretive project and had knowledge of sensitive information."

"So sensitive, it might be quite desirable to the wrong people," Ariel said, looking at Hakan. Then, the Israeli made eye contact with everybody in the room in turn. "As you and only a few select people know, MAX 18 recently killed five people in Moscow." Ariel let the words hang in the air for effect. "It could prove coincidental, but we can't rule out the possibility of a connection to Putin and Barsoukov here in Lafayette. They had the knowledge and they had the access to…"

"Boolshiiitt!" Afshor interrupted. He ignored Ariel and pointed a trembling finger at Ford. "You told us yesterday that the dead men in Russia were connected to a terrorist group. Trying to hook Ivan and Yuri into that scheme is like saying the Pope was the mastermind behind 9-11." He let out a short, arrogant laugh and slapped his hand on the table. "It's idiotic! It's perverse!"

"Calm down, Dr. Afshor." Phillip said. "PIGR's reputation is at stake here. We're dealing with a vicious virus—we can't rule anything out."

"What's your view on this, Dr. Öztürk?" Miranda's gray eyes gave Hakan goose bumps. He experienced a strange feeling of déjà-vu as cold sweat began to coat his face.

"I think...I believe...I have..." he stopped himself, realizing that he could not connect his thoughts.

"Are you all right?" Miranda asked.

"I...eh...I'm fine." He swallowed and rearranged his strategy. "I'm just troubled by Mr. Cohen's insinuation of a possible connection between my team to whatever took place in Russia." Experiencing the feeling of cotton balls in his mouth again, he drank more water. "Isn't it still feasible something other than MAX 18 killed those men?" Hakan warned himself to calm down. "As of yesterday nobody was 100 percent sure."

"We are now," replied Ariel. "The phone call I received just before I came into this meeting confirmed our suspicion."

"And zat iiis vot?" Afshor jeered.

"It was the aerosol form of MAX 18 that killed the people in Moscow."

"Impossible!" Hakan protested.

Ariel shook his head. "Not anymore," he said. "MAX 18 was cleverly hidden in two cans of men's shaving cream; a Russian brand I never heard of. The autopsies on the two terrorists revealed a large amount of alcohol in both of their systems. One guy in his drunken stupor apparently grabbed the wrong can to shave." The Israeli paused. "For a change, my country got spared a lot of possible casualties."

"Why's that, Ariel?" Ford asked.

"The two Russian terrorists were booked on separate flights for Tel Aviv the very next day. We have reason to believe they were on a suicide mission to release the aerosol on the planes," the Mossad agent said. "Thank God, it didn't come to that. Both flights were overbooked. Hundreds of people would've died of MAX 18."

CHAPTER 83

IT WAS PAST seven o'clock in the evening when Hakan returned home. He immediately went to the bathroom and turned on the shower. After washing off the day's exertion, he felt somewhat better, but knew more stress lay ahead. He put on a fresh change of clothes, ate a hastily made cheese sandwich, and brewed his favorite tea. His mind kept racing.

The three-bedroom apartment on Surrey Street was nicely furnished, but Hakan rarely noticed his living area. The rare hours he was at home were either spent working in a room converted to an office or catching five or six hours of sleep in his bedroom. The third bedroom was purposely left unfurnished; even the closet was void of any contents.

He looked at his watch. It was almost eight o'clock. He raised the volume on the classical music station, then carried two kitchen chairs and a small tray table into the empty room. With the lights off, he stood behind the half-closed blinds and peered into the well-lit parking lot three stories below.

Five minutes later, a light gray Mitsubishi Lancer pulled into one of the stalls marked "For Residents Only." A stout man, wearing blue jeans and a dark sports jacket, emerged from the vehicle. The man opened the trunk and took out a saxophone case. After closing the trunk and locking the doors, he proceeded toward the back entrance of the building.

Lost in thought, Hakan remained by the window and stared into the night. He recalled that at the beginning of the month, a entertainment agency out of New York City had rented a two-bedroom apartment in the building for their visiting clients—

musicians who were featured artists at a local jazz establishment. The fictitious New York agency paid one year's rent in advance.

A soft knock made Hakan rush to the front door. Dead-bolting the entrance door, he silently motioned his guest toward the empty bedroom.

Hakan gently closed the door of the spare room. He was pleased that the well-illuminated parking lot below provided sufficient light in the otherwise dark space. He could not help an involuntary smirk as he studied al-Fatah's latest identity.

"It's amazing," Hakan said in a hushed voice. "You really manage to look like an eccentric musician with your fake gray beard and ponytail."

The Saudi ignored the compliment. "When was the last time this place was swept?"

"Six weeks ago. Don't you remember, it was you who made the arrangement," Hakan said. "This room has been bare to the bone since I moved in here. Hard to put a device anywhere—we're safe."

"I've burned my tongue before while eating soup—one can never be too cautious. Remember that," al-Fatah warned. "Afshor already told me about the Mossad agent. Tell me more about the meeting."

"All of them, especially the Jew, grilled us about Putin and Barsoukov's private lives. I think we handled the situation as well as we could." Hakan shuddered. "I don't like what is happening. To be honest, I was very nervous today and felt like a sheep separated from its flock, surrounded by a bunch of snarling wolves ready to devour me."

Al-Fatah frowned. "I don't like to hear that you're nervous. You must at all times feel in control; if you look nervous, you'll look guilty like a thief wearing feathers on his head." He leaned forward. Flecks of gold flickered in his warning brown eyes. "Everything from now on depends on *you*."

"I know." Hakan squirmed. "I was hoping the explosion in Putin and Barsoukov's apartment building would be treated as an unfortunate accident. Instead, everybody now has become even more suspicious because these other careless snakes in Moscow died of MAX 18." Hakan began to gnaw on the inside of his lower lip. "What will happen if the hounds in the intelligence agencies find proof to connect the deaths in Moscow to Putin and Barsoukov?"

"They soon will forget about your dead colleagues and turn their attention to more important matters."

"Why is that?"

"Listen carefully. Toward the end of this month, a U.S. human rights delegation under the tutelage of the Reverend Jamal Keene is headed for a Middle Eastern trip. Their first stop is Iran." The Saudi leaned back into the hard chair and smacked his lips. "Their accommodations will be in the guest quarters of a palatial mansion in Niavaran." He cracked a smile. "You might remember the estate; a long time ago it used to belong to your traitorous uncle. It's been government property since we rid ourselves of the Shah."

"Niavaran?" Hakan repeated. "It's on the North side of Teheran, I believe. I vaguely remember. My father despised the uncle and my mother was forbidden to see her brother. Sometimes, though, she disobeyed and took me along." More thoughts from his disturbing early childhood flashed through his mind. The pain made him flinch as the memories ripped open some old scars.

Al-Fatah smirked. "The six Americans in the human rights group will perish in that house. They will die from the aerosol form of MAX 18 of which, thanks to you, my ingenious friend, we now have plenty. For the first time, Al-Saafi will not only claim responsibility—Al-Saafi also will indicate its next move."

Hakan held his breath as he visualized the ramifications.

"Extreme safety concerns will become of great importance in this country. With certainty, the surgeon general will stop objecting to the immunization program for top government officials." Al-Fatah stood up and pointed at Hakan. "That will be your moment—the juncture you have been waiting for. The dogs will beg you to save their lives and you will be given the pleasure to feed them; little will they know, they'll never bark again. When death stops their howling from pain and agony, chaos will already have taken over. The world of infidels will finally collapse from the foul stench of the whimpering animals' last breaths." Al-Fatah extended his arms. With his eyes closed and his voice building, he looked and sounded like an evangelist preacher. "We will have freed ourselves! Our efforts and sacrifices then will be rewarded by

Allah. We will watch the faithless turn into believers and our pure and beautiful caravan will expand throughout the Western world and go on and on and on."

NEW ORLEANS

...in January

CHAPTER 84

THE MOMENT MIRANDA and Phillip Portal were briefed by Ford on the MAX 18-related deaths in Moscow they initiated the meeting in Lafayette. Later that day, Miranda called Angela and accepted the invitation to spend the night at the Atwood house in the Garden District of New Orleans.

Sitting in the comfortable surroundings of Angela's home, Miranda told her about the cause of concern the latest parley at PIGR had stirred in her. "Hakan was calm and controlled throughout the meeting. He almost looked drugged, but I could tell he was nervous. He became visibly upset when Phil announced that the two Russian scientists will be replaced by two capable, highly regarded virology experts," she said.

"I could hear the tension in his voice when he called me just before you arrived tonight. He said he experienced a very difficult day from a challenging meeting but never mentioned your presence."

"It's good that he's not aware of our friendship."

"I assume the replacements for Drs. Putin and Barsoukov are to manufacture more of the vaccine?" Angela asked. "Who are these new scientists?"

"Two years ago, we successfully lured them away from top research facilities. Dr. Sidney Meister joined us from Israel and Dr. Victor Weizman from Illinois." Miranda lowered her voice. "Hakan was in obvious distress when he was told today about the replacements. I know he would've preferred to pick his own staff again, but we had to move fast. PIGR needs to be ahead of the game and prepared for what's to come."

Miranda was quiet for a moment. "Because of you I learned about the wisdom of my soul," she finally said. "I'm still experimenting with the discovery of this gift, but already it gave me peace of mind where the future of my family is concerned."

She spoke of her distress over her husband's illness and the paranoia she experienced about her children's safety. "With all the money that we have, I could not buy inner peace until I met you. I now can see the brighter light and am able to sense vibrations of comfort. It almost seems as if someone whispers words of wisdom into my ear."

"Isn't it awesome to know that in one lifetime one can make a major leap?" Angela asked. "You're one of the few selected who was ready for this kind of advancement."

"I keep thinking, though, with all your incredible insight and with the power of foresight, why can't you stop Hakan and whoever else is involved before things get worse?"

"Everything, no matter how ugly or beautiful, happens for a reason." The purple brightness began to flicker in Angela's eye. "Wherever we look, right here on this planet or anywhere in the universe, fundamental elements collide; one cause is busy producing and another is threatening to destroy."

"Is that the reason why even you can't interrupt the process?"

"You know the answer to that question."

Miranda nodded. "You're not allowed to exercise control over the most supreme principle of all things," she said. Then, a shadow of sadness moved across her face. "I've been so happy ever since I met you, but already I feel the threat of your destruction and it hurts that..." she sighed without finishing.

Angela smiled. "Maybe I can ease your pain by letting you in on a beautiful secret." She moved closer. "While this circle is still open, I'll need your help. But when the circle closes, my part of the soul will be sealed with its other part to start anew in the world to come."

Los Angeles

...in January

Chapter 85

Christopher grinned as he raced the used 1995 metallic gray BMW 325i convertible toward Santa Monica. Without the help of Peter Hines, the fellow OAA member and used car dealer, Christopher would have never been able to get hold of such a find.

His father protested when he became aware of the purchase of a luxury vehicle. "I don't care what kind of a deal Hines gave you. You're spending frivolously. Every one of your hard-earned pennies should be put in the bank to grow," Snow had scolded, clueless about the amount of money Christopher had received from Ribelli.

"Double-fucking son-of-a-bitch," Christopher swore. His smile disappeared as he thought of his father's deceit. "I'll never believe that cheap bastard again. For a few lousy dollars, he made me live in the dirt, dig the filth off the streets, and risk my future by delivering those stinking guinea pigs. Mr. Wannabe-Big-Shot-Snow is nothing but a fat liar, paying me shit for the disposal of disgusting bodies. While he pretends to be clean and honest, he stuffs his own pockets with mega bucks behind everybody's backs."

Christopher hit the brakes and came to a screeching halt in front of a red light. "He lied to me all my life, that double-crossing loser," he sneered. "After all these years, he suddenly wants to be my father, but now I know what Gary-fucking-Snow is all about." Christopher honked the horn at a slow-moving truck in front of him. "He'd better watch out, because I'm onto him and his picture-perfect, boring little family."

Finally able to pass the truck, Christopher allowed his thoughts to shift to more recent pleasantries. Aside from the car, he also had purchased furniture, a computer, and a brand new wardrobe, keeping his father in the dark about these acquisitions. "It feels really good returning the favor of deceit," he said, knowing his old man also was unaware of his son's exciting double love life. Christopher was still going out with Eva Browne, but only for the sake of securing his job at Browne's Funeral Homes and for keeping up the image in front of the rest of the OAA members. Eva meant nothing to him any more. As a matter of fact, she was beginning to drive him crazy. "Why does she call me twenty times a day, crying like a neglected bitch in heat?" he asked, slowing down as he neared his destination. "And then, when I do pay attention to prissy Ms. Eve, she attaches herself to my body like a wet rag." He shuddered, remembering their last time together.

He parked the car, closed the convertible top, and locked the door. As he approached the small house near the beach, he could see his true love interest through the open windows. His heart began to pump faster.

Zoë Wagner was not only what Christopher called the-hottest-to-drop-dead-for-gorgeous-chick-I-ever-went-out-with, she also came from an extremely affluent family. She was two years older and already in her senior year, but Christopher knew she fell for him the moment they locked eyes after a basketball game. He liked the fact that she was older and more mature, but even more enticing was the fact that she'd abandoned a three-year steady relationship because of him. She had definitely been the aggressor, and he made love to her the first night they went out on a date. It was by far the best sex Christopher envisioned possible. And when Zoë told him afterwards how turned on she was by his good looks and muscular physique, he daydreamed of a future with her.

He walked toward the house Zoë's father had purchased for her use while she was attending USC. When he saw her skimpily clad body leaning against the glass door, he felt a stirring in his groin. Without saying a word, he pulled her close and began to rape her mouth. He knew she loved it and welcomed her gasps and grunts. When she ripped his pants open, he lifted her off the ground and carried her bronzed body to a nearby soft sofa. While her legs wrapped around his waist, he briefly fluttered his fingers over her already hardened nipples and teasingly flicked his tongue in places that made Zoë scream for mercy.

Christopher forgot about the open doors and the possibility that their performance might be visible to anyone on the otherwise quiet street. He felt strong, powerful, and infallible. Like a conqueror, he not only triumphed in the joust of the highly stimulating maneuver of sex, but he also felt like Croesus, sure that the road to his future was now paved in gold.

Christopher didn't realize he had become careless in his new life. He not only was convinced he'd gotten away with the attempted murder of his brother, but he also was certain he'd successfully outsmarted everyone by participating in the recent murders of undesirable individuals and, by now, considered himself to be above the law. But had Christopher looked over his shoulder as he used to, he might have noticed the same dark blue Chevy that had been tailing him for the past five days.

CHAPTER 86

WHILE HIS SON was still frolicking with Zoë, Gary Snow was busy saying goodbye and shaking hands with his comrades after their three-hour assembly. The January OAA meeting had lasted longer because of the detailed planning for the upcoming yearly big celebration on April 20th, Adolf Hitler's birthday.

"I'm starving," said Browne, "I need beer and Wiener schnitzel. What about you?"

Snow looked at his watch. "It's late. I told Paula and the kids I'd be home around nine."

"Call her and say the meeting is still going on," Browne suggested. "Speaking of your kids, where was Chris tonight?"

Snow frowned. "Something at the university must've come up. He wasn't home when I called and reminded him of tonight's important assembly. Christopher knows I want him to get involved in some of the planning for four-twenty." Snow wagged his finger. "He better have a damn good excuse for not being here."

"I'm sure he does," Browne said. "He's always on time for work and often stays longer than necessary—unless..."

"Unless what?"

"Well, sometimes I tell him to leave early because of Eva," Browne admitted, grinning widely. "There isn't a day lately that my daughter doesn't complain about my working your son too hard. She blames me that she doesn't get to see him."

"Do you suppose he's with Eva tonight?"

"Wouldn't surprise me; they're crazy about each other."

"Okay," Snow acquiesced. "I'm gonna call Paula and tell her I'll be late. Why don't you ask the new guy to join us for dinner? He earlier expressed an interest to get together; he sounds like an interesting fella." As Snow dialed his home number, he watched Browne approach a tall, light-haired man in his mid-forties.

Thirty minutes later the three OAA members walked into the Golden Ox, a German-American Restaurant and Biergarten. The owner warmly greeted Snow and Browne, who were steady patrons, then welcomed their guest in German after being told the nice-looking stranger was a *Landsmann.* The small group placed themselves at the *Stammtisch,* the table reserved for regulars.

"So Manfred," said Browne after they were served a round of beer and had ordered, "let me properly welcome you to Los Angeles." He lifted his glass and toasted the newcomer.

"Please call me Manny," said Manfred Gruber. "Even in Bavaria they call me Manny these days."

"Your English is flawless." Snow said. "You don't even have a trace of an accent, unlike a good friend of mine." He recalled the sharp voice of Dr. Gottfried Geist.

Manny shrugged. "I've majored in languages—just have a natural knack for it, I guess. Who's your German friend? If he's another OAA member, I'd like to meet him."

"Eh…no…eh…he's not really a friend. I…eh…I've had some business dealings with him recently. I think he went back to Germany already."

"Are you talking about Dr. Geist, the…?" Browne choked on the question when Snow's foot kicked him in the shin under the table.

Snow looked relieved when he saw the waiter. "Ah, here comes our soup," he said. He waited until Manny was served. "Wait until you taste this. Bet you can't find liver dumpling soup like this anywhere—not even in Munich."

"You're right, it's delicious," Manny agreed and took a crisp bread roll from the basket.

Manfred Gruber, as he had been known for the past month, before had lived under the identity of Gabriel Penña. Prior to that, he was identified as François Dumont and John Caspar, just to name a few of his many aliases. His real name was James Deaner, an undercover FBI agent. His superiors, due to recent developments, had started to work closely with the CIA, mainly with Ford.

Tucson

...in February

CHAPTER 87

AS THEY DID every morning, Teeba and Clayton woke before six o'clock and, like every morning, found themselves in each other's arms.

"Less than two months," Clayton's deep voice was still sleepy. He ran his palm over Teeba's round belly. "I'm counting the days."

Teeba snuggled her face closer into his chest. She did not say anything; the intimacy of every moment with Clayton was too precious; she was aware there were but few left.

She watched his hands move from her belly to her breasts and then felt them tracing every vertebrae of her spine, caressing her thighs and sliding beneath her hips, lifting her closer to him.

"I love you," Clayton breathed. "I do love you with every fiber of my body. Your vital essence nourishes my soul."

Later, when he was preparing fresh grapefruit juice and Teeba was setting the small breakfast table, a thought interrupted him. "I don't know why, but lately I think more and more of Angela. It's a strange vibration I can't explain." He looked at Teeba. "I need you to help me understand once again."

"Angela and I—or rather the two parts of our one soul—are getting closer as our mission will soon be completed," Teeba answered. "I feel her vibrations stronger every day, almost as if our physical bodies are next to each other and we breathe the same air."

"It frightens me when you talk about the completion of your mission," Clayton said, handing Teeba a glass of the freshly squeezed juice. "You've told me that I'm part of your mission, but I still don't feel the purpose."

Teeba smiled. "Your part is bigger than you can imagine."

"Share with me what you know," Clayton pleaded and pulled her onto his lap.

"I don't have all the answers; you know that. But I do feel the ebb and flow of timeless knowledge. And throughout my continuous learning process I have advanced to distinguish between good and evil."

"Doesn't everybody see the difference between good and evil?" Clayton asked. "The question remains: Why allow evil?"

Teeba shrugged. "I don't know everything in the universal spectrum of divine knowledge," she admitted. "I've learned to wait until the information is made available to me." She kissed his forehead. "You, too, must be patient and give time a chance."

They sat in silence holding onto each other but were disturbed by the ringing of the telephone.

"Oh, that's Ebony." Clayton lifted his wife off his lap and stood up. He stopped and looked at her in surprise. "Did I just say that?" He shook his head. "Ridiculous. How could I possibly know it is Ebony?"

"You're sharpening your senses; you're now able to feel the vibration when somebody else is having a thought similar to your own," Teeba explained. "Ebony and you must be on each other's mind."

CHAPTER 88

ABOUT MID-MORNING, one of Agave High School's office workers stepped into Teeba's tenth-grade class.

"Sorry to interrupt, but there was an urgent call for you and you're supposed to call right back," the out-of-breath woman panted.

Teeba gave instructions to her students and excused herself.

"Teeba? Thank God they got you," Sugie was in obvious distress. "I just had a call from Detective Smythe, the one handling the investigation after you were shot." She began to cry.

"Sugie, please calm down. What can I do for you?"

"Well…they're coming to talk to Timmy again. I hoped it was all over but now it seems even worse," she sobbed.

"Why is that?"

"I'm really afraid. Detective Smythe is coming with someone from the FBI." She paused and then repeated shrilly, "The FBI! What do they want from us? I'm so worried about Timmy. You remember how he regressed the last time they tried to interrogate him. What should I do?"

"I'll help you and Timmy," Teeba assured her. "Where is he now?"

"Both children are at home. As soon as I called Abe, he cancelled his appointments and picked them up from school early."

"I'm on my way."

Chapter 89

THE LEVI HOUSE, high above Skyline Drive on Alvernon Way, was an impressive modern structure. Teeba pulled into the long driveway and parked behind the unmarked police car. A large water feature near the entrance supplied a pleasant sound in the tranquil setting of desert plants and trees.

Before she stepped into the house, Teeba lifted her gaze toward Finger Rock Mountain and fondly remembered her long hikes to the mountaintops. Way up there, in the most peaceful of places, her meditation had taken her back into times where she could see the forming of planets and the beginning of mankind. Standing in front of the Levi house, she was aware that, in this lifetime, her feet would never again crunch the stones on the small paths, nor would she ever smell the wildflowers, hear the wind, or see the rugged beauty of the desert again.

"Nice to see you look so well, Teeba. The last time I saw you was when you left the hospital," Detective Smythe said. "Congratulations, by the way. How soon are you expecting?"

"I'm due in April," she answered, shaking hands with the FBI agent who introduced himself as Frank Martin.

"I'm so pleased you're here. You were next on my list to contact, Mrs. Harris."

"Call me Teeba."

"Teeba, I'm glad to make your acquaintance." The agent released the handshake and got to the point. "We decided to try to talk to Timothy Snow in his own environment. I understand it's less distressing for him. I also was told that he calms down in your presence. Thank you for coming right away."

"Excuse me, but his name is Timothy Levi," Sugie corrected, her voice trembling. "My husband adopted him after we got married."

Abraham put his arm around Sugie. "And you adopted Mandy."

"Where are the children?" Teeba asked.

"In the playroom down the hall." Sugie's eyes welled up again. "Why do we have to put Timmy through this now? He's doing so well," she sniffed and took the handkerchief her husband handed her. "And why are you here?" She pointed at the FBI agent.

"Can we sit down somewhere, please?" Smythe suggested. "Agent Martin will explain his involvement."

"May I go to spend some time with the children? I'd like to prepare Timmy." Before she moved away, Teeba looked at Sugie. "He'll be fine," she promised.

Smythe and Martin followed the Levis into the great room where they seated themselves at a round glass table.

"Mrs. Levi, when did you last see or speak with your son Christopher?"

"Chrissie?" Sugie frowned. "I thought you came here because you've reopened the investigation of Teeba's shooting. I don't understand why you're asking about Chrissie."

"When did you talk with him last, Mrs. Levi?"

"He…I…" Sugie looked to her husband for help.

"Christopher has not been in touch with his mother since he found out about our wedding plans. He does not approve of our union," Abraham said. "He does not like the fact that his mother married a Jew."

"Did you know that your son is a member of an organization called the Order of American Aryans?"

Sugie's face went pale. "Oh no," she whimpered. "My ex-husband was involved in this terrible thing. He must've forced Chrissie to join after he moved to Los Angeles." She looked at Abraham. "That explains a lot of stuff, doesn't it?"

"Mrs. Levi, since you've had no contact with your son in several months, did you send him any money, by any chance? Like large amounts of money?"

"What? Of course not."

Abraham shook his head as well. "I make a very good living, but most of our money is being invested in the special programs and education that benefit both of our handicapped children." He looked at Martin. "You're aware that Tim is autistic, but maybe you didn't know that my little girl has Down's syndrome."

"Do you have any explanation as to how Christopher can afford to drive a BMW or how he has the means to purchase a very expensive computer system, brand new furniture, and fancy clothes?"

"I know he has a good job. Maybe his father helped him to buy new things?" Sugie suggested.

"We don't think so, Mrs. Levi. Neither your ex-husband nor Christopher earns enough money to substantiate these kinds of expenses. We've checked both their incomes and credit card activities." Martin raised his eyebrows. "We've reason to believe that your son Christopher has been involved in some illegal business."

Sugie grabbed her husband's hand. "Like what?"

"We're still following some leads; that's why we're here."

"If you're here to find out about Christopher, why do you have to unsettle Tim?" Abraham asked.

"I need your little boy's help, Mr. Levi," Martin said. "In the process of my investigation I've learned that Christopher on more than one occasion has bragged about being above the law. He's been boasting to a young lady about getting away with something pretty serious here in Tucson."

"Like what? What are you saying?"

"Well," Smythe cleared his throat. "From what Agent Martin has learned, it leads us to believe that Christopher might have been talking about the shooting incident at Agave High School last May."

"No, no, no…" Sugie cried.

"We would like to see if Timothy can recall anything. He's our only other eyewitness."

At that moment, the children, holding hands with Teeba, entered the room.

Mandy, trusting and friendly, walked up to the strangers. "Hi, what's your name?" she asked, and tried to climb on Smythe's lap.

Sugie got up and took Mandy in her arms. "Come sit with me, honey." She pressed her mouth into the child's hair.

Timothy remained standing in the middle of the room, stone-faced and serious. His head was cocked; his eyes focused on Teeba.

"These are the gentlemen who would like to ask you some questions. Is that okay with you, Timmy," Teeba asked.

"Yes," he said and began to rock.

Bending down to the boy's level, Teeba whispered, "Can I hold your hand and sit next to you?" Her closeness stopped the boy from rocking.

"Hi, Timmy. My name is Frank Martin." The agent spoke softly, trying to make eye contact with the boy. "Hey, I really like your shirt. You must be a basketball fan. I'd love to have a shirt like yours 'cause I'm a big basketball fan, too." He leaned forward. "Arizona has a great team. Do you get to watch them play sometimes?"

"Yes. Tim watch bas-ket-ball on TV." The words were chopped and monotone. The boy's head stayed cocked as he looked past the agent.

Smythe's eyes widened. He leaned close to Sugie. "I can't believe it," he whispered. "Several months ago there was a total lack of communication with Timothy; he severely regressed after the shooting. This is a much different child."

Martin continued his mostly one-sided conversation with Timothy, trying to win the boy's trust. Finally he said. "I hear you're doin' real well in school. Who's your favorite teacher?"

"Tee-ba," the boy answered immediately, in contrast to the pauses after previous questions.

"I can understand that. When I was your age, I wish I'd had a great teacher like Teeba as well," the agent said. "I bet you missed her when she was in the hospital for such a long time, didn't you?"

Timothy's head twisted further, his eyes rolled toward the ceiling. There was no response.

"Timmy. I'm here to find out who tried to hurt Teeba so it won't happen again. Can you help me?"

The child let out a short, agonizing wail and started to rock again. Teeba knelt down in front of him and began to hum a very slow tune. As soon as he heard the melody, Timothy stopped moving. Holding on to her hand, his brown eyes slowly shifted toward Teeba and he began to imitate the tune. Then, in his choppy monotone voice, Timothy began to sing.

"We call it Timmy's language. No one but Teeba can understand what he's singing," Sugie explained as tears rolled down her cheeks. "That's how they communicate." She wiped her face. "If you want to ask him any more questions, the best time is now."

"What a beautiful song," the agent said. "You and Teeba sing so nicely together." He held his breath. "If I had a close friend like Teeba, I'd be very upset if someone tried to hurt her."

The boy stopped singing but continued to hum the tune by himself. When he stopped, there was a breathless silence.

"Timmy?" Teeba initiated eye contact again. "You don't have to be afraid anymore. It's okay to tell what you remember."

"Tim-my, not Tee-ba. Tim-my, not Tee-ba," he repeated several times.

"What are you saying, Timmy?" Martin sat at the edge of his seat.

"Kill Tim-my, not Tee-ba."

Abraham clasped his wife's hands more tightly.

Martin crouched down next to the child. "Somebody wanted to kill Timmy, and not Teeba? Is that what you're saying?"

"Yes."

Sugie pressed her mouth into her husband's sleeve to stifle the moan.

"Who was it, Timmy? Do you remember?"

Another small wail escaped the boy's mouth. He moved his head in the direction of his mother, and with a sad expression he repeated over and over again, "Chris-sie, Chris-sie, Chris-sie, Chris-sie..."

Lafayette

. . . in February

Chapter 90

Everything was different—so different that it scared him. Hakan knew he had changed during the past eight months, finding it almost too easy to slip away from the teachings and principles of his faith. When he looked in the mirror, he cursed the stranger whose ideologies were confused and whose life had become a mess. What he once believed to be his life's significant aim, he now had trouble identifying as the true object of his attention. Yet, there was no backing out; more than ever, he now was the main character. He played the lead role and had to give his best performance in the final scene of the drama. He was well aware that the investors—his indoctrinators—waited behind the curtain, expecting him to deliver the long-awaited proceeds and glory.

He knew the disarray in his brain had started the day he met Angela. But whenever he tried to distance himself from her, his obsession and infatuation with her only grew stronger. He often wondered if he was experiencing love, a feeling that he was denied all his life.

He desired to be near Angela every waking minute. It was the only time when he felt clarity. But the mounting pressure at work and the controlling voice inside of him demanded that he focus on the final curtain, keeping him away from the woman that magnified the good in a world Hakan was taught to hate.

It was past ten in the evening and Hakan felt mentally and physically exhausted. He knew he would fall asleep within minutes, but also knew his troubling thoughts would wake him within three hours, making him toss and turn for the rest of the night unless he numbed his mind with a drug. He stared at the prescription, then gulped down the pill. Just as he began to undress his cell phone rang.

"I hope I'm not calling too late but I finished the data and could drop it off now since you said it was important." As always, Afshor talked fast.

Hakan cursed silently since Afshor's words made no sense. He realized it had to be an important coded message. He zipped up his trousers and re-buttoned his shirt.

Ten minutes later his doorbell rang and, with an exchange of a few words, Afshor pretended to drop something off. He wished Hakan a good night's rest, but instead of leaving, stepped into the apartment. Hakan rustled some papers and turned on the stereo system. He motioned Afshor to follow him into the empty room, and without turning on any lights, closed the door.

"What's this all about? It better be important," he said softly. He was sure his apartment was not bugged but al-Fatah's warnings had caused more paranoia in him. "Where were you all afternoon? I left you numerous messages and you never answered your page."

"I couldn't! They were waiting for me when I returned from lunch. They told me to get in the car and drove me to a meeting at the Al Nur Mosque in Metairie. They only now brought me back," Afshor whispered, his eyes darting around the empty room.

"What do you mean? How come they didn't contact me?"

"That's what I asked them, too. They told me you're too high a risk right now. From now on, nobody is going to contact you directly until D-day.

"D-day?"

"Doomsday, Death day…whatever," Afshor said with a half grin. "From now on they will get in touch with me and I'm to deliver the messages to you." Afshor chewed on his upper lip. He leaned closer. "To tell you the truth," he muttered, "I hate doing this. It makes me so uncomfortable that I sometimes think I'd like to abandon the whole thing. But I wouldn't do that to you; I know one hand alone can't clap."

Hakan felt his throat tightening. "Was al-Fatah there?"

"No!" Afshor shuddered. "There's this new arrogant Syrian, Abdul-Wahab. I was told to deal only with him from now on. He was the one giving me the orders; he told me that al-Fatah is in the disguise of a ghost."

"What does that mean?"

"Apparently al-Fatah prefers to keep invisible these days—extra, extra careful but still very much in command," Afshor whispered. "Here's a message for you from him." He handed Hakan another envelope.

Because of the darkness in the room, Hakan left Afshor alone for a few moments. When he returned he found the other man leaning his forehead against the cool wall. "Don't you feel well?" Hakan asked.

"I told you I'm nervous," Afshor hissed. "You're not only my superior but you've become my friend. I wish the whole thing would be over already. I wish I could leave this country now instead of later."

Hakan flinched when he heard his inner voice again. "A sheep that separates from the flock gets eaten by the wolf," he said, repeating what he thought he heard. He swallowed hard. "D-day, to use your term, will be soon. Everything is arranged for us to be safe once our mission is accomplished."

"Who knows if everything goes according to plan, though? What if something goes wrong while you're in Washington? Whom can I trust? I've bad vibes about this new guy Abdul-Wahab." Afshor said, gnawing on his lower lip. "Couldn't you suggest to al-Fatah in writing that it's okay to get me out of here as soon as we finish the vaccine production? I'd like to leave before you fly to D.C."

"It's easier to make a camel jump a ditch than to make a fool listen to reason," Hakan scolded. "So, don't be a fool now. The plan will work and you will have to play by the rules." He moved closer, his nose almost touching Afshor's. "Do what they tell you—they know what they're doing," Hakan said, putting a hand on Afshor's shoulder. "There's an old saying: *You'll always be safe if you listen a hundred times, ponder a thousand times, but only speak once.*"

Afshor swallowed and nodded. He gestured toward the papers. "What did al-Fatah say?"

Hakan told him, and then tore al-Fatah's memo into shreds. "By tomorrow morning this will be all over television and in screaming headlines of every newspaper."

Chapter 91

THE POWERFUL SLEEPING pill granted him five hours of sleep. Hakan had hoped for more, but as soon as he opened his eyes, he remembered al-Fatah's memo and bolted out of bed. It was before six in the morning when he switched on the television. He sat on the edge of his bed and watched the end of a commercial before CNN reported a tragic accident in Iran: The six-member Human Rights delegation under the leadership of the Reverend Jamal Keene had perished in a fierce fire, while asleep, in a suburb of Teheran. The terrible disaster was under investigation, but Iranian officials suspected old electrical wiring to be the cause of the fire.

Hakan switched to every available news station, but the reports were all alike—some focused more on the political careers of the six individuals who had died; other stations already were interviewing distant relatives or friends of the deceased. Hakan held his breath while waiting for the announcement of the claim by a terrorist group. But there was no mention of Al-Saafi; as a matter of fact, terrorism was ruled out.

Hakan quickly put on clothes and ran downstairs to fetch his newspapers. The headlines of the New York Citizen read *HOUSE FIRE NEAR TEHERAN KILLS ALL SIX IN JAMAL KEENE'S HUMAN RIGHTS DELEGATION—Iranian Authorities Doubt Act of Terrorism—U.S. Officials on Way to Iran—*. Hakan quickly scanned the article. He only glanced at the other similar headlines and reports of two different newspapers before returning to his apartment.

"It's a cover-up," he mumbled. "The Iranians must know it's a virus but have no idea about MAX 18; they're clueless about the disease and are scared of a massive outbreak."

Hakan knew that Al-Saafi had claimed responsibility and wondered how al-Fatah and the others were reacting to the repression of their proclamation.

"What'll be next?" Hakan wondered after he showered and dressed. He brewed tea while rereading the articles. "If this delays the plan, when will D-day happen now?"

He already had his briefcase under his arm when he decided to flick one more time through the TV stations. Given the hour—it was past eight in the morning—more reports kept coming in, but they revealed nothing that Hakan had not read, heard, or seen already. The last station he clicked on was KEY NEWS. Again, he noticed familiar footage, but right when Hakan wanted to switch off, the program was interrupted for a KEY News Alert.

"We just learned of a bizarre twist in what Iranian officials so far have called a tragic accident—the fire that killed Jamal Keene and his five-member delegation." An attractive blonde with glistening pink lips spoke in a very precise fashion. *"KEY's Scott deWitt is reporting live to us from Teheran with an exclusive story. Scott?"*

"Good morning, Susan. I'm already into the next day; it's three o'clock in the morning here in Teheran. Just about three hours ago, we learned what could indeed be a bizarre twist to what, until now, was believed a Teheran house fire in which the Reverend Jamal Keene and the other five members of his delegation were killed.

"About ten hours ago I was contacted by a man who only gave me his first name as Ali." Scott deWitt turned around and pointed to a van. *"I don't know who this now-abandoned vehicle belongs to but in order for me to get what Ali claimed to be newsworthy information, my cameraman and I were blindfolded and then brought to this location. Inside the van behind me, Ali detailed a scary scenario. He claimed to be affiliated with a terrorist organization called Al-Saafi. I was told it translates to "The Pure."*

"Al-Saafi apparently is in possession of a man-made virus much more vicious and faster acting than Ebola. According to Ali, one of Al-Saafi's cells—unbeknownst to the Iranian government—was hired to serve as the butler in the now-destroyed mansion, being used

as government guest quarters. This butler released the virus through the ventilation system after the members of the delegation had gone to sleep. Once infected with this agent, any individual will only live for a maximum of eighteen hours; that's why they named it MAX 18."

When Scott deWitt paused to take a breath, the anchor in the United States took the opportunity to speak.

"Are you saying this alleged terrorist group Al-Saafi has claimed responsibility for executing the six Americans? To my knowledge no official statement has been issued here in the United States. Have the authorities in Iran acknowledged this claim?"

"No, not yet, Susan, but I felt obligated to notify the local authorities, the Sharbani *and the* Savama, *here in Teheran. I let them know what I was told by this man Ali. You can imagine that my cameraman and I were thoroughly interrogated. The Savama—which is Iran's intelligence agency—just an hour ago released us. Fortunately they neglected to forbid us to report; that's why I took the first opportunity before they have a change of heart."*

"Fast thinking, Scott. What was the reaction of the authorities? Did you have the feeling they were aware of Al-Saafi's claim?"

"No, they gave no indication. However, according to Ali's speculations, the Iranian government fears the spread of the disease and a subsequent outbreak of public panic and hysteria. If this is all true, then we're dealing with a new, extremely fast-killing virus. Ali was confident the fire was purposely set by the local authorities to avoid a possible spread of this MAX 18. Ali seemed angry about the fact that the authorities so far have denied the claim of this new terrorist organization, Al-Saafi."

"Scott, since you were blindfolded, I assume you never did see this Ali. And since everyone seems to be in the dark about Al-Saafi, is there any other evidence to substantiate these people's existence?"

"Good question, Susan. I never did see Ali's face but he most definitely came prepared and brought more than adequate proof with him: he handed me six passports that belonged to the members of the Human Rights delegation. For further proof, Ali also gave me some of their personal belongings to substantiate Al-Saafi's claim of having killed the Americans. I would've liked to be able to show you these items, but the Iranian authorities made me turn everything over to them."

"Unbelievable, Scott. What a horrible story. Who discovered the victims?"

"Here's yet another strange twist, Susan. Again, I can only report what was told to me by Ali. The butler in the government's guest quarters, who supposedly is an Al-Saafi member, has a younger sister. This young woman is a government employee and has been working as a hostess in the mansion for some time. Al-Saafi used her fine and honest reputation to get her brother a job there as well. Ali stressed that the woman is in no way affiliated with Al-Saafi.

"From what I've learned, neither she nor any of the servants were supposed to leave the premises while the Americans were visitors in the mansion, but being a newlywed, she snuck out to spend the night with her husband. When she returned early in the morning, she heard the cries of the infected Americans and three other live-in servants. Since the virus apparently is extremely fast-acting, all of the people in the mansion were already too sick to move. Besides that, all the phone lines had been cut so nobody was able to call for help. The young woman first thought the sick condition of the Americans and the employees was due to a gas leak. She immediately opened all the windows and doors before running to the nearest house to use their phone."

"That information came from Ali as well?"

"No. I actually spoke with this young woman, as well as neighbors. We had good footage of those interviews but, together with the passports and other items, this too was taken away from us by the Savama."

"So the sister of the Al-Saafi cell is alive. What did she tell you?"

"I was only able to talk with her briefly. She was terribly shook up and I did not get to tell her about the implications made by Ali. Unless the government authorities have informed her by now, I believe she has no idea about her brother's affiliation with Al-Saafi and the fact that he is the prime suspect. What I did find out, though...her brother only recently returned to Iran from Damascus where he lived for several years—she says she believes her brother worked for the Syrian government."

"Do you think this young woman is a reliable source, Scott?"

"From what I've gathered she has a fine reputation and is getting high praise everywhere: Reliable, responsible, respectable. Her new

husband and she still live with her mother. Her father apparently died when she was a little girl; she says she can't remember him at all."

"Scott, am I understanding correctly that the brother knowingly wanted to kill his sister?"

"I'm sorry but we're still not clear on that."

"Okay, but how come she wasn't affected by the virus after entering the house? Did any of the authorities get infected? And what about you? Weren't you afraid of contamination by talking to the young woman?"

"To my knowledge, no one who later entered the premises caught the virus. Ali did mention something to the effect that this MAX 18 is self-limiting; in other words, it dies after a certain time of exposure to oxygen."

"Scott, you keep referring to either a 'young woman' or 'the sister.' Have you been able to find out her name? If so, then it must be easy to identify the Al-Saafi connected brother."

"I'm sorry Susan. Have I not mentioned names?" DeWitt looked embarrassed as he brushed a hand through his thick wavy hair. *"This all happened so fast and since I'm the only reporter chosen by Al-Saafi to make their claim known, my head is spinning from the developments here."*

"So you do have names?"

"Yes. The brother, who apparently released the MAX 18 virus, is known as Majeed Khatami. His sister's name is Farah; her married name is Sharif." DeWitt bent down and picked something out of a small bag. *"I was able to keep these pictures from the authorities. I don't know if the camera gives you a clear look at them, but these are the faces of Majeed Khatami, Farah Sharif, and their mother, Layla Khatami."*

Hakan's face was two feet away from the television screen. With his eyes wide in horror, he felt as if someone was choking him and held his hand protectively over his throat. He was staring at the faces of his wife, son, and daughter—the family he had denied ever since his identity was changed from the Iranian academic Dr. Sattar Khatami to that of the Turkish scientist Dr. Hakan Öztürk.

Washington, D.C.

...in February

CHAPTER 92

SMALL CLUSTERS OF people stood around the Oval Office, heatedly defending their views on the situation when President Daniel Goldman entered.

"Ladies and gentlemen, sorry to keep you waiting," he said with a bright smile, "but an hour ago, Rachel and I became grandparents. Our daughter in California gave birth to extremely handsome twin boys. Rachel and I just made their acquaintance via live video broadcast in the birthing room at the hospital," he beamed. "That's why I'm late; I couldn't tear myself away from the screen. Rachel is still cooing with the babies," he laughed.

President Goldman shook hands and accepted congratulations from his staff, as well as the CIA and FBI representatives.

"I know you came here to discuss a very serious matter." His tone of voice had changed. His gaze swept the room and fixed on Ford. "Any new developments?"

"Yes, Mr. President. Not only has the company been looking for the German scientist, Dr. Gottfried Geist, but Mossad actually has had him on its list for much longer. He was the mastermind behind the deaths of the young dance group from Haifa five years ago." Ford refreshed everyone's memory of the anthrax attack on the twenty Israelis before their final performance in Dresden.

"Acting upon a tip from Mossad, Britain's MI5 found Geist hiding in London. They interrogated him and were ready to extradite him today but, unfortunately, the German hung himself last night."

"Were the Brits able to find out about MAX 18 before this neo-Nazi killed himself?" the secretary of state asked.

Ford nodded. "Dr. Geist admitted to human experiments with MAX 18 in a converted warehouse in Los Angeles."

"Damnation!" the secretary of defense exclaimed. "What else did they get out of him? Any names?"

"British Intelligence was able to get the names of the other *so-called* scientists in the warehouse. Geist also talked about the OAA involvement. We're already onto all of them."

While Ford handed out folders that contained pertinent information, he continued, "When asked about Al-Saafi and MAX 18, the German suggested to the interrogators that they do the work themselves and find Farouk al-Fatah. Dr. Geist obviously slipped when he mentioned al-Fatah and most likely realized that he was a dead man anyway—so he killed himself."

"Any trace of al-Fatah?"

"Mossad, MI6, and all of our intelligence sources are looking for him; he'd be a gold mine of information. I know we're gonna get him. It's just a matter of time."

"That's the one thing we don't have: time!" the national security advisor said. "We've received another threat from Al-Saafi warning us that the Jamal Keene attack in Teheran was only the hors d'oeuvre to stimulate their appetite. They're now ready for the bigger portions of their feast. Do we have any idea who they want to target next?"

"Us of course!" the attorney general quipped. "But how will they approach us? They missed their chance at the State of the Union Address. Are they now going to get us one by one in our homes?"

"We can't rule anything out; these days the most impossible is possible," Ford responded. "From what we've learned, Al-Saafi seems to be everywhere. As preposterous as it might sound to you, there even could be a spy, a sleeper cell, working within or close to the government who has an entirely different identity in another part of the world."

A sudden uneasy silence filled the Oval Office.

Ford broke the spell. "Al-Saafi is a multi-ethnic, multinational extremist group. We're aware of thugs who converted to Islam while in prison right here in the U.S.; some of them might have joined forces with Al-Saafi. We learned from Geist that their monetary rewards are extremely lucrative. What better way to quickly make a lot of dough?"

"I'm sure you're doing your best again, Ford, but this time it seems like you're not getting to the heart of the monster fast enough," the national security advisor said. "I'm not trying to take anything away from your excellent reputation, but how long will we have to wait before you get to the bottom of this?"

"Try emptying the Potomac with a ladle," Ford replied. "The truth is, we may never reach the bottom in this stream of sludge, but we've interrupted or stopped the flow before, and we'll do it again."

There was another moment of silence. Then all at once, everybody in the Oval Office started to talk.

President Goldman intervened. "Okay, you need to calm down," he said. "I'm not underestimating the severity of the threat, but since government officials, especially the ones in my cabinet, seem to be Al-Saafi's next targets, we do have an option." He pointed at an open page in his folder. "I see that enough vaccines are available for this administration to be inoculated."

Ford nodded. "Yes, Mr. President, that's correct. I believe, for the security of our nation, you and your staff should volunteer and get protected by the vaccine."

"Excuse me! I'm still having a problem with this," the surgeon general, a personal friend of the president, protested. "Aside from the unfortunate beings that were used as guinea pigs in the LA warehouse, there've only been less than a handful of volunteers who received the vaccine. Granted, the scientists at PIGR showed no side-effects, but they might've just been lucky." He shook his head. "Look at the smallpox vaccine; we know it can cause severe problems—even death. I strongly object. The risks are simply too high."

"With due respect," Ford addressed the surgeon general, "you need to look closer at the data in the folder. By now, we've had many more volunteers at PIGR. I and my entire family felt comfortable enough to receive the vaccine; so did Phillip Portal, his wife, and their children." Ford grinned. "You know Phillip Portal very well. You also know that no one is more paranoid or cautious."

The surgeon general leafed through the folder. "Most everybody at PIGR volunteered to get inoculated except Dr. Hakan Öztürk, the man who developed the vaccine." He wrinkled his forehead at the president and then looked at Ford. "That doesn't seem to make any sense."

"Dr. Öztürk claims having suffered anaphylactic shock from various vaccines before. I agree, it seems ironic, but he believes his own vaccine may kill him." Ford pointed at a page in the folder again. "He does caution people who've experienced an episode of anaphylactic shock."

"Look," said President Goldman, "I've spoken with Phillip Portal at great length. Not only are we lucky that PIGR committed themselves to work with the CIA on this black project, we're also fortunate that Dr. Öztürk was able to develop the vaccine." The president narrowed his lips. "Phillip Portal gave me permission to tell you today that Dr. Öztürk also developed a new medication that could halt the progression of Lou Gehrig's disease." The president elaborated on Phillip's condition and the results from Hakan's compounds. "You see," the president finished, "Phillip Portal has been Dr. Öztürk's guinea pig twice already—both times with wonderful results. Ladies and gentlemen, I'm perfectly willing and feel very secure to receive the vaccine—the sooner the better."

The voices swelled up again. After further discussing the pros and cons, the majority of the people in the Oval Office agreed to be vaccinated against MAX 18.

"We can't possibly release this information," the secretary of state said. "Not until more vaccines will be available for health care workers and the general public."

"I'm not trying to create a panic, but ever since the KEY News exclusive from Teheran, the media is out of control and suspicious about anything being released anyway," Ford said. "I strongly suggest that this meeting be held highly confidential until further notice." He adjusted his large body in the chair. "I want to reassure everyone that we're doing our utmost to stop Al-Saafi before they have a chance to destroy anyone in this nation. No matter how hard they're trying to be inconspicuous, we'll find them."

Ford stood up; he knew his height would give his words more weight. "As we speak, arrests are being made. There are several members of the Organization of American Aryans who without doubt will supply us with needed information, which then will lead us to others."

Ford knew he couldn't talk about his instinctual certainty about successfully finishing this mission. Instincts were not facts, but they certainly had helped him throughout his highly successful career.

Los Angeles

...in February

Chapter 93

Christopher lay stretched out on his new leather recliner, crunching the just-emptied can of root beer. Not really interested in the basketball game anymore, he yawned at the screen of the fifty-three-inch Pioneer Elite digital television set, another recent acquisition, which almost looked too big in the relatively small space. The Lakers were losing by twelve points in the fourth quarter. He belched out loud and, in a high toss, threw the can into the wastebasket.

When he glanced at the time, his eyes involuntarily moved from the screen to the telephone, expecting it to ring any minute. A lazy smile crept over his face and deep in his throat a purr began to build like a contented cat that had just emptied the fish tank. It was only a week ago that he'd received another call from Argentina. Ribelli indeed had kept his promise.

"I need you to do another run for me," Ribelli had said over the phone. "As a matter of fact, I like the way you work, and if you're willing, I'd like to make you my partner."

At first Christopher hesitated, but when he heard what his share in hard cash was going to be, he changed his mind.

"Two hundred fifty thousand fucking dollars per delivery," Christopher laughingly reminded himself, and kicked his long legs in the air. "A quarter of a double fucking million bucks." He snickered and made boxing movements with both arms as he thought of the foreign account that Ribelli had established for him. "Soon I'll be a triple fucking millionaire." He clapped his hands together and jumped out of the chair.

At the same moment as his stomach churned with excitement, he thought of the despicable days living in the Tucson trailer with his mother. He had stopped talking to her the day he learned she was going to marry the Jewish orthodontist. Although Sugie had left biweekly messages, Christopher never bothered to call back. Then, to his surprise, the calls stopped two weeks earlier. As his mother's image lingered in his mind, he wondered why he hadn't heard from her since. Despite her alliance with a Jew, he missed hearing her chatter on his voicemail, giving him regular updates about life in Tucson.

Christopher still kept in touch with his old high school buddy, Buzz Nolan, who worked as a driver for Prime Produce. Buzz had said he made weekly deliveries with complimentary boxes of fruits and vegetables to the fancy large house in the Tucson foothills where Sugie and Timothy lived with their new family. "I still have trouble recognizing your mother, man," Buzz had said. "She looks incredibly good; really cool and elegant."

Christopher tried to picture his mother living in a mansion and looking like a lady. Somewhere deep inside of him was a pinching wish to feel her arms around him, but his resentment was stronger than the urge to be held.

"Enough," he said out loud, and replaced the image of Sugie with that of a younger woman. Christopher closed his eyes and began to grunt with desire. Zoë's beautiful face and body became so prominent in his mental vision that he believed he could detect her natural fragrance. He missed seeing the Amazon who, out of the blue, had excused herself in the middle of the semester to join her rich parents on a cruise. Christopher had not heard from her since, and felt a twinge of anger about her neglecting to phone him. But he quickly assumed it might be difficult to call from the private yacht far away in the Mediterranean Sea. He convinced himself that she soon would return to him. After all, every time they were together, it was Zoë who repeatedly told him that nobody ever before had turned her on as much as he did.

"She'll be back," he assured himself. "And when she's here I'll make her brains spin again." He imagined ravishing her body and showering her with extravagant gifts. *Now I can afford to buy her anything,* he thought and dreamed he was accompanying Zoë to her favorite stores, encouraging her to pick whatever she wanted. He fantasized how his new wealth would not only impress her but her fancy family as well.

When the doorbell rang, he knew it was Ribelli. Christopher laughed out loud when the chime reminded him of the tinkling sound of money.

CHAPTER 94

"SORRY MAN, BUT I was delayed and now I can't stay long," Ribelli apologized, flashing his strong white teeth. "But I promise, you and I'll soon celebrate our new partnership in style." He looked around Christopher's small apartment. "It's good that for the moment you'll continue living modestly in this area; you'll draw less attention this way." He slapped Christopher on the back. "I'm really happy I ran into you back in November. You and I are gonna do great together."

Christopher nodded. "I still have a lot to learn but I tell ya—I surprised myself how calm I was when I cleared customs. Thanks to your coaching, it all seemed so easy."

Ribelli elbowed him and winked. "Easy? Man, I'd say it was as silky and smooth as the lining in a coffin," he cackled. "My ideas are always dead on."

Back in Ciudad del Este, Ribelli had staged his own drug-related execution, making sure Tufan Keshishian was made aware of Ribelli's unfortunate destiny. During the following three months, he waited for his hair to grow so it could be slicked back into a ponytail, and used the time in South America to establish himself as *el patron*. He grew a full, neatly-trimmed beard that changed his looks entirely. Since establishing new identities was no problem among his many contacts in Paraguay and Brazil, he took the earliest opportunity to first fly to Mexico and then cross the border into the United States, where he met with Christopher.

Just like Ribelli used to smuggle the heroin in Keshishian's antique rugs, Christopher had started his first assignment by hiding close to twenty kilos of black tar heroin beneath the white satin lining of a coffin. The corpse, peacefully resting on ten to fifteen million of street-value dollars, was an old man who had lived on handouts. He made his first and final journey across the border from the dirty streets of Tijuana, dressed in a fine suit as he lay with folded hands on cushions of unimaginable wealth.

Ribelli, under the name of Alejandro Herrera, played the grieving son who was bringing his beloved father to his final resting place in Los Angeles. Prior to that, Ribelli had visited Browne's Funeral Homes where he picked out the most expensive coffin and spared no expense for the funeral.

After being told how proficiently Christopher conducted the transaction, Browne readily agreed to let Christopher accompany the distraught new customer across the border to pick up his deceased father. Ribelli even offered Browne a generous amount of money for the inconvenience of taking Christopher away from his job for two days.

The rest was easy. After Christopher brought the coffin into Browne's Funeral Homes, he removed the heroin during the night, took it to his apartment, and hid it in his Murphy bed.

Ribelli gave his fictitious father a beautiful and respectful funeral. A few grieving men and women, finely dressed strangers who had never met the corpse before, were paid to toss fragrant flowers onto the expensive coffin as it was lowered into the ground. The old Mexican inside, who for most of his life on the streets was kicked like a dog and cursed like a rat, had finally found luxury in death. Ribelli's cash, contacts, and clout had staged the first perfect scenario; many more were planned to follow.

"So your boss shows no signs of suspicion, huh?" Ribelli asked after they discussed the details of Christopher's next delivery across the border.

"Not at all; your call from Nogales didn't even raise Browne's eyebrow." Christopher made a puffing sound. "As long as he gets his steep prices, he doesn't give a fuck who gives him business."

Ribelli's eyes narrowed. "But we have to be careful. We can't use Browne's exclusively for the next few stiffs. I already have contacted a funeral home in San Diego. This time you'll be accompanying a cousin who died in an unfortunate diving accident." Ribelli flashed his big white teeth. "Here are your papers." He handed Christopher a new passport and other documents.

"When?"

"Next Thursday."

Christopher frowned. "I can't do it then. I have a big test on Friday morning and need to be at practice during the afternoon."

Ribelli leaned closer, shaking his head. "You can miss your test and practice. You just need to be sick for a few days, *amigo.* Why train for fucking baseball games that you might lose? Isn't a guaranteed home run across the border more important?" Ribelli cackled. "Actually, I'll be needing more and more of your time. Screw college and baseball. I'm offering you a career with benefits higher than you ever imagined."

Christopher gnawed on the inside of his lip and nodded. "Funny you should say that now. I've been thinking the same thing." He hesitated. "What about my education, though? Without a degree I won't achieve my goals. I've always dreamt of amounting to something big."

"What your eyes might see in only your dreams, your hand won't reach in real life," Ribelli said. "Don't be a fool, Chris! I'm handing you a pot of golden honey. You'll be able to lick your fingers for the rest of your life."

Abruptly Christopher lifted his head and smiled. "Fuck it!" he said. His aqua blue eyes sparkled like ice crystals on faraway glaciers. "I guess I can always pick up my studies later. Hey, by then I can afford private professors, don't you think?" He grabbed Ribelli's hand and shook it. "I'll be available full time as soon as you'll give me the signal."

They talked about future plans and when Christopher would have to relocate under a new identity. Then Ribelli looked at his watch. "Shit, I have to get going. Where's the stuff?"

Christopher pulled down the Murphy bed and lifted the blanket. There, neatly taped and arranged in double layers across the bed, was the new load of heroin.

"Beautiful sight as always," said Ribelli, and unzipped a duffle bag. "Help me pack it up."

There was movement in the silver van that had been parked for more than a week on the street below Christopher's apartment building. Two FBI agents adjusted their weapons while the third spoke into a headset. "We just received positive identification on Ribelli. It's definitely him who's up there with Snow. Let's take them down now." Two FBI agents emerged from the van while the third remained inside.

The doors to two other vehicles, parked near the van, opened, and six more agents hurried toward the entrance of the building.

Two minutes later the door to Christopher's apartment broke open. The two men inside whipped around, surprise and shock frozen on their faces as they found themselves staring at the barrels of eight weapons pointed at them.

CHAPTER 95

WHILE CHRISTOPHER AND Ribelli —charged with murder, conspiracy to commit murder, and drug trafficking—were handcuffed and arrested, Gary Snow and Roger Browne were meeting in a small house on South Crescent Heights, rented by their new OAA brother Manfred Gruber.

"So, you think you can help me?" Manny asked.

"I think it's doable," Browne said promptly, and turned to Snow. "What do you think?"

Snow's mind worked fast. He couldn't believe that in such a short period of time he would be so lucky and hit the financial jackpot again.

At first he had been skeptical of Manny Gruber, but when the newcomer's credentials checked out clean, Snow lent an open ear to the German. Only minutes ago he had learned that Manny was planning a major attack on Jews in the Los Angeles area in late September. It would be during the Jewish high holiday season, when the synagogues across the city would be packed with worshippers during Rosh Hashanah and Yom Kippur services.

According to Manny, some German neo-Nazi scientists had developed an agent that, after being put into a ventilation system, would cause irreparable lung damage and hopefully death, if left untreated. But before the plan could be executed, Manny said he needed to test the substance on humans.

A possible attack on Jews in the Los Angeles area was like music to his ears, and Snow was proud to be taken into Manny's confidence. Snow found it amusing that within less than a year, two Germans had turned to him for help. *This time it'll be a much easier task,* Snow thought. *After all, I have all the experience as to where and how to find worthless subhumans for testing.*

"What do you think, Gary?" Browne's voice brought Snow out of his thoughts.

Snow looked from one man to the other; then, he cleared his throat and nodded. "It's absolutely doable—after all, we've done it before."

"Hey, you're ready to let the cat out of the bag?" Browne elbowed his friend. With a wide grin, he looked at Manny. "You must have a good nose because you came to the right people. Like Gary says, he's an expert in finding what you're looking for and I own facilities to erase all the evidence."

"What do you mean? I don't understand."

Browne and Snow chuckled in unison. Then Snow told Manny about Dr. Geist and the purpose of the warehouse. He talked about Christopher recruiting homeless substance abusers and the scientific experiments that were performed on them.

"What kind of experiments?" Manny asked.

Snow shrugged. "They didn't tell me exactly. But I know they injected certain groups of people and had others inhale a fast-acting virus that put these folks into some horrible agony before they died a short time later. They also injected some of the scumbags in the early stages of occurring symptoms with an antidote that cured them."

"So some of them lived? What happened to them?"

"Once the experiment proved the scumbags recovered from the vaccine, their happiness was short-lived. I don't know what it was, but they got a deadly something mixed into their last supper," Snow said, grinning.

"Last supper? Good one, Gary." Browne laughed out loud. "And Browne's Funeral Homes made sure that no trace of any of them was ever to be found again." He explained about the cremations, handled by Christopher. "It was a neat operation—the perfect way to get rid of filthy slime."

While Snow and Browne began to negotiate the financially rewarding deal with Manny, three FBI agents sat across the street in a house on South Crescent Heights. They watched a screen and listened to the two OAA members agreeing to the facilitation to commit murder with Manfred Gruber, better known as Special Agent James Deaner.

LANGLEY

...in March

Chapter 96

"Congratulations accepted," Ford said into the phone, beaming. "The FBI got four of them in one day: Father and son Snow, Browne, and Ribelli. Interrogations have just started, but Snow Junior immediately caved under the pressure and is singing like a canary."

While talking, Ford typed a command into his computer to pull up Christopher's file. He stopped and found himself staring at the picture of Teeba Prime.

"I know this is not related to Operation Mayfly and of no interest to you," he continued his phone conversation, "but eight months ago the young Snow also attempted to kill his younger brother, but instead shot his teacher when she threw herself over the child to protect him."

"Glad to hear that with one swatter you guys killed two flies, so to speak." Ariel Cohen replied from across the Atlantic. "What would you say if I had more good news for you?"

"Please tell me you found Farouk al-Fatah?"

"Unfortunately the Saudi still manages to keep himself off any intelligence radar screen, but we happened to bump into the man who might lead us to Farouk's hiding place."

"No shit...you located Tufan Keshishian?"

"You're so quick, Randolph," Ariel teased. "One of our operatives spotted him in Teheran. He was on his way to Turkey and we notified the authorities there. Keshishian was arrested just over an hour ago at the airport in Istanbul."

"*Mazel Tov!*" Ford shouted. "We work very well with MIT and since the Turkish Intelligence is cooperative, they should start pumping Keshishian ASAP."

"If anyone can give us leads, it'll be him," Ariel said. "After all of this good news, you should be able to sleep like a bear. Head home, my friend, it's awfully late where you're at."

"Not yet. I still have work to do. Monday the president and the majority of the administration will get immunized against MAX 18. At least they'll be safe after Monday."

"By the way, since Israel is next on Al-Saafi's hit list, PIGR pledged to sell the vaccine to our government."

"That's news to me," Ford said, baffled. "Öztürk didn't say a word to me and lately I speak to him almost every day." Ford shifted uneasily in his chair. "On the other hand, why would Hakan tell me? It's the Portal's decision."

When Ford hung up the phone, he rubbed his forehead and felt the fatigue spreading fast through his body. *Ariel is right,* he thought. *Tonight, or what little is left of it, I will sleep like a bear.* He looked at the documents piled on his desk and began to put some of them away.

We're getting there, he said to himself as he scratched Ribelli, Snow, Browne, and Christopher from his most-wanted list. The few remaining names and faces that stared back at him were more than just sympathizers of Farouk al-Fatah. Ford suspected them to be organizationally involved in Al-Saafi's network.

I'll get you all, he vowed, but sensed something important was about to happen—something that might finally end his career in the CIA. He was more than ready for his retirement.

In his lifelong pursuit to interrupt planned catastrophes and crack down on international terrorism, Ford always seemed to know where to hunt, what to achieve, when to negotiate, and how to hinder. He had pleased his superiors and surprised his colleagues over and over again with his uncanny sense of direction. Many times his instinct caught him off-guard; he had no explanation for the preternatural feelings. It was as if he was guided toward the target by an invisible hand. He never spoke to anyone about it except to his wife—only Ginny seemed to be able to understand the bizarre mystique.

He kept looking at his handwritten notes on the most-wanted list while drumming his pen on the desk. "Something is still missing," he grumbled. "I know I'm close, I can feel it. But what is it?" He looked at the computer screen; Christopher Snow's file was still open.

Ford's gaze was drawn to Teeba's picture. He read again how she made a remarkably fast recovery from the coma, and that Timothy Snow recently identified his older brother as the shooter.

He had no idea why he felt compelled to keep looking at Teeba's picture, nor could he explain why he unexpectly also thought of Angela Atwood. He blinked when his mental image of Angela seemed to merge with that of Teeba on the screen.

Without taking his eyes off the screen, Ford began to write, and without looking down at the sheet of paper, realized he was adding another name to those on the list of most wanted.

The hair on his neck bristled and he shuddered. He stared at the name he had written and underlined: Dr. Hakan Öztürk.

"Impossible," he shouted into the stillness of his office. He wanted to scratch out the newly added name, but instead threw the pen across his desk.

"I'm overtired—my mind is playing tricks on me," he grunted. As he pressed his strong palms onto the armrest, propelling himself out of the chair, Teeba's eyes again attracted his, and once again, he believed he saw Angela's face as well. Another strong sensation took hold of him.

"If there's a connection between the two of you, what on earth is it?" he asked. Nothing made sense, and yet he felt a calming awareness. "It won't come to me tonight," he finally said, and shut down the computer. Then he locked up the important files and secured his office.

As he walked through the empty hallway of the company, he thought of his wife's favorite statement. Whenever Ginny needed time to figure things out, she adapted Scarlett O'Hara's final words from *Gone with the Wind*. For the first time those words fit his own circumstances. *I'll think of it all tomorrow. After all, tomorrow is another day,* he thought.

Lafayette

...in March

Chapter 97

"*Merde,* I have not slept in twenty-four hours; this operation has made slaves out of us," Afshor complained in French. "My nerves are sizzling and I can't think straight." He ripped off his lab coat and threw it on the floor. "I want to get out of here. I must get out of this country now!" He collapsed onto a chair, pressing his hands against his head.

Hakan stared at Afshor. Even though he was overly tired and his nerve endings felt raw, Hakan kept reminding himself that it was almost over.

"Get a hold of yourself," he hissed in Farsi. "Your crying will blind your eyes. Instead of finishing and fixing our situation, you're going to mess it up." He walked over to Afshor, raising his finger. "How many times do I have to remind you to keep kissing the dog on his mouth until you get what you need? Like every Muslim, you're a soldier in Allah's army. You must be strong."

"I know," Afshor whined. "But I can't stand the pressure. Don't you understand?"

"It's almost over; in forty-eight hours we'll be on our way to a new life. Until then we must protect the flame of the candle so it can brighten our days forever." Trying to control his shaking hands, Hakan reached for the bottle of pills in his pocket and handed it to Afshor. "Take one now," he said, "it'll calm you down."

Thirty minutes later they took two sealed containers out of the laboratory's walk-in freezer and replaced them with two identical-looking ones.

The previous day—under the supervision of the U.S. Surgeon General, the FBI, and the CIA—Hakan and his assistants had packed more than two hundred subfactor vaccines against MAX 18 into two PIGR containers, which were to be picked up before seven o'clock on Monday morning.

Accompanied by federal officials, Hakan was to take the vaccines to Washington where he was expected to inoculate the president and the administration.

But after everyone left the premises late Friday, Hakan and Afshor returned and replaced the vaccine with vials of MAX 18.

"How are you feeling?" Hakan asked as he helped carry the subfactor vaccines, packed in bags and on dry ice, to Afshor's car.

"Better, thank you. Can I keep the rest of your tranquilizers? I'm sure I'll need them to keep me stable through Monday."

"They're yours. I have more." Hakan carefully placed the bags into the trunk. "Let's go back to get the rest of the stuff."

They made several more trips to Afshor's car with boxes and bags.

"Is this it?" Afshor asked.

"Yes. The only thing left for us to do is erase whatever is left on the computers."

"I'm a step ahead of you," Afshor said. "There's virtually nothing on my computer—it's one big blank."

"I still have to do it." Hakan suppressed a yawn. "I not only have to eliminate everything, but I have to reprogram. The new information on my computer will be extremely confusing to anyone. It also will stall any investigation."

"The last thing they want to think about will be an investigation," Afshor mused. "There'll be chaos in this country without a government. Everything will collapse. It'll be a hellhole. You think Iraq and Afghanistan were bad after the infidels poisoned the territories? This'll be a hundred times worse."

Afshor left, driving to the Al Nur Mosque in Metairie where al-Fatah's men would take possession of the subfactor vaccines and other materials.

Hakan watched the car's taillights disappear and suddenly felt like a refugee, isolated and abandoned. He had been instructed not to contact Afshor or any other Al-Saafi member until he was safely hidden in Iran. A grip of temporary fear took hold of him and he shivered.

Knowing he would not leave his laboratory or office until Monday morning, he had brought two changes of clothes. Even though there still was plenty of work for him, he planned to take a few naps during the next forty-eight hours; he could not afford to appear jittery or feel tired when he oversaw the inoculation of the president.

But before he went to work on his computer, Hakan did something he had not done in a long time; he began to pray, reciting the words from Mahomet, in Qur'án I:

"Praise be to Allah, the Lord of creation,
The merciful, the compassionate
Ruler of the Day of Judgment
Help us, lead us in the path."

Chapter 98

It was the last time she would race her fire-engine red Porsche down the highway. She enjoyed the minutes that were left. She even smiled despite the sadness that overcame her earlier when she kissed and embraced her parents and Ella for the last time.

Angela was grateful she didn't have to resort to a painful exchange of words to let her parents know they would never see her again. On this last day of her life, she had received another illumination, a revelation that enabled her to communicate in a new way with her mother and father. No words were necessary to transfer the message; Ronald and Chantal Atwood at last comprehended the importance of their daughter's mission in this life.

Angela had given them the strength to accept the actuality that there is no end; she had calmed them with the gained awareness of the continuum of souls.

Arriving at PIGR, she parked her Porsche and stared at the building, especially designed for the CIA's black project Operation Mayfly. Then, she stepped out of the car and looked up at the charcoal gray clouds that had formed above her. Lifting her head, she chuckled as the first fat drops of rain fell on her face. She thought of her childhood when she and Ebony would stand in the Louisiana rain with their necks stretched, heads tilted upwards and their mouths wide open, pretending to receive heavenly liquids being poured by angels.

As the drops coated her face, she slowly walked toward the entrance, and before stepping under the glassed overhang, she looked one more time at the gloomy sky.

Then she extracted a master key card, supplied by Miranda Portal, from her pocket. Since it was Saturday, she knew that nobody other than Hakan would be working in this building.

She was familiar with the facility, but she realized she needed to punch in two different combinations for the other doors to open.

She closed her eyes and recalled the necessary information she had received from the unsuspecting man who prided himself on being her lover for the past eight months. Only two nights earlier the fire of the amethyst had hypnotically held Hakan's eyes, allowing her to sense what had been on his mind.

Standing before the secured gates, Angela pressed the four-digit number on the keypad and the door opened.

As if immune to gravity, she moved through the quiet corridors, looking like an elegant dancer in her final performance. She pirouetted around a corner and found herself standing in front of Hakan's office. She closed her eyes again and let her fingers move automatically to punch in the second combination. She opened the door softly.

Hakan sat in front of his computer, totally immersed in his work. Angela saw his body stiffen; she knew he had detected a fragrance well known to him. His head turned slowly toward the door, almost as if he was afraid to find what he did not think possible.

Angela closed the door behind her and with a second key card, deactivated the lock, sealing them into the sterile-looking room.

"What are you doing here?" he sputtered, shakily rising out of his chair. "How did you get in?"

"I came here to die."

"What?" He took several quick steps toward her. "What did you say?"

"The day you and I met was predecided. We are destined to die together now."

"Angela?" Like a tired old parrot, he cocked his head in confusion. "Are you feeling all right? What are you talking about?"

She walked around him toward the computer. Before he could interfere, she typed in a command and erased what he had been working on. She pointed at the empty screen. "All of that was a lie," she said. "No more deceit, Hakan. Now it's time for the truth."

He kicked the desk chair that separated them and jerked her arm. "What in the world do you think you're doing?" He pushed her against the wall. "What has gotten into you? Have you gone mad?" He hurried back to the computer and tried to override her last command, but the screen remained empty.

"Restore it," he hissed through clenched teeth.

"No, I don't believe that's an option. Your destiny at this moment has never been more clear." Standing in front of Hakan, she took his hands and looked into his angry eyes, allowing the fire of the amethyst to do the rest.

CHAPTER 99

HAKAN HAD NO control as he felt his body shake and bounce like a spineless puppet whose string was being mercilessly yanked and pulled by a pitiless phantom.

Don't allow her to do this, he heard a voice scream. *You're the puppet master. Fight her—kill her.*

"What is going on? Who are you?" He slurred his words as drool ran from the side of his mouth. His heart pounded; he covered his ears hoping to silence the inner command to kill the woman who had opened up a beautiful passionate world for him. "Why did you come here—better yet, why did you ever enter my life?" he agonized.

"I would have liked nothing more than for you to discover the pure core you were born with so you'd be able to work toward a greater purpose of life. But I was meant to enter your life when it was too late for you to change things. Long before we met, you chose to listen to the wrong voice."

He tried to ignore the beauty of the purple aura around her. "Are you a witch?" he yelled.

There was no reply, instead, the penetrating purple fire found its way into his brain and beyond again.

He staggered backwards toward the small refrigerator. He removed a vial and quickly inserted the needle. Then, he pointed it at Angela like a gun.

"Get out of here now or I will have to kill you." He felt tears running down his cheeks as the beautiful scene of the past eight months fast-forwarded behind his eyes.

Kill her before she ruins everything, screeched the voice inside him.

"I'm not here to ruin anything," she said.

Hakan froze. How could she hear the voice?

"I'm here to prevent a terrible tragedy," she said. "The moment has come for you to correct the mistake that became your life's goal."

He heard the voice again and slavishly repeated the words. "There's been no mistake," he said. "I'm brilliant, I'm the master of the game and it is necessary for me to complete my mission. Nobody is going to stop me." Hakan stepped forward, still pointing the needle at Angela. Through a fog, he saw her beautiful face. "I don't want to do this..."

"But you have to," Angela finished the sentence for him. "I know what your alter ego is telling you. All your life you've been listening to the wrong callings."

Not grasping how the purple fire in her eye affected him, Hakan stumbled toward her.

She's a witch. She's the enemy, he heard the voice scream. *You must kill her; you have no choice.*

As he fell forward, he jammed the needle into Angela's arm. Then, he remained motionless, watching the empty vial fall onto the white-tiled floor. He had injected Angela with MAX 18. "You made a fatal mistake by coming here; you gave me no choice," he stammered.

"My having to die today is not a mistake. There's a higher purpose behind this decision."

"You may have bewitched me before with your beauty but your witchcraft is lost on me now," Hakan said. "If you're so powerful, why don't you let your magic work and reverse the injection?"

"I must die so the future can happen."

Hakan's dark eyes bore into hers. "You're right," he said. "By Tuesday morning there'll be the beginning of a new future. This country will crumble like a burnt cookie. Too bad you can't be here to witness this new beginning for my people."

"I still have not been able to make you see," Angela whispered. "You became my destiny, but I've become yours as well."

When her eyes attracted his like powerful magnets, his body began to shiver uncontrollably. He tried to fight back, but this time the purple fire was too strong.

He stopped shaking when some strange and pleasant warmth seemed to blanket his brain. Then he felt as if the tepid liquid, like a waterfall, kept splashing down his spine before it spread its healing qualities into every cell and fiber of his body. Like a cleansing bath it washed away all of the hatred, anger, guilt, and pain.

When Hakan recognized the reality of his office again, he touched his body to make sure it was his. He searched for the demanding voice that had accompanied him most of his life but he could not hear it anymore. He had never experienced total tranquility before and wondered why the sudden peacefulness did not frighten him.

"What is happening?"

"I'm setting you free, Hakan. In your final hours of life you are able to act alone and do what is right," Angela said.

"How can I do what is right? All I know is what I've been programmed to do." He thought of the two containers filled with MAX 18 two rooms away. He thought of Afshor, al-Fatah, and everyone else connected with Al-Saafi. All of them were expecting him to deliver them and their cause from the infidels. Now, nothing seemed to matter; nothing made sense anymore. "If I don't finish what is expected of me, they will kill me," he said.

"They've killed the true you long ago. I will help you retrieve some of the good that once was in you. There's still time for you to make things right." Angela took his hands.

With awe he looked into the magnificent fire of the amethyst and, for the first time, felt its power. It was then that everything became clear.

"I understand what needs to be done next," he said moments later, and walked to the refrigerator, removing the only other remaining vial with MAX 18.

"When I hid two doses in here, I believed I might have to defend the project and myself. But I had no idea I would ever have to defend myself from myself," he said, looking at the vial delicately held between his fingers. "I worked so very hard for this." A soft moan escaped him. "Courage has never been my forte." He closed his eyes and inserted the needle into his arm.

He lifted his head and looked at Angela. "I've never loved anyone the way I loved you," he said. "In my wildest dreams I did not expect to become the cause of your death." He sank to his knees and began to weep. "You looked through me since the day we met; why did you wait so long? You could have stopped me months ago."

She shook her head. "We are spinning in a very particular circle of life in which many others are involved," she said. "If I had stopped you before today, I would have altered the outcome of good versus evil missions, causing even more damage." Suddenly, she doubled over and let out a small cry.

Knowing she was feeling the first sharp pain from the fast-acting MAX 18, Hakan held her. "Please forgive me," he pleaded.

"I have to die so the future can happen," she said, "but I do need your help."

His eyes followed hers, and he stared at the computer and the video camera above. He nodded, activated the video camera, and sat down in front of it.

He knew it would take hours to confess his involvement with Al-Saafi. He would start with describing the group's early stages in Iran and finish with where to find al-Fatah and the other operatives, some of them hiding behind government and clerical positions in Iran and other Middle Eastern and European countries.

While he talked for the camera, his fingers flew over the keyboard, typing every spoken word, reliving his scientific dream for the last time.

Since his eyes had been opened to another dimension, he was able to speak freely. As his speech became more rapid, his fingers were typing faster and faster. He realized how devilish his mission was and how foolishly he had feasted on the might of power, mistakenly feeling supreme and untouchable. He had created a biological monster, birthed it, and with loving hands cultivated its rapid growth. Now he knew that his monstrous brainchild would soon take the life of the woman he loved. His only consolation: MAX 18 would also kill its own creator.

"Before I die the horrible death I envisioned for the U.S. president and the current administration," he said, looking into the camera, "I, Dr. Sattar Khatami, will be sending my life's confession in its entirety to Ford."

Tucson

...in March

CHAPTER 100

AT THE SAME moment Angela experienced the first painful symptoms from MAX 18, Teeba gasped and reflexively pressed her hands on both sides of her round belly.

"This is it," she whispered, and slowly got out of bed. "Clay," she said louder, "it has started."

Clayton threw the sheets aside. Turning on the lamp, he blinked into the sudden brightness. "Now? But you're not due yet. It's too early."

"There's nothing I can do about the force of nature, my love."

Clayton hurried through the house, grabbing the necessary items and placing them in Teeba's big straw bag. Then he called The Women's and Children's Hospital.

"Please call Ebony. I promised to let her know the minute I go into labor," Teeba said. "It will be necessary for her to be with us."

Twenty minutes later, Teeba was given the routine checkup in a cheerful-looking room.

"Are you sure there's nothing wrong? I'm just not comfortable that she'll deliver six weeks early," Clayton told Dr. Kraemer.

"Everything is perfectly normal; see for yourself," the doctor motioned toward the monitors. "Your tiny family is in excellent health. Don't worry about a thing." He looked at Teeba. "I suspect it'll be a while since your contractions are still three to four minutes apart. I'll be back in an hour. If you need me, just tell the nurse."

Left alone with Ebony and Clayton, Teeba smiled at them. "This is a very important night—not only for Clayton and me but also for you, Ebbie."

"I know. I've never been present at a birth." Ebony pulled a chair close to the bed and stroked Teeba's hand. "And since I probably won't ever have babies of my own, this is a real thrill for me."

"You'll have babies," Teeba assured. "You'll have babies really soon."

Ebony laughed out loud. "From your mouth into God's ear—but shouldn't I find myself a husband first?"

"You're such a pretty, unique woman, Ebony," Clayton said. "Maybe you're working too many hours and don't give yourself a chance to meet the lucky guy who'll kiss the ground you walk on."

"Hey Clay, wake up! It's you who's putting the demand on me at work. Maybe if you ease up a little, I'd find the time to search for the father of my children," Ebony teased.

"Are you kidding? I can't imagine my day at the Institute without you. On second thought, forget the idea of finding a husband. I need you too much."

With closed eyes, Teeba listened to their dialogue, her face glowing with content. She spread her fingers over her belly like a Byzantine dome, permitting light and communication from four directions to filter toward the life inside of her.

Ebony lowered her voice. "Sssh, I think she fell asleep. Look at her symmetry; I imagine this is what angels must look like. I used to call her Sleeping Beauty when she was in coma."

"She's certainly been my gift from heaven. She's opened my eyes and ears to worlds I never thought existed. Soon she'll give birth to new life and another world will unfold for me. I can hardly wait." He took a step back and sank into a chair.

"Go ahead and rest, I'll stay awake," Ebony whispered.

"No, no. Tell me more about when you grew up with Angela in New Orleans."

Both Clayton and Ebony were so absorbed in their question-and-answer dialogue, they didn't notice the obstetrician returning to the room.

"How is it going?"

"Has an hour gone by?" Clayton shook his head. "We've been busy talking while Teeba's been resting."

"Well, the way it still looks, y'all might be here for some time," the doctor concluded. "Let us know when things change. I'll be nearby. One of my patients is about to deliver."

As soon as the door closed behind the doctor, Teeba opened her eyes. "Dr. Kraemer is wrong; it won't be that long."

"We thought you were sleeping, sweetie." Ebony stepped to the bedside and fluffed the pillow under Teeba's head. "But I should've remembered, you hear everything, even in your sleep."

"How are you feeling, Teebs?" Clayton asked, kissing her forehead.

Teeba inhaled sharply and held her breath. Her healthy coloring turned pale. "Oooh, oooh, oooh." The sounds were those of pain but her face showed no signs of it.

Clayton looked at the monitors. The infant's heartbeats were regular and the other monitor indicated no sign of contraction. "Darling? What's wrong?"

"The pain I'm feeling is Angela's." A silvery tear rolled over her soft skin. "I feel her dying a terribly tormenting death."

Clayton exchanged a quick glance with Ebony. "What are you saying, Teeba?" he asked.

Ebony took Teeba's pulse, felt her forehead, and looked into her eyes. Even though Teeba's vital signs checked out normal, Ebony said, "I'm calling the nurse to get the doctor back in here."

"No, not yet. Both of you, please look at me and listen." A purple spark escaped her right eye and a brilliant glow spread through the dimly lit room. "The circle has closed. The time has come."

"No!" Clayton protested. "I won't let it happen." He sank to his knees and put his face close to hers. "Not now Teeba, please. Not now or ever. I don't have the power to change things, but you can…" He softly kissed her.

"What are you saying?" Ebony cried. "What is happening? Tell me this is all a mistake."

"Life doesn't make mistakes. Things happen for a reason, Ebbie." Teeba squeezed her friend's hand. "This life has been a gift—another lesson I've learned." She watched as Ebony sank to her knees on the other side of the bed, opposite from Clayton. "I've been trying to tell both of you for some time that my mission will soon be over. And now the time has come."

Ebony shook her head. "If you told me, it went over my head. And although I've inherited my mother's clairvoyance, my senses aren't as sharp as hers." Ebony lowered her voice and caressed Teeba's belly. "I've never felt more connected to you than this moment."

Teeba took a deep breath and waited for a contraction to pass. "I want to thank both of you," she said softly. "Because of you, my father, and a few very special people, my physical existence has been an unforgettable voyage. But now my soul is guiding me to go home to unite with its other half."

"Please no," Clayton begged. "I can't think of a second without you. More so, the life you're about to bring into this world needs a mother."

"You won't be left alone, my love." Teeba willed herself to ignore the next labor pain. She reached for Ebony and Clayton's hands and joined them on her belly. "Be very still and listen to your souls," she whispered. "Can you hear the sweetness of the message?" Teeba smiled and closed her eyes. "There," she breathed. "You now understand that I must leave so the future can happen."

McLean

…in March

Chapter 101

Ford sat up straight in bed, staring through the darkness of the room. On the digital clock in the half-open armoire, he saw that the time was only six o'clock; he had slept less than three hours. He heard Ginny's even breaths and was glad his abrupt change of position had not interrupted her sleep. She needed the rest; as always, she had waited for him until he came home.

He had bolted from his sleep when he heard his name being called. Strangely though, it was not from a voice; there had been no tone to it. Yet, he could still hear the calling, but not in language or sound.

He believed he was seeing the images of Angela and Teeba again, bathed in a velvety purple aura. He wondered if the sounds that woke him and the purple vision were beyond a physical experience.

The time on the digital clock had only changed by one minute, yet it seemed as if the encounter had held him captive for much longer. Ford remembered how tired he was when he put his head on the pillow. Strangely, though, his senses now felt freshly sharpened and his body experienced a revitalized energy. He slowly moved off the mattress, but the soft rustle from the sheets caused Ginny to stir.

"Why are you up already?" she asked in a small, sleepy voice.

"I have to work on my computer. Go back to sleep, sweetheart. It's way too early."

Ginny stretched and yawned. "You're up, I'm up. I'll make coffee, okay?"

Ford smiled in the dark and kissed her.

As soon as he activated his computer, he saw that a message was waiting for him from Hakan Öztürk. It did not surprise him that Hakan would contact him; after all, ever since Operation Mayfly was established, they had been in fairly steady contact.

What surprised him, though, was that there also was a video message from Angela Atwood sent less than fifteen minutes ago. He could feel his heart beating faster as the strange experience of this early morning's awakening came into the foreground again.

Ford gasped when he saw Angela's face on his screen. Her eyes had sunk deep into the sockets. Dark circles contrasted sharply with her pallid skin tones. He held his breath when he heard her raspy, labored voice.

"Ford, I don't have much time, but I need to verify Dr. Hakan Öztürk's testimony and confession that he has sent to you separately. He and I have been locked in his office at PIGR for the past twelve hours. We both are infected with MAX 18 and will most likely have died by the time you have alerted the authorities. Once you have finished hearing and reading everything Hakan has sent you, there's a sealed document addressed to you that'll explain everything from my point of view. I'm certain you won't need any help to understand, but as a backup, Miranda Portal is expecting your call."

Ford sat paralyzed, finding it hard to breathe when Angela stopped talking, turning her face away from the camera. He heard rasps and coughs before she faced him again.

"Whatever happened here at PIGR, happened for a reason tonight. There was nothing I could have revealed earlier. What is important, though, is that Dr. Öztürk, of his own volition, chose to come forward and prevent an otherwise terrible tragedy."

Angela turned her head to cough again. With an obviously labored effort, she smiled into the camera. *"Enjoy your retirement, Ford—you certainly deserve it."*

Her last sentence was barely audible before the screen went blank.

Ford knew that time was of essence. He clicked onto Hakan's message and realized it was a simultaneous confession in writing, visual, and audio.

Three hours later, at his office in Langley, after making all the necessary calls and having alerted the White House and various intelligence authorities, Ford received the call he had been expecting.

It was Miranda Portal. Her voice was calm, but filled with sadness. "I met the agents at PIGR after you called me. Even though I knew it was not necessary, we outfitted everybody with biohazard gear; everybody except for me since I was vaccinated against MAX 18."

"Were they still alive?"

"Hakan had died about an hour before we got here. Angela is still breathing, but her neurological functions seem to be gone."

"Miranda, you said 'seem to be.' What do you mean?"

"I know she can still hear me. I have no proof but..." Miranda stopped, and then continued in a whisper. "I'm sitting next to her, cradling her head. I know she's aware I'm here; the hearing is always the last thing to go."

Ford envisioned the scene and shuddered. "I know you'll stay with her until she dies. Please tell her that because of her, I now understand what my lifelong instincts have been all about. I'm able to recognize who I am and why I'm here." He wiped his eyes and whispered, "Please let her know that I'm very grateful to have been part of her circle."

He heard his second line ringing but waited before he answered; he needed to get hold of his emotions. Finally, he picked up the receiver.

"We got Afshin Afshor in his apartment. When we broke through his door, we found him in a compromising position with another man," said an FBI agent in Louisiana.

Ford could tell the agent was grinning. "Is he talking?"

"Yeah, he's talking all right, although screaming would be a better description. The guy is hysterical; nervous as hell and sweating more than Mike Tyson in a spelling bee contest. But he's giving us what we want."

A calmness overcame Ford when he learned next that the Syrian, Abdul-Wahab, was arrested with other Al-Saafi cells in the living quarters below the Al Nur Mosque in Metairie. Containers loaded with two hundred vaccines against MAX 18, more than a hundred passports, eight million dollars in cash, boxes of blueprints, microfiches, computer disks, weapons, and ammunition, were confiscated from the cellars of the mosque.

Each time he crossed off another name from the most-wanted list, his heart felt lighter. When the phone rang again, Ford knew it would be the final catch of the day. The call came from Israel.

"Congratulations, my friend!" said Ariel. "Your information, combined with what we found out yesterday, helped us pinpoint al-Fatah's hideout in Teheran. Our Iranian friends have his compound surrounded. Even though they're expecting resistance, we know we're finally carving into the core of Al-Saafi."

At last it was over. Ford leaned against the thick-cushioned back of his desk chair.

He had accomplished his final mission. He picked up the phone to call Ginny and tell her the news.

"Randolph? I was just going to call you." Her words came fast and excited. "Turn on your television set. It's on every network."

"What is?"

"There's another one of those phenomenal natural occurrences in Tucson. A rumbling of the Earth without it registering on any scale. The whole desert is painted in these incredible variations of purple. You've got to look at it to believe it."

As soon as Ford clicked the remote control, he smiled. He felt the same vibration as he had experienced earlier in the morning. He stared at the small television screen. Surrounded by mountains that were covered with saguaros, Tucson sparkled in brilliant shades of purple.

Even though his eyes saw the footage and his ears listened to the reports, he was able to see and hear far beyond. Once again, he saw images of Angela and Teeba melting into one body, creating a beautiful purple flame. As the flame diminished in its strength, it gave birth to a new one—more beautiful than before. It was the beginning of another circle: The continuum of the fire of the amethyst.

Epilogue

Twenty-seven years ago, one soul went into two incarnations. Two different physical beings had a mission to accomplish. Without knowing each other's name or place of living, they shared the same reality. Their time flow became synchronized.

The moment Teeba gave birth to a baby girl, an unusual and rare pulmonary embolus caused instantaneous and irreversible death to the mother.

The attending obstetrician performed an emergency C-section to deliver the twin.

At the same time that Angela peacefully exhaled her last breath in Lafayette, Dr. Kraemer in Tucson cut the umbilical cord of the second baby girl.

Clayton and Ebony remained at Teeba's side until the end. When the nurses put an infant into each of their arms, they were overcome by emotion. Yet, holding the babies, they sensed a familiar vibration and could feel a revelation enriching them with a new gift of wisdom and knowledge that came from a world beyond human reality.

Ebony and Clayton looked at each other and through their tears comprehended the message: Angela and Teeba had to pass on so the future could happen.

Holding the infant girls in their arms, Ebony and Clayton saw the twin babies lifting their tiny eyelids. A colorful flicker developed in one of each of their dark eyes. The flicker soon developed into a bright purple flame. It was the fire of the amethyst.

And so it continues.